LIES THAT BIND

CJ STONE

BLOODHOUND
— BOOKS —

First published in 2022 by Bloodhound Books.

www.bloodhoundbooks.com

Print ISBN: 978-1-5040-8009-5

For Vicky, with love.

PROLOGUE

The strip light above him buzzed and flickered, the strobes like a slide projector. Each pulse brought a fresh image from his life to the forefront of his mind, the rhythm keeping pace with his increasingly heavy heart.

He strained to look down, could just about make out the tips of his toes, pointing to the floor. His bare feet scrabbled, trying to make contact with the edge of the fallen stepladder... so achingly close.

He coughed and writhed. The thick rope dug further into the tender skin around his neck, the rough fibres like a thousand razor blades, scraping, gouging. He winced. His feet flailed more desperately. He fought back against the pain, against the sadness and regret consuming him...

The flickering of the bulb above him slowed – perhaps an illusion caused by his own fading light.

His body relaxed, his muscles no longer tensed and straining, and a rush of acceptance swept through him. His body slumped against the noose. In his more relaxed state, the tips of his toes brushed against the cold metal edge of the ladder. His skin prickled.

Solid contact. A chance to change how this ended?

No, he realised with absolutely finality. The next second his toes slipped free. He didn't have the strength, physically or mentally, to try again. He was already too far gone, his eyes closing.

Deep down, he knew he deserved this.

CHAPTER ONE

JESS

'You youngsters, always your faces in your phones.'

I frowned at Nanna's comment. Faces *in* phones? For some reason my mind conjured a very literal interpretation of those words. I glanced to my brother, Frankie, across the other side of the cramped room. Cramped today, at least, given the guests we'd squeezed inside our modest five-bed home for my dad's birthday.

Frankie did indeed have his phone out, head down, shoulders hunched as he typed away. Nanna carried on talking, about the good old days, of course, but I struggled to listen properly. Usually I cherished these moments with her, even if I didn't always agree with what she had to say, but today I was simply too distracted.

Through old age, ill health and accidents, my eighty-seven-year-old Nanna – my mum's mum – was the oldest surviving family member we had. Something of a relic, a treasure of a bygone era.

That might sound a little strange, a twenty-year-old having a grandma of eighty-seven, but Nanna had been forty-four when she'd given birth to Mum. Very old, so I'm told, over and over.

Far too old to have a child. Much better to have them in your early twenties – Nanna relishes in telling me – when you're fit and healthy and when your womb is a bastion of wonderfulness and youthfulness, hasn't been stretched or torn or worn, or something like that. I grimaced at the thoughts building in my head.

I was nowhere near ready to be a mother, certainly not mentally.

'Have you got yourself a nice, young man yet, Jess?' Nanna asked, as she put a withered old hand onto my bare knee. Her skin was mottled, bruised here and there. She bruised so easily, scarily so really. I put my hand on top of hers and tried to give her my full attention, ignoring the little spat at the other end of the room between my parents – the reason for my distraction. Or one of the reasons anyway.

Had anyone else noticed?

'Not quite,' I said. 'There is a boy I like. We've been dating, but it's...' I didn't finish the sentence. How could I begin to explain all that to Nanna? I'd intended – had hoped to build the courage – to try and talk to Mum and Dad this weekend, but they'd been so awkward with each other. With me too. I hadn't told them anything. I didn't tell Nanna either. Instead, I said, 'He's really nice. Tall. Handsome. He's got green eyes that you could stare at all day. He plays football for the university team.'

Nanna smiled and nodded. 'He must be very fit then. Don't let him get away. The best ones get taken up quickly.'

'I'm sure they do.'

'But you'll be fine. You're clever. A degree? I can't believe it. My little Jess, getting herself a degree at university. Not many women in our family can say that. I never had the chance. Impossible in my day. Any man would be proud to have you.'

'That's very sweet of you,' I said, flattered by the genuinely heartfelt statement. I kissed her on the forehead. 'Do you want anything?' I held up my empty champagne flute.

'I'm okay,' she said.

I got up from the arm of the chair and moved across the room, smiling here and there. I walked past my dad who was now busy talking to Frankie – perhaps telling him to come off his phone. No chance I could get a private moment with him right now, even though, out of my parents, he was the one who I knew it would be easier to talk to, given the subject.

Instead I headed out into the hall, looking for Mum. I found her in the kitchen. By the sink, water gushing. She was alone, her back to me, her shoulders hunched and... quivering? Crying?

'Mum?'

She quickly reached out, stopped the tap, ran her forearm across her face before she spun around to me.

'Darling, are you okay?' she asked. She smiled brightly though the cracks appeared within a beat or two.

'I'm fine. Are you?'

'Me? Yes, just cleaning a couple of glasses. We always run out.'

There were indeed four washed wine glasses draining on the side, but I didn't buy it. The way she'd rushed out of the lounge, away from Dad...

I moved closer to her. She was jittery, as though she knew I knew something – which I didn't, even though I wanted to. I'd rarely seen her so awkward around me.

Actually, no, that's not true at all. But on an occasion like this, with all the family around, my mum was normally centre of attention. Hostess extraordinaire, running around filling glasses, feeding everyone until they popped, laughing, joking, getting the silly games and the dancing going.

As a young girl I always wanted to be just like her, in pretty much every way. I styled my hair like hers, tried to talk and walk and dress like her. Really, I didn't look much like her at all. She had high cheekbones, a little snub nose, piercing bluey-green eyes. I had dull brown eyes, a more rounded face, wider lips, darker hair. A face more like Dad's. I'd realised as I'd gone through my teenage years that I wasn't really much like her personality-wise either. More reserved, but also impulsive. Naive? Or was that simply my age?

Still, I continued to look up to her. I loved her warmth. Her kindness. I loved her exuberance on occasions like this.

Yet today she was just... a little bit flat. Less than flat. On edge.

I reached out and took her wrist and gave a gentle squeeze. 'If there was something wrong, you'd tell me, right?'

A strange flicker in Mum's eyes, but she pulled her face back to bright and breezy in a flash and swooshed her golden hair behind her as she looked over my shoulder. 'Hey, sweetie,' she said, and I knew from the saccharin tone and the way she stooped down, exactly who had just walked in.

Mum scooped Lily – my five-year-old sister – in her arms and Lily, in her pink Peppa Pig pyjamas, clung on with both arms and both legs, and buried her head.

'You're supposed to be asleep,' Mum said.

'It's too noisy,' Lily squeaked. 'All I can hear is Frankie doing monkey noises.'

I smiled. Yes, that definitely sounded like Frankie.

'But it's really late,' Mum said. 'Just shut your door and close your eyes and think nice things.'

'I can't shut my door because of–' Lily didn't finish the sentence. Instead she squealed in shock when a crash came from the dining room. Breaking glass. Followed by sarcastic cheers from loud male voices.

Then, almost in unison, 'Mum!' and 'Jane!' were bellowed from my eldest brother and Dad.

'Jess, could you take her back upstairs?' Mum said, trying to hand me Lily.

I hesitated. I always did. I wasn't any good with Lily. She was too... little. Even though I'd been so similar, at least at that age – another mini version of Mum – I didn't get her. And not just because she was so much younger than me, but because... she was a girl. Perhaps that's confusing, but even through my early girly years, I'd grown up with brothers around me. I had virtually no memories of my life before seventeen-year-old Frankie was born, not long after my third birthday, and I was nearly eleven when Tom – now nine – was born. In a really weird way, and as really weird as they both were in many – often disgusting – ways, I got them. I'd grown up with them.

But Lily?

'Jess, please?' Mum said in her exasperated tone. The one she used when addressing me as a child.

I reluctantly took Lily from her. My sister clung to me like a koala bear on a tree trunk, but as soon as Mum left the room to clear up someone else's mess – one of her life's duties – I bent down and dragged Lily off me. 'Come on then, Lil,' I said to her. She looked up at me, a little hurt, I thought, but then grabbed my hand.

I took her up the stairs, to her bedroom, tucked her back into bed.

'Will you read to me?' Lily asked.

'It's too late,' I said. 'Time to sleep now.'

She held the covers close to her head and nodded, her eyes big and round as she stared at me. My heart stung but I got up and moved to the door.

'Don't shut it all the way. It's too dark.'

'Okay.' I left an inch gap then headed back down. Mum was

already back in the kitchen, tipping the dustpan of broken glass into the bin.

'She really misses you, you know,' Mum said.

'I know.'

'She looks up to you so much.'

I didn't say anything this time and Mum glanced over at me. 'You should try spending more time with her. It's almost like you avoid it.'

'That's not it at all.' I could see my answer didn't convince her. I thought about further explaining but then felt the force of moving air behind me, like a tornado approaching.

'Out the way, sis!' Frankie shouted.

I just about managed to sidestep out of my galloping brother's path before he rushed past and around to the other side of the small kitchen island where he came to an abrupt stop, looking back over, a grin from ear to ear.

'I'm going to get you next time,' Tom blasted from behind me. He sounded angry enough, but his relaxed face told a different story.

'Come on now, boys,' Mum said, glaring at both of them in turn. 'This is how the last accident happened. You need to calm down. Tom, it's nearly time for your bed anyway.'

'Awwhhh, seriously?' A petulant eye-roll and shrug of the shoulders from him.

'I was just getting a drink,' Frankie said, moving to the fridge. 'He won't leave me alone.'

'Can I have one?' Tom asked.

'It's too late for you. Frankie, another beer, really?'

'Please?' Frankie mock-begged, the can already in between his prayer hands.

Mum sighed. 'Fine. But it's the last one.'

He smiled then went to leg it out of the room when Tom made a move on him.

'Boys!' Mum shouted at the top of her voice. They both came to a stop before slowly moving out, but we both knew they'd be back at it any second. Tom was Frankie's little shadow, followed him everywhere, and Frankie loved it. Loved the attention he got, perhaps mainly because outside the four walls of our house, away from family, he was as introverted as I was.

'How about you?' Mum asked.

'What?'

She nodded to the empty flute on the island worktop.

'I shouldn't,' I said. 'I've got an early train back tomorrow.'

My turn now for the Mum glare. 'I really wish you'd booked something later. You knew we were having everyone over.'

I didn't say anything. Whatever explanation I'd given – particularly the truth – would only have upset her, even though I really did want to talk to her about... no, I wasn't thinking about that now.

'Just a small one,' I conceded.

Mum filled the glass to the top. Filled herself one too.

'Come on, it's time to give Dad his present.'

'Didn't we do that already?'

Which of course we had, three hours ago, when he'd had his presents off us all plus his cake with forty-eight candles, which Lily had blown out for him, pretty much one after the other, slobbering all over the icing as she did so – much to the amusement of my immature brothers.

'We did. But I've got him a special something too.'

'For his forty-eighth? Not exactly a big one, is it?'

Mum's eyes pinched as she looked at me, as though I was being hard work. 'Come on,' she said.

In the dining room the table was now pretty much cleared of the food from earlier, just the cheese and biscuits and a few other scraps remaining.

Everyone gathered around, drinks in hand, fifteen of us in

total. A nice family unit, even if we weren't all close to one another. Still, it was nice to have everyone together. With Nanna struggling as she was, there wouldn't be many of these occasions left.

I gritted my teeth in irritation at my own grim thoughts. I looked over at Nanna, sunk in an armchair in the corner of the room. It looked like she'd never get out of there. She certainly wouldn't without help. Not after the three whiskey and waters she'd had. At least it was only three. She'd asked for more, but I'd given her a little bit of cold tea in the glass instead, sweetened it up with a bit of sugar. If she'd noticed, she hadn't said anything. Probably wouldn't to me.

'I just wanted to say a special thank you to all for coming today, so close to Christmas as well; I know everyone's really busy, but...' My mum paused. She looked so uncomfortable. I didn't know why. I felt embarrassed for her. 'Andrew, we've been together for so long, and you know how much I love you. Not everything's been plain-sailing, and, without saying too much to everyone, this year has been a little more challenging than most.'

'You're not pregnant, are you?' Uncle Duncan shouted out.

I tightened the grip on my glass – anger. Mum shot him a look too. But I was more concerned about Mum's words than Duncan's heckle. I'd sensed something wasn't right, but what was she talking about? And why was I so in the dark?

I looked over at Frankie, grinning like a buffoon still as he squeezed Tom's shoulders to hold him in place. If either of them knew anything was wrong with our parents, they didn't show it.

'I felt like you needed a little something extra,' Mum added, quite lamely, as she looked at Dad.

'Sounds like it's your lucky night, Andy!' Duncan spewed. 'Make sure you use protection.'

I winced at his words. Dad looked pissed off too, but as

always, no one said anything to Duncan. We were all too nice, and no one wanted to cause a scene by calling out his imbecilic nature. Families, eh?

Mum took the envelope from the table and handed it to Dad. He had a grin on his face, but also looked a little dubious. He opened the envelope. Took out the piece of paper, unfolded it. His eyes went wide. 'Wow! Italy? The Grand Prix? Are you serious?'

Mum clasped her hands together and nodded. Her eyes welled. Mine too.

Dad reached forward and grabbed Mum and pulled her close to him, and for a few seconds their hug appeared genuine and loving and heartfelt and completely natural. But when they parted... something in their eyes. Distance, coldness. Mum stepped away. Dad grabbed his beer and took a heavy swig and the two of them simply drifted apart as people carried on with the night.

I watched them – my parents, my rocks – for a few more moments, my heart aching. It was true I'd acutely noticed their awkwardness with each other today, and I wasn't sure what had caused it now, but in reality I knew the distance between them had grown, slowly, incrementally, for some time, what they'd lost irretrievable.

I also knew it had all started because of me.

CHAPTER TWO

ONE WEEK LATER

S unday afternoon in the Red Lion was something of a tradition for the four of us. What had started at the beginning of our second year of university as a means to overcome our weekend hangovers, by drinking copious amounts of orange juice and lemonade while filling our stomachs with a classic Sunday roast, had turned into a regular, all-day social. Not an alcohol-fuelled, all-out bender, but more of a chance for us four girls – flatmates since the start of our second year – to sit and relax and wax lyrical about everything without interruption and, on good days, without thinking about the stresses and problems beyond the walls of the pub.

Of course, over the one and a half years of uni that we'd been housemates, there'd been plenty of ups and downs, twists and turns in our relationships with one another. Starting year two as a tight-knit foursome, in a few months we'd come to the end of our third year – the end of university entirely for some of us – and without doubt tension and strain had crept into the group dynamic here and there. Would we remain best of friends beyond next summer? Probably not all together, yet I'd certainly miss these moments.

'I saw Blake last night,' Gemma said, looking over the table at me. 'At Clink.'

Clink. One of our regular haunts that on a Saturday had a 90s night that was always at least three quarters students. Except I'd stayed in on my own last night; had missed last week too when I'd gone home for Dad's birthday. I blamed my latest absence on period cramps. A lie, which I think the others knew really, though no one had called me out.

'Jess?' Gemma prompted.

'What?'

'What's going on with you two? I thought you were getting serious.'

'Not really.'

'He seems to think so. He wasn't happy you weren't out. Says he hasn't seen you all week. Not since you came back from your parents.'

Dad's party. Yes, I'd gone home to celebrate with him, to celebrate with all my family, but I'd also wanted – needed – the opportunity to speak to him and Mum, get their advice and their comfort. But I never breathed a word to them.

No, that's not quite true. I got so close with Dad. In the morning. As we stood awkwardly in the hall, waiting for my taxi to take me to the station because Dad was too hung-over – probably over the limit still – and Mum had taken Lily for a walk.

I'd built myself up to talk to him. I think he knew something was wrong...

Then he'd gagged, dry-heaved, and as the taxi pulled up he rushed off to the toilet, face green.

'It's been a busy week,' I said to the girls.

Cath scoffed at that. I don't think she'd meant to be snide toward me, the reaction was intended more as light-hearted, and the sunken look on her face when I glared at her seemed to confirm that.

'I saw him talking to the hockey girls,' Natasha interjected.

'Yeah, they were all over him and his mates,' Cath said.

'As usual,' Gemma added.

It was true. One of Blake's best friends was dating the captain of the women's hockey team, so naturally Blake found himself around them a lot. Did I trust him with them? Not one hundred per cent. Was I bothered? Yes and no.

'Seriously, Jess, what's with you two?' Gemma asked. 'It was only a couple of months ago I bet Cath a tenner you and Blake would be the first out of all of us to get married.'

Cath laughed. Natasha looked shocked. Gemma smirked. I felt sick. I hoped none of them noticed.

'We're only twenty. I don't think that's going to happen,' I said.

'Because.'

'For one, because he's set on moving to London next year. He's already got a job lined up.'

'And you're what? Going back up north?'

Up north. My home town. Graystone. A little place of less than ten thousand about twenty miles from Leeds, the nearest big city. Not rural exactly, but also not exactly a hip and happening place. Did I want to end up back there? No. I'd deliberately gone to university in Bristol, a big city – to me at least – to experience something different from home. I'd always thought that was what I wanted.

Now?

'I haven't decided,' I said. 'But London?'

'What's wrong with London?'

'Nothing. I just never... I don't see myself there.'

'I thought you had a couple of offers from–'

'Let's just... I don't want to talk about Blake. Not today.'

Yes I'd had job offers from two banks in central London, but I wasn't even sure I wanted to be in finance, even if it was a natural progression from my business degree. Yet if not that, then what else?

Three years of my life wasted, most likely.

My friends stared at me. As though I was a problem somehow. For all of them. Or perhaps a misfit. The odd one out. Or maybe they all just sensed I'd closed myself down from them, even if they didn't know the reasons.

Why couldn't I confide in them? My best friends. Nor my parents. Why did I have no one in my life close enough to me that I could talk to openly and freely...

'Shall we get another bottle of Prosecco?' Cath asked.

'I'm up for it,' Gemma answered.

I checked my watch. 6pm. 'I think I'm going to walk back,' I said. 'I could do with getting a couple of hours revision done tonight.'

'Revision? A few days before we break up for Christmas?'

'I'm a bit behind,' I said. 'Sorry.' I got up from the table, put down twenty pounds which more than covered my costs, then walked away. I heard their whispers as I went. Concern, for sure, but mostly aggravation. I was annoyed at myself. I knew I'd been a lousy friend recently, but how could I tell them all the things going on in my head? Was anything in my life where I wanted it to be?

Car windows glistened with frost as I headed home, icy strands stretching across the glass like giant spider webs. I put my head down into the thick furry neck of my winter coat, hands in pockets, trying to eke out some warmth. We only lived half a mile from the pub, pretty much every house I passed on the streets of 1950s semis was full of students. The main campus was just the other side of the small park. I didn't see anyone I recognised as I walked, and an eerie feeling built

15

as I neared our road. I never liked walking alone in the dark, even at a reasonable time of night, even in such familiar surroundings.

I heard footsteps behind me. Glanced over my shoulder. I spotted a broad-shouldered figure, ten yards back, striding purposefully.

I crossed the road to the other side. Slowed down. The man went on past. I stayed on the wrong side of the road until I reached my turning, then dashed back across. I didn't see the dark shadow coming at me from my right, from behind a parked van, until the last second.

My heart raced, my body tensed and primed, I let out a little yelp of... something.

'Jess, it's only me.'

'Fuck, Blake, I was about to...' I didn't finish. About to what? My hands were out of my pockets. My fists balled. But what? Blake was six-two and athletic. I was an unfit five-seven and probably weighed little more than half as much as he did. It wasn't as though I could out-box him, out-fight him, out-run him even. Out-scream him?

'You okay?' he asked.

'Not really. You scared me.'

'Sorry, I didn't mean to.'

'What are you doing here?'

He looked confused by that comment. 'I was under the impression my girlfriend lived on this street.' He looked around, shrugging, holding his hands up, as though for confirmation from the people who weren't there. I rolled my eyes. He reached out and took both my hands. 'I missed you last night.'

I whipped my hands back. 'Yeah, sure you did. Is that why you were cosying up with Lauren and crew?'

He looked amused more than anything, which only made me all the more angry. 'You look hot when you're jealous.'

I huffed and walked off, but he was soon by my side. 'You know I would never do that to you?' he added.

'Do I?'

'Seriously? Have I ever?'

'How would I even know?'

'Well I'm telling you, I haven't.' Anger now. Or irritation at least. 'And I wouldn't be so bloody stupid as to do it when I know your friends are there, watching my every move.'

I stopped, he did too. I gave him my best pissed-off glare. 'Okay? So it's only because my friends saw you that you didn't fu–'

'That's not what I said.'

We stood in silence for a few seconds. I really didn't know what else to say.

'I wish you'd just let me in,' he said. I had no response to that. 'I haven't seen you properly for... it feels like an age.'

'It's only been a couple of weeks.'

He shook his head. 'But it's even longer since we–'

'So that's why you're here. Hockey girls not putting out for you?' I stormed off again.

'You know, you've got a real attitude problem.'

'Yeah?'

'Yes. You have. Whatever's going on in your head, I'm not the bad guy.'

'This isn't about good and bad, Blake.'

'Then what is it about?'

'It's... I...' How could I ever explain to him when I couldn't even explain to myself?

'I would have gone with whatever decision you wanted,' he said. 'You know that. I told you that. So to now push me away like this. It's bullshit, Jess. And I think you know it.'

We reached the gate to my house. We both stopped on the outside.

'What you mean is you copped out,' I said. 'Left the hard decision to me.'

'That's not fair.'

'Isn't it?'

'I just want you. More than anything. That's all. I still do. I love you.'

Did I believe him? I wanted to. And I wanted to reach out and grab him and squeeze him and have him squeeze me back and have him tell me everything was okay, and *we* would be okay, and...

'I need time to think.' I opened the gate and walked away from him. I opened the front door, stepped inside, my heart in pieces, perhaps the one person who could help mend it for me right there behind me, if only I let him...

Except when I turned back around, he'd already gone.

I shivered, then closed the door. My phone buzzed in my pocket as I took off my coat. I expected it to be Blake. Or even one of the girls, asking me to come back to the pub, or at least asking if I was okay.

'Frankie?' I said under my breath.

Not at all like my brother to call me. Ever.

'What's wrong?'

He didn't answer my question straight away. Not with words anyway. Instead all I got through the tinny speaker pressed to my ear was the most horrifying, stomach-churning cry of anguish. And it came again. Again.

I fell back against the wall. Slid down to the ground. 'Frankie... What's happened?'

'Jess,' he shouted, in between sobs. 'Jess, you've... got to come. It's... I think he's dead, Jess! Dad's dead.'

CHAPTER THREE

'What's happened? Where are you?'

'He's... we're in the garage. He's... he's hanging.'

Nausea rushed through me. Images flashed in my mind. Grainy, dark, like in a twisted horror movie, my dad's features ghastly in the dimly lit space – milky eyes bulging, face purple.

I shuddered. Got up from the floor, ran up the stairs to my bedroom. 'Where're Mum and the kids?'

The kids. Tom and Lily. Our younger siblings. Not really the same as me and Frankie. I was an adult. Frankie very nearly. The other two were so young, so intrinsically tied to our parents still.

'I've... I don't know. I... I... just got home...' A pause. 'Mum?!' he shouted out as though perhaps she was there after all.

'Frankie, focus.'

'Jess, what do I do!'

'Check his pulse.'

'What?'

'Frankie, check him!'

'I... can't.' Horrific silence... 'Nothing. There's nothing!'

I shut my eyes in despair. 'Cut him down!' I shouted.

Frankie didn't say anything, but then a wave of doubt, of panic, washed over me. Cut him down? Was that the right thing to do? 'Frankie, you have to try!'

'Please, just come home.'

'I'm on my way. Cut him down. Try CPR. I'll call an ambulance. I'll call Mum too. I'll... I'll go straight to the hospital. I'll see you there.' I ended the call, frowning at my own parting comment. Meet him at the hospital? As though the paramedics would rush Dad there, rather than... the morgue? As though there was a chance he could be saved...

There had to be.

I called 999, then Mum as I whizzed around the room packing a bag. The call to Mum went to voicemail. The next three too.

Minutes later – I don't know how many – I climbed into an Uber outside. Frankie called back. I looked at the phone, weighing heavy in my hand. A large part of me didn't want to answer. I didn't want to hear or see anymore. I wanted to crawl away somewhere dark, warm and safe.

I answered the call anyway. I realised then I couldn't leave Frankie alone like that.

Not ever.

'Frankie?'

'They're taking Dad.'

'Who? Where?'

'The paramedics. He's in the ambulance already.'

'Go with them.'

'I... there's police here too. I think they're taking photos.'

Strange thoughts whirred. Frankie had cut Dad down, just as I'd told him to. A crime scene investigator was photographing the garage – what did that mean? Had we made a mistake?

'Let me speak to them?'

'What?'

'The police. Let me speak to them.'

'I can't. I need to go with Dad.' A pause. 'Jess, I've got to go. I'll call you back.'

'Frankie!'

'Just get here soon. Please.'

'I will. I promise.'

Those last words haunted me for the next few hours. Sunday night was perhaps the worst possible time to attempt to get a train home, particularly so close to Christmas. Sunday service, problems on the line, replacement carriages. There were only two more trains that night. The 19:10 and the 21:10. At seven thirty the platform was crammed, the first train delayed due to leaves on the track somewhere, apparently.

Mum remained out of contact. Until my phone buzzed in my hand as the already packed train finally chugged along the platform toward me.

'Mum?'

'Jess... Jess, can you hear me?'

'Only just. Where are you?' Did she even know?

'I'm on my way.'

'Home? Or the hospital?' I assumed the hospital, but... 'Mum?'

'I ca... hear you... ry well.'

'You're cutting out. Where are you?'

Once again I got no answer to that.

'Mum?'

I looked down. The call had ended.

I should have taken a taxi all the way from my uni house in Bristol to the hospital in Leeds. Two hundred miles, give or take. I had no idea how much it would have cost – one hundred pounds, five hundred – but at least I would have been home more quickly.

In reality, no sooner had I boarded the horribly full train carriage my phone drained of battery. I didn't have a charger, the crowded carriage didn't even have charging points, and I spent the whole long, stuffy journey lost in a world of morbidity and questions of why my dad would kill himself.

Try to kill himself. *Please.*

I hadn't even managed another call with Frankie, and could only presume he – and Dad – were both at the hospital, rather than at home.

Mum, Tom and Lily?

I rushed across the hospital forecourt. A&E was hard to miss with its big, brightly lit sign. I sped inside. Reception desk to my left. Waiting area to my right. I was about to go to the desk when I saw him, sunken in a chair, on his own.

Frankie looked up at me... I've never known my brother to appear so small and lost.

'What's happening?' I said, striding over to him. A few heads turned my way, perhaps noting the desperation in my voice.

'I... I don't know.'

'Where's Dad?'

He shook his head.

'They brought him here? To A&E,' I said. 'You told me the paramedics were taking him in the ambulance.' The doubt in his eyes, the doubt in my own words...

Frankie reached forward and we wrapped our arms around one another and held each other like I don't ever remember holding my brother before.

'Where's Mum?' I asked.

'I don't know,' came his muffled response, his head on my shoulder.

'I spoke to her earlier. Hours ago. She was travelling home.'

He pulled back, doubt – worry – strong in his eyes still. 'From where?'

I didn't respond. I turned around to look over to the reception desk. 'I need to know what's going on.'

I went to move away from him then paused when I spotted a female police officer wearing a thick, bright yellow jacket coming in through the outer doors. I froze and turned to Frankie as my brain scrambled for some answers. Those same thoughts as earlier whirred once more. Was Frankie in trouble for having cut dad down so soon? Was I?

The police officer looked like she was about to go to the reception desk and for a fleeting moment relief bubbled deep down in my gut, but then she looked over and made a beeline for us and my heart seemed to stop for several beats.

'Jessica and Frankie Evans?' she asked, pity rather than suspicion in her voice, which made me all the more concerned.

'Yes,' I croaked, feeling Frankie nudge into my side as though for comfort.

'I tried to reach you at your home, but... I'm so sorry. There's been an accident.'

Neither I nor Frankie said a word. I couldn't if I'd tried.

'Your mum and brother and sister were in a car crash.'

I grabbed Frankie's hand. He squeezed hard.

'Where's Mum?' Frankie asked, sounding on the verge of breaking down. If not for the shock, I think we both would have.

The police officer slowly shook her head.

I glanced at Frankie's pained face. I knew what her words meant, even if I didn't understand. I didn't understand at all.

What was happening? 'Lily? Tom?' I asked, not sure I even wanted an answer.

'Your brother's a real fighter,' the police officer said with a strange optimism.

But no mention of Lily. No mention of her being a fighter. Sweet little Lily.

Tom was alive.

Mum and Lily – and Dad – weren't.

CHAPTER FOUR

L ooking back I don't know if the events of that fateful Sunday happened in slow motion or fast forward. My memories of the day, in some respects, are so detailed and vivid. I can smell it, feel it, remember minute details, like how many people were in the waiting area in the A&E at various points, what they wore, what they ate and drank. But that detail is at odds with how the day actually shot by in real time. How I went from drinking and eating in the Red Lion with my uni friends in the afternoon, to several hours later falling asleep on a chair next to Tom's hospital bed having learned of my Dad's suicide, and the car accident which had taken my Mum's and Lily's lives as they'd raced to come home.

The next few days definitely didn't race. They dragged. Dragged me through hell. I didn't want to be awake. I didn't want to see anyone, do anything.

The day Tom came home, a week later, was the day I thought perhaps there'd finally be some brightness returning to what was left of our lives.

In a way that was true, but I really wasn't sure it'd be enough for any of the three of us.

Tom, all things considered, was incredibly lucky. As the car flipped and crashed along the A-road, he'd suffered numerous injuries. A double rib fracture. A broken wrist. Severe bruising to his legs, but no broken bones there. A bad concussion, a horribly bruised face, but he had his life – and no long-term physical damage, the doctors thought.

'I still don't understand how,' I said to Frankie as we stood by the door to the lounge and watched our little brother. He was sitting on the carpet, reaching distance of the TV, watching his favourite programme – *Teen Titans Go*. Usually the show had him in hysterics. Today he watched glassy-eyed, not moving a muscle, not saying a word. He'd barely spoken a word in the last seven days. His reaction to the trauma wasn't just heartbreaking, it was disturbing. I wanted the old, lively Tom back. Not always happy exactly, in fact Mum and Dad often said Tom had no in between. He was full-on all the time, either full-on energy and happiness, or full-on bad mood and temper.

Now... he barely displayed any emotion at all most of the time.

Would, could the real Tom ever return?

'How what?' Frankie said, looking at me quizzically.

I moved away, into the kitchen where the island remained piled high with cards and flowers from family, friends, neighbours, people we'd never even met. I couldn't even bring myself to open the envelopes.

'I don't understand how Tom was okay,' I said. 'Why?' I was asking my seventeen-year-old brother as though he had expertise in car crash investigation.

'He was really lucky,' Frankie said.

He was. Undoubtedly. But I still didn't get it. And I wanted to know more. But I didn't just have questions over how Tom had survived a car crash that had killed two others rattling inside my mind, but so many other questions too. Why had Dad killed himself? Did anyone know how he was feeling? Did Mum know? Frankie? Could we have stopped him? Where was Mum going that Sunday night with Tom and Lily? Did Tom know? I wanted to ask him, about that day, the journey, what he remembered of the crash, but... too soon. I couldn't make him relive that horror.

'Was... everything okay?' I asked. 'Between Mum and Dad?'

'Obviously not,' Frankie said.

'Obviously, but—'

'This was totally out of the blue to me,' Frankie said, fixing a strange look on me.

'Do you think... do you think he really did it?' I asked.

Frankie didn't answer, but continued to hold my eye, making my insides turn over. I couldn't be sure whether the look was threatening or accusatory.

Did he think *I* had something to do with it all?

The next morning I left Frankie in charge of Tom – they weren't going anywhere. Tom wasn't up to it, either physically or mentally. Movies and snacks, again. At some point we'd move on from that, but I wasn't yet sure when. The doctors, police officers, the relatives we'd spoken to, had all said we had to keep normality for Tom – at least as far as we could, as far as his injuries allowed. The more he kept to a normal routine, the more easily he'd settle and begin living his life again. Technically he still had three days of school before the Christmas holidays, but I'd asked him over the weekend if he wanted to go and he'd simply looked to the floor and shook his head and cried. It would have been a trial for him anyway, given his broken wrist and banged up ribs.

Frankie – in his first year of A-levels – had already finished school until the new year, so he was, in a way, easy to sort out for now. January was the target for both of them to return to school.

As for me and my life at university? I had no clue. I didn't even want to think about it. I'd already made the decision to make sure my brothers were okay, first and foremost. I could deal with me later. Plus, my focus on the boys felt like a good coping mechanism, because it at least kept my mind off our shared trauma, which I struggled to face otherwise.

Denial? Perhaps.

I drove Dad's car into town. I'd been a named driver on his insurance since I passed my test a couple of weeks before my nineteenth birthday, though this was the first time I'd ever been out in his BMW on my own. Not only that, it was the first time I'd driven since Mum's accident, and my heart raced the whole way, even though I drove ridiculously carefully, and slowly, ignoring the many glares and flashing headlights and beeps from the other road users. Such unnecessary aggression. Had those attitudes – self-entitlement, mostly – contributed to what happened to Mum?

I was made to wait in the dull reception of the police station. A couple of hard steel chairs, a small coffee table with self-congratulatory police magazines. A water cooler in the corner, the plastic of the cabinet pink around the edges from age or wear, the whole thing grimy. After nearly half an hour a plain clothed woman I knew as DS Holster came out. She was short and fit-looking, a grey trouser suit, dark brown hair pulled back tight. An uncompromising face – probably necessary for a detective – but she did smile, kind of, as she approached me.

'Jess?' she asked as I got to my feet.

'Yes.'

'I'm DS Holster. We met before, at the hospital.' She said the words as though it'd been a non-event and I'd have no chance of remembering her, as opposed to the most eventful and horrifically unforgettable day of my life.

'I know,' I said.

The smile faltered a little.

'Please, follow me.'

She turned and I walked behind her, through doors, along corridors, to a room. A room where they interviewed suspects? The space had a single barred window, a table, three chairs, no big mirror like on TV, but was that because of the CCTV camera in the corner?

'No need to be nervous,' Holster said. She looked about the room, a little apologetically. 'Sorry, it's not a big station and half of it's being refurbished, so this is the best I can offer.'

'It's okay,' I said.

'We can go out if you prefer? I'll buy you a coffee.'

'It's fine, really.'

'Okay then.' She sat forward and clasped her hands together. 'What can I help you with?'

I let out a sarcastic laugh. 'Time machine would be nice.'

Holster frowned, concerned. 'How are you holding up, Jess? We can find you any help you need. You just need to say.'

'Do you know what happened? To my Mum and Lily? The accident?'

Holster unclasped her hands, sighed, sat back. 'You're asking about the crash?'

'Yes.'

Holster sighed again. She stared at me strangely, like a psychiatrist might with a deranged patient. 'It was a simple accident,' she said. 'I know that's not comforting to you, but it happens.'

Not comforting? I don't know if it was or wasn't.

'There were no other cars?' I asked.

Holster shook her head. 'We've reviewed CCTV footage, a

29

crash scene investigator went over everything at the site. There was no evidence of any other vehicles being involved, or having caused the crash. Your mum... she was more than likely going too fast. She lost control on a bend. It's a notorious spot and it was pretty frosty that night. Skid marks showed where she tried to... to avoid crashing.' Holster shook her head again, a pained look now on her face.

I realised I was clutching my hands too tightly. I let go and looked down and saw the little lines of reddened flesh on my palms where my nails had cut into the skin.

Did I feel relief to know Mum's and Lily's deaths were pure accident? That no one else had caused it?

No. Because someone had caused it still. Mum had. Somehow I felt even worse knowing that.

'If she was speeding, driving too fast...'

I couldn't finish the sentence. Holster reached across the table, as though to take my hand for my comfort. I didn't move. After a few seconds she took her hand away again.

'But Tom survived,' I said. 'I don't understand.'

'He was on the other side to Lily and your mum. Their side was... it was more badly damaged when the car rolled.' She really struggled to say the words, though I felt that was only because of the effect she could see – or imagined – her words had on me. The connotations sent a wave of nausea through my gut. 'Somehow the side Tom was on remained more or less intact. He was very, very lucky.'

I shook with grief as tears rolled again. How many tears had I shed these past few days? I hated my vulnerability, but what was I supposed to do?

'Is something... what are you thinking, Jess? About the crash?'

I laughed. A very odd and subconscious reaction, though Holster didn't bat an eyelid. I couldn't decide whether her calmness was a good thing for me or not. 'I don't know... I don't know why she was so far from home,' I said.

Now Holster reacted. A questioning flick of an eyebrow. 'She was rushing to the hospital, I imagine.'

'No, but... before that. Before I spoke to her.'

I paused, thinking.

'Go on,' Holster prompted.

'Where she crashed was nearly an hour away. On a Sunday night... it doesn't make...'

'It was outside her routine?'

'As far as I know. I mean... I don't live with them now. Didn't. Didn't live with them.'

'Friends or family near there?'

'It's south. I guess it's the way she'd go to visit me. My aunt and uncle too. But... I don't know.'

Holster nodded.

'Honestly, Jess? I don't think you should beat yourself up about this. As I said, this was an accident.'

Unless she meant to do it, I thought but didn't say. Though that didn't make any sense. When I'd spoken to her that time on the phone... she'd been so distraught. Plus Holster had mentioned about the skid marks. Mum had tried to save herself. Save Tom and Lily.

'What about my dad?' I asked.

'He took his own life. We're not looking into it further.'

The finality with which Holster said this annoyed me. As though she was attempting to pre-empt my questions, as though she didn't want me to go down the path of suggesting maybe his death wasn't suicide, that perhaps someone had killed him. Despite there being no evidence of anyone else having been there, no evidence of a break-in or anything like that. Despite the note he'd left us all, in his unmistakeable, barely legible handwriting.

31

'I don't know why he did it,' I said.

'I can't imagine how you're feeling, but this is often the way.'

Was she speaking from personal or professional experience?

'Suicide is often out of the blue for many family members and friends. Perhaps for the very fact that the victim internalises. They can't share their darkest thoughts with others. And sometimes... it's because they don't want to be dissuaded.'

I closed my eyes as a wave of thoughts hit me. How long had Dad planned this? Could, should, I have done more? Mum, Frankie too?

'I'm glad you came to see me,' Holster said, shaking me back to my new grim reality. 'But really none of this is a police matter anymore. This must be incredibly hard for you, but please at least take some comfort in that.'

I couldn't speak. I felt so foolish, childish. She was basically telling me I was there wasting her time.

'I can't imagine what you're going through, Jess, but there's so much help out there, available for you. If you need me to–'

'I'm sorry for taking your time,' I said, getting to my feet.

'Don't be silly.'

I turned to leave.

'Jess, don't torture yourself. Take the help that's on offer. You'll need it. For you, and for your brothers.'

Don't torture myself? Except it wasn't about me. It was about my family and our shared tragedy. I'd already decided to lock away my own grief as long as I could in order to get us through. And I wouldn't let it out until I had some answers.

CHAPTER FIVE

W hen I arrived home Tom remained in the lounge, in front of the TV. He barely moved when I said hello. I hugged him. I'd do that as much as I could from now on.

I found Frankie in the kitchen, sitting by the island, playing on his phone.

He saw me, carried on typing for a few seconds then put his phone onto the worktop and sighed. 'Everyone's going out tonight,' he said. 'A Christmas party at Icon.'

Icon. The only real nightclub in our town. A grotty, smelly place full of teens – the club, not the town. Well, mostly at least. I'd loved Icon at his age.

'Go if you want,' I said to him, even though the very thought of going to a club, drinking and chatting, felt so alien to me, so far out of reach. 'Please, don't feel like you can't live still.'

He looked at me, but didn't say anything. I moved over and took the stool on the adjacent corner to him. He looked over at the flowers, the cards. The envelopes I hadn't managed to open were now torn apart, the cards in a small pile by Frankie.

'Who are these people?' he said, almost disgusted.

So far in the past seven days we'd had plenty of knocks on the door. Had our distant family members like Duncan and Sarah phone over and over, offering their condolences, but it wasn't much, and in truth that was fine. I didn't want them butting into our lives, and I'd pushed back on any attempts at planned visits from anyone.

Other than my brothers, the family member I felt most sorry for was Nanna. Frankie and I had been to see her at the nursing home she lived at, not far from us, and I'd visited her once on my own too before that, while Tom was still in hospital. She'd been strangely quiet on both occasions. She'd barely said a word. For years she'd suffered from dementia, far worse at some times than others. Had she even processed what I'd told her? One of the things that had stuck with me most was a simple sentence she'd repeated on both occasions. *Everything happens for a reason.*

Actually no, that wasn't the sentence that stuck with me most. One other, even more prominent, remained forefront in my mind, if not for the words, then certainly for the tone of delivery.

They never leave us. Not really.

I shivered.

'I'll go then, if you really don't mind?' Frankie said. He looked so uncomfortable as he spoke.

'It's really not a problem,' I said, even though I couldn't imagine why he'd want to go and party, but that didn't mean I should stop him. After all, we'd been explicitly told to stick to normality for Tom's sake, so why not for Frankie and me too? 'Just don't be back too late. And you need to text me every hour.'

He didn't look impressed by that. But I knew that Mum would have insisted on the same. Just thinking about that caused my eyes to well.

'Okay,' he said, to my surprise. He left the room.

I stared over the cards and flowers once more. I picked up the most recent arrivals. Read the messages of condolence. I recognised some of the names, such as Mum and Dad's cousins who I'd met maybe two, three times in my life. Some others I could see the link, such as a neighbour from a few doors down, who'd signed off the card with their name and house number, showing they weren't at all close to my parents or me and my siblings, but I guessed everyone on the street was talking. Other names I had no clue about at all, like Jannette, from a local church group, saying we should go to Mass and that God and Jesus could help us get through this.

I slammed that one down, though I wasn't quite sure why.

Then my eyes rested on the now well-thumbed piece of paper. A5, lined. Ripped from one of the corporate logo emblazoned notepads that Dad used to bring home from work on a regular basis. We must have had ten, fifteen of them lying around the house in various states of use.

Did it mean anything that he'd chosen something so ubiquitous, so without apparent worth to him or us, to write his last words?

I reached over and took the paper, unfolded it and stared down at the scrawl.

My dearest Jane, Jess, Frankie, Tom and Lily. Please forgive me. I'll miss you all.

No sign-off even. Just those fifteen words, a third of them simply our names. His whole life, and death, boiled down to something so basic and... inexplicable.

I continued to stare at the words, looking from letter to letter. Yes, my dad's handwriting was unmistakeable, but... I shook that thought away and instead concentrated on the message. The more I read the note, the more just three of the words stood out, looming larger and larger each time.

Please forgive me.

But forgive him for what? For killing himself and leaving us all alone?

Or had he meant something else entirely?

CHAPTER SIX

FRANKIE

He lay back on the bed in Meg's room. She remained sitting perpendicular to him, back to the wall, her bare legs, sticking out from her short skirt, tangled with his in his jeans. In the other corner of the room, Katie sat on Ali's lap, squeezed in on an oversized bean bag. Meg's bedroom was small, about the same size as the box rooms Tom and Lily had at home. That Lily used to have. Other than the bed, much of Meg's room was taken up by the desk, upon which sat her laptop, a clutter of schoolbooks, and a chaotic selection of make-up. Thirty or more photos were spread out across the wall above the desk, depicting various highlights of Meg's teen years.

Frankie liked it in her room. Liked the way the space felt, smelt, the way *he* felt there – even if the rest of the house was, in all honesty, a bit of a dump. A basic two up, two down, the only other bedroom belonging to Meg's dad. Not the most pleasant of men.

Was it better to have a horrible dad than *no* dad, though?

'What did you tell her, then?' Ali asked, snapping Frankie from his thoughts.

'Said we were going to Icon.'

Ali raised his eyebrow with a grin. Frankie looked to Meg. She wasn't impressed.

'So you found it more easy to explain to your sister that you were going for a midweek bender at a nightclub, than to tell her you were going to your girlfriend's house?' Ali asked, enjoying Frankie's awkward moment.

'That's because she doesn't know about Meg, does she?' Katie asked, or more just stated really. Given the tone of her voice, she clearly didn't approve.

'She doesn't know, yet,' Frankie confirmed. He reached over and took Meg's hand. She didn't resist but she did take her legs off him. She pulled her skirt down a little before curling her feet under her. 'It's not like that,' he added. Like what? 'It's not as though I'm that close to Jess.'

He felt bad as those words passed his lips, imagining how his sister would feel to know he'd said that.

'Then what's the problem?' Katie asked, clearly wanting to stick up for her friend. 'Why is it better to lie to her?'

'Doesn't have to be a lie,' Ali said. 'We *could* go to Icon.'

Both girls glared at him. A little unfair, Frankie thought.

'Seriously, Frankie, why are you lying about Meg?' Katie asked again.

Frankie didn't answer. He shuffled closer to his girlfriend. She rested her head on his shoulder.

'I'll tell Jess. When it's right.'

Except he didn't know when that would be. And the problem wasn't really why he hadn't told Jess. He hadn't told his parents about Meg either. Why? He really couldn't be sure. Yet his reasons for lying to Jess weren't only to do with the difficulty in explaining about his girlfriend, were they? The problems in his life were far more serious than a burgeoning relationship his family knew nothing about. That's why he'd come out tonight, to get away from it all.

'You got another one?' Frankie asked Ali, who nodded immediately, no doubt what he meant by the question.

Ali took the spliff from the top pocket of his shirt. 'Last one though.'

'I'm not sure we should,' Meg said. 'It'll stink in here.'

'It's only one little joint.'

Meg sighed and lifted off Frankie. 'Maybe. But I want something to drink first.'

He held her eye for a few moments. He got what she meant. Yes, she wanted something to drink, but she wanted him and Ali to go and get it from the shop. She wanted a girlie chat with Katie. Probably about him.

'You okay?' Ali asked as he and Frankie trudged slowly along the cold, dark and quiet street.

'Not really.'

'You seem more pissed off than upset.'

Was he?

'Maybe because I knew something was going on.'

'How do you mean?'

'With Mum and Dad. And with Jess too. I told you about the party last week.'

'Your dad's?'

'Not just that. Something had been wrong with Mum and Dad for a few weeks. Sniping, arguing, barely able to be in the same room together.'

'You think that's why... why your dad...'

Frankie closed his eyes and squeezed his fists together in his coat pockets. He'd never forget walking in to see his dad like that. And he'd never forgive himself for not going home earlier that night.

He'd been at Ali's house, Katie and Meg there too. For the last two months, with him dating Meg, the four of them had become something of a clique. Two couples, two sets of best friends. Katie had wanted to be home for a family dinner that night, and Frankie and Meg had left a little before she needed to go in order to give her and Ali a bit of alone time. Frankie could have gone straight home from there. If he had, he would have been back a good thirty, forty minutes earlier. Enough to save his dad?

But would he just have killed himself another time?

Possibly. Yet that wasn't the point. The point was that he'd first walked Meg home. And even then he'd delayed. Her dad was home that evening, so Frankie couldn't go in. Already dark out, in the middle of winter, they'd snuck around the back of the house, shared a few kisses in the grotty little yard. Shared a little bit more than kisses, actually. Frankie had wanted to take it even further still, but Meg held him at bay – worried about her dad hearing them – and eventually persuaded Frankie that he needed to go.

He'd gone away from her house that night frustrated. With her, for not letting him stay longer. How stupid and childish that all seemed now. If he'd just...

No, he couldn't keep thinking like that.

'Frankie?'

'Sorry,' he said. He'd been miles away. He got his thinking back on track. 'The thing is, when Jess came home that day for the party, everything was even weirder. Mum and Dad with each other, but Jess with them too. None of them would tell me anything, but Jess knows something.'

'You think she caused it?'

What would he do if that was the case? Could he ever forgive her if she'd done something to cause their dad to kill himself? But what could that possibly be?

'I'm going to find out,' Frankie said. 'One way or another, I'll find out what she did.'

They arrived at the run-down little corner shop. Really much of this part of town was run-down, from the cramped terraced houses, mostly with unkempt yards, to the small recreation ground forever littered and with broken play equipment.

Somehow Meg had blossomed from this area though. It did happen. A diamond in the rough, some people would say.

His diamond.

A buzzer sounded as they pushed the door open. The burly shopkeeper, behind a Perspex screen for his own protection – the necessity of which only went to show the quality of the usual clientele – eyeballed Frankie and Ali as they stepped through and toward the selection of cheap beer and wine in the far corner.

Frankie's heart rate steadily built as he looked over the booze.

'How much you got?' Ali asked.

'Tenner.'

'Same. Vodka'll probably be better.'

'Yeah,' Frankie agreed, though all the spirits were behind the counter so they'd have to ask the guy for that.

'Let's get some snacks too.'

They grabbed a couple of large bags of crisps and popcorn then skulked off for the counter.

Shit. As they turned the corner Frankie spotted someone else there. He hadn't noticed him before, too focused on getting to the booze.

Dylan. Of course it had to be Dylan, in this part of town. Frankie put his arm out across Ali's chest, intent on halting their forward progress and making a quick retreat back out of sight.

But Dylan's head twisted and he set his beady eyes on them.

A silent glare before he took his change from the shopkeeper and headed out without a word.

'Don't stress it, man,' Ali said. 'It'll be fine.'

Since when was anything fine around that piece of shit?

'Come on,' Ali said, giving Frankie's coat sleeve a little tug. Even more nervous than before, the two of them sauntered up to the counter, the shopkeeper glaring at them the whole way.

'One of those vodkas, please,' Ali said, pointing to the cheapest offering. Ali was nearly always the front man. Although a few months younger than Frankie, his face was undoubtedly a little older looking, plus he had some decent facial stubble. Plus he had a top-quality fake ID if it came to that.

The shopkeeper didn't make a move for the drink. Instead he continued to glare at Ali, then to Frankie, then back to Ali again. 'You're eighteen?' the guy said.

Ali laughed. 'Twenty, mate. I've been in here loads. Don't you remember?'

Definitely a lie. He'd been in twice before with Frankie, who could see no reason why his friend would have been any other time. Ali lived the other side of town. The nicest part of town. The biggest houses, the best cars. Frankie's home was in the middle, both physically and in every other sense.

The shopkeeper glared at Frankie again, then mumbled under his breath before he turned and grabbed one of the vodkas. Frankie tossed the crisps and popcorn onto the counter then handed out the ten pounds. All a little too eager, he realised, given the stern look Ali gave him.

The shopkeeper shook his head. He knew. Didn't he? Still, he gave them the change and Frankie couldn't have grabbed the goods and headed for the door any more quickly.

Except he stepped outside and then wished he'd taken a little longer.

He spotted Dylan, sitting on a low wall. And he wasn't alone. In the dark, and given their dark clothing and their hoods, Frankie couldn't be sure who they were, but two others lurked with Frankie's nemesis.

'You don't live around here,' Dylan said. He rose from the wall and stepped forward. His two companions, both with drinks in their hands, got to their feet too, though stayed by the wall.

Frankie and Ali stood their ground, even if a large part of Frankie wanted to turn and bolt. That would only add fuel to Dylan's fire.

'I know why you're on our turf,' he said, only a couple of steps away as he came to a stop. He spat on the ground. 'She putting out for you yet?'

Frankie said nothing.

'Fucking loser. She's about the easiest ride I ever had. She doesn't like you, mate.'

'You spend a lot of time thinking about my girlfriend?' Frankie asked.

Dylan's face twitched. 'Yeah I do. I spend a lot of time thinking about her riding on me.'

Frankie held his tongue as Dylan's friends burst out laughing. Ali took hold of his friend's arm. Frankie wanted to go, wanted nothing more than to get out of there. Well, perhaps he wanted to smack Dylan in the face too, but he couldn't exactly do that, could he? Especially not here.

'How's things *hanging* with your dad?' Dylan asked, to another round of guffaws from his friends. The two of them high-fived each other as they pointed and cackled.

Frankie's muscles tensed, his legs shook, it was a big battle to not launch himself forward.

'You must be a really shitty son for him to be that desperate to get away from you.'

'No need for that,' Ali said, half stepping in front of Frankie.

'At least I had a dad,' Frankie said. 'Do you even know which scumbag your mum was fucking before she shat you out?'

Not the wisest move. Dylan bolted forward. Ali stood in the way, took an arcing fist to the side of his head as he tried to hold Dylan back. The two friends moved forward too. Frankie was stuck in two minds...

Then the door to the shop swung open and the bulky shopkeeper stepped out, bat in hand. 'Get out of here, you little shits!'

Ali threw Dylan off him. For a moment they were all caught in a stand-off, before Dylan's friends grabbed their leader and pulled him away.

'Next time, Evans,' Dylan drawled. 'I see you around here again, I'm gonna knife you.'

'Just keep on walking,' the shopkeeper shouted as the three shuffled off, thankfully in the opposite direction to where Frankie and Ali would go. 'And, you two, I'm not here to save your arses. Now piss off before I call the police.'

Ali actually blew him a kiss. Frankie grabbed his mate, and the both of them hotfooted it away.

Frankie's legs remained shaky with adrenaline. The amped feeling didn't fade for a few minutes. Then fear set in. Dylan was not a good person to have as an enemy. For years he'd been in more scraps than anyone else at school, and luckily Frankie had flown low enough under the radar to never get on the wrong side of him.

Until Meg.

'He's got it in for me,' Frankie said.

'What do you expect? You basically stole Meg from him.'

'Come off it, it's—'

'I'm joking, mate. But you know he still thinks she's his.'

'They weren't even together properly. At least not according to her.'

'Has she ever... has she talked to you about him?' Ali asked.

Frankie didn't want to think about that. He knew the two of them had had sex, a horrible thought really, but it wasn't as though he and Meg were going to go through the sordid details with each other, were they? Dylan was history. According to her at least.

Except that psycho apparently didn't agree.

They made it back to Meg's unscathed, Frankie almost relaxed by that point, and found the two girls on the bed, in fits of giggles. The boys unpacked the goods and soon got down to it, all four of them on the bed as they drank through the vodka. They persuaded Meg to let them enjoy the last joint. They talked, laughed, and Frankie generally felt bloody good for the first time in a long time, even if his trauma, his grief, remained there right under the surface, ready to rise up if he stopped at any point to think of life outside Meg's room.

By the time they'd worked through the booze it was already gone ten thirty. Frankie became even more dejected as he sent Jess his latest update text. The fun was almost over. Meg's dad would be home soon, and he'd not even got to spend any time just with her. As he looked up from his watch, Ali caught his eye, perhaps understanding. He leaned over and whispered in Katie's ear.

'Come on then, handsome,' she said, before planting a kiss on Ali's lips. 'Let's leave these two lovebirds on their own.'

Smiles and hugs all around before Ali and Katie were gone. Frankie lay down on the bed. Meg cranked the window a little further open, despite the chill coming inside from the night.

'Still reeks of weed in here,' she said. She jumped onto the bed and into Frankie's arms and he held her, and they kissed for a few moments before she pulled back.

'Are you sure... is this really okay for you?' she said.

'What?'

'Like... so soon after–'

'Of course it is.' He went to kiss her again but she shuffled further back.

'I don't know how you can cope. If–'

'Come on, we don't have long.' He went to kiss her again but then they both froze. She'd heard it too. The car engine outside.

'Shit,' they both said in unison.

'He's early,' Meg said, jumping off the bed in a panic.

Frankie glanced at his watch. Definitely early. Her dad didn't normally get back from work until half eleven. Frankie needed to go. Ryan Lambert was a dinosaur, over-protective dad, big and mean. Kind of how Frankie imagined Dylan would be in years to come.

Not for the first time, Frankie wondered how someone as beautiful as Meg, and as kind and intelligent as her, had turned out as she had. From her mother? Possibly. Though Frankie had never met her. A druggie, apparently, she'd run away from home when Meg was five, never to be seen again, leaving her in the care of her nasty, vicious dad.

Somehow she'd nonetheless turned out as she was, even if her home situation meant dating her was tricky to say the least.

'Come on, Frankie!' Meg said.

He grabbed his coat. Grabbed the bag with the empty vodka bottle and snack wrappers. He pushed his feet into his shoes, no time to lace them. Meg pretty much shoved him toward the open window.

The sound of the front door opening and closing echoed.

Frankie reached the window. Had one leg out when he turned back to Meg.

'I could always just go down the stairs,' he said to her. 'You could introduce me properly.'

She looked at him like she had no clue whether he was joking or not. In a way, he wasn't so sure himself.

He kissed Meg on the lips then swung around, dangled and dropped down. A well practised move now. He scuttled off away from the house. Looked back to the window. Meg waved before closing it and moving off out of view, probably to greet her dad and fob him off with how she'd been doing homework all evening, or some other bullshit fib.

Frankie straightened up and stopped and looked up and down the quiet road. No one in sight at this time of night. Thankfully. No sign of Dylan and his gang. A very big plus.

He pulled the hood over his head. Looked around him once more, then, hands in pockets he moved across the road to the narrow snicket that ran between two rows of houses, leading to the next parallel street. Away from the sporadic street lights, he faded into the darkness of the alley.

He stopped. Turned. He pulled up against the wall. Calmed his breathing. Inside the pocket of his coat, the fingers of his right hand rummaged and then wrapped around the handle of the flick knife. He felt a little safer at the feel of the cold metal.

His eyes settled back on Meg's house across the way. His plans with her were spoiled, but given the last text he'd sent to Jess, he still had plenty of time before he needed to head home.

Plenty of time to do one of the things he liked most of all.

Watch.

CHAPTER SEVEN

JESS

Frankie had left the house just before 8pm. I'd managed to get Tom into his dressing gown by then, and he'd brushed his teeth but was back to watching TV as Frankie headed out. It wasn't long ago Tom had worn pyjamas to bed every night, whatever the weather, but now he vehemently claimed to be too old, and would sleep in nothing but his boxer shorts, even on a frigid winter's night.

Tom's usual bedtime was eight o'clock, though at weekends he stayed up until nine. I really didn't know what the protocol was supposed to be now. Should he get to stay up to whenever he liked? Should we keep to his routine as another example to him of life going on as 'normal'? Should I even have tried to get him to bed earlier? At least that way, in sleep, there was less time for him to have to face our dark, new reality.

'Shall I take you up?' I said to Tom when his latest programme finished. Nearly 9pm.

He looked at me with glazed eyes and nodded. A surprise reaction really. 'Piggyback?' he asked.

'Why not.'

He got up from the floor and I got up from the sofa. I turned around and he climbed onto my back, holding on with just one arm. He was heavy. Too heavy for me to really carry him like that, though I loved to do it for him whenever I came back to visit.

Did Mum and Dad do it every night?

'Blimey, Tom, you're eating too much,' I said as I achingly rose up. 'No more burgers for you. Salad only.'

'Meanie,' he said, playfully hitting my side before resting his head on my shoulder. I smiled at the comfort of his body close to mine, though I soon wiped it away when I moved to the hall and saw my relaxed, happy face in the mirror.

Too soon.

I powered up the stairs, my legs seriously aching by the time we reached the top. The landing light was already on. I flicked the light on in Tom's box room too – a mirror image to Lily's small space right next door. When we'd moved into the house it'd been one decent sized bedroom, easily big enough for a double bed, but when Lily came along and Tom was forced to share, my parents eventually asked a builder to split the room in two.

Tom climbed into his single bed, tucked in the corner of the room, pulled the Star Wars duvet to his neck. I knelt down by his side.

'Where's Frankie?' he asked.

'He went out with some friends.'

'Why?'

'Because it's important we still do the things we like.'

'Can I?'

'Can you what?'

'Still do the things I like?'

'Of course.' I reached forward and ran my hand through his

messy, light brown hair, pushing his quiff back and up. With closely-cropped hair at the back and sides, his hair was super stylish, like the footballers he idolised, and he was incredibly handsome for a nine-year-old, even if he was too young to realise it. 'What would you like to do?'

'I dunno,' he said. 'Bowling? Cinema?'

'We'll do both. I promise.'

'Both? Tomorrow?'

'If you're good. And if there's time.' I leaned forward and kissed his forehead. 'Night, night.' I walked to the door and turned off his light.

'Jess?' he said.

I paused. 'Yeah?'

'Do you think they're watching us?'

I shuddered at the question, though I wasn't sure why, even if the words did remind me of what Nanna had said.

And anyway, what did Tom want the answer to be? None of us were religious particularly, we didn't go to church or anything like that. We'd never before had serious conversations about heaven, hell, the afterlife. Did he *want* to believe his parents were now up in the sky somewhere, looking down? If not heaven, then... did he want to see the *ghosts* of his parents?

Or was he terrified at the possibility?

'I'm sure wherever they are, they're watching over us,' I said, hoping that would quell him. 'They'll see all the good times. And they'll keep us safe. They'll always be with us. Always.'

In the darkness I couldn't gauge the reaction on his face.

By eleven thirty I decided I'd had enough of watching TV on my own. Not that I'd been paying attention to the screen much. My phone hadn't been out of my hands. One, because I was waiting for Frankie's supposedly regular messages, and two because I decided, with nothing better to do, to work through the backlog of messages and emails from friends and the like. My uni girls were all asking after me, offering help, wanting to know when I'd be back. It wasn't that I wanted to ignore them, I really didn't, but I couldn't even begin to deal with the thought of university, and I didn't want any of them making the trip up here to see me.

Blake had tried numerous times to contact me too. I'd tried to placate him in response, rather than ignore him, but I hadn't spoken to him, and really couldn't face that part of my life right now.

I'd also received messages from my friends at home: Jamie and Kristen, the power couple, and Ed, my geeky soulmate type, and Hannah, my best friend since we were at nursery together. People I'd grown up with, went to school with, who I'd been so close to before university. But our lives had drifted apart in the last two and half years. I wasn't even sure how they'd known about what happened as I hadn't directly told them. Each of them had messaged me separately, plus I'd received well wishes through our not so well used group chat on WhatsApp. They all wanted to meet up with me. At some point I'd want that too, though I didn't know when, or whether to do so with them all at once or one at a time.

I was so confused.

I left the decision hanging and headed upstairs, leaving the hall light on to help Frankie when he came back. Which would be when? The last message I'd had from him was time-stamped 10.22. More than an hour ago.

I moved across to Tom's room. Sound asleep. Despite his new, quieter self, I was still so proud of him, of his strength and resilience.

I went to go to my room but instead found myself at Lily's

door, staring inside to the dark and empty and eerily quiet space. It still smelled of her. A distinctive sweetness that I think came from her shampoo.

Shit, I hadn't even thought about when, how, we'd clear out her room. Mum and Dad's too.

I shook my head. No, don't think about that now.

I looked into the room again. Turned on the light. From the doorway I looked over her toys, her bed, her teddies. I could hear her voice, see her, feel her. It was true there'd always been an awkwardness between me and Lily – entirely one-sided – though my heart ached for her now. I wanted nothing more than to hold her, squeeze her, play with her, have her painfully brush through my hair as she explained in great detail how she would be a hairdresser one day.

I sobbed, standing there, thinking of her, thinking of all the times I should have tried to be closer to her.

Until my phone pinged. Frankie.

I'm okay. Back soonish.

Soonish? Probably a couple of hours then, I thought with an eye-roll, though at least he was out there, living.

I looked back to Lily's room once more. I turned off the light. But as I did so I was sure a shadow flashed across the room from left to right and I heard a faint whisper.

I gasped, stepped back. Stared. My eyes ever so slowly adjusted.

I stood and listened. The house was horribly quiet. But I'd heard something. A rush of air perhaps? No, it had sounded so clear... my name. A soft, female voice.

I reached out, turned on the light once more...

Nothing there. Nothing had moved.

Of course it hadn't.

I turned away this time, before I turned the light off, then rushed across the lit landing to the bathroom. I quickly got myself ready, moved back out. Glanced to the darkness beyond Mum and Dad's partially open bedroom door. I shook with irrational fear.

I rushed across, couldn't look inside their room as I grabbed for the door handle and pulled the door closed. A waft of cool air billowed out as I did so. I shivered. The air caught in my nostrils.

It smelled just like them.

———

I was only half asleep an hour later. How could I get a deep sleep with so much darkness not just in my head, but outside my room, so much emptiness. A five-bedroom house, for years so busy and bustling. Tonight it was only me and Tom. Only Frankie was missing from the previous few nights but it still felt so wrong, so lonely.

I hated it.

Yet somehow I succumbed to tiredness. My phone remained gripped in my hand, my low bedside light still on, when I woke with a start, my body jolting upright. Groggy, disorientated, it took me a few seconds to figure out what was happening.

Then the scream came again...

'Tom!' I shouted, jumping from the bed with a jolt. My phone came out of my grasp and clattered to the floor. I left it, raced for the door, across the landing. The door to Mum and Dad's room remained closed. Frankie's door remained open. He wasn't home yet? I reached Tom's room and slapped haphazardly at the light switch.

Tom was sitting up in the bed. His knees to his chest, his eyes wide. He rocked back and forth.

'There was someone here,' he said, pure terror in his voice. 'Someone was in my room.'

I rushed over to him, sat on the bed and grabbed him and held him. I looked across the room as irrational thoughts blared in my mind – the shape in Lily's room, that voice...

'No one was here, Tom. It's just me and you.'

'No, Jess, there was a man. I saw him. Standing in the doorway.'

I shivered. Then jumped at the bang downstairs.

'Frankie?' I shouted out. No answer. My heart pounded my chest. 'Frankie!'

More of a shriek now.

Then the shadow in the doorway...

'Bloody hell, Jess,' Frankie slurred. 'I was trying to be quiet.'

I was as angry as I was relieved to see him.

'Frankie, check the house,' I said to him.

For a few seconds he looked at me like I was an idiot, but then his demeanour changed. He must have realised what was going on by the petrified looks on both mine and Tom's faces. 'Okay. I'll go check.' He rushed off.

Tom and I didn't move. My little brother clung to me like I couldn't remember him doing for years. I listened with intent for Frankie, for anything else. The house remained painfully quiet around us as we waited.

Then I heard soft padding up the stairs. I held my breath until Frankie reappeared in the doorway.

'It's fine,' he said. 'Everything's fine.'

An overstatement, perhaps, but his words still brought genuine relief.

'What's going on?' he said.

'Nothing, just a bad dream.'

'It wasn't a dream!' Tom protested, wrestling away from my grip.

'The alarm's on downstairs,' Frankie said. 'And everything's locked tight.'

I released Tom fully and looked at him. 'Yeah?' I said to him. 'You happy? There's no one else here. Just us.'

He nodded, though looked far from convinced.

I got up and he lay back. I tucked him in and moved to the door.

'What the hell was that?' Frankie whispered to me.

'He just got freaked out.' I looked over the banisters to the darkness below. Tom was freaked out? What about me?

'Yeah, well, I'm knackered,' Frankie said, turning to move off.

'Was it good?'

He faced me again and gave a reluctant smile and nodded. 'Actually, yeah, it really was. Night.'

'Night,' I said as he wandered to the bathroom.

I flipped Tom's light off. 'Jess?' he said. I looked back at him. 'I don't want to stay in here tonight. Can I... sleep with you?'

I didn't answer straight away. Mum would have said yes. Dad would have said no. If I agreed tonight then how could I ever go back on that? He'd be with me every night, according to Dad's school of thought at least.

But he's only nine, Mum would have said. *Give him the comfort he needs.*

'But only for tonight,' I said.

He shot up off the bed and toward me.

'Promise?' I said.

He nodded and I grasped his hand. We walked along the landing. We neared Mum and Dad's room. The bedroom door was partially open now, the darkness beyond thick and sinister.

I heard that whisper again, the end of my name long and

drawn into a hiss, though this time I knew it was only in my head. With a chill running through me I picked up the pace and pulled Tom along to my room.

CHAPTER EIGHT

The knock on the door came at 8.55. Still no sign of Frankie arising at that point though I'd been up with Tom since before seven. The queen-sized bed in my room was big enough, in theory, for the both of us, though in practicality neither of us was used to sharing, and Tom's limbs seemed to extend unreasonably when he was asleep. That, together with the jitters which had remained with me after Tom's 'episode' meant I'd slept horrendously. Again.

'Who is it?' Tom asked as I walked past the lounge on the way to the front door.

'Just the solicitor. I think.'

It was. A rotund, bald man in his fifties by the name of William Talbot. I'd met him once before, last week, and I didn't like him. The way he sucked in air before spoke. The way he fiddled with his fountain pen non-stop. The way he eyeballed me, eyes flitting up and down me, examining.

'Morning,' Talbot said as I opened the front door. I noted the omission of the word 'good' to his pleasantry.

'Come in,' I said.

I showed him through to the dining room. Tom looked at us curiously as we passed, though remained rooted. Talbot and I took chairs opposite each other at the dark wood table. He smiled as his eyes wandered over me – baggy jumper on today, deliberately – and he put his briefcase down on the table. I winced at the scratching sound. Dad always hated anything hard touching the wood directly like that. I didn't say anything.

'How are you keeping?' Talbot asked.

'Shitty,' I said.

He gave me an odd look. 'I imagine so.' He shuffled about with some papers.

I watched him silently for a few moments. I wanted to be relaxed but I found something about his manner off-putting. Not just his wandering eyes but his... I didn't know. 'Would you like a drink?' I asked.

He looked at me and smiled. 'No, I'm fine, thank you. The reason I'm here is that I do have some updates for you on your parents' affairs.'

The look on his face told me it wasn't all good news.

'Okay,' I said.

'Perhaps start with the bad news,' he said with a poorly placed chuckle. I didn't react. 'Your father had a life insurance policy, as we discussed last time. I've checked the policy detail over and over, and spoke to countless people at the insurer, and I'm afraid there won't be any payout.'

I clenched my teeth shut as I thought. The policy was worth more than £200,000. 'But you told me–'

'I said it's normal for newer policies to pay out even for a suicide, and this insurer does just that for new customers. But your father's terms were never updated from when he first took this policy out. He's had it for nearly twenty years and there really isn't a way to argue against what's in black and white. I'm sorry.'

'There's nothing you can do?'

The way he held my eye unnerved me. 'If there was, I'd tell you.'

'We really need that money,' I said. 'For the mortgage.'

Talbot sat back and sighed. He continued to stare at me in a way that made my insides curdle a little. I folded my arms across my already amply covered chest.

'You don't have to do this, you know,' he said.

'Do what?'

'I don't know you personally, Jess...' I cringed at his use of my first name, '...but you're young. You're still at university, aren't you?'

'Yes.'

'Your brothers need a guardian, at least until Frank is eighteen, but the council run a fantastic foster service, I hear. I can put you–'

'I'm not letting my brothers go into care,' I said, with such force as to cause Talbot to pause.

'It might not be your choice,' Talbot said.

'How?'

'Look, this isn't my area. I'm a probate lawyer, but I do come across similar situations from time to time. I know a good contact at the council, if you want me to put you in touch and get a head start on seeking guardianship. But regardless, if you're intending to take custody you'll have to go through the official process. Someone in the social care department will have to sign off on this and you'll have to prove not just that you're capable, but that you'll be able to provide, financially, for you *and* for your brothers.'

'I'm not stupid, Mr Talbot,' I said.

'I can see that.'

'Can you help?'

He pursed his lips and swung his head from side to side as

though in thought. 'I like to do my best for my clients. And I like you, Jess. But we can come onto that after.' He grabbed some more papers and pushed one across the desk. 'I've done some calculations for you. The money and assets your parents had will be split equally between the three of you, according to their wills. The biggest asset by far is this house, but there's also a substantial mortgage on it.'

I looked at the eye-watering numbers. The size of the debt made my insides curdle even more.

'The current mortgage is over £250,000,' he continued. 'That gives equity of about £150,000, based on a crude valuation.'

'What does that mean for us?'

'You could sell, use the capital to buy or rent something smaller.'

'We're not moving.'

'Jess, you might have to, unless the mortgage company agree to transfer the debt to you. But you're not even in work.'

'I'll get work.'

He looked at me dubiously. Actually, no, it was more that he looked at me like I was a dumb child. I wasn't. I wasn't dumb, I wasn't a child. I was young and inexperienced in these matters, but that wasn't the same thing.

'Your father's got a good pension. A final salary scheme. Having spoken to the provider, they'll pay out a lump sum to the estate. Two times his final salary, according to their scheme rules. Close to £100,000.'

I didn't know whether that was good or bad but it certainly sounded like a lot.

'I'll put it toward the mortgage,' I said.

Talbot nodded. 'You'll get a payout from the insurer for your mother's car too. Plus she had a smaller pension. Together with their savings you might scrape together another fifty, seventy-five thousand. I need to get final figures for some of those areas, but you'll still be well short of the mortgage balance. And you'll still need income every month to support you all.'

'Jess?' I turned to see Frankie at the door. He looked tired, he also looked worried.

'It's fine, Frankie, we're just going over some things.'

He didn't look happy, but he mooched off without another word. I felt a little bad. I was sitting there deciding his future for him. But even if I wasn't technically my brothers' legal guardian yet, I was their big sister.

I was all they had.

'We're not moving unless we absolutely have to,' I said. 'This is our home.'

Talbot sighed again. 'If you're happy for me to do so, I can ask some questions to the mortgage provider, and I'll get the final figures for the other areas we discussed so you know exactly where you stand.'

He scooped up the papers from the table.

'And I'll look for a job,' I said, determination gripping me. 'I'll make this work.' The finality in my words made me feel queasy. Work? What work was there in Graystone for a twenty-year-old with no experience? And was I really saying I'd walk away from my degree, just like that? Two-and-a-half years wasted, debts mounting up?

Yet I'd made the choice pretty much on the day of the accident that I had to be there for my brothers, no matter what, no matter the consequences for me.

Talbot finished tidying and stood up from his chair. I showed him to the door. 'Take care, Jess. And don't put yourself under too much pressure. It's the last thing any of you need.'

I said nothing. He reached out and I shook his hand. His

fingers were chubby and clammy. He smiled at me in a sickly way.

Soon he was gone.

Tom remained oblivious to the meeting. I found Frankie fixing himself some toast in the kitchen. 'So?' he asked, not turning to look at me.

'So what?'

'What's going to happen to us?'

'Frankie, nothing will happen. He was just going over some of the numbers.'

'I heard what he was saying. We're broke, aren't we? We'll have to move.'

'No. We won't. I'm going to look after you.'

I moved up to him and he turned. I expected to see a worried, perhaps even teary face, but he was angry.

'What if I don't want you to?' he said.

His words shocked me. 'But–'

'You're the one who wanted to go to university. You're the one who didn't want to live here anymore.'

'That's not how it was–'

'You're my sister; you're not my mum.'

His toast popped up. Frankie ignored it and stormed past me. I didn't know what to say, so I said nothing.

Tom was standing in the doorway as Frankie blasted past. 'Are you leaving us?' he asked, on the verge of tears.

'No, of course not.' I moved over to him and crouched down to his level.

'Then why is Frankie mad at you?'

I really didn't know the answer to that. 'This is just hard for us all,' I said.

'But you can't leave us,' Tom said. 'Promise me you won't.'

'I won't leave you, Tom. I promise.'

Except doubt pervaded my words. Frankie's words echoed, so too did Talbot's. Despite them both, I wouldn't leave my brothers.

The big problem, I knew, was that perhaps the decision was beyond my control.

CHAPTER NINE

W e didn't make it bowling, even though I'd told Tom the previous night that we could, and despite his continued eagerness. I'd probably spoken a little flippantly, in trying to calm him, but I felt he was too physically fragile, much to his annoyance. The three of us did enjoy the cinema in the evening though, and a much better sleep than the night before, despite the vast amounts of sugar swimming through us all from the various snacks we'd had. Perhaps tiredness had finally caught up with us – though for Frankie was it just a hangover?

I'd questioned myself a few times whether I'd been too relaxed in letting him go out drinking, and so late, on a Monday night. He was only seventeen. Would he have listened if I'd said no? He'd grown up so quickly while I was at university, from a scrawny, spotty fourteen-year-old to a handsome, but still pretty scrawny, young man. At seventeen Mum and Dad had let me go out to pubs and bars on occasion – or had they just resigned themselves to the fact? But did I need to keep Frankie reined in, particularly given what had happened to us?

Even at twenty years old I knew only too well the temptation to turn to alcohol as a mental soother. According to the therapist my parents had sent me to between the ages of fifteen and when I'd left for uni at eighteen, I had an addictive personality. I hadn't agreed with her at the time. I'd never smoked, I'd never really taken drugs except for the couple of times my friends had persuaded me to try. But my relationship with alcohol had been a little more rocky.

One of the key episodes leading to my therapist's conclusion came when I was sixteen. I'd had a tough time at home and at school. Exams were looming, boys – or a boy – were becoming a problem for me. Distraught, I went out with my friends one night with the sole intention of obliterating my troubled mind. My parents didn't even know at that point that I was already sneaking into bars at the weekend. I'd only tell them I was going to Hannah's or Ed's house. Instead we were nearly always first in the queue for Icon when it opened at nine thirty, where they had a two-for-one happy hour on all cocktails to entice early revellers. It worked. I got blind drunk and by 11pm, I was outside the club spewing up sickly sweet vomit. The worst of it was that most of the drinks had been bought for me – and Hannah – by a group of twenty-something-year-old lads. Despite my state, one of those kindly chaps had tried to take me home with him. I didn't even know where Hannah had got to at that point.

Luckily for me – and I've never really thanked him properly for it – I was rescued by Kyle, the older brother of my on/off friend, Kristen. He'd got into a taxi with me to my house. Had more or less carried – or more likely dragged – me to the front door where he'd stood, knocking, until my dad had got out of bed to answer the door.

Kyle had taken an earful – apparently. Shoot the messenger, as they say. I passed out on the sofa with a towel and a bucket by me, and my mum watching over me through the night.

The next morning... I'd never experienced that severity of

hangover before. I wanted to bury my head in the ground. I wanted to pull my insides out, my stomach ached so badly. It took nearly two full days to recover. I swore I'd never drink again. I swore to my parents I'd never drink again, that I'd not put myself in such a vulnerable position again.

They agreed with my sentiment, and grounded me for two months. At the time I thought they were unreasonable, that their anger was misplaced and they should have been more considerate. As I got older, I realised just how reckless and, in a way, inconsiderate I'd been, and that their anger had really only been concern.

Sixteen was when my rollercoaster relationship with alcohol began, but I hadn't had a drop since Mum and Dad and Lily had died. I'd deliberately stayed strong, because I didn't know whether, once I started, I'd be able to stop.

'Are we going yet?' Tom asked, breaking me from my thoughts. He already had on his shoes, coat, hat, gloves and scarf.

'Is Frankie even up yet?'

'He's having breakfast, but he says he doesn't want to come.'

I wasn't happy about that. 'Wait by the door,' I said. I got up from the sofa and headed through to the kitchen where Frankie was standing with a bowl of cereal, looking out of the window to the frosty garden beyond. 'Morning.'

He turned to me, face passive. 'All right, sis.'

'Tom's ready to go.'

'I know. I said you two could do it without me.'

'Because?'

'Because I don't really fancy it.'

'But we said we'd do this together.'

He shrugged. 'You don't really need me.'

'No, but I want you to come.'

'It's always about what you want, isn't it?' He brushed past me, knocking into my shoulder. Milk spilled out of the top of his bowl as he went.

'Frankie!' I shouted after him. 'You're going to clean that up.'

Nothing from him. I moved out after him. Found him plonked on a sofa. 'Frankie?'

He ignored me. Then after a few seconds turned. 'What?'

'Why are you pissy with me? Again? We had a good night last night.'

'I'm not pissy with you.'

I sighed. 'I'm not the bad guy here.'

'And I am?'

'I didn't say that.'

He carried on eating.

'Will you come with us, please? For Tom?' I looked over at my younger brother, standing expectantly at the front door. What was Frankie trying to prove by doing this? 'Frankie?'

He'd been fine last night at the cinema. Was this just teenage mood swings?

He got up from the sofa, walked toward me. The look he gave scared me. I stepped out of the doorway and he headed on past.

'Pick us a good one, Tommo,' he called out as he walked back toward the kitchen.

'Sure thing,' Tom shouted back.

More pissed off than I wanted to show, I took Tom and we left.

A week too late. At least according to the shop assistant at the garden centre. We tried three different places but they were all the same. Row after empty row where I expected to see lines of thick, bushy, deep green Christmas trees, but all they had left were the stragglers that no one wanted. In the end we had to settle for a barely five-foot thing that Tom said looked like a turkey after a fight with a cactus. That had made me laugh at least, though I couldn't quite picture what he meant.

Still, even the puny little thing was a hassle to get into Dad's car. My car. It was now my car. Dad didn't need it.

Either way, the boot was shallow and we had to put the back seats down and squeeze the shrivelled tree in as best we could, losing a good portion of its already sparse needles as we did so.

As we drove home, Tom's face didn't hide his disappointment. I'd built this up for him. Telling him we'd still have a magical Christmas, just the three of us, with Mum, Dad and Lily watching over. I knew, deep down, he didn't really believe in Santa anymore, but I'd wanted to try and play on the old traditions this time, tell him how we could make a great day of it, and getting our tree and decorating it would be the start of all that.

Then Frankie had bailed on us, and now we had the world's shittiest tree.

'I'm sorry,' I said to Tom.

'Dad always got one of the really good ones,' he said, his face glum.

'But I'm sure he would have gone much earlier than we did. That wasn't really...'

I trailed off. Wasn't really what? Why hadn't Dad got a tree already? Strange thoughts rumbled. When I'd seen him at the party, we hadn't exactly had a heart to heart, hadn't shared any tender moments – something I'd forever regret now – yet I'd definitely sensed that something wasn't right, at least between him and Mum. Was he already thinking that day about what he was going to do? Had the decision already been made in his mind and it was only a matter of time? But then if that was the case, why *hadn't* we shared a tender moment? Why hadn't he told me he loved me, hugged me, wished me well, if that was the last time I'd ever see him?

Why hadn't he bought us a fucking decent Christmas tree already?

'It's not that bad,' Frankie said, chucking another handful of crisps into his mouth. I stood by his side to admire our handiwork. He was right, really. The tree wasn't *that* bad. Not as bad as I'd feared when we were shoving the thing into the car, nor when we were dragging it back out again. With all the lights and decorations on it looked... passable.

No, it was better than that. It was... nice. Festive. And, despite the horrible circumstances, the last couple of hours with the boys had been fun. We had a longstanding Evans family tradition of putting up the Christmas tree together. Christmas songs on the stereo, Mum and Dad would share a glass – or more – of fizz, the kids would get bowls of snacks to munch through. That tradition had carried on right through, although I'd missed the last two occasions as I hadn't been able to get back from uni on time. And I had no doubt that, even for the few years before that, in my late teens, the occasion hadn't felt quite as special to me as before. Which had also coincided with Lily and Tom being the youngsters, and centre of attention, I guessed. Christmas was, after all, more for the kids, wasn't it?

This time we'd foregone the sparkling wine. There hadn't even been a question asked about that between me and Frankie. We hadn't foregone the snacks, though. We had bowls of nuts, crisps, trail mix, Skittles, M&Ms, Quality Street. Near empty bowls now.

'Do you want to do the honour,' I said to Frankie, handing

him the star for the top of the tree. Dad usually did that, as he was the only one who could reach the top of the much taller trees we were used to. Now Frankie was the man of this house.

He somewhat reluctantly took the star from me, and easily reached the top of the diminutive tree to put the decoration in place.

'Tom?' I said to the little one, who sat eagerly by the plug socket. He flipped the switch and the lights twinkled into life and we all smiled.

But then, as we all looked to one another, the happy, jolly faces slowly faded. I tried to be strong, and to keep the moment going, but the rush of memories nearly knocked me off my feet. I wanted to try so hard to make this Christmas work for the three of us, but the sense of loss was so great, and so painful.

I'd do my best, but I really wasn't sure I had the strength to pull my brothers through to the other side.

CHAPTER TEN

S nack bowls refilled a few times over, we'd settled in to watch *Elf* – a long-running family favourite – in the early evening when the doorbell rang.

I looked to Frankie.

'Not for me,' he said with absolute surety. Still, I'd kind of wanted him to answer it, given Tom was laid out on me and Frankie was in the armchair on his own. Plus, it was dark out, and I just...

The bell rang again as I manoeuvred Tom off me. Out in the hall I looked to the door to see a tall figure beyond the glazing, caught in the orange glow of the porch light. A man, I thought.

I opened the door. 'Ed?' I said, in shock.

'Hey, Jess.'

A few moments of awkward silence followed as we took each other in. I'd only seen Ed a handful of times in the last couple of years. We'd been friends for forever, we had so much in common, yet for various reasons we'd drifted – particularly since I'd left Graystone for university two hundred miles away.

'What are you doing here?' I asked. The words came out accusatory. I hadn't meant that.

Ed's creased forehead showed his offence. 'Sorry, Jess, I didn't mean to upset you. I only wanted... to make sure you're okay.'

'Not really,' I said with a strange laugh.

He gave me a look of concern at that. 'I didn't want to keep doing this over text,' he said. 'I don't know if you're busy, but... do you want to go for a walk or something?'

I looked back over my shoulder. I'd wanted to make a night of it with the boys. But would they really notice if I went out? They were all set up for the night anyway, and I felt like I'd had no time to myself the last few days, forever running around after those two. Is that how Mum had felt for the last twenty years?

I pushed back the well of emotion as I thought of her motherly nature.

'Give me a sec,' I said to Ed and headed back to the lounge.

'Hey, boys, is it okay if I pop out for a bit? For a walk with Ed?'

Frankie didn't even look up. Tom burst out laughing at the TV – the scene where Will Ferrell unintentionally taunts Peter Dinklage's character by calling him an Elf. One of my favourite scenes. I smiled too, but then Tom turned to me and his face dropped.

'You're going out?' he said in such a way as to suggest he couldn't cope with the idea.

'Not for long,' I said.

'It's fine,' Frankie chimed in, still not looking at me.

Tom said nothing, just gave me his best doe-eyed look.

'I'll be back soon, okay?'

———

The night air was cold and hazy. Ed, his slimline six-foot-two frame towering over me, had on a thick parka but no hat to cover his exposed ears and head. I liked his new look, quite a change from his younger years when he'd simply had a flop of hair, no particular style.

How Frankie was now, reminded me a little of how Ed had been back then. A tall, slender, but not at all athletic frame. Neither was sporty really, both preferring music, both were clever. Ed had widely been considered a geek at school, and had taken plenty of flak from the 'cool' kids because of it. At school he'd always been shy and quiet, kept his head down in class and in the corridors. Outside school he was kind and caring and quite funny in an endearing way.

But he had changed. That geeky, boyish look had gone. He'd thickened out a little and now had stubble and tattoos reaching up his neck and covering his lower arms – when they were on show at least. His hipster look, his designer clothes, were quite at odds with the geeky boy I'd known for so long. I couldn't quite reconcile the two in my mind, or decide which Ed I preferred.

'How are you holding up?' he asked, looking down at me and shaking me from my thoughts. I quickly looked away, realising I'd been staring at him.

'Horribly,' I said.

He reached out and put an arm around me. I didn't move away even though I wasn't one hundred per cent happy with the gesture.

'You can talk to me anytime you want, you know.'

'I know.'

'We might not be as close as we used to be, but that doesn't mean I won't always be here for you.' He took his arm away. Perhaps because I pulled to the side a little.

'How's life for you, anyway?' I asked.

'Me?' he said with a chuckle. 'Nothing changes here, Jess.'

CJ STONE

I sighed when he said that. Of my circle of friends, I was the only one who'd chosen to move away from home for university. I'd always wanted change. None of them had, which was why they all stayed in Graystone. Now I seriously questioned whether I'd made the right choice.

Since school, Ed had joined a local accountancy firm on a training contract, skipping uni altogether. Hannah and Jamie had gone to universities within commuting distance, initially staying at home with their parents, though Jamie had since moved in with Kristen, who worked in a call centre. I'd previously – quite snidely – thought that was something of a comedown for her. Kristen had been the classic pretty girl in school, even though she was – mostly – decent with it. She hadn't cared about exams or anything like that so a lot of careers ended up out of her reach. But she'd still done the hard work of getting a job and had stuck to it, and now I felt foolish for ever thinking like that, for ever putting myself above her.

I desperately needed a job and I'd happily take what she had.

'Job's okay?' I asked, sounding lame.

'It pays,' Ed said. 'I've got my own place now. An apartment. One of those new-builds off Theakston Avenue.'

I vaguely knew where he meant.

'Renting?'

'No. The real deal. Mortgage. I'm proper adulting now.'

'You could afford one of those?'

He shrugged. 'I managed to save a fair bit these last couple of years.'

Of course he had. He'd lived with his parents while earning a full-time salary. At twenty he'd moved out and got a mortgage on his own apartment. Meanwhile I was tens of thousands of pounds in debt with student loans. What did that say about the education system?

'You're living on your own?' I asked.

'Pretty much,' he said.

A bit of a strange answer.

'Come on, this way,' he said.

We entered the park. Not a big park, it was quiet at night. Victorian-esque lanterns lit up the twisting path to the large pond, but either side of that the grass and shrubs were bathed in black. The park was a perfect hangout for teenagers, particularly later in the evening, though at only 7pm a few dog walkers remained out, even on a cold, winter's night.

We took a bench overlooking the inky, rippling water.

'I can't imagine what you're going through,' Ed said as we sat side by side.

An awkwardness crept over me at his words, his manner. I liked Ed. I really did. He'd been such a good friend over many years. But there'd always been something else under the surface: his longing for me. Sometimes I didn't know how to deal with him, found myself forever second guessing his words, looking for an ulterior motive.

I hated that I did that. It wasn't really fair on him, and also, why did it bother me so much? It's not like I was a catch. I didn't have lines of boys at my door clamouring for my attention. I should have been flattered, not put off.

'I don't have a choice but to get through,' I said. 'All I can do is take each day at a time.'

'But what are you going to do?' Ed asked. 'You're going back to uni, aren't you?'

I glared at him. 'I can't leave my brothers.'

Ed looked confused. Why did people think it strange that I wanted to stay and care for them? Was it that hard to understand?

Or did they simply doubt me?

'Will they let you defer or something?' he asked.

I didn't know. I hadn't even asked the question. I was too busy just surviving to think about that. 'All I know is I can't go back yet,' I said. 'I have to take care of Frankie and Tom.'

'Frankie's eighteen next year, I mean–'

'He's still a child. Legally. He needs a guardian. I'm going to do it.'

The force of my statement caused Ed to pause. He continued to look at me, unconvinced by my words, but clearly not sure what else to say to me about it.

'You must have a mountain of debt,' he said.

I laughed at that, though I found the situation far from funny. 'Tell me about it,' I said. 'Plus the mortgage on the house, etc., etc.' I put my head in my hands.

'I admire your bravery,' he said.

'It's nothing to do with bravery.'

We both went silent and I sat back upright. With my hat and thick coat on, and hands in warm gloves, I couldn't really feel the cold much, but Ed hunched his shoulders and rubbed his hands together and then shivered.

'It's freezing, isn't it?' he said, shuffling a little closer to me.

'It's not that bad.'

'What happened between you and that guy? Blake, was it?'

I shut my eyes. *Ed, please don't do this.* 'I can't think about that right now. I thought we were going out to take my mind off things?'

He looked a little offended at the glare I sent his way. 'Sorry, yeah. You're right.' Then he smiled. It lit up his face. No doubt his maturing looks made him handsome, especially when he relaxed like that. 'Do you remember this place?'

'The park? Of course.' I'd been hundreds of times.

'Yeah, the park.' He looked around him, as though calculating. 'But I'm pretty sure it was this bench too, right?'

I'd thought the same thing. The park was a regular hangout for teenagers, now and in the past. We'd come here loads back then, when we were just that little bit too young to get into bars regularly, but old enough to go out on our own, and old enough to convince the odd shopkeeper to sell us alcohol. We'd get cheap cider and vodka and whatever else we could afford and come out in the cold and dark and drink in the park. All very childish really, but at the time we felt so rebellious and cool, like we were the first teens to ever achieve such feats.

But it wasn't those many giggle-filled times that Ed was referring to, I knew, but a more specific occasion.

'I'm pretty sure this is the bench, isn't it?' Ed prompted once more when I didn't say anything.

'Where you professed your eternal love for me,' I said with a slightly uncomfortable laugh.

'Where I tried to kiss you and received the most ferocious slap ever.' He smiled as he rubbed his cheek. 'I'm sure I can still feel it now.'

I didn't react to his words. I knew he was trying to make light of the moment from several years ago, but the problem was I had quite a different memory of it to him, apparently. I'd just come out of a bad situation with someone else. It was only a few days before that big bender at Icon saw me grounded for two months. I was tipsy, I was upset, I was in tears. I needed comfort and consoling. What I got was one of my best friends with his arm around me, kissing my neck. Then he'd kissed my lips. Then when I half-responded, more stunned than anything, his hand had slid under my jumper.

That was when I slapped him. Shouted all manner of abuse at him until Jamie came running over to see what the issue was.

Probably a big deal over nothing really. We were young, both drinking, and it wasn't like he'd done anything seriously bad. He'd just misread the signs. Except he was very good at misreading the signs. Tipsy Ed was often lover-boy Ed when I was around. By the time it was coming close to us leaving school, I'd avoid being alone with him after we'd been drinking because I couldn't take the same old every time.

'Jess? Sorry, have I upset you?'

'No. It's fine.'

'Do you... want to talk about anything? I mean, about... what happened?'

Did I? Other than DS Holster, I hadn't really done so with anyone, and even with her I'd remained cagey once I realised she had no real interest in exploring *why* that night had turned out as it had.

'Your dad... I still can't–'

'What if he didn't do it?' I blurted.

We both paused as Ed stared at me curiously. 'What if he didn't kill himself?' Ed said eventually.

'I've thought about this for hours a day and I can think of nothing that could have caused him to kill himself and leave us all behind like this. He wasn't that... selfish.' I cringed at that last thought, my words not really explaining my feelings properly. Ed didn't say anything, but he looked seriously uncomfortable. I was too. I didn't know how to express what I was thinking, and honestly I didn't know why I was now trying to with Ed. Perhaps the fact he was removed from the situation helped?

'What did the police say?' he asked.

'Case closed. No evidence of foul play. But... it doesn't make sense.'

'Perhaps... it must be a struggle to understand.' He went to put his arm around me – comfort? – but I shoved him off.

'There was a note. It looks like his handwriting, but... how hard is it to fake handwriting? Or what if someone made him write it? Or what if he did write it, but it was about something else entirely, not because he was going to kill himself?'

Could that make sense?

'What did the note say?'

I relayed the words. Ed said nothing.

'I looked for the notepad,' I said.

'The notepad?'

'The note was written on a piece of paper from one of his work notepads. I looked through all of the ones I could find. I don't know why, but I wanted to find the one. I thought it might help, to know where he was when he sat writing those words. I looked for the indentation from the note in the paper below, but I couldn't find any evidence in any of the notepads I've found.'

'So what are you suggesting?'

'That... that... I don't know. Did someone take *that* notepad because it would somehow implicate them otherwise? Fingerprints or whatever. And it's not just that. What about the rope? I'm not saying I know the contents of our garage off the top of my head, but rope like that? I can't see any reason why Dad would have it, which means if he killed himself he had to have bought it just for that purpose. When? From where?'

'Have you checked credit card statements, bank statements?'

'I don't know where they are,' I said with a sigh.

'You spoke to the police about this, though?'

'Not really.'

'Because?'

'Because I knew they'd think I was being irrational. And they already told me they weren't looking into it any further.'

We both went silent. I thought for a while then looked up at Ed. 'What do *you* think?' I said.

He didn't answer for a while. 'I think beating yourself up over the reasons why won't help you move on.'

I sank at his words, and I sensed his dismay in my reaction. But he'd spoken the truth, at least, and I couldn't fault that.

I looked at my watch. 'Do you think we could go?' I said.

Clearly disappointed, he nodded. With sceptical thoughts still rumbling in my mind, we both got up from the bench.

CHAPTER ELEVEN

FRANKIE

As soon as the front door closed, Frankie shot up from the sofa.

'Where you going?' Tom said, looking up from the TV, the little boy lost gaze.

'I need to pop out.'

Normally Tom would have actively encouraged this. Frankie had done it plenty of times in the recent past, when Mum and Dad were out, and Tom relished the chance to be home alone, to be the big boy. The look on his face tonight suggested otherwise.

'Please? But you can't tell Jess.'

Tom didn't look happy about that prospect at all.

'You'll be fine. I won't be long. I'll give you five pounds if you keep quiet about it.'

'Five pounds?'

Frankie saw the temptation in his eyes. 'Yeah. Put yourself to bed when the movie's done. The fiver's yours in the morning.'

'But... what if...'

'You'll be fine. You've got the penknife I gave you, haven't you?'

'Yeah.'

'Keep that close, just in case.'

Frankie didn't hang about to hear any more of Tom's complaints.

Did he feel bad for his little bro? Yes, without doubt. But they both had to return to some sort of normality, didn't they? Tom would be fine. Being younger, the loss he'd suffered would naturally affect him differently – more severely? Except it wasn't Tom who'd found Dad like that. It wasn't Tom who had the *what if* thoughts.

And anyhow, Frankie was doing this for his brother in a way. Tom was too young to figure this all out. Frankie wasn't.

With his dark coat on, hood up, hands in pockets, Frankie slunk through the streets. He'd watched from the window which direction Ed and Jess had gone in, and then taken this gamble. The gamble paid off. He caught up with them a couple of hundred yards down the next street. Not hard, they were walking much more slowly than he was. More like a lover's walk. Ed close to Jess's side, the arm of his coat brushed against her shoulder every now and then.

Where were they going? A pub, or café?

No, very oddly, they ended up walking into the park. The park? The dark, park? On a cold December's night? Very odd indeed. But then that was Ed. Odd. He always had been. One of Jess's best friends for as long as Frankie could remember, but Frankie had never liked him. Ed wasn't a stupid guy: if anything he was super clever. A proper geek. But for all his cleverness he was also super sneaky. The kind of guy who'd say or do anything to get into a girl's knickers. And for as long as Frankie could remember, Ed had had his dirty eyes on Jess.

The thing was, Jess wasn't stupid either. She knew fine well about Ed's intentions, about his lust for her, yet for years she'd strung him along, pretending they had a perfectly normal friendship. Which of course they did, from her side at least. Perhaps Jess just liked the attention, liked the power it gave her.

Ed and Jess walked along the twisting path. Frankie stayed on the grass, in the shadows, all of ten yards behind them. They had no clue he was there, even if Jess looked around nervously every now and then.

She shouldn't have been nervous about what was around her, but about the man she took a seat with on the cold bench. Frankie came to a stop by a thick trunk.

What the hell were they doing? Ed was such a creep. Next he'd be trying to kiss her, trying to get his hand up her top.

What would Frankie do if he saw that? Would he rush over and smack the guy, or stand and watch with interest? He really wasn't sure.

He spied from his dark spot. Their voices drifted over but he wasn't quite close enough to make out any words. Could he get closer still?

He didn't. Instead he simply stood and watched, and watched, his brain tumbling with thoughts, his annoyance growing by the second.

This was just another example of how he knew Jess wasn't being straight with him. The way she'd sneaked off into the night with Ed, to have whatever this private chat was about. What did Jess know that she wasn't telling him? And was she spilling all to creepy Ed? Telling him everything, and her own brother nothing, about what had caused their dad to kill himself. An event which had directly caused Mum's accident too.

It had, hadn't it?

Frankie remained deep in thought when Jess, quite abruptly, stood up from the bench. What the hell? Had he missed something? Had Ed tried it on after all?

He didn't know, but he watched, not moving, to see what would happen next, his heart rate building a little. Were they heading home already? Possibly, they were certainly going back out of the park the same way they'd come in.

Frankie followed them to the exit. Left would take them back toward home. Right toward the town centre and perhaps another destination.

Left.

Crap.

Frankie rushed out of the park, went right, then left. Broke into a jog as he moved along the street parallel to where Ed and Jess walked. After a couple of minutes he slowed, took another couple of turns to get back on track for home. The last of those turns he made a little more nervously than the others, as he looked further down the street, trying to spot his sister and Ed in the distance. No sign of them.

Good?

Either they were going really slowly or they'd gone somewhere else after all.

Nothing he could do about that now. He rushed on home, took the final turning onto their street, the house just a few doors away. One last glance over his shoulder before he headed across the road. But as he turned back he didn't spot the looming figure until it was too late.

Frankie barged into the man and sent him stumbling.

'What the–'

'Jesus, I'm sorry,' Frankie said, jolting in surprise. He went to hold his hand out but the man managed to recover and not fall to the ground. He brushed himself down. Shorter than Frankie, but the guy was stocky with a bulky winter coat. No hood, but a woolly hat covered his head and in the thin illumination of the street lights his face remained partially hidden.

'Sorry, man, I didn't–'

'Don't worry about it,' the guy said before stepping past Frankie.

No time to dwell. Frankie watched the man for a beat before he rushed on. He arrived at the front door. Still no sign of Jess behind him. He headed inside. Stripped off his shoes and coat.

Bloody hell it was warm. Just because he'd rushed home?

No. He put his hand to the radiator in the hall. Blazing hot. Tom had turned the heating on, the little git.

Frankie moved to the lounge door. The light was on but no Tom inside. He went back to the bottom of the stairs. Walked halfway up. No light on in Tom's room.

'Tommo, I'm back. You okay?'

Shuffling, but no response.

Fast asleep. He was a good kid.

Footsteps outside. Frankie rushed back down the stairs and into the lounge. He quickly spread out on the sofa and turned on the TV just as the muffled sound of Jess and Ed's voices drifted over.

As he sat and listened, trying to calm his breathing and his heart, Frankie's brain rumbled with thoughts. Mainly about his sister, and what was going on with her, but increasingly about what had just happened outside too.

That man. At first Frankie thought he'd made a simple mistake. Distracted by looking behind him. But the more he thought about it, the more the situation felt odd. Why was the guy just standing there, like that?

It wasn't only the situation that was on his mind though, but the man's face. Yes, it was pretty dark out, but something about him, the familiarity of his features, had unsettled Frankie.

Where'd he seen him before?

CHAPTER TWELVE

JESS

'I really didn't mean to stress you out,' Ed said as we stood on the doorstep.

'You didn't. I'm just not me right now.' I reached out and patted his chest. Sometimes it was like dealing with a wounded puppy with Ed. 'I'm glad you came over. Perhaps we should all get together. In a few days maybe?'

'After Christmas?' he said, immediately perking up. 'That'd be great. It's not like I'm going anywhere.'

'See you then,' I said. We hugged. Despite the strangeness that had preceded it, the embrace wasn't awkward at all. In fact, it felt really good. Familiar. Which was odd, because it wasn't familiar at all, really.

'Take care,' Ed said as he moved off down the drive. 'Call or text anytime.'

I waved him off then headed inside.

The house was dark, but warm. Frankie had turned the heating on. Dad would have blasted him for doing so at this time of night. The heating was scheduled. End of. If the house was cold after that you either put the fire on in the lounge or you put an extra layer or two on.

I moved on through. No sign of Tom. I found Frankie curled on the sofa watching some movie with blood and guts spewing on the screen. I turned away. Not my kind of thing.

'Tom's in bed?' I asked.

'Yeah,' was the only response I got.

'Well done,' I said to him. Not to be mean, or to be challenging. I genuinely meant it.

'I know how to look after my own brother,' Frankie said, clearly pissed off with my comment. 'I'm not a kid.' He glowered at me.

'I know you're not.' *Even if you act like one most of the time,* I thought, but didn't add.

'How was Ed-nimble-fingers?'

I cringed. Why had I ever explained that situation to my kid brother? Well, no, I knew why. I hadn't told him at the time, Frankie had been way too young then to be thinking about stuff like that. I'd told him more recently. When he'd got into a similar situation as Ed. Similar to a certain extent anyway. He liked a girl at school. A girl who was a friend, who was happy being his friend, but who Frankie wanted more from. He'd come to me, his older, university going sister, for advice. At the time that had made me feel really mature and responsible. Despite our differences, he clearly looked up to me and felt comfortable asking about the things he couldn't go to Mum and Dad about.

Now he certainly couldn't.

I chastised myself for that last thought.

The point was, he'd come to me for girl advice. I'd told him my story about how not to do it. Told him to be respectful and just ask her. Tell her how he felt and see what happened. Don't be creepy. Don't assume. Don't just try it on. And if he decided to reveal his thoughts at all, be prepared that it might affect the friendship.

I honestly didn't know if my advice was sound, if he'd really taken it on board, or how that story had panned out. I'd never asked. I felt a little bad about that.

'It was fine,' I said. 'It was nice to see him. Nice to get out.'

'No wandering hands then?'

I wasn't impressed with his attempts to rile me, but I tried not to show it. 'No,' I said. 'Ed's a good guy. A good friend.'

Frankie snorted.

'I'm going to go upstairs and read.' No response now. 'I'll turn the heating off for you.' I did so, locked up downstairs and made my way to my room. I left the light off as I moved across to the window to close the curtains. I paused, fabric in hand, when a shadowy figure scooted out of sight, beyond a car parked on the road. I kept my eyes on that spot. Not sure what I'd seen at first. A figure, I thought. A tall, dark figure. Ed?

Or was it just an animal? Or a trick of the eye caused by headlights from a car somewhere further along the street?

I stood and stared, unnerved, but saw nothing more. Whatever I'd seen, if anything at all, had been swallowed by darkness.

I pulled the curtains closed, shivering as I did so, then whipped around to look across my unlit room. I rushed to the door and flipped on the lights, spun, looking over *my* space. My safe space.

My heart raced. What was wrong with me?

Then came Tom's hollow scream...

I hotfooted across the landing. Frankie was already at the bottom step as I reached Tom's door.

'Jess!' Tom screamed, his panicked voice even louder than before.

I turned on his light, looked across the room as though ready for an attack by... something. Then I rushed over to him. I hugged him, much like the other night when he'd last had a nightmare.

'It's okay,' I said. 'I'm here. You're fine. Everything's fine.'

'Except it's not, though, is it?' Frankie said, sullen, as he stood in the doorway. 'Nothing here is fine.' He walked off.

I gritted my teeth in anger. Tom sobbed.

'It was just a dream,' I said to him, hearing doubt in my voice.

'It wasn't a dream,' he said. 'I saw him. Standing right there.' He pointed to the other side of the room.

'There's no one there, Tommo. No one in the house but you, me and Frankie. Same as the other night.' I tried to sound persuasive but I wasn't even to my own ears. *I* didn't believe in ghosts.

'You're not listening to me,' he said, anger taking over. 'I saw him. Standing right there. I'm not stupid. I'm not making it up. I really saw him.'

'Saw who?'

'Dad. I saw Dad.'

CHAPTER THIRTEEN

'What do you think he saw?' I said to Frankie the next morning as he sat watching the sports news on the TV. Tom was up in his room, playing with his Star Wars Lego, recreating some big battle.

'What do you mean?'

'That's twice now, that he says he saw a man in his room.'

As much as I wanted to simply refute Tom's claims, and find logic to explain, I had no doubt he had seen *something*. And I'd sensed myself, more than once, some sort of presence recently. Someone, something watching us. Me.

I'd seen, I'd heard, I'd *felt* it.

But what?

'He said he saw Dad,' Frankie said.

'You don't seem too bothered.'

Frankie glared at me. 'Bothered about what?'

I thought about telling him. Telling him about what I'd experienced too. But would he look at me differently? Would he lose respect for me? I wasn't sure I could afford that.

'Is he okay, do you think?' I asked, taking a different course.

Even I felt foolish for asking my seventeen-year-old brother this, as though he were a mental health expert.

But... who else did I have to ask? And really, Tom was growing up so fast with me being away at uni. He'd changed a lot since I'd left at eighteen, and I wasn't sure if his poor sleeping, his claims of seeing things in the night, was only a result of the trauma he'd suffered, or a longer pattern of night terrors that I simply didn't know about.

'You know him better than I do,' I said, a lump in my throat. 'Has he ever... does he normally have nightmares?'

Frankie frowned, looked at me like I was an idiot. 'Dad killed himself. Tom was in a car crash that nearly killed him, and *did* kill Mum and Lily. He's messed up. What do you expect?'

I didn't like his tone, or the way he looked at me, his eyes squinted with irritation. 'So that's a no then?' I barked back.

'What was the question?'

'Did Tom have these nightmares before... before...' I struggled to say the words.

'No,' Frankie said. 'Before Dad hanged himself, before Mum and Lily died, Tom slept great. Go figure.'

I shook my head. Frankie rolled his eyes and looked away.

'But...' I wanted to ask more. I wanted to have a real, reasonable conversation with him... why was he being like this with me?

The doorbell rang.

'I'll get it,' I said. Frankie didn't shift a muscle.

I opened the door. A squat lady, thick curls in her black hair, wearing a poorly fitting suit, stood on the doorstep.

'Jess Evans?' she asked.

'Yes.'

'Eleanor Thornby from social services.'

'Oh, I wasn't...'

'Is this a good time?'

'For what?'

'To come and talk to you? Your brothers?'

I glanced over my shoulder. A good time? With Frankie being off with me? The house a mess? Tom only a few hours after thinking he'd seen a ghost of his dad looming over his bed?

'Come in,' I said stepping aside.

Eleanor waddled inside. Didn't take her shoes off as I shut the front door. She carried on along the hall without waiting for an invitation and stood in the doorway to the lounge. 'You must be Frankie,' she said.

A grumble in response. Eleanor introduced herself. I moved up to her and looked beyond to see Frankie's still grumpy face. I tensed up. If he wanted to, he could make this so much more difficult for me... but why would he want to?

'I'll come and chat to you soon, yeah?' Eleanor said. 'I just need to borrow your sister for a few minutes first?'

'Whatever,' Frankie said, before turning back to the TV.

Eleanor faced me again, her smile a little less warm than before, a little more suspicious. 'And Tom is?'

'Upstairs, playing,' I said.

She looked up there, but said nothing.

'I can get him?'

'It's fine. Is there somewhere quiet we can talk?'

We ended up in the dining room, sat in the same positions as I had with Talbot the other day, although I felt a whole lot more nervous this time.

'Please, Jess, don't look so worried. I'm not here to cause you problems.'

'But... sorry, I don't mean to be rude, but... why are you here?' I hadn't made any initial contact myself with the authorities. I'd simply been too busy, and perhaps a little reluctant. But the fact was we hadn't even buried my parents and Lily yet and thinking about the future with any real clarity was a near impossible task, the cloud of grief hanging over me too thick to allow any space for doing so.

'This is just an initial visit. To meet you. To see how you're all getting on. To understand what you'd like to do next. You're at university, aren't you?'

How did she know that?

'Yes. But I won't be going back. At least not in the short term.'

'Oh?'

'I mean, I haven't properly looked into the process yet, but I want to seek guardianship of my brothers. I want us all to live here still.'

She smiled and nodded, though it wasn't a happy, welcoming smile. Condescending.

'It must be best for them, right?' I said. 'I read somewhere that wherever possible, in questions of custody, stability is the most important thing for young children.'

'It is, you're right, but there are many considerations. And your brothers aren't really that young.'

We went silent. I thought she might have mentioned what some of those considerations were, but instead she simply stared at me. 'Is there anyone else in the family who might seek custody? Who might challenge your application?'

'No,' I said. 'It's me or foster care.'

She nodded. I questioned my own response. Was it true that we had no one else? What about Duncan and Sarah? Although they lived hours away, and would they even want the boys.

'I want to do this,' I said. 'I'll make it work. I just need to prove it to you.'

'You'll need to show me you can support yourself and your brothers. Financially I mean.' She looked around the room. I knew what she was thinking. Big home for a twenty-year-old to afford.

'As soon as Christmas is out of the way, I'll be looking for a job,' I said.

'And I'll need to make assessments of the living arrangements here. Of the likely mental health implications, and needs for all of you, given... given the circumstances.'

I didn't say anything. I really didn't know whether I should have done. Mental health? I was hardly one to talk, plus given mine and Tom's nightly sightings... what did that all mean for my plans?

Eleanor sighed and sat back in her chair. 'Like I said, this is just an initial visit. Nothing to worry about, and I won't try to cause any problems for you, Jess. I can only imagine the suffering you've been through, but I can sense how much you love your brothers. If there's anything I can do to help you, I will. I don't want to break up a family unit. My only question for you, is this: do you really know the personal sacrifice you'll have to make? Once this is done, there won't be any going back. Whatever future you thought you might have, university, a good career in a big city, might look very different for you if you're placed in charge of your brothers.'

'Whatever future I thought I'd have is already gone,' I said. 'It disintegrated the Sunday evening I got a phone call from my brother to say my dad killed himself, the same night I learned my mum and sister died. There's no going back now. No changing the past for any of us. I'm staying right here where I belong. I *will* be here for my brothers.'

Even if they didn't want me to be, a voice at the back of my head said, an image of Frankie's angry, distrusting face flashing before my eyes. Would my own brother try to scupper everything?

If he did, what would happen to him and Tom? What would happen to me? As I sat there, nerves and doubts taking hold, I really didn't know the answers.

CHAPTER FOURTEEN

I watch Tom cleaning up. He's helping out in the kitchen. He has these moments. Most of the time he's still babied a little, likes everything to be done for him, his particular way. Crusts taken off his bread for sandwiches, apples peeled and cut into slices. He causes a fuss most mornings if you ask him to do his own cereal. Get box. Take a handful of cereal. Put in bowl. Add milk. Too much for him. But then he'll say, 'Shall we bake a cake today?', or similar, and when he puts his mind to it, and wants to do something, he's really quite handy. He doesn't just stand and watch, he thinks, and takes charge.

We're making cookies. They're already in the oven, and he's washing up while we wait for them to bake. The smell is amazing. He finishes rinsing the mixing bowl and places it on the drainer. I can see there's still cookie mix all down the side of the bowl. I'll have to redo most of what's drying probably, but he's really tried at least.

He dries his hands on a tea towel and turns to me, eagerness on his face.

Then he glances at the cooker – the clock? – and glares at

me. 'It's too late, they're going to be burned!' he shouts, angry at me.

He's right. Five minutes past due. I've been distracted, watching him. He rushes to the oven. Pulls open the door. Grabs the baking tray with his bare hands.

'Tom, no! It's hot!'

He pulls the tray out, grasping it tightly in both hands. He turns to me. His face a look of horror. His hands are steaming, sizzling.

'Dad!' he screams. 'Dad, help me!'

Dad's there. Standing right next to Tom. But he's not moving. He's looking down at his son, a horrible grin on his face.

'Dad, please!' Tom begs.

Why won't he help?

I race over. At least I try to. But my legs are heavy. Stuck? Like wading through treacle, I'm so in shock. The table is in the way. Chairs too. I clatter across. Tom is screaming, crying.

Dad looks on as his son suffers.

I finally reach Tom and swipe the tray from his grip and the soft cookies splat to the floor as the tray bangs and crashes.

Tom is screaming in pain. He turns over his hands. His palms are blood red, blistered and bubbling.

I look to Dad. A snide, knowing look fixes on me...

My eyes sprang open. I stared at my ceiling, images of the dream fading, but not the uneasy feeling in my stomach, the horror and helplessness I'd felt at seeing Tom in so much pain but not being able to help him.

And what was with Dad? I knew it was a dream, but...

I looked over the bed. Alone. That was right. I'd brought Tom into my bed again the night he'd claimed to have seen the ghost of Dad in his room, but last night I'd persuaded him to stay on his own. Not an easy task, but I'd remained dogged, and determined not to create a bad habit of him not being able to sleep in his own room.

Apparently last night had gone more smoothly, both for him and me. No visions. No voices, even if I did shudder a little just at the thought.

I looked at my phone. Half eight. Late for me.

I stayed in bed a few minutes more, getting my mind in some sort of order, before I pulled myself up and grabbed my dressing gown from behind the door. As I walked along the landing I realised from the light streaming into the boys' rooms that both were already up, their curtains opened.

I headed downstairs. Found Tom on the lounge carpet, whizzing cars around. He was even dressed. A surprise.

'Morning,' I said to him.

'Hi,' he said without turning to me.

'Where's Frankie?'

'Dunno.'

'Have you had breakfast yet?'

'No.' Then, as I went to move away, 'Can you do it?'

That dream flashed in my mind.

'Sure.' I walked to the kitchen. Expected to see Frankie there, munching away on something. He wasn't. But I noticed the door to the utility was open, and cold air from the poorly insulated space – essentially a lean to – wafted in.

I shivered as I moved over. Then stopped in the doorway. Frankie was there, at the other end of the little room, standing with the door to the garage wide open. Standing, staring into the space inside. He hadn't heard me. At least he didn't show he had. He simply stood there, motionless, trancelike.

And I stood there, watching him. A little freaked out.

'Frankie?'

He didn't respond.

'Frankie?'

He sucked in air and slowly turned to me. I couldn't read the expression on his face.

'You okay?' I asked.

'Yeah.'

He walked past me, back into the kitchen. I stepped forward to the garage door. Goose pimples rose on my arms and legs as I gazed inside – I hadn't been in there at all since...

I quickly closed the door and with a rush of fear darted back into the warm kitchen.

Frankie was there. Facing away from me. Hunched over, his hands on the kitchen counter.

'Frankie?'

'Why did he do it?' he said.

I didn't answer, even if I'd asked myself the same question over and over. I'd said it out loud to DS Holster that time, and I'd even spoken to Ed, not just about why, but about my doubts.

Why couldn't I open up to Frankie about my dad's death?

Frankie took his hands off the counter and turned to face me, his agitation clear – because of my lack of answer?

'Why did he do it?' Frankie asked again.

'I don't know.'

'Don't you?' he said, his face screwing further. 'Are you sure about that, sis?' He hissed the last word, the sound reverberating through me, before he turned and walked out.

CHAPTER FIFTEEN

The funeral was exactly as horrible, painful, miserable as I'd feared it would be. I just didn't want to be there. Couldn't look anyone in the eye, didn't want to engage in conversation. Thankfully I think most people either got that, or just felt the same way as I did anyway. The time passed by in a fog of tears. Inside the chapel, or whatever they called it, I watched solemnly as the caskets disappeared one after the other from beyond the curtains of the crematorium, Lily's little wooden box so small and delicate. At the sight of that the sobs in the room heightened, almost unbearably so – my own included.

Soon it was all over and I found myself outside in the drizzle with my brothers, looking down at the small plot of land where the ashes would later be buried.

'It doesn't seem right,' Frankie said. Pretty much the first time he'd spoken since we arrived.

'What doesn't?'

'Mum, Dad, Lily. All of them crammed into this little space. It doesn't seem right. It doesn't seem fair.'

'Nothing about this is fair,' I responded.

'I'm not talking about *you*,' he sneered. 'I'm talking about them. It's not fair on them. Did they even want to be cremated?'

How was I supposed to know the answer to that? There'd been no conversation with Mum and Dad about it, had there? Nor had Talbot suggested that my parents had laid out their desires for burial within their wills. I was left to make the thankless choice, and, in the end, I'd gone for the far cheaper option. Did that make me a horrible person? I really didn't know. But what I did know was that our family finances were far from rosy, and the idea of spending thousands on something when we didn't need to seemed reckless.

I also knew neither Mum nor Dad were deeply religious, so we hadn't needed a large, religious ceremony or anything like that, and I struggled to see why they would have been offended at the idea of cremation.

Apparently Frankie didn't agree with my choice, judging by the shitty attitude. Or maybe he just wanted to vent. Again.

We used to get along so well. Why did he seem to hate me now?

'I don't want to be burned,' Tom said. 'It's horrible.'

I couldn't say anything to that.

'Don't worry, Tom, you won't be,' Frankie said, putting his arm around his brother.

'What if they were still alive? What if they were in the fire but couldn't get out?'

'That wouldn't happen,' I said. Both of them glared at me. 'They weren't alive. They can't feel anything anymore. It wasn't really them.'

My words didn't come out as I'd intended, and I could tell they did nothing to ease my brothers' tension or suffering, nor had they done anything to ease mine.

The house was busier for the wake than it had been not long before for Dad's birthday. That sat uncomfortably with me, even if everyone in the house was there to pay their respects, the distant family members would surely have come to Dad's birthday if they'd been invited, wouldn't they?

That said, the fact so many people were there wasn't down to me, but Aunt Sarah, who had done a great job in getting the word out about the funeral. She'd also helped out here and there, from afar, with the funeral director, and in organising the small ceremony.

She'd reached out to all sorts of people from my parents' lives, from work colleagues, to rarely seen cousins and second cousins and old friends who I'd perhaps met only a couple of times in my life, if at all, and didn't even have contact details for. She'd also helped out with catering. Nothing too difficult or extravagant, but she and Duncan had arrived early in the morning with bags full of bread and snacks and other titbits and had spent a good hour or so before the funeral prepping the sandwiches and getting the dining table in our home ready for after.

Given the effort I'd said they could stay the night, as they had a near three-hour road trip home again later, but Sarah had politely declined.

I was happy about that really.

I was busy not being busy by the dining table, eating a small square of tuna and cucumber sandwich when Duncan rolled up to me, his manner and face sombre. But moments ago he'd been having a much more light-hearted conversation with two of Dad's friends from university. Two men I'd never met before today.

The upbeat moments were fine with me. I didn't begrudge anyone who wanted to smile and joke and reminiscence fondly today. In a way I just wished I could too. It just seemed odd that Duncan had mirrored my mood as he came over.

'You're doing a great job, Jess,' he said, standing by my side to look out over the room.

'You and Sarah did most of the hard work.'

'It was nothing. But I didn't mean today, I meant with everything. You've really shone for your brothers.'

'I'm not sure I had a choice, but thanks.'

He looked at me quizzically. I don't think I really got Duncan that well. Sarah was my dad's younger sister, though the two of them had never really been that close, from what I'd seen. Not that she wasn't nice, I always felt she was really warm and caring toward me and the other kids, but there'd been an ongoing tension between her and Dad that I think stemmed back to when their dad had been ill with cancer, when I was really small. Sarah had lived much closer to him, had seen him much more than Mum and Dad had before he'd died. I'd never really asked much about it – yet another facet of my family's life that I'd perhaps never know about now.

Sarah married Duncan when I was five, a couple of years after my granddad had died, and at the time I'd thought him handsome and suave. He drove a sports car, wore nice clothes, was always really chatty with me, and jokey. It was only as I grew older, and particularly in my teens, that I started to see him as more conniving and... just a little bit creepy. In particular his boyish, and often borderline racist humour grated on me, and I knew it had done with Mum and Dad too. In fact, Dad was the only person out of all of us who I'd ever seen call Duncan out over his tasteless jokes, though such occasions were few and far between.

Dad wouldn't have chosen a man like that as a friend, and neither would I, but Duncan was still family, and I think he definitely cared about us all.

'I was talking to Sarah about you and the boys,' he said to me before taking a swig from the beer bottle in his hand. 'I feel really bad because your lives have been thrown into chaos and we're so far away.'

'It's fine, really.'

'But what are you going to do? I mean, with your degree for starters? Are you going back?'

Why did this feel like a fishing exercise? And how many times would I have to answer the same questions?

'I haven't figured out yet how it'll work. But I can't leave Tom and Frankie.'

'No, I guess not.'

'Technically Sarah is next of kin, isn't she?' I said, and he squirmed a little. I wasn't sure that was correct, but still...

'You know? We had that same conversation. I mean, neither of us is the parenting type...' He laughed then. I didn't know why really. But it was true, they didn't have kids and I'd never expected them to. They just didn't... seem right for it, '... and I know in theory we could take you all down to live with us, but it'd be just as far for you and uni. We'd have to pull Tom and Frankie out of their schools here. We'd have to sell our house and try and buy something bigger as we've only got three bedrooms–'

'Duncan, it's fine. I wasn't expecting you to actually take us all in.' Though I had quite enjoyed watching him dig like that.

'Yeah,' he said, rubbing his neck. I sensed relief more than anything. 'So how's it going to work then? With the house and everything?'

He'd got over the hurdle of not having to foster his niece and nephews. Now onto finances, I presumed. I guessed he wouldn't really want to help out there, if he could afford not to. Sarah and Duncan ran a property management company together. I didn't know the ins and outs of how it worked, but I knew they were pretty well off. Their house – was it really only three bedrooms? – was this big, old Georgian thing. Tall ceilings, wood panelling, tasteful decoration. All a bit old worlde for me, but definitely not cheap. And Duncan always had a nice car or two, like the Aston Martin they'd arrived in today. I didn't know much about cars but I knew it was expensive, even if it wasn't brand new.

Yet Duncan was a 'tight arse', as Dad used to put it. Never the first to get his wallet out for drinks. Always the one to quibble to the penny on a restaurant bill. Made a fuss about the expense of staying in a hotel when they came to visit if we already had other rooms taken by Nanna and the like. Dad used to get really riled by that, especially as my parents weren't exactly loaded, even if they were comfortable financially.

'We'll get a few payouts,' I said. 'Pension, insurance and things. It'll all go toward the mortgage, and I'm hoping I can get whatever's left to pay transferred over to me.'

'So you'll still be in debt?'

'I expect so. Quite a bit. Student loans too. And I need to find a job to keep us going.' I sighed. 'So it really doesn't look like the degree is ever going to happen now.'

'Wouldn't it be easier to sell this place and get something more affordable?'

'This is our home,' I said to him, not far off a growl behind my voice.

'I know. Sorry. I shouldn't have said that.' He sighed. 'We really want to help out. Any way we can. Let me talk to Aunt Sarah about it.' He put his hand onto my shoulder. 'We're not going to let any of you suffer any more.'

His surprisingly heartfelt words sent tears to my eyes. I'm not sure he noticed, because the next moment he'd turned to walk away.

I did my best with pleasantries and making sure everyone

was fed and watered, but really I felt immeasurably lonely in my own home during the wake. After only a few minutes of eating and talking to relatives, Tom and Frankie had shut themselves away in their rooms – Tom on his PS4, Frankie on his laptop – and I hadn't seen either for ages. That was fine. This was hardly an event for them to enjoy. But it did put an extra burden on me. As the host, I had nowhere I could disappear off to, even if I really did want to.

I moved from the kitchen to the lounge where Nanna was on a sofa next to another old lady, who I think was the widow of my granddad's cousin, or something like that. Someone Sarah and Duncan knew.

I'd collected Nanna from her home earlier in the day, and now at 5pm I was already considering whether it was time for me to run her back. I watched the two of them for a few moments, no words spoken between them. On opposite sides of the family, they'd probably never met before today, except perhaps at the odd wedding or previous funeral. Despite the lack of conversation between them, Nanna seemed surprisingly bright and alert, as she had done most of the day. As though this really was a celebration – as the funeral director had tried to put it.

Duncan came into the room and wandered back over to me. 'Got any more beers?' he said, wafting the empty bottle my way.

One of the many things I hadn't really thought about for this occasion was alcohol. It'd never really occurred to me to get extra beer and wine in to 'celebrate' the deaths of my parents and Lily.

'There's probably another box in the garage,' I said. 'I'm sure we had some left over from Dad's birthday.'

'Do you want me to–'

'I'll get it,' I said, stepping in front of him. It didn't seem right him going in there, where my dad was found. Forever tarnished, the garage felt like a private space now, only for me and the boys. Like a shrine.

Not that I *wanted* to spend time in there. In fact the very idea terrified me.

'Thanks, Jess, you're a star.'

I walked off, back through the kitchen, into the perennially chilly utility room. I opened the door to the garage. Light drifted into there from the utility room and I stood and stared. I hadn't set foot inside since that fateful day. I'd made it this far before, but no further. I looked over the space, thinking, reminding myself of how I'd found Frankie the other morning in this exact same position. What had been going through his mind then? Was he having the same doubts as me?

I took a big inhale then made the move. Tried not to look up to the rafter where the noose had been tied to.

I felt sick. My legs were weak.

I couldn't stop myself. I imagined the moment. The moment my dad – or someone else? – had kicked the small stepladder away. The small stepladder now innocently propped over in the corner. I imagined the agonising seconds that followed. My dad choking, squirming. Was he in pain? Did he regret it? Was he desperately hoping for someone to rescue him in those last moments?

Or was he at peace the whole time?

I wanted it to be the latter, except that meant he really didn't want to be alive, to be a part of our family, a part of my life, and that thought made me feel even worse. Even more empty.

And what about the impact of that day on Frankie? I'd heard his screams on the phone, they were terrifying enough, but to have actually walked in and seen first-hand... I couldn't even bear to think how Frankie had felt in that moment. In the moments that followed as he tried desperately to get Dad down and tried, unsuccessfully, to revive him.

All the while I'd sat in a taxi, or stood on the train, worried as hell, but not really *part* of it.

Me and the boys had all suffered, but had I underestimated the traumatic impact on Frankie of actual finding Dad like that? Not just finding Dad, but then him being alone for so long, before I'd finally arrived at the hospital, where Frankie had taken the extra hit of knowing Mum and Lily were dead too...

Enough of the morbid. All I had to do was get the beer and get out.

I made a pathetic, anguished squealing sound as I rushed across the floor to the wine rack in the corner, beside which sat two boxes of San Miguel.

I grabbed one of the boxes.

Felt a rush of wind behind me.

I turned.

The garage door slammed shut and plunged the space into blackness.

CHAPTER SIXTEEN

I screamed. I dropped the box. Bottles crashed and banged. I spun. Ran for the door. Grasped in the dark for the handle. Why hadn't I turned on the light?

I found the handle. Yanked the door open. Fell out into the utility room gasping and panting. Fell into Duncan's arms...

'Christ, Jess, are you okay?'

I couldn't speak. I sobbed into his shoulder, my whole body shaking in fear.

'What happened?'

I tried to pull myself together. Pulled myself off Duncan. Looked back into the garage. The light was on now?

'I just... I just...' I glanced back to Duncan. He looked over my shoulder, into the garage, concern on his face – for me – but also confusion as though he couldn't figure out what was going on.

Neither could I.

'I got spooked,' I said, deciding to leave it at that. But I'd felt something. Someone. Had *heard* them. Movement at least. I was sure of it.

Someone. Something. I didn't know. Which was why I didn't say anything more.

Regardless, he nodded, as though he understood.

But then... beyond him I saw no one else coming to see about the commotion. Had anyone else even heard?

Why – how – was Duncan right there?

'Don't worry about it,' he said. 'Go and sit down. I'll clean up.'

I wanted to say no, but I didn't say anything. Duncan moved inside. He grabbed a broom and a mop and bucket and moved over to the widening pool of spilled beer.

Everything seemed so... normal in there now. But those few seconds, alone, in the dark where my dad hanged himself, it was as though the darkness had taken shape, swirling around, stifling, choking, crushing...

Alone...?

Had I been alone? I tried to shake the feeling away. I needed to be logical. How had the door closed? The utility was a draughty old place, perhaps–

'Jess, go and relax, please,' Duncan called out, not looking at me as he spoke.

I did so. I wanted to get away from there. On shaky legs, I moved back through the kitchen, to the hall. I spotted Frankie standing there at the bottom of the stairs. He'd changed from his black suit into jeans and a hoody, his hands stuffed in his pockets.

'What happened?' he asked.

'Nothing. I dropped some beer.'

'You were in the garage?' he asked.

'I was getting a box from in there.'

'And you just dropped it?'

'Yeah.'

'Just like that? No reason?' He sounded so... almost confrontational, but what did he want me to say?

'An accident,' I said.

'Yeah,' he said, before heading up the stairs.

I went back into the lounge. Nanna remained there, her new 'friend' still next to her, though her head was tilted to the ceiling, her eyes closed, her mouth wide open as she snored in her sleep. Nanna looked over at me. No smile on her face now. Her eyes were dark and hard, glassy – soulless.

Despite my unease, I moved to her. Sat down on the chair arm and put my arm around her shoulder. She turned her head to look at me, flinched, her face brightening, and looked a little surprised, like she hadn't known I was there.

'Jess?' she said. 'Jess, how lovely to see you.'

'You too, Nanna.'

'What a spread you've got for us.'

'Aunt Sarah did most of the hard work actually.'

'Your mum too.'

'Mum isn't here, Nanna. Nor Dad and Lily.'

'Don't be silly, dear. This is their home.'

'Nanna, they died. Remember? That's why we're here today. You were at the funeral earlier.'

She stared at me, undisturbed, but didn't say anything. What was happening in her head? Her dementia had started in her early sixties, even before I was born. I remember when I was young, people thought it was quite funny. She'd say the strangest things. And ask the same questions over and over. 'How's school, dear?'. Or 'What are we having for tea?' Just basic things like that. We used to laugh at her confusion sometimes – *with* her. But she'd deteriorated a lot since then, and her confusion had become more of a burden, for her and for others, even if she mostly acted brightly.

Given the gravity of the situation, I thought she'd remember about Mum, Dad and Lily the first time I told her in the home, though I knew that day, and since, that she wasn't quite there yet, even if she had just witnessed the funeral. Somehow something hadn't fully clicked in her mind, though I also really didn't want to have to keep on explaining about what had happened – the task was simply too painful.

She reached out and put her hand into mine. 'Lovely spread,' she said again.

'Thanks,' I said with a smile.

'Your mum always knows how to treat us well.'

'Mum's not here, Nanna. Nor Dad and Lily. Remember?'

'Don't be silly. I saw them in here not long ago.'

'Not today, Nanna.'

'Yes, today,' she said, a little more harshly, her eyes pinching. 'Lily was running around right here.' She laughed. More of a cackle. 'She's such a sweet thing. So much like you.'

She locked eyes with me. Something behind her glazed irises terrified me.

'They're still here, Jess,' she said, almost a whisper now. 'They'll always be here.'

CHAPTER SEVENTEEN

FRANKIE

Not the worst day of his life. It was pretty clear which day that was. But the day of the funeral without doubt sat right up there. Frankie mostly avoided everyone, spending most of the afternoon in his bedroom, only coming out every now and then to go to the toilet or to get food and drink. Honestly he felt quite pleased with how Jess took the lead in handling everything, not just in the sense that she – together with Sarah, apparently – made all the arrangements, but how she'd been happy for him to spend so much time in his room while all the guests were downstairs. He'd expected her to want him to be down there too, to mingle and chat and to decrease her own burden. Apparently not.

Did her laid-back attitude have anything to do with guilt, he wondered?

He called Meg while in his bedroom. He'd already texted her on and off through the day.

'I can come over if you want,' she said. 'To keep you company.'

He really did want that, but unless he could sneak her in,

then he'd have to explain to Jess who Meg was, and today really wasn't the day for doing that, he didn't think.

'I wish you could,' he said.

'Why won't you just tell her. Why is it a problem?'

'You haven't told your dad,' he said.

'That's different,' she responded, clearly not happy at the comparison. 'Your sister isn't an overbearing bully.'

No, Jess definitely wasn't that, but she wasn't as squeaky clean as she liked to portray either.

So why wouldn't he tell her about Meg, then? Mainly because their relationship had nothing to do with Jess. Things were weird right now, and Jess was, apparently, intent on sticking around and being his and Tom's 'guardian', whatever that really meant. But he'd be eighteen in a few months. He loved Jess, but she was his sister, and that was all she'd ever be. She didn't need to have a say in his private life. Even the thought of it was just... weird.

'Dad's working every day up until Christmas now. You can come over here one night.'

'I'll try.'

He sighed. They both went silent. Until Meg asked, 'How's your brother?' A bit of an odd question really.

'Same,' Frankie said.

'So he's still seeing things.'

Was that the explanation? No doubt Tom had been creeped out a couple of times recently. Properly creeped out. He seriously thought he was seeing ghosts. Poor kid. Or was it all just a cry for help?

No. Tom wasn't that good at acting. Whatever he thought he'd seen... Tom at least truly believed it, and Jess had clearly been spooked too. As for him? he wouldn't say it to another living soul, but the house felt so eerie now, like the walls were watching...

Frankie shivered, glad no one was around to see it. 'I'll be over one night soon,' he said, 'I promise.'

'You should talk to him about it,' Meg said. 'Find out what he's thinking. You're his big brother.'

Frankie thought about that for a few moments. Actually she was right. He'd do that.

After ending the call, Frankie mooched about in his room for a while before deciding to emerge for some food. And because, while he really wasn't interested in socialising, he was interested in watching Jess. He still believed she wasn't being straight with him. Could he glean anything today from who she spoke to and about what?

He found Jess in the dining room, talking to Duncan. Even though Frankie had come downstairs to get some food, he didn't go in there, instead continuing to the empty kitchen. He grabbed a Coke from the fridge and a packet of crisps from the cupboard and went back out again. He made it to the bottom of the stairs when he heard the voice behind him.

'Hey, Frankie,' Aunt Sarah said.

He turned to her. That perpetual look of concern on her face. 'Hey.'

'You're going back to your room?'

'Yeah.'

'Are you okay?'

He shrugged.

'You don't have to shut yourself away.'

'Not really a fun occasion, is it?'

She sighed. 'You can talk to me if you want. About anything. Anytime.'

She spoke genuinely enough, as though she really cared. But did she? It's not like she and Duncan had been that close to him growing up. He saw them two, three times a year max. They didn't really know him, and she hadn't really been that close to his mum and dad either, even if she did share blood with his dad. So why pretend now? Why not just say it like it was?

'I... I don't mean to pry, but is there a problem between you and Jess?'

'Why are you asking?' Frankie said, his suspicion not hidden at all.

'It's just... you seem quite tense with each other. Or more you to her, really.'

Frankie gritted his teeth. 'It's not exactly an easy time for us.'

'No, absolutely not. But your sister... she's really stepped up. For both you and Tom. Try not to be hard on her.'

Was this really happening? Who the hell was Aunt Sarah to call him out like that? 'I'm not being hard on her,' Frankie said.

Sarah pursed her lips, making it clear she didn't believe him. 'She's lost a lot, Frankie. Perhaps more than you realise.'

What on earth was that supposed to mean? 'Do you know why Dad did it?' Frankie asked, deciding to put her on the spot.

Sarah squirmed. Looked like she'd made a mistake in coming out to speak to him.

'He was your brother.'

'You shouldn't ask yourself that,' Sarah said, shrinking a little. 'It won't do you any good to dwell.' She reached out and put her hand on his arm, as if to offer comfort. As if that touch was going to make the situation of losing his parents and sister any better.

'Why shouldn't I ask?' Frankie said. 'I think I should be asking everyone. The people in this house are the people who knew him the best in the world. If no one here knows–'

'We can't know what truly goes on in someone's head, Frankie.'

'You're telling me you have no clue why? That you never suspected?'

'I really didn't,' she said, shaking her head, her lips trembling a little – a wave of sadness?

'Well somebody did. I know it.'

Sarah didn't say anything.

'And where was Mum going that night?' Frankie asked, and saw the twitch on Sarah's face.

'What do you mean?'

'Six o'clock on a Sunday night? Travelling fifty miles away from home with Lily and Tom? They had school the next day. Where was she going? Why?' He really wanted to ask Tom that question too, but hadn't built up to it yet, not wanting to set him back. But he would soon. He had to know.

'You shouldn't do this to yourself.' Sarah sounded more desperate now.

'Heading south. Same route she'd have to take to go to yours?'

Sarah shook her head but Frankie's attention was stolen by someone coming out of the dining room. Jess. She was too preoccupied to look up to see Sarah and Frankie as she headed off to the kitchen.

'I'm going back up,' he said to Sarah before turning away from her.

But he'd only moved up a few stairs before he stopped again. Sarah had already retreated to the lounge. Jess was out of sight, but Duncan skulked out of the dining room, and into the kitchen. What was that sneaky sod up to?

Frankie took one step downstairs before he heard the crash and Jess's scream. The whole house went silent for a moment, before hushed conversations started up again. Strangely no one burst out of the lounge or dining room to go to Jess's aid.

Except Duncan was already in there with her. Already there to offer a helping hand.

Frankie hovered on the stairs, wondering whether to go to her or not. Moments later Jess came back out. No Duncan. Her face was white. She looked terrified.

'What happened?' Frankie asked.

'Nothing. I dropped some beer.'

'You were in the garage?'

'I was getting a box from in there.'

'And you just dropped it?'

'Yeah.'

'Just like that? No reason?'

'An accident,' she said.

An accident? Or had Duncan done something? If not Duncan, then what?

Once again Jess wasn't being straight with him, but she was clearly spooked about something. Properly spooked. His mind went back to the conversation with Meg. To Tom's creepy sightings. To the way he himself felt now in his own home. What the hell was happening in this house?

'Yeah,' was all he said to Jess.

Then Frankie caught the eye of Duncan, standing in the background, glaring over as though not happy about brother and sister talking.

So what was his story?

Frankie looked away and headed on up the stairs and back to his room. But not for long. After a few minutes he lightly stepped out onto the landing. All was quiet downstairs now, the drama over with. He moved along the landing to his parents' room. Grasped the handle and pushed the door open. He felt a little sickly as he sneaked inside, but he was determined to do this. Determined to find out what was really going on.

And he knew exactly where to start.

CHAPTER EIGHTEEN

JESS

I didn't tell my brothers about Nanna's spooky words. Was I freaked out? Yes. Did I believe in ghosts? I hadn't before, but given events in Tom's room, the way I'd felt in Lily's room and what I'd thought and heard in there, my own room too, the garage... I was certainly becoming more and more unnerved in our home, even if I hadn't asked Nanna exactly what she'd meant. Instead, the more rational part of my mind put her words down to the confused ramblings of dementia.

The irrational part of my mind, however, subconsciously whirred out of control, day and night.

Tom's unsettled nights continued in the days that followed the funeral, though he didn't explicitly claim any more ghostly sightings. I too didn't see or hear anything unearthly, though, never really feeling settled, I also tried my best to move around the house with lights on where at all possible, tried to spend as little time alone as I could. At night we got into a pattern of pretty much one on, one off for him coming into my room. That was a compromise, wasn't it? I definitely slept better on the nights with him in my bed. Insisting on him sleeping alone every night likely would only have led to reduced sleep for all of us, though I was becoming increasingly concerned about his night-time fragility. Mine too. Should I see a doctor about it?

On the morning of Christmas Eve, Tom got out of my bed a few minutes before seven. No matter his night-time troubles, little could be done to prevent his early morning alertness. I decided to stay put and try and get some extra rest, partly because of genuine tiredness, partly to while away some of the hours of the day. I knew today, and tomorrow, would be especially tough for us, and shortening the day by sleeping through it was one way of coping, I guessed.

It was nine thirty before I rose out of bed – seriously late for me. Frankie was already up too by that point. I'd expected my brothers to be in the midst of TV or video games, but when I went into the lounge I found them huddled on the sofa, staring at the laptop screen propped on Frankie's thighs.

'Morning,' I said.

'Morning,' Frankie responded, not looking at me.

'Jess, Frankie thinks we really do have ghosts,' Tom said, a little excitedly.

I shot my eldest brother a look.

He turned to me, nonplussed. 'There's some really cool stuff here,' he said. 'Did you know humans believed in ghosts for thousands of years. They reckon at least as far back as some of the ancient Mesopotamian religions, before written records even began.'

'Mesopotamian?'

Frankie shrugged.

'How would anyone know about it if it was before written records?' I asked.

He gave me a quizzical look. 'Across pretty much every religion, old ones and new ones, there's references and examples of ghosts. The belief that there's a human spirit, separate from our physical being goes back... forever. I mean... how is it so common if it's not true? All these people, from different places, different times, but with similar beliefs.'

'Probably because thousands of years ago people didn't know how to explain the world around them. Everyone believed the earth was flat until a few hundred years ago.'

'Some people still do,' Frankie said.

'But, Jess, some of these stories,' Tom added, animated. 'They sound so... similar.'

'Similar to what?'

'Basically there are loads of reasons why ghosts might exist,' Frankie said. 'Sometimes it's because the dead person was wronged so their spirit stays in our world, either to get revenge, or just because they're stuck. Like, what's the word?'

'Purgatory?'

'Think so. So, like, if you don't bury a body properly, or something, the spirit can become trapped, not able to enter the afterlife.'

'The afterlife? Since when have you–'

'Look at this one,' Frankie said, pointing to the screen that I couldn't see, then clearly reading from it as he spoke. 'Pliny the Younger... I... whoever he was, he wrote about a house in Athens, 2,000 years ago. The house was bought by a philosopher... Athen... Atheno... Athenodorus, who thought it was haunted. He kept seeing this ghostly shape, of a man in chains. Then one night, he followed it outside and the ghost indicated a spot on the ground. When Athenodorus dug up the area, he found a shackled skeleton. The haunting stopped after that, once the skeleton was given a proper burial.'

'Mum, Dad and Lily did have a proper burial,' I said, quite defensively. Was that what this was about? Frankie still angry about the cremation? Though really I just wanted him to stop talking about ghouls. Even in the daytime, the thoughts whirring in my mind as he spoke made my heart judder.

'That's not the point,' Frankie said, sounding a little frustrated with me. 'There's another story here.' He typed away and I was in two minds whether to entertain this anymore or close it down straight away. 'Oxford, in the 1800s. Mallory House. The servants regularly complained to the lord of the manor about being haunted at night. They kept seeing a woman and child, both draped in white. The lord wouldn't have any of it. In fact, he was really horrible and said if anyone else talked about it, he'd not pay them. But the servants knew something wasn't right. The ghosts always appeared in the same spot, in the kitchen. One night the cook, who was preparing for a banquet the next day, followed the ghosts outside, to the vegetable garden. They found the bones of a mum and daughter there. The lord of the manor had killed them.'

I shook my head, exasperated. 'Frankie, that's basically the same story, rehashed. How many times has the same story been told in different ways?'

'Isn't that the point?' he said, as though it was me not getting it.

'What if something bad happened with Dad?' Tom said. 'What if that's why he's coming to us, because he's trying to tell—'

'Tom!' I shouted, shaking my head. Both of them stopped and looked at me, a little shocked by my raised voice. 'Tom,' I said, more calmly. 'Do you think you could give me and Frankie a minute?' They continued to stare at me. 'Go and play on the PlayStation or something.'

That did the trick. Tom shot up off the sofa. 'How long have I got?' he asked.

'I don't know. An hour?'

'Only an hour?'

'Tom, please.'

He skulked off.

Frankie glared at me. 'What?' he said.

'Are you serious?'

'Yeah,' he said. 'It's you who was asking about Tom's nightmares. I'm trying to help. You should look at this. Seriously. Maybe... maybe it really is real.'

'You don't believe that.'

'Don't I?'

'And even if you did, you can't go filling Tom's head with that... nonsense. He's struggling enough with sleeping at the moment. Telling him ghosts are real isn't exactly going to help that.'

I moved over to him, went to tip the laptop lid closed but Frankie shifted it away from my reach.

'He's struggling because he's terrified,' Frankie said. 'He's struggling because his parents are dead. Maybe this will help him.'

'Thinking that Dad really is standing in his room at night? You think that's going to help him?'

'Why not?'

'Please, Frankie,' I said, trying to tone down the combativeness, 'this isn't the way.'

'Says you.'

'Yes, says me! I am in charge here now.'

'In charge. Like we're your little slaves, having to follow everything you say.'

'That's not what I meant at all.'

'Whatever.'

Frankie closed the laptop lid, got up from the sofa with the computer in his hand.

'We don't need to battle each other,' I said. 'We all need to *help* each other.'

'I *am* trying to help,' Frankie said before brushing past me. 'Are you sure *you* are?'

123

Frankie shut himself in his room. Tom remained upstairs too, playing on his PS4. Despite me staying in bed late as some sort of avoidance technique, I did want Christmas Eve to be a nice, family day for us all. But I left them both to it for a couple of hours. Pottered downstairs, tidied up, read a book, thought.

My brain rumbled with the ghostly stories my brothers had relayed to me. Did I believe them? I didn't want to, but what I'd heard had struck a chord. I still couldn't understand why Dad would kill himself. So naturally, if he hadn't done it, someone else had. Could that explain the eerie presence in our home? His wronged soul remaining in our world until the truth was discovered?

I needed to be more open with Frankie about my suspicions, but I'd have to find the right time. Perhaps not over Christmas, though.

In my room, I also fended off some texts from Aunt Sarah. Since the funeral she'd sent me a few – out of real concern, I thought – asking us if we wanted to spend Christmas with them, either at their house or ours. I'd politely declined, but she was becoming quite insistent. I held my ground. Why? I'm not really sure. I think I wanted to show everyone, myself and Frankie in particular, that I could do this. Christmas was just one day, but if I could get the three of us through it, successfully, then didn't that show that I really could take care of my brothers? That I really was a responsible enough adult? Silly, but that was how I felt.

As lunchtime approached I decided it was time to get us all back together. I headed upstairs. Frankie's bedroom door remained closed, so I went to Tom first. He was busy playing Fortnite, his favoured game of recent times. If it was up to him he'd play it for a whole day, and I knew Mum and Dad had had multiple battles with him over the game, which they said was addictive and nearly always stressed him out rather than giving him real enjoyment. I didn't have a strong opinion about the game, and hadn't witnessed anything too severe when he'd been on it. In fact, over the last few days whenever he'd played he'd simply sat, a little zombie-like, hands and fingers moving at speed but otherwise entirely still. Though that wasn't only Tom when he was on Fortnite, that was him most of the time now, a certain quietness and sadness ever present.

I kind of wanted to see the Fortnite tantrum that Mum and Dad had told me so much about.

'Probably enough for one day, don't you think?' I said to him.

'I'm in a game,' he responded, robotically.

I moved over and sat on the edge of the bed and watched the screen for a few seconds, the bright, cartoon images. An arsenal of guns exploded onto the ground when Tom annihilated one of his competitors. I couldn't really see why the game appealed so much, but I'd never been a big gamer.

'The things Frankie was showing you earlier,' I said, 'you know none of that is real, don't you?'

Tom didn't answer, just kind of growled as his fingers moved up a gear, nearly warp speed as he... I'm not sure. It looked like he was building, a structure going up around his figure, springing out of the ground from nowhere really.

'Tom?'

'No!' he shouted, slamming the controller down. 'That's impossible! I hit him already!'

On the screen I saw his player down. The shooter taunted with a victory dance as Tom's final position was displayed.

'Second place? That's not bad, is it?'

He smacked the controller again. 'It's terrible. I'm terrible. I hate this game.'

Tears flowed as he rocked on his knees. The reaction had come from nowhere. I slid off the bed to the floor and moved to him. When I put my arms around him he initially tried to shrug me off but after a few seconds his resistance faded and he turned and buried his head into me as he sobbed.

'Tom, come on, it's just a game,' I said, though I immediately felt foolish as I knew really that the extreme reaction had little to do with Fortnite. Wasn't it? Unless this was what Mum and Dad had talked about.

Tom didn't say anything. Neither did I. We continued to embrace as he slowly calmed.

'What's the matter, Tommo?' I asked. 'You can tell me. You can tell me anything.'

He still didn't say a word.

'Is it because of what Frankie was showing you?'

A slight nod, I thought.

'Did it scare you?'

A shake this time.

'Then what?'

He pulled away a little to look up at me. 'I haven't seen him for ages.'

'Dad?'

He nodded. 'That night, when he was in my room... what if I scared him away?'

'Tom, come on. Ghosts aren't real. Dad wasn't in your room.'

His face creased, but it was more exasperation than annoyance. 'I know what I saw, Jess. He was here. And... I'm really scared now.'

'There's nothing to be scared of,' I said, not really feeling my words.

'No, Jess, that's not what I meant. I mean, I'm scared that he won't come back. I want to see them again. I *have* to see them again. But what if they don't come back now? What if they never come back? What if it's all my fault?'

'Nothing's your fault, Tom.'

'So... you think they will come back? You think I'll see them again?'

I simply didn't know what to say to that. We sat in silence for a few moments. I knew what I wanted to say, but I was worried the words wouldn't come out right. 'The night of the crash,' I said, trying to sound calm and carefree. 'What did Mum say to you? About where you were going.'

'She didn't,' he said.

'She didn't?'

'She didn't tell us where we were going. Just told me and Lily to get in the car.'

'What about Dad?'

'I don't know where he was.'

'He wasn't in?'

A shrug.

'Mum said nothing else at all?'

'She... she did. She said, *I have to get away from that man.*'

'That man? Dad? Had they had an argument?' There'd certainly been tension between them the last time I'd seen them.

'Was she angry?' I said. 'Or afraid?'

'I... I don't know,' Tom said, sounding more dejected, on the edge of breaking down, likely as he relived that horrific night.

I decided not to push it, but his words remained tumbling in my mind.

CHAPTER NINETEEN

As I left Tom's room, more than anything I was angry at Frankie, for encouraging Tom's ideas about ghosts, even if what they'd found did leave me with even more questions. Regardless, it surely couldn't be healthy for a young, grieving boy to not only have it reinforced that ghosts were real, but that it was possible for him to see the ghost of his dead dad. Not only was the whole thing bizarre and creepy, it also heaped way too much pressure on Tom's already burdened shoulders. Now, apparently, he was actively wanting to see the ghost of Dad – and Mum and Lily too? So what happened when he didn't? Disappointment, self-doubt, perhaps something worse if he came to believe that the lack of their ghostly presence was down to him, something he'd done wrong. That the spirits of his parents were punishing him by their non-presence.

I had to find a way to bring him back to rationality, and I knew perhaps the most persuasive way of doing that was to play down the presence of ghosts – even if I couldn't be sure what I felt myself anymore – and getting Frankie on board with me. Perhaps not the simplest of solutions given his attitude with me of late.

I eventually managed to coax Frankie from his room, though we didn't have a chat about my plans for Tom. I wouldn't let it slide by, though. Me and Frankie had to provide a united front for Tom. For all of us really, and Frankie's determination to battle with me had to change.

Still, we really tried to have a positive afternoon, despite the obvious holes in our family. We watched a Christmas movie, we played games – charades, Scrabble, Monopoly, cards. We laughed, a lot, we had a few grumbles and paddies about losing games – not from me – but mostly we bonded and did exactly what we'd always done on Christmas Eve. Despite everything, I felt better than I had at any other time since that Sunday night.

Come early evening we were taking a break. I was mentally exhausted, perhaps from the battle to stay positive. Not pretending exactly, but it didn't come easy. Tom remained in front of the TV – was he getting too much screen time? – while I once again tidied, got things ready for dinner. Frankie had disappeared upstairs as usual.

With a lasagne in the oven for tea, and the table set out all ready to go, I went upstairs to check what he was up to. With Tom busy, perhaps I'd get a chance to have the much-needed conversation.

The door to his bedroom was open. He wasn't inside. Odd. So where was he? Not in the bathroom, not in Tom's room either. I moved across the landing. The door to Mum and Dad's room was ajar an inch or so. For days on end now I hadn't managed to bring myself to even look in there, never mind go in, but as I stood by the door I heard movement beyond.

I pushed the door further open. I spotted Frankie inside, kneeling on the carpet by the wide-open cupboard doors.

'What are you doing?'

Frankie, shocked, turned around to me, but his look of

surprise faded quickly to typical teenage flatness. 'What does it look like?' he said.

I reluctantly took a step into the room, trying my best not to look around, in particular to not look to the bed where my parents used to sleep.

Instead my eyes rested on the small piles – boxes and bags – on the carpet by Frankie. I knew immediately what they were. Presents. Christmas presents that Mum and Dad had bought for us all. For each other too? Sickness rose up in my throat. 'You can't do that!'

He paused and glared at me. 'Why not? This stuff's for us.'

'But...'

'They wanted us to have this. They bought it all for us. What are we supposed to do? Just leave it in the cupboard forever?'

I squeezed my eyes shut, trying not to think about what it all meant. Trying not to think about my Mum and Dad, in the shops or scouring the internet looking for presents for their kids. Presents they'd never be able to give. Not able to see our smiling, grateful faces.

When I opened my eyes again I was staring at the pile that perhaps had the most in it. Or, at least, the presents were generally bigger in that pile. Big boxes, crammed with big plastic toys. A lot of pink. Lily's presents.

My heart shuddered and I wiped at my eyes. I moved closer, not really thinking. 'How did you know?' I asked. A strange question really.

'They always put our stuff in here. Dad pulls the shoe rack forward, stuffs everything behind. Same for birthdays.'

I shook my head, a little disgusted by my brother. How long had he been sneaking in here to check everyone's presents before the date? He seemed so... casual about it all.

'They might have bought all this for us,' I said, 'but that doesn't mean they wanted you snooping, did it?'

He returned his glare to me. 'Yeah, well, they're not here anymore, are they?'

I shook my head in disbelief at his lack of feeling. Without thinking I sat down on the bed. A waft of Mum's scent was thrown into the air. I ran my hand over the soft duvet cover, but couldn't look back to the pillows, as though if I did so I'd be violating Mum and Dad somehow.

Instead I glanced over the other piles. Mum and Dad always treated us so well at Christmas, pretty much whatever we asked for. In a strange way I felt a bit foolish for not having thought about doing what Frankie was doing. After all, we were on a tight budget, weren't we? I'd been out and bought both the boys a little something from me: a book and PS4 game for Tom, a Red-Letter Day voucher and some chocolates for Frankie. Looking at the array of presents Mum and Dad had bought made me feel even more foolish. They'd even bought Tom the same game I already had.

'They got me driving lessons,' Frankie said, not looking at me. 'They got you–'

'Please don't tell me.' Although I'd already spotted the jewellery box. 'Will you wrap the things for me and Tom?' I asked him.

Frankie shrugged. ''Spose.'

'I'll take the things for you.'

'Not much point really, but whatever.'

I gritted my teeth. Was he trying to rile me? I picked up the pile of presents intended for him.

'Do you think they'd already got each other something too?' he asked me, looking around the room now.

'I don't know.'

'What should we do with it?'

I thought for a moment. 'We shouldn't do anything.'

'But–'

'No buts, Frankie. Please don't go looking.'

He didn't say anything. Wouldn't even hold my eye.

'Frankie, I'm serious. It's not right.'

'It's not wrong, either. We can't just leave everything in here, like this, forever. They're not coming back, Jess. They're dead.'

Now it was my turn to say nothing. Because as harsh and unfeeling as I found his words, I knew he was right. 'But... for now, please?' I said at last. 'When it's time, we'll do it together. We'll clear out this room, Lily's too. But we'll do it together. Yeah?'

He didn't answer.

'Frankie?'

'They'd bought all this stuff,' he said.

A question? I wasn't sure.

'If they'd got all this stuff, that means they'd planned to give it to us... so why...'

He didn't finish. I understood where he was going. Why would Dad buy us presents he never intended to give us? I'd thought the same thing. Yet he hadn't got the tree, had he? Perhaps... perhaps those two contradictions were evidence enough of his internal struggles.

Perhaps they were evidence of something else...

I shook the thoughts away. 'We can't torture ourselves by thinking about it.'

Frankie glared at me. 'I need to know *why*,' he said. He picked up Tom's presents and mine, then moved on past me.

After a few moments of uncomfortable silence I put his things back on the bed and quickly put Lily's presents back in the wardrobe. I'd deal with them another time.

The clothes inside smelled so much of Dad it made my head spin. As I closed the wardrobe doors those earlier conversations about ghosts loomed in my thoughts, the spooky words of Nanna, the eeriness I'd felt in the garage...

I hurriedly pushed the cupboard doors shut, grabbed Frankie's things and ran out, pulling the door closed behind me with a bang.

I shut the door to my bedroom, put Frankie's things on the desk, then lay back on the bed. I didn't cry. I wanted to, but I think I'd cried so much the last few days that there weren't many tears left in me. After I don't know how long I decided to pull out the boys' things from the drawers in my room and wrapped up the presents, leaving Tom's duplicate game to the side. I'd get a refund and let him choose another one.

The doorbell rang downstairs. Strange, at 5pm on Christmas Eve. I had a flashing thought that perhaps Duncan and Sarah had come, intent on doing the right thing – according to them – by spending Christmas with us, despite me repeatedly putting them off.

I reached the landing before Frankie called up. 'Jess, for you. Apparently.'

Apparently? Odd thing to say. I moved down, eyes focused on the open front door, on the figure standing just beyond the threshold, revealed several inches at a time with each step I took. A pair of smart trainers, jeans...

Below in the hall, Frankie passed by and looked up at me. 'Popular as ever with the boys,' he said, a little snidely.

The figure at the front came fully into view a couple of steps later. Out of anyone, for some reason I most expected to see Ed standing there. Jamie even, given Ed had broken the ice with my home town friends already, and the others would all surely think I was now okay to be approached.

The person I hadn't expected at all was Blake.

CHAPTER TWENTY

'Blake? What are you doing here?' I asked him. Perhaps I didn't need to say it in such a questioning tone, but both surprise and annoyance got the better of me. Particularly when I looked down to the two big, black bags by his feet. He shuffled nervously. He had his hands stuffed in the pockets of his bomber-style jacket, the collar raised up around his neck. His hair hung lazily over his brow, how it naturally did, all of the time, a look other lads spent time and money perfecting. That was the thing with Blake. So many things came so effortlessly to him. His looks, intelligence, sporting prowess. Girls? Not that he was arrogant or conceited about all that, one of the very reasons why I felt so drawn to him in the first place. Well, that, and the fact he was ridiculously hot, particularly when he set his velvety blue eyes on me. Like he did now, as if to placate me.

'I came... I brought some things for you,' he said. 'From home. From uni I mean.'

'You went through my room?'

He squirmed. Clearly he hadn't expected the conversation, the reunion, to go like this, but I didn't know what to think.

'We've hardly heard from you,' he said. 'The girls are really worried. I am too. I didn't know when you'd be able to get back. I wanted to help.'

'Don't give him such a hard time,' Frankie called out from somewhere behind me. 'Where's your Christmas spirit, sis?'

Blake glanced over my shoulder, smiled a little at my brother, until he caught my eye again.

I looked beyond him. To the parked car on the road. He had another lengthy journey to get back to his home tonight. It's not as though our house was on the way from Bristol for him. My eyes rested on a darker spot on the street beyond his car, though I wasn't sure why. Was someone there, lurking? I couldn't tell in the dark.

'You'd better come in,' I said as a chill spread through me.

Nervous relief extended across Blake's face as I stepped to the side. He picked up the two bags and then dropped them again on the tiles inside the hall. I shut the door and ushered him through to the kitchen. Where Frankie was standing by the kettle. Was he intent on taunting me?

'Want a drink, Blake?' Frankie asked, pure nonchalance.

Blake looked a little uncertain. How did Frankie even know his name? Had the two of them already shared a brief conversation or was it only because I'd blurted the name at the door?

'Blake, this is my brother, Frankie. Frankie, this is Blake from uni.'

'Yeah, I know,' Frankie said. 'So? Drink?'

'Just a quick one,' Blake said. 'I can see I'm disturbing you. I can smell your tea in the oven.'

'It won't be ready for a little while yet,' Frankie said. 'Tea? Coffee? Beer?'

'Coffee, please. Bit of drive still. Could do with the boost.'

'To where?' Frankie asked.

'Cheshire.'

Frankie nodded. 'Want one, sis?'

'I think I'm going to have a glass of wine,' I said, grabbing a bottle of red from the rack in the kitchen. Both Frankie and Blake gave me a weird look, but enough was enough. I needed something to settle me.

And it was Christmas Eve after all, right?

'Have a seat,' I said to Blake, indicating to the stools by the island, still in two minds about the whole thing. Why had Blake come tonight? Was I glad he was here?

I poured a large glass and put the bottle on the island. I sat down and watched Frankie taking an age doing the coffee for Blake. Apparently he enjoyed my discomfort.

Finally, with the drink done, Frankie turned back to us, nothing for himself. 'See you later then,' he said with a grin before heading out. He left the door to the kitchen wide open. I took a drag of wine then got up, moved over and pushed the door to. Not fully closed. That would only make Frankie all the more suspicious.

Would he try to eavesdrop?

'I'm so sorry,' Blake said, standing up from his stool as I walked back across. He stepped toward me and I didn't resist as he reached out and took me in his arms.

I didn't say anything, didn't move for several seconds as he held me, his touch warm and tender. I hadn't expected to see him tonight, I hadn't wanted to, really, but I'd missed his touch, the way my body fitted into his taller frame. The feeling of his long, muscle-hardened arms around me.

He released me. I would have stayed there longer. We both took our seats. I took an even larger mouthful of wine.

'How are you?' he asked.

'We've had a nice day, today,' I said to him with a meek smile.

He shook his head. 'I can't even imagine what you're going through.'

He looked across the room. To the closed door leading to the utility room and garage. Did he know the details – I certainly hadn't told him – or could he simply sense what had happened here? In there. A cold draught from that direction raised the hairs on the back of my neck. Thoughts and images of ghouls and ghosts flashed as my eyes danced across the room and to the darkness beyond the windows. More wine.

'I'm sorry if I upset you,' Blake said. 'By going into your room.'

The thought made me feel weird. My room at uni. My private space. Blake, not exactly my boyfriend, not anymore, rummaging through there when I wasn't around. Did I have anything in there I didn't want him to see? Not that I could think of, but that wasn't really the point.

'I was starting to run out of clothes,' I said, which was certainly true. The day I'd left for home I'd packed in a few seconds, only a small bag with virtually nothing in it, and in recent days I'd been relying on the rejects which had stayed in the wardrobe here, gathering dust, while I was at uni.

'The girls are really worried about you,' Blake said again. 'Me too.' He reached across and put his hand over mine. I didn't resist.

'You didn't have to come all this way,' I said.

'I wanted to see you.'

I didn't say anything, though I struggled to hold it together and I think Blake could see that. One reason I'd fallen for him was his kind and caring nature, and sitting with him now, my natural attraction to him was undoubtedly still strong, I found it hard to figure out why it had all gone so wrong.

No. I knew why. The problems were down to me, and those

problems, in many ways, felt all so insignificant now in comparison to what had happened here.

'What will you do next year?' Blake said.

'In January?'

He nodded.

'I've got to stay here. My brothers need me.' I was almost sick of answering that question now. As if any doubt remained about what I would do. 'Before you ask, I've no idea what that means for me. For my course, for graduation next year. Do I need to defer? Go back again the year after when Frankie is eighteen and can look after Tom? Can I switch to a uni near here to finish off? I haven't a clue. But I'm staying here for now. My brothers need me. We can't lose this house. I won't have them taken into foster care. There's no one else who can look after my brothers but me. I'll get a job; I'll do what I need to do. For them.'

The room fell strangely silent. Blake held my eye. I felt a little embarrassed by my little monologue, but I just wanted to get it all out there, to avoid any more follow-up questions. The future wouldn't be easy. The future would be a sacrifice of everything I'd worked for at school, and over the last two-and-a-half years at uni. But I belonged at home.

'You're amazing,' Blake said. 'Whatever happens next, your brothers are in the best possible hands.'

To avoid showing the emotion on my face I picked up the wine and finished off what remained in the glass. Then poured another. Blake gave me a dubious look.

'I'll do whatever I can to support you,' he said. 'The distance isn't a problem. I'm here for you, Jess. Whatever happens next, whatever comes after graduation, I want to be part of your life.'

He reached out for my hand again. This time I did take it away, because I spotted the shadow at the kitchen door. Frankie.

He walked in without hesitation. Made a show of checking his watch. 'Think that lasagne's just about ready, isn't it?' he said.

I looked to the clock on the oven. Actually it had a couple of minutes left. Frankie probably knew that.

Tom followed inside in hot pursuit. He stretched his arms into the air as though he'd been asleep. 'I'm starving,' he said. Then he looked to Blake and paused, as if he hadn't realised I had company. Probably because he'd been so engrossed in the TV.

'Tom, this is my friend from uni. Blake.'

Blake flinched a little at the word 'friend'.

'Do you want to eat with us?' Frankie said to Blake. 'It's a bloody big lasagne.'

'Frankie, language!' I said. Tom smirked.

Blake looked at me, as though searching for the answer.

'It's going to be way too late to eat when you make it home,' Frankie said.

I still didn't say anything.

'If you're sure,' Blake said, holding my eye.

'We're sure, aren't we, Jess?'

I said nothing, just poured myself some more wine.

I couldn't be sure of Frankie's intentions on being so overtly nice and accommodating to Blake, but the end result was – unexpectedly – a net positive. Despite the issues between us, I'd missed Blake. I missed the way he made me feel. I missed his touch. His inquisitive nature. His humour. His presence. Honestly, I missed just looking at him, his wide jaw, those deep blue eyes, the little freckles that lined his nose that gave him a boyish charm at odds with his manly physique.

Not so long ago I'd imagined introducing him to Mum and

Dad. I'd really quite wanted to, I could well have imagined the look on my mum's face when she first set sights on him; tall, handsome, athletic, kind, intelligent. Everything a mum would want for a daughter. The idea of Blake meeting my siblings hadn't been such a big thought, but over the near hour we sat at the table together, with Blake on such natural form, a wave of sadness grew and grew inside me as I watched Blake bond with Frankie, and in particular Tom.

Blake had a younger sister, twelve years old, and in the past I probably would have said he'd therefore have been more in tune with Lily than Tom. Yet by the time Tom scuttled off to watch more TV, Blake was my little brother's new best friend, and pretty much had my brother's whole life story. They'd bonded over everything from favourite movies, to video games, to football, to favourite fast-food restaurants, to cringeworthy – but quite funny – knock-knock jokes.

'I'll wash up,' Frankie said, getting up from the table.

'I'll give you a hand,' Blake said, going to get up.

'Don't worry about it,' my brother replied, waving the offer away.

'It's getting pretty late,' I said to Blake.

He looked at his watch and his face dropped. 'Yeah,' he said.

It took a couple of minutes to get him to the front door. I sensed his reluctance. Despite me trying to get rid of him, a large part of me felt the same, but what was the alternative? He stayed for Christmas and missed out on his own family time? His mum and dad and sister would be devastated. And I knew now – from horrific personal experience – that those family times were more precious than anything.

Plus, I still had so much to figure out before I properly let Blake back into my head and my life. If I ever did at all. I hadn't even considered our problems recently.

CJ STONE

'I'm glad you came,' I said to him as I held the front door open.

'Any time.' He looked beyond me. 'Bye, lads!'

Frankie called back in turn from the kitchen, but Tom came scurrying out of the lounge and right up to Blake and gave him a big hug that took both me and Blake by surprise.

'Merry Christmas,' Tom said before rushing off again.

'Merry Christmas!' Blake shouted out.

Then we stood in silence for a few awkward moments. Blake reached into his pocket. Took out the small, wrapped parcel. 'I should have brought something for the boys,' he said. 'Sorry. But this is for you.'

I hesitated before I took the gift. 'You didn't need to.'

'I wanted to.'

'I haven't got anything for you.'

'I wouldn't expect it.' He reached forward and I responded and we shared another hug, more brief than before, more awkward too.

'Speak soon, yeah?'

'Yeah.'

'Merry Christmas.'

'Hopefully.'

Then he turned and walked off toward his car. I waited on the doorstep. The chill of the night had goose pimples spreading over my skin, the darkness outside still and silent. I watched him drive off, then I looked across the street once more, to that same dark spot as earlier.

No. No one there now. But earlier?

With a wave of disquiet I closed the front door, blocking out the creepy thoughts.

'Nice chap,' Frankie said from right behind me, making me jump.

I turned to him. 'Quite an act you put on,' I said to him, playfully hitting his arm.

He put his hand to his heart. 'Me? What about you?'

'What about me?'

I went to move away, Frankie blocked my way.

'He's the one, isn't he?'

'The one?'

'That's got you all messed up?'

'Messed up? Thanks.'

'You know what I mean.'

'Do I?'

'So are you going to tell me?'

'There's nothing to tell.'

I pushed past him.

'I don't believe you,' he called as I walked off. 'The truth will come out eventually.' He said it as though he really wanted to know the truth. As though it would help him. Help him understand the problems our parents had, and why our dad killed himself. Help him understand me.

On the contrary, I was damn sure he didn't want to know *my* truths.

And I sincerely hoped he never would.

CHAPTER TWENTY-ONE

Christmas morning went by about as well as I could have hoped. I'd made a deal with Tom that he had to stay in bed until seven thirty, as otherwise he would have been up who knew when to tear his presents open. In the end it was closer to eight when he came to my door to see if I was awake. I was. We all got up. The lounge, with the lights and tree and the presents underneath, looked so nice, though I thought that the piles the boys had were a lot smaller than in previous years.

We got through the presents quick as ever, both boys happy with their haul, and then we settled down to a morning of playing with their new things, interspersed with snacks and TV.

We scheduled a video call with Duncan and Sarah for eleven, and sat in a line on the sofa to speak to them. They'd left some small presents for each of us when they came up for the funeral, and had sent a card each in the post, though asked that we not open anything until they could see us.

After a brief chat we got down to it. Another video game for each of the boys. Some racing game for Tom, and an eighteen-rated zombie blood-fest for Frankie that he seemed about as happy with as any other present. I'd have to make sure Tom got

LIES THAT BIND

nowhere near that. For me a necklace, to go with the much nicer one that Mum and Dad had bought me – which naturally had made me horribly teary – and the perhaps a bit too expensive bracelet that Blake had bought me. I already had both of those on. I'd texted Blake a thank you, felt a little awkward in doing so. Should I call him later?

'It's great,' I said to Duncan and Sarah.

'Just a little something,' Sarah said. 'Do you want to open the envelopes next? Boys first.'

The boys were straight at it, tearing eagerly. A card with a cheque inside for them both.

'Fifty pounds, nice!' Tom said.

'Yeah, thanks,' Frankie said, a little less enthused as he wafted the paper in the air.

'Jess?' Sarah prompted.

I opened the envelope. Took out the card and the cheque. Spotted the five and the zero and at first thought that was that. Except I followed along. Another zero, another, and another before the decimal point.

'What the...'

I quickly pulled the cheque out of sight of Frankie next to me. Why? I don't know, but it didn't seem right him seeing. I was speechless. £50,000? An obscene amount. In some ways quite grotesque really, as a present.

But also an amount that could literally change everything for us.

'I don't know what to say.' And I sounded stunned, more than excited or anything else.

'I told you I'd have a word with Aunt Sarah,' Duncan said. 'To see what we could do to help out.'

'How much is it?' Frankie asked me.

'A lot,' I said. 'Too much,' I added as I looked back to the screen.

'It's the least we can do,' Sarah said. 'We're here for you. For all of you.'

Of course I was happy with the money: £50,000 was huge, but I really didn't know how to react to it. Giving such an amount wasn't normal. What was I supposed to do? I'd have to have a private chat with Sarah before cashing the cheque, though I knew, if we were able to keep it, then the money would make such a huge difference in paying off the mortgage and helping us – me in particular – to move forward with my plans to look after my brothers.

But did the money mean we'd be forever indebted to Duncan and Sarah? Not an ideal position, but I couldn't afford to turn the money down either.

Somewhat stunned, I passed the rest of the day in a mixture of TV, games and eating and drinking, plus a quick trip out to see Nanna. Me and Frankie shared a few drinks together through the day; beer and wine, though we both remained pretty dialled back. After a couple of glasses of wine I decided to quietly explain to him about the money, when Tom's ears weren't listening, and also to reinforce that it didn't mean we could go and splash out on nice things, but that the money was to help keep our roof over our heads. He seemed to get it, even though he'd begged for *just* a thousand each to get something for ourselves. I'd refused that, but perhaps he had a point. Perhaps we could take some out for a holiday even?

We held a toast to Mum and Dad and Lily more than once during the day, at key moments like when we were pulling crackers at the dinner table, when Frankie lit the brandy over the Christmas pudding, each time with tears in our eyes. But we made it through. I got the boys through. An exhausting day, a special day, a haunting day, knowing what we were missing, a bewildering day given the money from Duncan and Sarah, and more than anything I was glad when it was over and I could climb into bed.

I couldn't sleep though. My brain was wired. Perhaps because of the wine. Often when I'd had a few glasses it gave my brain extra fuel. Time had rolled past midnight as I lay in the bed, on my side, eyes open as I looked over to the door to my room. I couldn't be sure if I'd drifted off moments before, but alertness had reasserted itself over me. Why? I didn't know, but my eyes rested on a strange shadow in the corner of the room, next to the door.

As of late I'd been leaving my door open a little, so I could better hear Tom. I also left the landing light on, and the lines of illumination poking in through the gaps between door and frame partially lit the room – probably affecting my sleep really – but somehow that light didn't reach into the corner where my eyes were focused. An empty corner of the room, nothing there but a small chair, I knew. So what could I see? A shadow from outside, perhaps? A tree branch. But we had no big trees that close to the house.

As my heart rate ramped up, the shadow seemed to sway and swirl, fluid in motion. I slowed my breathing, trying not to make a sound. I clutched the covers a little more tightly around my neck. I couldn't take my eyes off that spot.

Then came the voices. Shallow, soft. My heart pummelled my ribs. Clammy sweat built on my skin. I strained to hear. A voice. Definitely a voice. Memories of that time in Lily's room whirred in my mind. What were they saying? Too quiet to be from in my room. Not from the corner. Not from that shadow that still swirled in and out like a slowly pulsing heart. As I continued to strain, a piercing sound built in my ears, pressure rising, crushing, causing me to wince.

But was the sound there at all or just a reaction to my tension?

When it became too much, in a moment of reckless bravery, I threw the covers back and jumped out of the bed and rushed toward the corner of the room. As if to... what? Attack thin air?

Yes. That's exactly what I did. I swooshed my arms through the air. Reached out and touched the chair. Reached further and felt over the wall. Nothing there.

I spun back around. All alone. So what had I seen? There was nothing else in the room to even create a shadow here.

The voices continued to drift. Or, just one voice, I now thought. I shuddered. The same voice as I'd heard in Lily's room? I really couldn't be sure. I really hoped not.

I stepped out onto the landing, could place the voice more easily from there. I tensed as I moved past Mum and Dad's room. Nothing at all came from Frankie's. Nor Lily's, I realised with huge relief.

I reached Tom's door. Could hear his voice even more clearly now. Not scared at all. A conversation. A one-sided conversation.

'Tom?' I said, stepping into his room. A surprised shuffle in the bed as a swathe of light burst into his room from the landing.

'No! What are you doing?'

At the panic in his voice I put caution aside and rushed through the partially lit room, searching, on edge, every shadow, every dark corner, pulsing and jumping out toward me. I reached the bed but Tom shoved me away. I backtracked to the door and slammed on the light.

'Tom, what the hell?'

'You made them go away! You made them leave!'

'Who?'

'Mum and Dad,' Tom said, glaring at me, his eyes welling.

'They came back. They came back to see me. But you've scared them away.' He buried his head in his pillow, sobbing.

I didn't sleep properly the rest of the night, one ear trained for any more voices, my eyes half open, gaze resting on that dark spot in my room where the shadow never reappeared.

How?

I was glad when 7am wound around and I heard Tom moving across the landing. As tired as I was, I decided to get up.

After a bit of TV, which we watched in silence, I fixed us some cereal, building up the courage to ask him about the night before, which had apparently unsettled me a lot more than it had him.

'I'm sorry for disturbing you last night,' I said. Strange words really, and I couldn't believe that was the best I'd come up with.

Tom didn't respond.

'You saw Mum and Dad?' I asked. 'Together?'

He nodded. 'They wanted to say Merry Christmas.'

'What about Lily?'

'It was too late for her, she's only five,' he said, as though I was a moron for not realising that.

'It was pretty late for you too.'

'But they can only come at night.'

'Did they say that?'

'It's obvious, isn't it?'

I couldn't find any words to answer that. It surprised me how Tom spoke so calmly about it all. He hadn't been scared in the night. He genuinely thought he'd been having a conversation with the spirits of his dead parents.

Clearly, that comforted him.

It terrified me.

I promised Tom that we'd go shopping on Boxing Day. He not only wanted to swap the game I'd bought him – though I claimed the duplicate was from Nanna – but he also wanted to look for something to spend his money on. Not only the fifty pounds from Duncan and Sarah but another seventy he'd accumulated from the wider family.

'What are you thinking of getting?' I asked him as we entered the somewhat dilapidated 1970s shopping centre in town. A sizeable proportion of the units were closed down for good, although it did have a few of the national chains that might be found in larger and more illustrious shopping centres in bigger cities, albeit on smaller scales and with much smaller ranges.

'Not sure,' Tom said.

I'd asked a couple of times already, and he'd given similarly bland responses on each occasion, though I could tell by how he led me that he had a plan in mind.

'Then which shop are we going to?' I asked.

'How about Argos?'

The centre did have a small unit for the catalogue outlet, though in my experience most of the items in the catalogue usually weren't in stock, only available at the much larger store on a purpose-built retail park a few miles away.

'Sure,' I said. 'But there are better places to get computer games from.'

'I know. I don't want a game from there.'

'Then what?'

He shrugged.

We reached the store and Tom ran in and up to one of the catalogues and began flicking through.

'If you let me know what you're looking for I can help you.'

'I'm fine,' he said, his face screwed with concentration as he went back and forth, no particular plan I could see.

I decided to just relax. It wasn't as though we were in a rush for time. Several minutes passed until Tom finally settled on a page. I leaned over to take a look, expecting to see one of the toy pages open.

No. Electronics.

'What are you after?' I asked him.

'I want to buy a camera.'

'I thought you had Dad's old digital one?' Not a very good one. Eight megapixels, I thought. A camera that Dad had bought probably before Tom was born. I remembered him using it on a holiday to Sardinia when I was seven or eight. I'd really wanted to use the camera but Dad refused as it was his new plaything and he didn't trust me. Instead I was given a disposable that I don't think we ever got developed. Dad's old camera was certainly good back then, but nowhere near as good as the cameras on cheap smartphones now. Still, Tom had been delighted when Dad passed it down to him a couple of years ago.

'No,' Tom said. 'That got put in the bin. It was rubbish.'

'Oh,' I said, with a strange feeling of mourning, not for the camera, but at the memories of that part of my younger life.

'Not that kind of camera,' Tom said. 'I want a video one. Like a CCTV.'

Hardly the typical object of desire for a young boy. 'Why on earth would you want a CCTV camera?' But as the words passed my lips, the answer dawned on me.

'For my room. In case I miss Mum and Dad when I'm asleep. I want to see them; I want to know when they've been.'

I didn't know what to say. I looked at the open pages. Glancing over the selection, I noticed that he could easily afford one. A pack of two or three even.

'If you're seeing them anyway, then–'

'*I'm* seeing them,' Tom said. 'But you and Frankie aren't.'

I thought to the shadow I'd watched so closely, nervously, the night before. To the moment in the garage too. Lily's room. No, I hadn't seen Mum and Dad. But what *had* I seen, felt, smelled, heard in our house? My heart jolted a couple of times at the mere thoughts.

'You two haven't seen them, and I know *you* don't even believe me.'

'Tom, it's not that I don't be–'

'This will prove it. This will show you that I'm right.'

'I'm sorry, Tom. It's... don't waste your money on that. Please?'

'But I need you to believe me.'

'I do believe you.' Did I?

'Liar. You don't.' He glared at me, my own hackles raised such was the force of his look.

'I said no, Tom. You're not getting that.'

He didn't say anything.

'Sorry, but no,' I added.

'You're so mean.' He slammed the catalogue closed and stormed out.

CHAPTER TWENTY-TWO

Thankfully I managed to calm Tom, even if I remained anxious. An iced doughnut and a hot chocolate and a quiet fifteen minutes did the trick for him, and we headed off to another shop to get him not one but two more PlayStation games. He still had plenty of Christmas money left over after that, but given he had nothing else he really wanted – other than a CCTV camera – I managed to persuade him to keep the rest in his money box. As we made our way home, he actually seemed pretty pleased with that idea, gleefully telling me that he now had over £500 in there.

'If you need anything for the house, I could help,' he said.

'That's a lovely thought,' I said, ruffling his hair, 'but it's your money. Keep it for when you need it.'

I wondered where that comment had come from. I'd been very careful not to mention money problems directly in front of him, but had he overheard something? Or had Frankie said something to him?

Either way, it appeared his view of our financial situation was only from a nine-year-old's perspective if he thought £500 could see us through.

'We're back,' I called out to Frankie as we opened the door. He'd said he wasn't going anywhere, so I expected him still to be home.

He was. In the lounge. Though as I strolled in he quickly shuffled in his seat, a little too slow to get back into an apparently relaxed position. He looked up at me, guilt in his eyes. I glanced first to the TV. Had he been watching something he shouldn't have?

I moved into the room. 'What's going on?'

'Nothing,' he said, a bit too defensively. He was spread out on the sofa, leaning on his hand, his elbow on the chair arm to prop himself up. As though covering that corner, beneath him.

'Frankie?'

Tom came into the room.

'Give us a minute, Tommo?' I said to him. He didn't seem impressed by that but the look I gave him told him I wasn't playing and he moved off as I stepped closer to Frankie.

'What were you doing?' I asked.

'Sis, seriously? What's your problem?'

Cleary he wasn't going to tell me. So I shot forward and stooped down and pushed my arm out underneath him, underneath the cushion he was intent on covering.

'What the fuck!'

I ignored his protest. Wrestled against his strength to push my hand further down.

Got it. I think he knew that too because his physical resistance waned and I pulled the device out. A phone?

For a moment I stood confused. But then I realised. A phone. But not his phone.

Dad's.

'Frankie, what the hell?'

He took advantage of my surprise, jumped up off the sofa and swiped the phone from my hand.

We squared off. I wanted to wrestle it off him again, but he was bigger, stronger than me, and he had a fire in his eyes that unsettled me.

'What are you doing?' I asked.

'Nothing wrong.'

'Where'd you get that?' Strange thoughts whirred. Since Dad had passed, I hadn't once considered what happened to his phone. Had it been on him at the time? If so, had the doctors given it to Frankie at some point? That had happened with Mum's. Her smashed, unusable phone had been passed back to me by the police, and I'd stashed it away in my room, not sure what else to do with it. I hadn't even thought about Dad's...

'I asked you a question?'

'It was in his room. Bedside drawer.'

'You went back in there? After I asked you not to?'

'You don't get it, do you? You're not my parent.'

'That's your answer?' I said. 'You're ridiculous.' But more than anything his words pierced me. I wanted to turn and walk away and hide on my own and cry. Instead I continued to hold my ground. 'You broke into it?' I said.

'It's not breaking in. I guessed his code. It took me a while, but...' He trailed off and shrugged.

'Why?' I asked, shaking my head.

'Why? Because of *you*. Because of Mum and Dad. Because you were all keeping things from me. And I want to know what.'

'You have no right.'

'I want to know why my dad killed himself. I want to know where Mum was running to that night with my sister and brother.'

'Running?'

'Come on, Jess, you know something. You must do, or you must at least have thought the same thing. Mum was miles away from here. Where the hell was she taking them on a Sunday night?'

'And what's your theory, Columbo?'

'Columbo?'

'Doesn't matter,' I said with a sigh.

'My theory is I'm in the dark,' Frankie said. 'And I don't like it.'

'So you're rummaging through Mum and Dad's private things for answers? Don't you see how horrible that is?'

'They're dead, Jess! Nothing up there is "theirs" anymore. Nothing in this house. Nothing in this world. They're gone! Forever!'

'The fact you can't even see how wrong this is...'

'The fact you can't give me a straight answer to anything. To the beef between you and Mum and Dad. To whatever the hell is happening with that Blake guy?'

'Blake? That's got nothing—'

'How'm I supposed to believe that?' He tapped on the screen. 'Look. Look at these messages then tell me again that I'm being stupid. That I'm paranoid.'

He turned the screen to me but when I went to take the phone he pulled it back. I squinted to see the small writing. The first one a text from Dad to Mum:

We need to figure this out. We can't keep lying to everyone.

The response from Mum:

We can't tell him. It'd destroy him.

Another one from Dad:

Not just him. It'll destroy everything. But what choice do we have?

156

'See?' Frankie said, pulling the phone back. 'And there's more.' He turned the screen to himself and scrolled before twisting the phone back to my view. Mum to Dad at the top this time.

Please don't do anything stupid. We'll get through this. I promise. I love you.

The response from Dad:

I don't even want to think about it anymore. About anything.

Then later another from Dad:

What have we done?

My heart thudded painfully with each word I read. I scanned over the messages another time, then read them more slowly a third time. I imagined the anguish of them both. My dad in particular.

'This was right before...'

The words passed my lips without me even thinking.

'Three days before,' Frankie said. 'I haven't been through everything yet, but–'

'But, Frankie, this doesn't even tell you anything. These messages could be about *anything*.'

Though I didn't even believe that myself. I'd doubted Dad had killed himself but... these messages were confirmation at least that there'd been something seriously wrong. Weren't they?

Frankie glowered and slipped the phone into his pocket. 'I'm not an idiot,' he said. 'It might not be clear what they're talking about, but I know it was something big. I want to know what was going on.'

'Me too, but–'

'This is your chance, Jess. This is your chance to tell me what you know.'

'I don't know anything.'

'So none of this is to do with you? None of it is to do with Blake?'

'Blake? I told you already–'

'I know what I saw with you two.'

'Seriously, Frankie, Blake has absolutely nothing to do with this.'

'This?'

'With Mum and Dad. Why would you even think that?'

'Then what? What do you know?'

I held my tongue and shook my head.

'I'm going to find out,' he said. 'Even if you won't help me, I'm going to find out everything.'

And as he brushed past me, I fully believed his words.

CHAPTER TWENTY-THREE

FRANKIE

'You're serious?' Meg asked as they lay on her bed.

Another late night of work for her dad, though tonight Ali and Katie weren't invited over. Just Meg and Frankie, exactly as he wanted. He ran his hand over her back, across the fabric of her spaghetti strap top. Her legs, in even thinner and tighter leggings, were draped over his as she liked to do. The lights were off, though the window was open, orange from the street light drifting in to add to the small array of tea lights Meg had set out. With the window open, a chill in the air had taken hold, even with the heating on full, but with their bodies so close to one another neither cared.

'About what?' Frankie said.

'This ghost thing?'

'I'm serious that Tom believes it.'

'But he's not scared now?'

'He is and he isn't. I think it depends, but the other night he was talking to them. Like, properly talking to them, a full-on conversation.'

'What do you think?'

He didn't know how to explain that. Did he believe in

ghosts? Not long ago he'd have said no without thinking. But he'd watched scary movies before. In the dark, at night. Probably everybody had. Probably everyone had felt spooked at some point in their lives. A shadow watching them. A presence in a room. A strange chill. An unexplained creak.

Well, that was simply how it felt in their house every single night now. Did that make it real? Certainly the response in him, Tom and Jess was real.

'Frankie?' Meg prompted.

'I don't know,' he said.

'What about Jess? I bet she wasn't impressed that you were encouraging Tom.'

Meg spoke with real familiarity about Jess, even though they'd likely only ever met in passing in a school corridor. As far as Frankie knew, the two of them had never shared a single word of conversation. Everything Meg knew about Jess she knew from Frankie, yet her intuition seemed spot on most of the time.

'I wasn't doing it to spite her,' Frankie said, which was only half true really. He'd known that showing Tom that stuff about ghosts on the internet would take the youngster down a certain path. That Jess would rather have denied, denied, denied and told Tom that his sightings were all a load of crap, that there was no way he could communicate with his dead parents, even if she too was clearly freaked out in the house now. So yes, he'd done that with Tom knowing that Jess wouldn't approve, but that wasn't the main reason why. The main reason was that he wanted to help Tom, but he also wanted some explanations for himself, and once he'd started reading about spirits and ghosts and the link – often broken – between life and whatever came after, a lot of things really had started to make sense for him.

Did he believe in ghosts?

A lot more now than he ever had before, though he wasn't sure he could say that out loud to anyone.

'You know what you could do?' Meg suggested.

'What?'

'Get an Ouija board. My aunt used to be into all that. She did seances and everything.'

No. He didn't want that at all. He'd seen a movie where they'd carried out a seance, had used an Ouija board that some evil spirit had taken control over, the medium in charge of the seance unwittingly opening a bridge from hell, or something. The demon had killed half a dozen people in various brutal ways. He wasn't after blood and guts and demons wanting his soul, he only wanted to know what had happened to his dad, and his mum and sister.

'I couldn't do it,' he said. 'It's not...'

He couldn't finish the thought.

'Then I tell you what,' Meg said. 'There's a fortune teller at the Christmas Fair–'

'A fortune teller?' Frankie said, smirking. 'You mean, like, crystal balls and all that?'

'My aunt knows her,' Meg said, looking offended. 'She's really spiritual. It's not the same thing as a seance, nowhere near as intense, but she might be able to help. Might be able to give you some answers or help you in some other way.'

Really, he only wanted to shut this conversation down now. Too weird, but also too unsettling. Actually he just felt embarrassed, the more he thought about it. What would his friends think if they knew he was talking about stuff like this to Meg?

What would Dylan think?

Frankie tried to shake thoughts of that prick. Why had he even gone there? 'You can't tell anyone,' Frankie said, holding Meg's eye. She smiled at him, but then her face turned serious, probably because of the force in the look he gave her. 'Seriously, Meg, you can't tell anyone about this. Please?'

'I won't,' she said, cupping his face in her hand. 'You can trust me.' She reached up and kissed him. 'And I love that you can tell me, and only me, these things. I'm not going to spoil that.'

She kissed him again, more lingering this time. Frankie kissed her back, but his mind dwelled for a few seconds on that l-word. He wasn't sure how that made him feel. A little nervous, more than anything.

He soon forgot about that when she shuffled her body closer to his, pressed up against him. She pushed her hips further forward as the kiss intensified. He slipped his hand down to her waist. Slowly moved his fingers up, underneath her top. She didn't resist. So he moved up further, toward her chest. She murmured, so he carried on, fondling her breast over the top of her bra. Then, as he kissed her neck, he slid his hand down again, to the rim of her leggings. Pushed his fingers beneath the thin fabric.

She squirmed and pulled back. 'No,' she said.

'What?'

'Not that.'

'Not what?'

'I'm not ready for that.'

Frankie sat up, not hiding his annoyance. 'Why not?'

'I'm just... not. I want to. With you. But, not yet. Not like this.'

'Like this?' He looked around the room. 'What's wrong with this?' Hadn't she laid out all that romantic crap for this very purpose?

'I don't want to, okay?' she said, more forcefully now, probably a direct reaction to his own rising irritation.

'I don't get it,' he said with a huff. 'After two months all I get is a few kisses, but you'll screw an arsehole like Dylan Farrelly after a few vodkas.'

'Seriously?' She shoved him, both hands, nearly enough force to topple him off the bed.

'Yeah, seriously,' Frankie said. 'So what's so fucking great about Dylan? You'll have sex with him. We've been going out for ages and I'm still–'

'I thought you were better this.'

'Better than what?'

'Better than him.'

'That makes no sense.'

'Doesn't it? You have no idea what happened with Dylan. Think about it, Frankie. Think about why I'd want to wait, with you.'

Frankie didn't want to think. Certainly not about her with Dylan. The idea made him mad as much as it made him feel sick. 'All I know is I'm not good enough for you. But apparently he is.'

'Maybe you're right.'

They both glared at each other. Frankie stood up off the bed.

'Just go,' Meg said, turning away from him.

So he did.

He was too angry, too wired to head straight home. As he walked, his brain rattled with the conversation he'd just had with Meg. Initially thinking of all the things he could have said to her to 'win' the argument, he started to think about what had actually happened. About why she was reluctant to sleep with him, what it meant to her.

It didn't take too long to figure he'd been an arsehole. Hadn't listened. Hadn't wanted to hear her excuses, again. Excuses, yes, but that didn't mean she didn't want to be with him. He hadn't even tried to understand her point of view. He'd only thought of himself.

Idiot.

In two minds as to whether to head home or go back to hers and grovel for forgiveness, Frankie kind of lost track of where he was going. He headed on past the corner shop that he and Ali had gone to a few days before. No sign of Dylan and gang there tonight, but they'd be skulking around somewhere, nothing better to do. With his hood on, and keeping his head low, Frankie carried on, enjoying the feeling of danger of being in the wolf's lair.

He took a couple of turns to arrive on the street where Dylan lived. A pretty much carbon copy of the street where Meg's house stood, with narrow terraces lining both sides of the road, though these homes didn't have front yards at all, the doors opening directly onto the street. With cars crammed either side, the compact nature of the street made it far too open, too obvious really to stand and watch anywhere.

He passed on by Dylan's home. Number 132. Lights were on in the front window. Curtains open, a TV on. No sign of Dylan in there though as he passed.

He carried on going, took the right turn at the end of the road, then another. An alleyway ran behind the houses, providing access to the backyards. No street lighting, the alley stank of rubbish and piss, and bins were everywhere, litter strewn. A couple of banged up cars were parked there – abandoned? Broken glass embedded in cement topped every one of the high walls that enclosed the small yards. Rudimentary but effective security.

Frankie tried to figure out which of the gates belonged to Dylan's home, but he saw no numbers and he lost count. He'd have to do another recce. Thought about doing it there and then, until up ahead two figures turned into the alley.

Shit.

They were too far away, it was too dark, for him to see who they were, though after a few steps of calculating, he realised they were shorter, slighter than him. Kids. Though in this part of town, that didn't exactly mean an absence of threat.

He could turn and head back the other way, it wasn't too late...

He didn't. He kept his head down as the duo closed in on him. They walked slowly, nudging each other every few steps. Definitely smaller, younger than him. Boys. Twelve, thirteen, perhaps.

Their chatter died down as Frankie neared, only ten steps or so separating them.

'All right,' one of them called out.

Frankie said nothing.

'I said, all right, wanker.'

Frankie's heart sank. Not all kids in this neighbourhood were tearaways, but some most definitely were. Trust his luck to have found two of them.

He went to pass them. The boys came to a stop.

'He called you a wanker,' the other one said.

Frankie ignored them, carried on.

'He's not a wanker. Daddy tugs it for him. Fucking paedo.'

'Piss off you little gits,' Frankie blurted as he turned his head to them, immediately regretting his mistake. But the mention of his dad...

'You what?'

Frankie kept on going.

'Get him, Aitch.'

Frankie heard the quick footsteps behind him. He turned to see the lankier of the two rushing toward him. To do what?

Frankie, caught off guard, lifted his arm, and swiped the kid with the back of his hand. Not a forceful slap, but enough to cause him to reel away.

Frankie turned and ran. He sprinted around the corner as the two kids yelled out at him, shouting all manner of expletives. He took another turn, back onto the street of terraces. Looked left and right. A few people dotted about. Run or walk? He jogged for a few seconds but then slowed down, trying not to draw attention.

He headed on past the shop. Stole a glance through the windows to the inside. No one he could see beyond the glass except for the shopkeeper.

A place of solace? The guy had saved him once before...

Voices behind him.

'Oi, Evans!'

Dylan. How the hell?

Frankie burst into a sprint. But he was already out of breath from his initial run. And he was hardly known for his athletic ability. He looked behind him. Two people in chase. In the dark he couldn't tell which one was Dylan. Most likely the one at the front. Dylan was a runner. A footballer. A swimmer. Rugby. Anything that involved physicality, and didn't require brain power, Dylan excelled at.

Sex?

Why had he even thought that.

Frankie took the turn onto Meg's street. Why? Could he go to her door, seek refuge there? But even if she did let him in, Dylan was close enough to see. He'd likely only sit in wait for Frankie to leave.

What else could he do though?

By the time her house was in sight, Dylan had closed the gap to all of five yards. No chance Frankie could even get inside Meg's in time.

He took a chance and raced across the street, right in front of a car which screeched to a halt, horn blaring. Would the move gain him some ground? A little. But not much.

No sign of the second chaser now. Had he given up?

Dylan wouldn't.

Frankie darted into the snicket. Thought about stopping in the dark to launch a counter-attack. He didn't. He carried on going, back out onto the next street. But by that point Dylan was in touching distance.

Frankie spun around, came to a stop, hands held out in defence. 'Please?' he said.

Dylan came to a stop too. Pure rage on his face, the shadows created by the orange light above him giving a truly sinister edge to his features. 'What did you say to my cousin?'

'Your cousin?'

'Big man, are you? Say it to my face. Say what you said to him, to my face, you piece of shit.'

'I'm sorry, Dylan. Please.' Frankie took a couple of steps back, looking all around, hoping for a saviour from somewhere, but the street was deathly quiet.

'I've had enough of you.' Dylan launched himself forward.

Frankie cowered and Dylan sent an arcing fist to his face. Frankie didn't have the nous to block and the fist caught him on the nose and he stumbled back.

Dylan lined up for another shot, but Frankie managed to back step further, out of the way of the glancing blow, but then smacked into the bonnet of a car with a thud.

Nowhere to go...

He pulled his arms up to his face, ducked his head, like he'd seen boxers do in the ring on TV. Dylan smacked him, again, again. Pummelled him. A shot got through the defence and split Frankie's lip.

How the hell was he supposed to get away?

In his pocket. The knife.

'Hey, you two!' came a gruff shout from behind Frankie. A pedestrian, or someone at their front door?

Either way, the interruption caused Dylan to halt the beating and he stepped back and looked behind Frankie. 'Fuck off!' he said, challenging.

Frankie took the chance, he turned and ran.

Or at least tried to, but Dylan grabbed for his coat. Tugged him back. Frankie spun, trying to release himself. He couldn't. But without thinking he reached out and grabbed Dylan's wrist, spun around again and yanked forward and sent Dylan stumbling... right into the path of an oncoming car.

Tyres screeched. The car missed Frankie by... nothing really. It didn't miss Dylan, the front corner banged into his hip, sending him sprawling. Not a high-speed crash, but still...

Frankie didn't hesitate. He sprinted away. Looked over his shoulder to see Dylan groggily getting to his feet, the driver out of the car, helping him up.

'You're dead, Evans!' Dylan shouted out. 'Dead!'

Frankie didn't look back again after that, simply kept on running, all the way home.

CHAPTER TWENTY-FOUR

JESS

I'd only gone upstairs to quickly check on Tom. He'd been in bed for nearly two hours and I hadn't heard a peep from him, which somehow made me even more unsettled than if he'd woken up screaming at seeing a ghoul, or if I'd heard him chatting away to the ghosts of my parents.

I peeked inside his room. Dark and quiet. I could hear him breathing, could only just make out his form in the unlit room. I left him to it. I should have gone downstairs again, but instead I found myself in Lily's room, sitting on her bed in the dark, staring about the place, wanting... what? To see *her* little ghost? To see Mum and Dad?

I really didn't know anymore.

I felt alone. I *was* alone tonight, but I felt horribly alone. Without me really realising it, Frankie and Tom had become my rocks recently, my eldest brother in particular, even despite his mood swings with me – was that all his up and down attitude boiled down to? Hormone-led teenage mood swings? The point was, I don't know if we'd ever spent this much time together, certainly not with me as an adult, and now tonight, with Tom in bed, and Frankie out of the house, I really did feel brutally lonely.

Quite why that meant I chose to go and sit in Lily's room, in the dark, I'm not sure. Maybe because with my brothers around me all the time, me in charge of them, a task which was way harder and way more all-consuming than I'd imagined – how had Mum and Dad coped with four of us? – I perhaps hadn't given myself any proper time to grieve for Lily.

A tear rolled down my cheek. I didn't wipe it away. No point anymore. I picked up a teddy from her bed. A little lion that she'd brought back from a zoo when on holiday with Mum, Dad and Tom the summer before last. I hadn't been on that holiday, nor Frankie. I knew how much she loved Lion though, how she couldn't sleep without him. Holding the little teddy, thinking about Lily and that holiday without me, I realised I'd missed so much of her short life. I hadn't even been home for half of it.

A mistake I'd never be able to rectify.

I put the teddy to my nose and sniffed. Sweetness. Like ripe strawberries. Lily. I hoped the smell would never fade.

I clutched Lion close to my chest and sighed.

I could remember the day that each of my siblings was born. Frankie's birth, when I wasn't quite three, was now the most faded of those memories. In the run-up to his arrival I'd been so desperate to see my new brother. At that age I think I was a stereotypical little girl. I loved the idea of babies, and mothering. I had dolls and a little pushchair, and the idea of having a real, live baby in the house had me enthralled. I was so excited when Mum went into hospital, and I remember my dad trying to temper my eagerness, warning me that we had to be patient, keep our fingers crossed that everything went okay.

It did. Frankie was born without any hitches. But having a baby brother was nothing like I'd expected. When I first set sight on him, all bundled up in a tiny little cot, his bright red, almost purple face all scrunched and screwed and wrinkled, I cried. I cried and whined and complained because he looked horrible. Not a cute little baby at all, nothing like my dolls. And when we got home and over the next few days I realised how much he cried, how much he slept, how much he smelled of poo, how much of Mum's time he took away from me, I really began to dislike him quite a lot.

I don't think I ever really got over that disappointment. I quickly realised Frankie wasn't my little toy, so I kind of just left him to himself, and by the time he was growing older, I'd moved on from babies anyway. Plus, the three-year age gap, together with the gender stereotypes that the adults in our lives struggled to move us away from, meant we just kind of drifted and stayed apart most of our childhoods. Siblings, with plenty of angst and tension. Yes, we'd enjoyed some wonderful shared moments, like Christmases and birthdays and holidays, but we certainly weren't friends. He was my brother, and I always loved him, but we were never hugely close, never shared any similar interests or anything like that. Never held any big conversations, heart to hearts. Did we really know each other at all?

Then Tom arrived, and things really did change. At eleven I thought of myself as mature for my age, I think a lot of older siblings are probably put into that bracket, whether rightly or wrongly. But I didn't want another brother. What was wrong with just the two of us? I'm not sure Mum and Dad were necessarily expecting a third child either, as I remember there being a lot of tension in the house in the build-up to Tom being born. Mum wasn't religious at all, but I do know she held very strong views on abortion. Not views I agreed with, but she couldn't bear the idea of ending a foetus's life.

I didn't really understand all that back then, I just knew Tom being born was bad for me.

Anyway, Tom came along, and somehow all that pre-birth tension – the arguments and the tears and fights between my parents – disappeared almost immediately. At least in my memory. Mum and Dad loved Tom. They doted on him way more than I remembered them doing with me and Frankie. Despite my initial hesitation at losing even more of my parents' time, I thought Tom was great too. Even though I hadn't wanted another sibling, I really loved him. Loved helping Mum with him, feeding him, taking him out in the pushchair. I even changed a few nappies. As he got older I remained close to him through his toddler years, almost as though he was the little baby, the little brother that I'd wanted all those years before with Frankie, but which I'd probably been too young, too immature, too needy and jealous, to properly appreciate.

Plus Tom, personality-wise, was always so happy, relaxed, with none of the angst that often existed between Frankie and me, the much closer age gap naturally causing more friction.

Tom was a star.

And then, a few years later, came Lily.

I was already well into my teens, nearly sixteen when she was born. GCSEs on the horizon, a plan for A-levels and university already mapped out in my mind beyond that.

Now, looking back, I knew my mistakes. At the time, really right up until the recent tragedies, I'd been so preoccupied with myself, exams, getting ahead and pulling away from the family and Graystone to make my own future.

I'd missed Lily's life in the process. Her whole, short life.

I heard movement outside the room. Flinched at the unexpected sound as my heart rate ratcheted.

No, nothing scary this time. The front door. Frankie was home. Earlier than I'd expected, though I was a little glad about that.

I carefully put Lion back in place on the bed, stood up and

wiped my eyes then headed down the stairs. No sign of him in the hall or lounge. I found my brother in the kitchen, coat and shoes still on, standing by the sink, his head down near to the running water which he splashed over his face.

'Frankie?'

He didn't respond. I moved closer and he turned the tap off and grabbed a tea towel and dabbed at his face. He turned to me. I spotted the red smudges on the towel first...

'What the–' I went to rush to him, concern sweeping over me, but he held a hand up and glared.

'Don't,' he said. 'I'm fine.'

'You don't look fine? What happened?'

He tilted his head up, to stop the blood from pouring from his nose, I presumed. With his dark coat on it was hard to tell for sure how much was on him, but spots of the fabric glistened with wetness.

'I fell over.'

'Yeah, right. I'm not an idiot.'

'It's nothing, seriously.' He went to walk past me but I stood in his way.

'This isn't nothing. You need to talk to me.'

He held my eye. With his head tilted, his eyes pointed down, the look was seriously peculiar.

'You didn't go to Ali's house, did you?' I said. He'd told me he was going over there to watch a movie. I couldn't smell booze on him, so I didn't think he'd been to a bar, but it was a hell of a movie to come back looking like that.

He didn't answer my question.

'Frankie, what's going on?'

'I got jumped.'

'By who? Around here?'

'No.'

'Well not around Ali's either.' Ali lived in one of the nicest streets in the town.

Frankie sighed and huffed and looked like he was struggling with something. I only wanted the truth.

'I was at a girl's house.'

Okay. That was a start. Still didn't explain the bloodied face. 'I'm presuming she didn't do that to you. Unless she's a black belt and you tried it on when you shouldn't have done.'

I meant that as a joke but the strange look on his face suggested I'd actually hit on something. Which part?

'She lives over on Goose Avenue.'

Goose Avenue. It took me a moment, but I knew where he meant. That made a bit more sense. 'You were jumped?'

He nodded.

'Did they take anything?'

He shook his head.

'We should call the police.'

'No!' His face screwed – fear? – before relaxing a little. 'No, please. It's nothing.'

We both went silent. I knew he didn't want to be in the room with me. Fine, but I wasn't finished. In the end I moved out of the way and he shuffled past, avoiding my eye.

'Can't wait to hear all about her.'

He didn't say anything to that.

CHAPTER TWENTY-FIVE

I'd already made plans to meet up with my friends the next night before Frankie had arrived home battered and bruised. As the evening rolled around I thought about cancelling, or at least postponing, but Frankie insisted I should go. He'd been fine through the day. He had a swollen lip – the cut had crusted over – but that was the only visible damage. Other than that he seemed a little quiet, embarrassed, I thought.

I remained in two minds, but felt I did need the break, and a change in company.

I'd found out nothing more about the incident the night before, nor of the girl whose house he'd been to, though he had confirmed her name was Meg and he liked her and he'd been seeing her a few weeks. Even telling me that seemed an effort for him. Why the big secret? I was pleased for him, even if the revelation didn't explain how he'd been beaten up, and even if it did only go to show how little I knew of his private life.

I put thoughts of my brother aside.

I'd seen Ed before Christmas, with that awkward walk to the park, but I hadn't seen my other home town friends since before my life had turned upside down. I looked forward to the reunion with Jamie, Kristen and Hannah, even if I knew that the group dynamic held plenty of tension, going back quite a few years. In many ways I thought it odd – unlikely, really – that we stuck together still as one group, though I knew the reason why. Hannah. My best friend for many years, Hannah was lively, bubbly, friendly, a bit of a party animal. She was just lovely; everyone liked her, and she held us all together, although perhaps only in the same way that paper covers a crack-filled wall.

Or perhaps they all remained super close to each other, and only I was the outlier.

Plaza, the bar in town where we were meeting, a trendy little new place, lots of fancy cocktails on offer, a chic, woody interior, had opened after I'd started uni. I'd been a couple of times before but it held no real sway over me, not like the other pubs and bars that had been the backbone of my late-night revelry in the time before I'd left home. For my friends though, Plaza was a favoured choice – just one example of how our lives had diverged.

When I walked in I realised I was the last to arrive. Hannah spotted me first and jumped up from the bench and ran over to me and threw her arms around me. We both giggled as she swung me around.

'You look...' she stepped back to take me in, '...gorgeous. As ever. Love the hair.'

'Thanks,' I said, brushing the loose strands away from my face. I hadn't really made much effort, but I appreciated the compliment nonetheless. 'You too.'

She'd put on weight and it definitely suited her. In the past we were almost like sisters, in height, shape, hair, clothes, but her face was rounder and more mature now, and her chest... Bigger. That was for sure, and she definitely wanted to flaunt it with the low-cut top. On the other hand my chest seemed to have shrunk despite my extra recent pounds. How was that possible?

Hannah took my hand and pulled me over to the large, thick wooden table. Bench on one side, sofa on the other, two little chairs at either end. Odd set-up, but I found most things about the bar odd.

Ed sat at one end of the table, a little bit distant from the others, both in space and in mind.

Jamie was sunken into the sofa, a nearly empty pint glass in his hand. Kristen, glitzy dress on, was next to him, but sitting forward.

None of the others initially got up as I came over. A few half smiles, but a far more muted welcome than with Hannah. Not because they weren't pleased to see me – I didn't think – but because of the context.

'Hi,' I said to them all.

'I'm so sorry, babe,' Kristen said as she got to her feet and gave me a hug.

I pushed the well of emotion back and then took a seat on the bench next to Hannah.

After her initial glee, she too now looked more sombre. 'How are you holding up?' Hannah asked, putting her arm around me.

I shrugged. 'It's not great, really. I can't even describe it, but... I just want to get away from it for a bit. You know?'

'I bet you do,' Kristen said, reaching her hand over the table. 'You poor thing.'

I smiled meekly.

Jamie stood up from the sofa. Wobbled a little bit too. How many had he already had? 'I'll get some drinks,' he said. 'Ed?'

'I'll give you a hand.'

'Prosecco good for you?' Kristen asked me.

'Yeah, sure.'

Jamie and Ed headed off to the bar.

'So you two are going well,' I said to Kristen.

She gave me a weird look. 'Great, yeah.'

We both held each other's gaze, caught in a moment of awkward silence. I hadn't seen them since they'd moved in together, so I thought my comment was a valid conversation opener, but Kristen clearly saw differently.

'You'll have to show me your apartment some time,' I said.

'It's not an apartment, it's a house.'

'Oh. That's great. I'm really pleased for you both.' I smiled and she smiled back and the awkwardness returned.

'How are Tom and Frankie?' Hannah asked.

'About as well as you would expect. Tom was really shaken by the crash, but he's a fighter.' I cringed at my own words. *A fighter.* I hated that saying. He wasn't a fighter. He was damn lucky to be alive, but was horribly traumatised.

'I've seen Frankie around,' Kristen said. 'Not since, you know, but... he's so big now. Proper little man.'

I wasn't sure what to say to that. Jamie and Ed came back to the table, and I was pretty glad really, to get me out of the uneasiness. Hannah poured glasses of Prosecco for the girls, the two lads both sipped from their pints. Everyone sat forward to the table, eyes turning my way, as though to give me a grilling.

'Are you home for good then?' Kristen asked.

'I really don't know. I need to look after my brothers, so....'

She shook her head, sympathy I thought.

'So you won't get to finish uni?' Jamie asked.

'Not yet. I'm going to have to look for a job. To help support us. So if any of you know of anything that's going.'

I laughed nervously. The others didn't follow suit.

'Actually, weren't you saying there were some vacancies at your place,' Jamie said, nudging Kristen.

She pulled a face, though it wasn't clear why.

'I'm not sure that's what Jess would be looking for,' Ed said, quite snottily, though I think the edge was directed to Jamie, rather than me.

'What's that supposed to mean?' Kristen responded, clearly offended.

Ed's cheeks reddened and he sat back in his chair, taking a large swig of his beer. 'I didn't mean it like that. Just that...'

'I'll look at anything really,' I said, trying to bring a sense of peace, though the looks I received suggested perhaps my words didn't have the desired interpretation.

'Can't believe you're back,' Hannah said, her brightness exactly what we all needed. 'We've really missed you.'

'Bet you never thought you'd be mucking it with us around Graystone again,' Kristen added. 'I know you really wanted to get away and make something big out of yourself.'

I couldn't think of anything to say in response to that. Was she trying to rile me, or was I being overly sensitive? I simply smiled and took a big gulp of my glass, pretty much emptying it.

Jamie topped it up. The conversation lightened, thankfully, though after an initial flourish of catching up, I took a bit of a back seat as the drinks went down, and time wore on. I just wasn't quite... one of them.

I spent a lot of time watching my friends, this odd little group. One thing I did notice was Ed's relative distance from everyone. With me and Hannah on the bench, and Jamie and Kristen on the sofa, Ed at the end of the table appeared separated from us, and the increasingly bored look on his face cemented that.

I also found the dynamic between Jamie and Kristen intriguing. At school they had been something of a power couple. If we'd been in America they surely would have been prom king and queen. Kristen was gorgeous. Naturally light hair, dead straight, which she'd dyed blonde as long as I could remember. She had lovely tanned skin, a tall, slender figure that she always showed off with tight and skimpy clothing, and she would never leave the house without designer clothes and make-up. I'd envied her so much at school. Still did in a way. At five-seven and not in the best shape, I cut a paltry figure next to her. Kristen was the type of girl – young woman – who would relish a beach holiday where she could strip to a tiny bikini to show off her bod, and share the snaps daily on Instagram. I was far from fat but way too self-conscious for that, preferring to hide behind my clothes. Probably a realistic size twelve, I wore size fourteen a lot of the time just so my clothes weren't too tight in all the places I hated – bum, thighs and belly essentially – though I still had plenty of size tens in my wardrobe that I was determined to get back into one day, once I'd restarted a sensible diet and exercise regime.

Certainly I wouldn't be doing that anytime soon.

Did Kristen have to stick to a strict healthy lifestyle or was she just freakishly lucky? Kristen had the looks, but she'd never been that smart – at least not academically – and I sensed in the past she'd been as jealous of my exam prowess as I was of her looks.

Then there was Jamie. Not as tall as Ed, under six foot, but he looked like a movie star. Perhaps a much younger Brad Pitt, surfer version, blond highlighted hair, naturally muscular figure, but not overly bulky. And he was clever. Better results than me even. He could have gone anywhere, done anything.

He'd chosen to stay at home. To be with Kristen.

I'd fancied Jamie since I first got into boys aged twelve or thirteen. I think every single girl in school had fancied Jamie at one point or other. Fancied? I'd been infatuated with him at several points in my life, would have done anything for him. I think he knew that. Kind of like Ed with me, in a way, which was strange to think.

Kristen had ended up with Jamie, but she wasn't the only girl who had history with him...

'You okay, hun?' Hannah asked me. I snapped from my thoughts. Glanced to Ed who glared at me. I had a moment of panic. Had I been staring at Jamie as I thought?

'Yeah, fine,' I said.

I smiled at Ed but he didn't respond. He looked away as he downed the rest of the beer in his glass. He glanced at his watch then got to his feet. 'Sorry, guys, I've got to shoot.'

'No worries, man,' Jamie slurred, not rising from the sofa.

The other girls and I gave Ed a hug of sorts before he left, clearly in a sulk about something. Or was that just me reading too much into it?

'Always sneaks off just before his round,' Jamie said, finishing his beer.

'Is he okay?' I asked to no one in particular.

Hannah opened her mouth to speak but Jamie got there first. 'Think he's just got himself in a pickle,' he said with a laugh.

'Sorry?'

'Probably gone off to Claire's, all in a state about what to do.'

'Claire?'

Everyone stared at me.

'Claire,' Jamie said, as though I was a doofus. 'He's been seeing her for months. Pretty much lives with him in that crappy little flat.'

Why hadn't Ed mentioned her to me? Why had no one?

'You didn't know?' Kristen asked, surprised.

'Of course she didn't,' Jamie said. 'Ed was keeping his options open, the little player. And now you're back, Jess, he's got a real dilemma.' He swayed to his feet. 'Anyone else for another?'

I declined, but Hannah and Kristen asked for another bottle and I knew they'd probably be filling my glass up.

'And a water, please?' I said to Jamie before he swaggered off.

Kristen leaned over and said something to Hannah that I couldn't hear. To deliberately exclude me? I needed the toilet anyway. I checked my phone as I went. Nothing from Frankie or anyone else. I sent him a message, just checking in, and also one to Ed, to double check if there was a problem.

No response from Ed as I came back out the toilet, though Frankie sent me the short but affirmative *All good*.

Jamie remained at the bar. At the other end of the room, Hannah and Kristen were nuzzled close together on the bench, giggling. I smiled to see them both so happy and at ease. I really wished I could be part of that.

'Jess,' Jamie said as I neared him. He stared at me in the mirror behind the bar. I moved over.

'You need a hand?' I said.

'Not really.'

'Oh.'

He continued to stare at me in the mirror. Not a friendly look. 'We're really happy together,' he said.

'You and Kristen?'

He nodded.

'Great,' I said, sounding lame. Looking lame too, I realised when I glanced at myself in the mirror.

Jamie turned to face me. 'I'm not messing, Jess. I can't lose her.'

'And you're telling me because?'

'You know why.'

I scoffed. 'Seriously? You always did have an over-inflated opinion of yourself.'

'Whatever, Jess. Just so you know, me and her are unbreakable.'

'Clearly not given this weird conversation.'

He grabbed my hand. Squeezed hard. 'Don't mess things up for me.'

That pissed me off. I yanked my hand away. 'Why would you even think–'

'Because I know you've always wanted me.'

'Get over yourself, Jamie. I'm not sixteen anymore.'

He shook his head. I went to walk away but he stuck a leg out to stop me.

'She doesn't know,' he said.

I knew what he meant. 'That was years ago,' I said. 'It's never going to happen again, believe me.'

'But she doesn't know. And she can't know. Do you understand me?'

'Piss off.' I stamped on his foot. That made him move his leg. I knocked into him, spilling some of his beer as he picked it up. I headed on past, back toward the table.

Hannah had noticed. She stared over at me, concern spread across her face. I sat down at the table, trying my best to clear my head, to not let that idiot spoil the night for me. For all of us.

'Jamie okay?' Hannah asked.

'He's pissed as a fart,' Kristen said as she moved back to the sofa.

'You're not wrong there.'

'Ladies,' Jamie said, coming back over with his beer and a bottle of Prosecco. His face had relaxed. As though nothing had just happened. He sat back down and I took a glass of wine anyway, just to try and calm me.

I'd managed half of the glass before my phone vibrated with an incoming call.

Frankie...

CHAPTER TWENTY-SIX

FRANKIE

He'd given Jess the truth, but not the whole truth. Quite honestly, his private life wasn't her business, but he didn't want to lie to her either. He'd mentioned about Meg – just the basics – but nothing more about the incident with Dylan. He also hadn't told Jess that he'd invited Meg over to their house while his sister went out.

She arrived half an hour after he'd put Tom to bed. Good timing, because the little nipper had just gone to sleep. He'd checked on him when she'd texted to say she was five minutes away. She texted again when she arrived at the front door and he walked softly across the hall tiles to let her in.

Meg had a devilish grin on her face as he opened up. Her face was nicely made up, her hair tied back. He could eat her up. But when she looked at him her seductive pout changed to concern.

'Frankie?'

He held a finger to his lips and pulled her inside, closed the door as quietly as he could. He led her to the lounge, then closed that door behind them too.

'What happened?' she asked.

No point in lying to her. If anything, he wanted the sympathy, and to show her what a bastard Dylan was.

So he told her. Most of it. Not the part about him lurking around the back of Dylan's home, or about the brush with those young boys, but about Dylan chasing him, attacking him. Unprovoked.

Ninety-nine per cent truthful.

'I hate him,' she said. 'I really hate him.' She took off her coat. Stunning. A short denim skirt, sheers tights, a little pink top.

'Did you tell Jess?'

'Not about Dylan. Just that I got jumped.'

'Did she believe you?'

'Not really.'

Meg shook her head as she continued to stare at his swollen lip. She sighed.

'Let's forget about him. Do you want a drink?' he asked. 'Wine?'

'Definitely.'

'I'll be right back.' He headed off to the kitchen. Poured two large glasses of rosé wine. When he got back to the lounge, Meg was on the sofa, but still looked concerned rather than relaxed. He gave her a glass; they clinked then gulped. He sat next to her, took an inhale. The perfume he'd got her for Christmas.

He went to kiss her neck.

'You need to be careful with him.'

He pulled back. 'Dylan?'

'He's mental. I mean... properly mental.'

'You're telling me.'

'Please, be careful?'

'He hates that you're with me.'

'He doesn't get a choice what I do,' Meg said, looking angry.

'I'm not sure he agrees.'

She shook her head and took another gulp of wine. 'Our dads are mates,' she said. 'Did you know that?'

'I didn't realise your dad knew his dad.'

'He does. Doesn't live with him, but he and my dad go way back. We actually used to have playdates, years ago. Can you believe that?'

That explained a lot. Dylan had probably been into Meg for years.

'His dad is as horrible as Dylan is,' she said. 'Seriously.'

As horrible as *her* dad too? 'In what way?' Frankie asked.

'Nasty. Violent. Leary.' She shivered. 'Dylan had no chance.'

'You say that as though you feel sorry for him.'

She didn't deny that. Instead she looked around the lounge. This was the first time she'd been to his house. Before, when Mum and Dad had been home, there'd never been a chance to sneak her over. What a grim thought, he realised, closing his eyes.

'I love it,' she said, enthused but a little bit sad too. 'Your home, it's just... I'd love to live somewhere like this.'

'It's not that great, is it?'

'It is to me.'

He'd never seen his family as being that well off, not compared to the likes of Ali who lived in a five-bed mansion with electronic gates and a two-car garage, but he guessed, compared to Goose Avenue...

'I could give you a tour,' he said. 'Show you my room.' He flicked his eyebrows playfully.

She laughed. 'Your brother will hear us.'

'He's fast asleep.'

'I'm pretty comfy here, to be honest,' she said, arching back on the sofa, pushing her chest up. She pulled her hair from the bun and swooshed it about, then, toes pointed, lifted her legs from the floor and onto him.

How could he resist? He dove in for a kiss. She giggled and put her arms around him and for a few moments Frankie forgot everything.

Until thoughts of the night before crept into his mind.

He pulled away and looked down at her. 'You okay?' he asked.

She smiled. 'Yeah... if you want... we could try something else?'

If he wanted? He wanted nothing more.

Thank you, Dylan, you twat. Perhaps the cut lip had given him the sympathy card he needed.

He went back for another kiss and soon had his hand up under her skirt. He slowly wrestled with the top of her tights, edging them down. She sank her hand into the back of his boxers, pulled her fingers around to the side, moving further toward... He gasped. Was this really finally happening?

A scream.

A horrible, harrowing, pleasure-sapping scream.

Frankie jumped up. The scream came again.

'Jess! Jess!'

'Shit.'

Noting the look of horror on Meg's face, Frankie spun and dashed for the door. He yanked it open, moved for the stairs, took them two at a time. Tom's door was wide open. Not how he'd left it?

Tom was sitting up in the bed, shaking with fear. Frankie flipped the light on.

'Frankie! There's someone here.'

Frankie's shoulders slumped. Even one glance over the room confirmed no one was there – no ghost either. At least not now, with the light on.

'You're fine, mate. Honestly. It's just me and you.'

He moved over, but Tom's face remained petrified, his eyes darting this way and that.

'I thought you wanted to see them again, anyway?'

Tom looked at him like he was an idiot. 'It wasn't Mum and Dad. It was someone real. A man.'

Frankie sat on the end of the bed and looked back to the door.

'There's no one here, look.'

'You're not listening to me! I saw him. I saw a man. Standing right there, looking at me.'

'Bud, you–'

Then came the scream from downstairs.

'Frankie!'

Followed by a crash and a bang.

'Don't move.'

He jumped back up. Tore down the stairs. Nearly lost his balance and went head over heels. Somehow he managed to stay on two feet. He held on to the banister to swing around in the hall. Spotted movement in the kitchen. Meg? He dashed that way.

Meg stood in the kitchen, a mess of rosé wine and broken glass by her feet, her face pale. Her body shaking.

'Out there.' She pointed to the patio doors at the back. One of them was ajar. 'I saw someone, in the garden.'

Shaking now too, Frankie inched closer to the partially open door.

What the hell was happening?

Should he get a knife from the rack behind him?

He kept on moving forward. He'd never been so frightened. When he was two steps from the door he lunged and grabbed the handle and pulled the door closed and locked it. He then rushed across and pressed the switch for the patio light.

He stared outside. No one out there.

'I saw him, Frankie. I swear. There was someone out there in the garden.'

He believed her, even if he could see no one now.

'They must have... they must have jumped the fence,' Meg said, stepping closer to the patio doors.

The fences either side, and at the back, all led to other gardens. Easy enough to jump over, but not exactly freedom beyond.

Frankie had a moment of panic. The patio door had been open... perhaps she was wrong about the garden. Perhaps she'd seen a reflection. Was someone still inside?

He turned and looked down the hall, his heart racing in his chest.

No. They couldn't be. Surely not. Whoever it was had been upstairs. They ran down and out after that.

But then why hadn't he seen them?

He turned back to Meg...

'Who was it?'

'I... I...'

'Dylan?' he asked. That was his immediate thought. After all, the guy had threatened Frankie with death, hadn't he?

'I... I don't know.'

She broke down in tears. Frankie moved over to her and grabbed her and cuddled her as she cried. He was on the verge too. He really didn't know what to do. He'd never been so scared.

Someone had been in his home.

Who? Why?

After a few moments, not sure what else to do, he took his phone from his pocket and called the one person he could think of who could help.

Jess.

CHAPTER TWENTY-SEVEN

JESS

I ran all the way. More than a mile, with uncomfortable shoes, skirt, big coat. But there'd been no taxis at the rank in town, no Uber available for fifteen minutes. And the desperation in Frankie's voice...

I found him and his girlfriend in the lounge, on the sofa huddled together like two lost lambs. We wouldn't even get started yet as to what she was doing there, and dressed like that.

'Talk to me?' I said, out of breath, the skin beneath my clothes clammy even if my hands and my face were ice cold from the wintry night-time air. I stripped off my coat. Could feel my clothes sticking to me.

'Tom saw someone, in his room,' Frankie said, barely able to hold my eye. 'Not a ghost, Jess. A man. A real man.'

'He's upstairs?'

'The man?' Frankie asked with a shiver.

'No, dumbo, Tom?'

'In bed.'

I headed up. But not before bolting the front door. Every single light was on upstairs, including Tom's. He was lying on his belly in the bed, reading a book.

'You okay?' I said to him.

He looked at me and nodded as though nothing had happened.

'Probably time for lights out now, don't you think?'

He pushed the book off the bed and turned over, head on pillow, and looked at me.

I sat down on the bed and ran my hand through his messy hair. 'What did you see?'

'A man.'

'Can you describe him?'

'It was pretty dark.'

'But you're sure it was a man?'

He nodded.

'Frankie said you screamed.'

Another nod.

'You don't seem too scared now?'

'I was having a bad dream. I didn't expect to see him there.'

'Did he talk to you?'

A nod.

'What did he say?'

'Hi, Tom.'

'Really?'

A nod. This was beyond weird, and even with the light on I felt ridiculously creeped out. Had he really seen a man, or just... something. Either way Tom didn't seem bothered now at all. What was going on in his young mind?

'Did he do anything to you?' I asked.

'Like what?'

'I don't know.'

'He was just standing there. He doesn't want to hurt me.'

What makes you think that? I wanted to ask, but I didn't want to dampen his new-found confidence and calmness by exposing to him just how vulnerable he was, and how much worse the situation – if what I was hearing was true – could have been.

It was true, wasn't it? Otherwise Frankie and Meg's reactions wouldn't have been so severe, surely.

Given the last few days, I really didn't know anymore.

'I'll leave you to it,' I said, getting up from the bed. I moved to the door and turned off the light. 'Night, night.'

'It's the same man as before,' Tom said.

'What?'

'The same man I saw the last time, before Christmas.'

'You're sure.'

'Yeah.'

'I'll leave the landing light on.'

I didn't know what else to say.

I left his door half open. I checked over the upstairs rooms, Mum and Dad's included. All windows locked, no sight of anyone or any signs of anything untoward. Still not feeling particularly settled I headed back downstairs where Frankie and Meg remained on the sofa, exact same position as before. They appeared far more disturbed than little Tom.

'He seems fine,' I said.

'It was... horrible, Jess,' my brother said.

Meg nodded as she gripped his arm.

'Run me through it again.'

They looked at each other.

'We were in here,' Frankie said, a little cagily. I could guess what they'd been up to. 'Tom screamed. I rushed upstairs. He said about the man. He was really scared, Jess. I thought it was just him seeing ghosts again, but then... then...'

'I went out to the kitchen not long after he went up,' Meg said, taking up the baton. 'To get some more wine. As I walked in I saw the back door... kind of move, and a... a shadow. Well, no, a man, running away from the house.'

'Was the door open already? Unlocked I mean?'

'Definitely not open,' Frankie said. 'And I don't remember unlocking it.'

No. Nor me.

'I reckon the guy came in through there,' Meg said. 'Sneaked upstairs. Then when Tom screamed he hid until Frankie was up there. Then he ran. Only I spotted him.'

It made some sense. But the biggest question remained. Who had been in the house and why? Both why were they in the house, and why had they gone up to Tom's room?

I shuddered at the thought. This couldn't just be Tom imagining things anymore. Not given Frankie and Meg's story. Unless they were bullshitting me. But why would they do that?

Did it have something to do with Frankie's beaten face? No. That made no sense. If so, he wouldn't have called me. He would have tried to hide that anything had happened.

Only one conclusion worked this time. Someone – an intruder – had really been in our house.

'Have you checked everywhere downstairs?' I asked. 'The garage?'

'Not the garage,' Frankie said, looking at me with fear in his eyes.

'We'll do it together.'

We left Meg on the sofa. We moved gingerly to the back. I glanced in the dining room briefly. All clear in there. In the kitchen I checked the patio doors. Locked. I noted the pile of glass in the dustpan. I looked to Frankie.

'Sorry.'

'It's only a glass.'

We moved across to the door for the utility room. I opened it, and braced for the inevitable wave of chilled air. I moved inside. Opened the garage door. Frankie reached out from behind me and took my other hand, his skin warm and clammy as he held on tight. I turned on the light...

We both heaved a sigh of relief.

'There's no one here,' I said.

'No,' Frankie said. 'Not anymore.'

I quickly looked away from the garage as I turned off the light, then closed the door.

Despite the explanations from the three of them, which were all consistent, I really had no clue what had happened while I'd been out.

One thing I did know: neither me nor Frankie would get much sleep that night.

CHAPTER TWENTY-EIGHT

F rankie and Tom remained behind the closed lounge door as I showed DS Holster and her forensics colleague to the door. I'd called the police the previous evening, but after a brief visit from a PC – who decided everything was fine, at least in so far as there was no immediate threat – we were left to wait until the morning for a more full response.

'What will happen now?' I asked Holster on the doorstep. She turned to me.

'We'll get back to you on whether we have any prints that don't belong, and I'll get a PC to do some rounds with neighbours to see if there were other break-ins or if anyone saw anything. It's possible someone might have some CCTV that helps, but other than that, there's not a lot we can do. No forced entry. Nothing's been stolen. No one is hurt.'

She spoke clinically, unfeeling, creating doubt in my mind as to whether she believed me at all about the intruder.

'Is there anything else you can tell me?' Holster said. 'I can see you're troubled.'

I thought for a few moments as I watched the forensics guy pack his cases into his car.

'What if my dad didn't kill himself,' I said.

Holster's face screwed. 'Jess, I didn't mean–'

'But did you look, really?' I asked. I probably shouldn't have done, because I immediately noted Holster's more defensive look, as though I'd questioned her integrity.

'Is there something you know?' Holster asked.

'It just... doesn't make any sense. And now this.'

'You think the intruder you claim you saw is connected?'

Claim. Like she didn't believe me. Us.

'I don't think he wrote that note,' I said, which wasn't strictly true, but I had to try something.

Holster glared at me, looking annoyed. 'That's not what you and your brother told us before.'

'I know, but I've had chance to look at it more closely. I... I just...'

'Jess, I understand–'

'I don't think you do.'

We both went silent. Holster held my eye. I didn't think she was trying to be unhelpful, but it wasn't as though I was giving her anything concrete.

'Do you think... at least, do you think your forensics team could look at some other items.'

'What items?'

'My dad's notepads–'

'Notepads? What–'

'If we can find the pad where he took that paper from for the note, perhaps there's someone else's prints on there? The ladder too. The rope that was used for the noose. Do you still have that? The thing is, I looked in the garage for the rest of that rope, I mean, was it really just that one section, perfect length for a noose, or was it cut from another longer piece? But I can't find any rope anywhere. And when did Dad even buy that thing?'

Holster stared at me. I had no clue what she was thinking. That I was crazy and losing it?

'What about CCTV on our street or around here? Maybe there's–'

'Jess.'

I stopped talking and slumped, looked down to my feet. After what seemed like an age, Holster sighed. She turned back around to her colleague, who remained standing by his car, checking his phone.

'Harry, can I borrow you again?' Holster shouted to him, before turning back to me. 'Go and get the things you mentioned. We'll check them for prints. But I'm doing this more to calm you and show you there's nothing to find, more than anything else.'

'Thank you,' I said, before turning and rushing off.

An hour later, feeling a lot calmer, the boys and I sat together with our breakfast.

'Meg seems nice,' I said to Frankie, trying to steer their thoughts away from intruders and the police – I hadn't explained to them about the extra work I'd given Holster, though I did want to find the right time to talk to Frankie about it.

'Is she your girlfriend?' Tom asked, munching on his cereal, somehow the brightest out of the three of us. Strangely, I think he'd liked the fact the police had been. Did it make him feel safer, or did he just enjoy the drama?

'Yeah,' Frankie answered, not looking up.

'I thought I heard a girl downstairs,' Tom said. 'Before I went to sleep.'

Frankie glared at his little brother. I wasn't sure why.

'No need to sneak her in next time,' I said. 'Just ask.'

Frankie shrugged. 'Next time? Probably scared her off for life.'

'I don't think so. I saw the way she looked at you.'

Frankie's cheeks reddened a little.

'You've done well for yourself. She's really pretty, and you're... well... you.'

He did look at me now and me and Tom laughed. Frankie tried not to but eventually broke out into a smile. He got up from the table to hide it, taking his empty bowl with him.

I wanted to talk more about the night before, the man, but I didn't know what to say. I also hadn't mentioned to Frankie about me asking Holster to look more into Dad's suicide. I really wanted to, but how?

'What are we doing today?' Tom asked.

'We could go to the fair later?' Frankie suggested.

'Yeah, the fair!' Tom responded.

The Christmas Fair. Not my favourite place, but... The same fair rolled into our little town a couple of times a year. Once during the summer holidays, and once during the Christmas holidays. Consisting mostly of creaky old fairground rides, along with a few food stalls and other odds and sods, at Christmastime the fair took on a much more festive feel, with real Christmas trees, a Santa's grotto, big blow-up snowmen, and non-stop Christmas music played from the waltzer and further broadcast over loudspeaker. Probably more fun before Christmas Day really, while the kids were all so excited with the idea of Santa and presents, but what did I know? Kids loved it there, as did groups of young teens.

One big reason I really didn't like it was the mud. And the cold. Held at the same recreation ground in both seasons, I could count on one hand the number of times in all my years the site hadn't turned into a mud bath.

That said, I was probably only fifteen or sixteen the last time I'd been, and that was with my friends. Even longer since I'd gone with my brothers.

'Yeah, let's do it,' I said. 'We'll go this afternoon.'

'More fun when it's dark,' Tom said. 'With all the lights.'

My thought too. Though the idea of being out in the dark didn't enthral me. Still, I didn't say anything to disagree.

'I want to pop to the shops this morning, if I have any takers?'

'The shops? Again?' Tom asked with a groan. 'What for?'

'You'll see if you come with me?'

———

Tom did come with me. Frankie didn't. I questioned whether he'd be sneaking Meg over again while I was out. I don't think he appreciated that. Tom did.

But even though I'd made light of the situation between Frankie and Meg, I wasn't taking lightly the events of the night before. I was troubled. Scared. The police would do what they could to help us figure out who had been in our house, but I wanted to take more active precautions too. Which was why we headed back to Argos.

'What are getting from here?' Tom asked as we walked in, both suspicion and just a little bit of hopeful anticipation in his voice.

'I thought about what you said the other day. About the camera. About wanting to see Mum and Dad. I decided... well, I think you're right. I'd like to see them too.'

He eyed me, a little bit of distrust, but he didn't say anything.

'I'll pay for it even, how's that?'

'Really?' he said, his face brightening in an instant.

I bought a wireless camera system. Two small video cameras, battery powered, that connected over wifi to a central hub, and could be controlled by a smartphone. Frankie helped me set it all up. I'm sure I could have done it easily enough myself, but I asked him for assistance to give him a bit of responsibility really.

We put one camera in Tom's room, in the corner by the door, facing down into the room. We put the other in the corner of the kitchen, facing the patio doors.

'How do I see it?' Tom asked as he watched Frankie on the stepladder, fiddling with the set-up buttons.

'I'll have it on my phone,' I said to him. 'Frankie too. The cameras won't be on all the time, but we'll set it at night, when we're asleep. We can watch what it captures on our phones the next morning.'

'It'll record the whole night?'

'Not if we want the batteries to last. It starts recording when it senses movement.'

'How does it know?'

'It's very clever,' I said.

'Infra-red,' Frankie added. 'It's a type of light.'

'But it'll be dark at night,' Tom said, looking really confused. 'So it won't work in my room.'

Frankie rolled his eyes. 'It's not visible light,' he said. 'Not to us. People give off heat, yeah? Your body is warm. The cameras see that warmth, like a glow.'

The explanation didn't do anything to ease Tom's perplexed look. 'But Mum and Dad won't be warm, will they? Ghosts are cold.'

A fair point? I hadn't thought about that. Frankie looked to me, as if for assistance in explaining the unexplainable.

'I'm sure it'll work just fine,' I said to him.

'That's it,' Frankie said. 'Both of you stand really still.'

Tom froze, facial features and all. Held his breath.

'Now wriggle.'

Tom did a jelly dance and I burst out laughing. The camera unit blinked once to show it'd picked up the movement and had started recording. A ping came through on my phone to let me know motion had been detected.

'Let me see!' Tom said, excitedly.

I opened the app and he took the phone off me to see the screen and he laughed as he watched himself over and over.

He handed me the phone back as Frankie came down from the ladder.

'I can't wait for tonight,' Tom said, before rushing off.

Frankie and I shared a look.

We were all set, cameras ready, Tom ready too.

Who or what we'd capture in the night, I really didn't know.

We set off for the fair at 4pm, and by the time we arrived it was fully dark out and the lights at the fair twinkled and danced while music blared. Coming nearly a week after Christmas Day it all seemed a bit OTT to me, but what did I know, because Tom's face – big wide smile – was a real picture.

I felt pretty happy too, really, and the mud I expected wasn't there at all. Perhaps because of the recent cold weather which meant the grass underfoot was frozen solid.

I noticed a few familiar faces as we wandered around, including some people from my year group at school. I nodded and smiled a few times, a couple of odd words spoken here and there. I wondered whether any of them knew what had happened to me, to us? I knew nothing about what had happened to them the last couple of years, but then my family's tragedy had carried a very small feature in the local online news pages, if anyone actually read those, and in such a small town, I expected gossip to travel like wildfire.

At least no one said anything to me about it.

I also noted Frankie smiling at people I didn't recognise. Girls mostly. I'd never expected my quite introverted brother to be an object of affection but apparently he was.

'I asked Meg to come,' he said to me after a smile to a pretty red-haired girl.

'Oh,' I said, not really sure what to think. Actually, no, I did know what to think. I'd thought we were doing this together, the three of us, though I wasn't really annoyed. Mainly I was glad that he had someone, and that he was acting... normal. 'What time?' I asked.

'Five-ish,' he said. 'So we've got a bit of time first.'

'Let's get to it then,' I said. 'Tommo, where to?'

We let Tom lead the way for nearly an hour. Dodgems, three times over, doughnut stand, water squirters, the world's smallest rollercoaster – not officially, but I couldn't imagine a smaller one. I hadn't had so much fun since... I couldn't really remember. Certainly not with my family, which only once again gave a painful reminder to me of what I'd missed over the last couple of years, and what I'd now never get back with Mum, Dad and Lily.

Frankie, though, I felt only gave us seventy-five per cent attention. Certainly plenty of smiles and laughs, but I sensed a distraction too. Was that only because he eagerly awaited his girlfriend's arrival? Or was it more that he was trying to avoid someone, as he seemed really on edge at times?

I'd maybe ask him about that later.

'What next?' I asked.

'Can we eat?' Tom suggested.

'Didn't we already?' But then I spotted what he had seen. A

burger stall, right in front of us. The smell wafted over as we neared.

I looked to Frankie, to get his buy-in, but he stared at his phone screen, paying us no attention.

'She's here?' I asked.

'Yeah,' he said, looking a little embarrassed. 'Catch you in a little bit?'

'Sure.'

He headed off even before the word had finished forming in my mouth. Fair enough. 'Burger then?' I said to Tom.

We both got one. Not my favourite food, honestly, and not from a stall like that where it was hardly going to be the best quality sourced product, but it made Tom happy, and it filled a hole in my stomach so I wouldn't have to worry about making dinner later.

We went straight back to the dodgems. Perhaps not a great idea on bellies filled with doughnuts and burgers, but certainly better than the waltzer – my least favoured ride of all.

I spotted Frankie and Meg, hand in hand, as we came back off the cars. She looked cold. And nervous. I couldn't be sure if they'd intentionally come our way or if they'd made a mistake, though they didn't try and slink off.

'Hi, Meg,' I said to her and she gave me an awkward smile in return. 'Have you two been on anything?'

'Not yet,' Frankie said. 'Just been walking around. But there is something I thought we could try?'

'All of us?'

'Yeah.'

I couldn't read his mood. Nervous, more than anything else.

'Lead the way.'

We headed around a corner and stopped by this curious looking wagon. Rounded, wooden, like the type I'd seen in old movies, from the Wild West. Or belonging to olden day travellers.

The whole thing, compared to the glitzy, often garish rides that dominated the fair, appeared understated. No twinkling lights, no music, just a little sign:

Palmistry. Fortune telling.

'Here?' I said to Frankie.

He tried to look cool, and shrugged at me. 'Never tried it before.'

'My aunt knows who does it,' Meg said. 'Heidi. She's really nice.'

'What is it?' Tom asked, looking seriously doubtful, probably because of the apparent lack of excitement versus everything else on offer around us.

'It's a fortune teller,' Meg said, reaching out and taking Tom's hand. 'She can see into the future. She can see *your* future.'

'How?'

She flipped his hand over and ran a finger across his delicate skin. 'Palm reading,' she said. 'Every person's palm is unique to them. If you're clever enough to understand the differences, you can see everything a person has done in their life, and what's going to happen to them in the future.'

Tom's smile dropped, though I wasn't sure why, and he pulled his hand back and looked at me.

'You don't have to believe it,' I said to him. 'You don't have to do it either, if you don't want to.'

I looked to Frankie, part curious, part annoyed. Clearly he'd planned this, what with Meg tagging along and everything, and the fortune teller being someone she knew, but why had he been so cagey? Why hadn't he just said something to me before?

And why did he even want to do it? Fortune telling didn't

seem like his thing at all, unless he was only trying to please Meg.

'Would you like to try?' she said to Tom.

Tom, still a little reluctant, glanced across to the closed door of the wagon. He gulped. 'Will you come with me?' he said to Frankie.

'Yeah, bud. We can all go in, if you want?'

Frankie looked over at all of us. I really wasn't sure I wanted to go in either, but...

Tom took Frankie's hand and they moved toward the steps below the door.

CHAPTER TWENTY-NINE

The inside of the wagon somehow seemed far bigger than I'd imagined, like an optical illusion. Like the Tardis on Doctor Who. I hadn't looked properly on the outside, but I wondered whether the back of the quaint little wagon we'd seen was actually attached to something else.

The four of us stood in the room, a simple table in the middle, covered in a black cloth. Black and red cloth hung from the walls and ceiling too. A couple of soft lights up high, together with an ornate lamp on the table, provided the only illumination in the space that smelled... weird. Like a mixture of potpourri and curry spices.

The wagon felt strangely quiet, subdued. Eerie.

The woman came out from a curtain in front of us, from where, who knew. I'm not sure what I'd expected. A witch-like person? A stereotypical old hag, hunched, haggard? I had no clue really, I'd never done this before, had no idea what kind of person specialised in this. This? Which was what? Cheating people out of a few pounds by feeding them some bullshit?

But the woman who came out wasn't what I expected at all. Not old. Perhaps mid-thirties. An elegant black dress, dark hair flowing down the sides of her face. She had a kind smile, but piercing eyes made more prominent because of the dark make-up – very similar to Meg's actually.

'Welcome,' she said.

Meg stepped forward and the two of them held each other's hands. No hug, but a brief and very quiet conversation before Meg let go and went back to stand with Frankie. I watched my brother's girlfriend with just a hint of suspicion but when she caught my eye, she only smiled at me happily.

'Who'd like to go first?' Heidi asked.

Frankie and Tom both looked at each other, then me.

'I'll do it,' Tom said, for some reason looking more enthused now than he had done on the outside. Tom took the seat in front of us and the lady – Heidi – sat on the seat the other side of the table. She didn't look anywhere but directly at Tom. I shuffled forward a little to make sure I could hear.

'Put your hands on the table,' Heidi said, that smile still on her face as she placed her forearms flat on the black cloth.

Tom, more hesitant once more, put his arms out and Heidi twisted them so his palms faced up. He looked over his shoulder at me, a little nervously, as Heidi ran her finger over his palms. Over a few silent seconds, her smile faded to neutrality. Or perhaps seriousness.

'You poor boy,' she said to him, a slight shake of her head. 'So young, but you've seen so much.'

The room fell silent. I held my breath.

'You were hurt. Badly hurt. Not very long ago.'

Well, that much was obvious, given Tom still had strapping on his wrist.

Tom nodded. 'A car crash,' he said.

Heidi momentarily held his eye before returning her focus to his hands. 'But you're a good boy. A happy boy. Don't lose

207

sight of who you are. Those tragic moments won't define you. Your future can still be bright.'

I looked over to Frankie, the expression on my face supposed to show him my growing agitation and scepticism. He ignored me.

'I see a man,' Heidi said, and I tensed a little. 'A man, and a woman, very important in your life.'

'Mum and Dad?' Tom said, and I really wished he hadn't because he was only giving her fuel.

'They love you. They miss you, but they're still with you, always close by.'

Bollocks. She was supposed to be reading him, not telling him about other people.

Heidi suddenly looked up to me and I froze.

'I see it on his union line here,' she said to me. I looked down. 'See it here?' She pointed to a spot on Tom's hand. 'The union line, together with the lifeline, tells me all about your relationships.'

Apparently that explanation was for me, rather than Tom, but the way she'd sensed my doubt was... unnatural.

'There's also a fate line here,' she said, moving her finger to a different spot, 'a heart line, a head line. Each is different for every person, and the way they start, finish, overlap each other, tells me everything I need to know.'

'What about my future?' Tom asked.

Heidi smiled and returned her focus to him, said nothing as she moved her fingers back and forth. Then her face soured a little, a shake of the head.

'I see someone else. Another man.' Tom glanced at me. I tried to show no reaction. Heidi shook her head. 'Darkness follows him. A lot of darkness, in his past. In his future too.'

I tensed. Despite not believing a word she said, I didn't like where this was going. Plus, Tom was nine years old. Give him something to grasp. Fame or fortune, or at least happiness and a wife and kids perhaps in the future.

'Don't go with the man,' she said to Tom with a surreal bluntness as she grasped Tom's forearms. Her face turned, heavy lines appearing as she glared at Tom. 'You must stay away from him... if you can.'

Heidi whipped her hands away and Tom jumped in shock. Then she glared at me. 'You need to look after him. You need to protect him.'

I said nothing. She looked back to Tom, and in an instant her features relaxed again. 'That's all, my dear. There's happiness for you. If you can just find it.'

An odd parting comment. Tom turned around, a startled look in his eyes. He got up from the chair and I ruffled his hair. 'You okay?'

He nodded, but didn't say anything as he moved to Frankie.

'Who's next?' Heidi said.

I'd had enough already to be honest, would have happily walked out there and then, but I sensed the little clique the other side of the room – Frankie, Meg, and Tom – wanted to carry on.

'I'll go,' Frankie said, stepping forward.

He took the seat and Heidi took his hands and I looked from them and over to Meg and Tom, my brain whirring. That initial little exchange between Meg and Heidi earlier, what was that about? And Frankie had clearly planned to come here. Was Meg a stooge, relaying information on me and my brothers to this apparent fortune teller?

How else could she have known about the man? About Mum and Dad?

I realised I'd already missed the start of Frankie's reading, so engrossed in my own thoughts.

'So much burden on such young shoulders,' Heidi continued. 'But you're stronger than you realise.'

I rolled my eyes. Hadn't she pretty much said the same to Tom? Yet as I completed the gesture, Heidi flicked her gaze my way once more, and my heart stuttered.

'Please?' she asked, as though she'd heard my doubting thoughts and it'd disturbed her work.

'Sorry,' I said. *Why?*

'There's a lot of good in you,' Heidi said to Frankie. 'It's always been there, always in control, but you mustn't let it fade because of the challenges you've been through.'

Frankie nodded.

'There's a battle in you. A torment. I see your struggle.'

She paused and held Frankie's eyes, almost as though she'd entranced him. Neither spoke a word for what seemed like an age. I wanted to get out of there. I wanted to be sceptical, but it felt so... real.

'There's a crossroads ahead of you,' Heidi said. 'It will define you. Two paths you could take. One of lightness and happiness, one of darkness and pain and misery, for you, and for others.'

She went silent. I sensed Frankie's nerves now even though he didn't move a muscle. Could he move, or had she hypnotised him somehow?

'You can only take one road, and you won't be able to turn back after. But be careful, my dear boy, because it might not be clear at first which is which.'

She nodded and her eyes pinched as she stared at him. Frankie seemed enthralled, but despite the strange and eerie tension in the room, I wanted to question what I was witnessing. Her words were so non-specific, weren't they? And not really much different to Tom's reading, to be honest. *You might have a light future, you might have a dark future, you might not know which path is which?*

How anyone was supposed to take anything from that, I really didn't know.

And yet the mood and the sincerity in her manner and her words...

When Frankie was finished, he stood up and turned to me. I saw the washed-out look on his face and genuine fear in his eyes, and I knew he'd taken the words to heart.

Heidi's words meant something to him, really meant something, and on realising his reaction, a wave of prickles shot down my back.

'Jess?' Heidi said.

I flinched at her voice. And her use of my name. Had Meg told her while I'd been deep in thought?

'Okay.' I took the hot seat. Placed my hands on the table. Heidi's remained out of sight. I caught her gaze.

'Relax,' she said to me with a crooked smile, the light from the lamp on the table casting freakish shadows across her face. 'I know when I see someone who doesn't believe. But that doesn't mean you won't get a suitable reading.'

I nodded.

'If you relax, and listen, you'll see.'

See what?

She spent a couple of minutes running her fingers over the lines of my hands, no words, just a few murmurs and hmms. She took her time, a lot longer than with the boys.

Or were my own nerves simply slowing time?

She let go and caught my eye again. She shook her head. 'I know the tragedy affected you all,' she said, and I again wondered how much she'd known about us beforehand. 'A horrible tragedy for any person, but particularly for three siblings so young.'

I gulped. Even if I didn't want to believe in this woman's powers, it didn't make sitting there any more relaxing, make it any less intense. My heart rate steadily built, my skin had become clammy. The walls seemed to close in a little with each breath I took.

Intense? More so than I ever imagined, like she'd hypnotised me – as I thought perhaps she had with Frankie...

How was she doing it? I could barely move. Barely breathe.

I was scared. Horribly scared.

'Jess, you have to let go. Holding the grief inside will destroy you. Destroy your future.'

I swallowed hard, trying to hold my emotions together. I couldn't cry here, like this, in front of Frankie and Tom and Meg and this woman.

'I understand,' Heidi said. She took my hands again. Not to continue the reading, but to offer comfort. It didn't work. 'I understand why it's more painful for you than for Tom and Frankie. But please, don't let the pain you hold inside destroy what you have left of your family, and of your life.'

I whipped my hands away and found the strength and focus to stand up from the seat.

Enough was enough.

Had Frankie put her up to this?

I glared at him. He looked shocked. I didn't sense Heidi behind me. I jumped in shock when she wrapped her hands around my waist, her palms flat out against my belly. A kind of reverse hug, except she wasn't hugging me, she was... I don't know.

'Jess, Jess,' she whispered, or more like hissed, as she moved her hands slowly around my belly. 'My poor girl. I feel it. The life lost, still inside you. I feel it. Devouring you. You have to find a way to release it.'

'Get off me!' I shouted, yanking her hands away and pulling

from her grip. I spun around and glared. Heidi looked distressed. At my reaction, or what she'd felt in me?

'Jess?' Frankie said.

I shook with fear and rage. I couldn't get my breath. As I stared at Heidi her shape morphed, her features shifting and... oozing. The room swayed and pulsed around me. I couldn't breathe...

'Jess?'

Frankie's hand on my shoulder gave me a bit of clarity.

'Just leave me alone! All of you!'

I shrugged him off and dashed outside on wobbly legs.

CHAPTER THIRTY

Fresh air. I needed it so badly. I jumped down the steps, tears already flowing, my legs heavy. I only made it a few more steps before I collapsed onto a cold, soggy wooden bench. I didn't care. I couldn't stand up. I wheezed, trying to breathe, my chest was tight, a stabbing pain beneath my ribs. I put my head in my hands. Wanted to scream.

'Jess, what the hell?'

I felt the arm around me. I hadn't even heard or seen him come out, but Frankie was sitting next to me. I looked up. Tom and Meg were in front, concern etched on their faces as they looked at me; the mess.

'Hey, Meg, do you think you could take Tom for a bit?' Frankie said.

Meg smiled and nodded. She took my little brother's hand and they headed off.

'Talk to me, Jess,' he said, taking his arm off me and clasping his hands together. He ducked his head as though trying to look at me, but I turned away so he couldn't.

'Why did you do that?' I said.

'Meg and Tom?'

'No, idiot. Why did you make us do that?'

'I didn't make you do anything.'

'But you told her. You must have done.'

'Told who, what? Heidi?' he said, sounding a little angry. 'I've never met her before.'

'And Meg? What did you tell her?'

'About what?'

'About us!' I said, raising my head and my voice. 'About me!'

He looked offended, but I'm not sure I bought it. 'Why did you want us to do that?' I asked.

'I thought it would help.'

'Who?'

'Tom. Me. Maybe even you. I thought it might help us all to understand.'

I shook my head. Did he really believe his own words? Or was this all a ploy to get to me. Why?

'Jess, I swear, I didn't bring us here to upset you. I'm really sorry. I wanted... I'm so confused too. I don't know what's happening with Tom. In our house. To any of us. I thought... perhaps...'

We both went silent. I didn't know what he was trying to say. Was he suggesting he really now did believe in ghosts, the occult, whatever? That he'd hoped for some reinforcement of that by going to see a fortune teller?

'But what she said to you.' He shook his head, looking down to his feet. 'I want you to talk to me. I want to help you. Please?'

I didn't say anything, even though I knew my silence wouldn't be enough. Not this time.

'When she held you,' he said. 'That wasn't normal, was it? That's not palm reading. That's... what was that? Even Meg said she was shocked. Scared too. *I'm* scared, Jess. For you.'

I looked at my eldest brother. Such a strong young man in some respects, but so vulnerable now too.

'I'll tell you something, Frankie, but it goes no further. You have to promise me.'

'Okay,' he said.

'And I'm only telling you because...' I trailed off, because I didn't really want to say what I'd thought, which was *because maybe it'll get you off my back.* 'This has nothing to do with anyone else though. Nothing to do with what happened.'

He frowned, as if that wasn't what he expected, or wanted, to hear.

'A few weeks ago I found out I was pregnant.' I bowed my head.

Frankie took a long inhale as though he needed to build up to hear this.

'I really don't know how. I'm on the pill...' I cringed. Talking to my brother about my use of contraception? Could this be any more awkward? 'The doctor says it can happen. Like, I don't know, one in a thousand or something.'

I paused. Frankie said nothing. He held my hand. His touch really did help. 'You had an abortion?'

I closed my eyes and nodded. A sacrifice. A selfish sacrifice, made by me, for my own future.

'It's okay, Jess. You didn't do anything wrong.'

Didn't I? 'Whether it was right or wrong, isn't really the point.'

'Was it Blake's?' Frankie asked.

I nodded. Who else? I'd only ever slept with two people.

'Does he know?'

I nodded again. 'The truth is, I don't even know what he wanted. Not really. I didn't want to know, because I didn't want to have the conversation with him. I didn't want to talk about it, or even think about it. I only knew I couldn't do it. I couldn't... not at that time.'

I wiped at my eyes, but surprisingly found they were dry. I

guess there were only so many tears to shed. That idea made me feel all the more empty.

'Mum and Dad didn't know?'

'I wanted them to. Of course I did. But Mum... she wouldn't have...'

'She loved you more than anything,' Frankie said. 'I know she wouldn't like the idea of abortion, but she would have understood. For you.'

I shook my head. I didn't agree. 'They sacrificed so much for me. If Mum had known...' Once again I didn't finish, for fear of saying something I couldn't.

'I think Blake really likes you,' Frankie said. He put his arm around me again.

'Maybe he does. But this wasn't supposed to happen for us. It's changed everything. I'm not sure we can ever go back.' Perhaps that was the saddest part of all.

'I'm glad you told me,' Frankie said. He took his arm back from me and we held each other's eye. He didn't look very glad. He looked... a little bit angry, more than anything else. 'But, Jess, please, no more secrets.'

I nodded. A far more easy response than having to lie.

CHAPTER THIRTY-ONE

FRANKIE

Frankie held mixed feelings about the trip to the fair. He certainly hadn't gained from the palm reading what he'd expected, nor would he say he'd enjoyed the experience at all. What had started as seemingly mundane with Tom, had turned very real for him. The words about the two paths, one of dark and one of light, had struck a chord in his core. He hoped he hadn't shown that to the others, even if, as he'd stood from that chair, his heart had fluttered with unease and uncertainty.

What about Jess? Nothing she could have done to hide her reaction. Frankie hadn't intended the experience as a means of outing her. He really hadn't. What he'd really hoped for was more substance about what was happening at home, with Tom's ghostly sightings, and all the other creepy stuff going on around them, because mysterious intruder aside – Dylan? – Frankie still knew all was not right in their home.

But Jess's reaction to Heidi's words... he'd known instantly that the fortune teller had hit on something with Jess.

Then had come the revelation. A big one, for sure, and he felt truly heartened that Jess had chosen to talk to him as candidly as she had. He realised how hard that must have been, how much trust she had placed in him to do so, and he did feel for her. He was male; he'd never have that feeling of a living thing inside him, so he couldn't fully comprehend what she'd gone through, how she was feeling now, but he could see the significance to her.

The abortion was a big thing, and Jess had tried to deal with it all alone, which had probably only made things even more difficult for her after the death of their parents.

But then, wasn't that the problem? She'd dealt with it alone. Mum and Dad hadn't known. Even if they had, Frankie really couldn't see how Jess's abortion could have sent their dad over the edge to killing himself. So it explained very little really.

There was something even bigger that he still didn't know about, something that had caused the tragedy they were all now struggling with.

Frankie genuinely appreciated Jess's earlier openness, but the more he thought about it, the more he realised he didn't believe that her reaction with Heidi matched the explanation. Not fully. She was still holding back.

He wouldn't stop digging. Not yet.

He'd stayed at the fair with Meg after Jess and Tom left. He'd hoped to be able to go over to hers, to pick up where they'd left off last night at home. But no, her dad had a day off, so it was a no-go. After an hour or so on their own, he walked her home. He'd wanted to walk her as an excuse to spend more time with her, though in a way he wished he hadn't as she seemed so... distant. Ever since they'd come out of the fortune telling. Why was that?

He wondered as they walked toward Goose Avenue whether he'd have another run-in with Dylan tonight. He once again had the flick knife in his pocket, just in case. Would he use it this time? Last time he hadn't even taken it out of his pocket, even when Dylan had attacked.

No. No sign of Dylan at all. Frankie was part tempted to sneak back toward Dylan's house after dropping Meg off, but decided against it.

It had to have been Dylan in their house last night, didn't it? The bastard had broken in to have another go. Frankie wouldn't let it slide.

Tom was getting ready for bed when Frankie arrived home. He spoke a few words to his brother and sister before he headed up to his room. His brain muddled with differing thoughts, he went to his bedside table. Opened it. Frowned. He shuffled closer on the bed, dug his hand in, rummaged about.

Not there.

He looked around his room, thinking. No. He'd definitely left his dad's phone in the drawer. A hundred per cent.

Dad's laptop? He'd put that in his wardrobe. He headed there. Felt under the piles of clothes.

Still there.

What did that mean?

He sat on his bed a while, thinking, while Jess finished Tom's night-time routine next door. He waited a few minutes more. Then he sneaked out onto the landing. Of course, he could go and ask Jess directly, or...

He moved across, looking down to the hall below. No sign of Jess, the sound of the TV drifted up. He reached Tom's room. All quiet in there.

He retreated to the far side of the landing, left the light off as he slipped into Jess's room. He hated to do this, but he had to know.

With his heart thudding away, a constant film of sweat on his forehead and down his back because of his nerves, he searched and rummaged through her things, being as silent as he could. A couple of times an unexpected creak caused him to freeze.

She never came up, though, but nor did Frankie find the missing phone.

Angry, dejected, confused, he headed back to his room. Lay back on his bed.

Jess had known about the phone. She hadn't approved. She hadn't known he also had the laptop. An old one, that Dad had replaced a year or so ago with the laptop they usually kept in the lounge. That was Dad's too, really, but more like a family computer in truth. Nothing incriminating on there – Frankie had already searched all over. Why Dad had kept the old one, Frankie didn't know. Nor did he know whether it even held anything of interest. He wanted to find out, except he hadn't yet been able to get access to it because of the password, so he'd simply hidden it in his wardrobe until he could figure a way.

Why had the password changed?

Jess hadn't known about the laptop, she had known about the phone. The laptop remained in place; the phone was missing.

A coincidence?

Or Jess had taken it from him.

But why?

CHAPTER THIRTY-TWO

JESS

I open my eyes, though I'm not sure why at first. The room is pitch black. I can't see a thing. I lie still. Slowly, barely, the room comes into focus.

I realise why I woke up. A sound. Music. Distant, drifting into my room, toward me. From where?

I sit up in the bed. It's so dark in my room, outside it too. No lights are on in here, or the landing. Not how I left it. I've been leaving the landing light on every night for Tom.

Who turned it off?

More importantly, why is there music playing?

I reach out for my phone to check the time. Why? I don't need to know the time, but somehow just knowing that one thing will help to ground me as I recover from my untimely wake up.

My phone isn't there.

The music gets louder and I turn my head to the open door in a panic. No. Nothing there. Nothing but that music. A sweet, melodic voice. Female. French, I think. There's a background crackle as though it's playing out of an antique gramophone.

I rise out of the bed, take nervous steps forward.

I'm scared. The house feels so dark, empty. Yet Frankie and Tom are here, aren't they?

And there's that music...

I reach my door. I can see down the stairs, just about. No lights on down there either, I can only see because of the sparse moonlight drifting in through the landing window, and in through the patio doors downstairs in the kitchen.

Across the landing from me the door to Mum and Dad's room is closed. So too Frankie's. And Tom's.

Lily's, by the head of the stairs, is wide open.

I move over that way, trying to be silent. I'm a few steps across when my foot sinks on an ever so slightly loose floorboard.

Creak.

I freeze. The music pauses...

No. It doesn't. Just a break. Or was it?

I'm so confused, terrified too.

I reach Lily's door. Black inside. But I hear breathing. Tiny, little breaths. I can't go in. I'm too frightened.

Perhaps the sound is just Tom, right next door.

It has to be. But as I stare I'm sure I see a shape rising and falling inside, on the bed in the far corner of the room.

I look away. I don't want to know. It can't be real. Lily can't be here.

I move down the stairs. The woman's voice is more clear now. So beautiful. But haunting too. I don't understand the words, but I feel them. Sadness. Regret. Despair.

I reach the hall. The tiles are ice cold to the skin of my feet and each step sends a shiver up my legs, into my spine. I breathe out. The air is so cold I can see my breaths.

The music comes from the lounge. The door is closed. I push it open. A soft light on in there. I never leave the light on in there at night. Long shadows reach out toward me from the table light, but there's no one inside.

I walk in. The music is so loud now. How have the boys not woken up?

I head to the stereo. My legs are weak, the ground distant.

I press the power button and the room plunges into silence. I can't even hear my breaths, I'm trying so hard to be quiet.

Then a creak behind me. Not a floorboard. A door?

I spin on the spot. The lounge door remains wide open. But I heard the noise. Distinctive. Hinges. A door.

And the music?

Someone is in the house.

With panicked breaths, my body shuddering, I step forward again, the sound of my own breathing breaking through now and making me even more nervous.

My eyes focus out in the hall. The little diagonal door, that leads to the understairs cupboard, is directly in front of me.

Directly in front of me, and open an inch or two.

I don't know why but I go forward still.

No, I do know why, because I have to get out of here. I have to get past that door. Up the stairs to my brothers. To safety?

I'm a yard away when I see movement. I hear that same creaking noise again.

I freeze. Watch.

The gap between the door and frame ever so slowly widens. Ever so slowly. Did it even happen at all?

I squint, push my head forward, staring at the gap, I just want to get past and away...

But the door bursts open...

A roar of rage. A dark figure lunges. A face. Open mouth. Teeth bared. Anger.

He comes at me. Speed. Surprise. Viciousness. Terror.

There's nothing I can do...

It's...

It's Ed.

I opened my eyes. But I didn't move. I didn't scream. I couldn't. Fear had paralysed me. My breaths came hard, like I'd run a mile. My body felt clammy. My eyes moved about the room. My room. My space. Relief? No.

Because I wasn't alone.

The figure stood in the doorway. A silhouette with the bright light of the hall behind them. A big, looming figure, looking down on me.

I went to scream, to jump up, but, just like in that dream, I couldn't find the strength.

I did manage to whip my hand out from under the covers to turn the bedside light on.

'Frankie?'

He squinted at the light. Me too.

'What the hell?' I said. 'What are you doing?' I jolted up in the bed, pulling the covers with me, still recovering from the nightmare.

Or was this still part of it?

'I heard you,' he said. 'You were making these really weird noises.'

'What noises?'

'Just... groaning. Moaning.'

Perhaps I had been. But he'd just been standing there... looking at me. Perhaps I was overthinking it, coming straight out of the dream, but seeing him there, like that, really freaked me out.

'I'm fine,' I said. I looked at my phone. Gone 2am.

'You sure?'

'Yeah.'

'Okay then.' He lingered. Didn't he? I wasn't exactly with it. What was with him?

Then, without another word, Frankie turned and ever so casually walked away.

CHAPTER THIRTY-THREE

I slept in until after nine the next morning. Not my intention at all, although I think my troubled mind needed it, and it wasn't as though I'd enjoyed good sleep. Not until after 6am, at least, when I heard Tom going to the toilet, and somehow the onset of morning told my weary brain that I had nothing left to be scared of.

Downstairs Tom had fixed himself breakfast. Quite unusual. He seemed quite upbeat. Frankie wasn't up, though by the time I'd finished my toast and headed into the lounge with a cup of tea, there he was, lying on the sofa in his dressing gown.

'Didn't realise you were here,' I said.

'I wasn't.' He didn't look at me.

'So?' Tom said, looking around at us from his position on the floor.

'So?' I answered.

'What did you see?'

My tired brain took me back to my dream. To the cupboard under the stairs. That music which I could still hear in my mind.

To Frankie standing over me, staring...

No sooner had I sat down on the two-seater adjacent to Frankie had Tom bounced onto the cushion next to me.

'Je-essss!'

I looked at him, not quite with his train of thought yet.

'The camera!' he said. 'Did they come? I tried my hardest to stay awake but I couldn't.'

As I finally understood, the images from my sleep vanished.

I really didn't know if it was good for his mental health to be so bought into the idea of trying to see the ghosts of his parents. Frankie looked over at me and shook his head, despondent.

I checked the app.

'Nothing, Tommo. Just the notification I got when you first went to bed.'

Last night within half an hour of me leaving his room, I'd had the ping on my phone. The camera had started recording when he jumped out of bed, waving his arms in the air. The over-the-top movement suggested to me that he'd already made a more subtle attempt before that. I'd watched him in real time for a couple of minutes until he'd climbed back into bed.

'Show me,' he said, pulling the screen toward him. He initially smiled as he watched himself goofing around.

'I told you it'd work,' Frankie grumbled. 'You don't need to set it off deliberately.'

Tom's face soured. 'Is that it?' He pushed the screen back my way.

'Yeah. It didn't capture anything else.'

'But... that isn't all of it.'

'All of what?'

'It stopped before I got back into bed.'

Had it? I remembered watching in real time.

'It only records for a minute,' Frankie said.

'A minute after the motion stops, I think,' I added.

I replayed the recorded file again. Sure enough it ended

with Tom still messing, out of bed. A minute and twenty-six seconds total length.

'Didn't you go to the toilet too?' Frankie asked. 'Early this morning.'

Yes, he had. That was when I'd finally properly relaxed.

'I didn't even get a ping for that,' I said to Frankie. 'Did you?'

He shook his head.

'Great. Night number one and we have glitches already.'

Tom sank next to me. 'I knew we'd miss them. I knew it wouldn't work in the dark.'

'It's not because of the dark, you idiot,' Frankie said.

Tom growled at him. He picked up the cushion from the sofa and tossed it at his brother's head before he stomped out the room.

Frankie batted the cushion away and smirked.

'What's with you?' I asked.

'Nothing.'

'Then why the bad attitude?'

He didn't say anything. Once again I thought back to the night. To Frankie standing there, staring at me in my sleep at 2am.

'No need to take things out on Tom. Let's try and help him, yeah.'

'If you say so.'

'Yeah, I just did. Can you check both the cameras for me?' I asked him. 'Make sure they're actually working still.'

'Guess so.'

We both went silent for a few moments. What was his problem? But I didn't want us falling out.

'You got any plans today?' I asked.

'Dunno.'

'Fair enough. Then can you stay in and look after Tom? I need to run some errands.'

He groaned. 'Don't be too long. I'm not staying in all day.'

'You said you have no plans.'

'Well I'll make some.'

I rolled my eyes at him as I got up.

I moved to the door. I stopped a couple of steps away as my eyes fell on the cupboard under the stairs. The door was closed, as it normally was, but that dream, the vividness of it, the music and the melodic woman's voice filled with regret and sadness, burned away in my mind once more.

What I should have done was reach forward and open the door and clear up for my panicked brain that nothing lay inside there but clutter. Probably not even any space for an adult to lurk in.

Instead I dashed out of there and across the hall, squeezing my eyes shut.

I found the solicitors' office in town, not far from Plaza, taking up the first floor above a bakers and a hairdressers. Not a big place at all, with a small open-plan space for four paralegals – or whatever the underlings were called – three of those spaces occupied by young women; and two offices for the head honchos, one of which was Talbot. Each of the office doors was closed, each of them had a little brass name plaque. The sole receptionist – another young woman – let me in through the security locked door and showed me to a seat in the corner next to her tiny reception desk, where I sat, staring at Talbot's door.

I glanced across the young women in the office. All deep in concentration doing whatever it is they did, all were classically pretty, nice suits and tight blouses, make-up, neatly styled hair. I wondered about the small firm's intake criteria.

Perhaps if I dressed nicely and put a bit of make-up on then I could get a job with them, I thought dryly.

More than fifteen minutes after our scheduled appointment, Talbot's office door finally opened. He didn't move from there as he looked over, smiled and beckoned.

I got up and headed toward him, aware of his keen eyes on me, as they had been each time I'd met him now. Was that his manner with everyone? I really had no barometer to compare against, though I did notice a couple of the other workers glance up at me as I passed, though I couldn't read the looks they gave me. Sympathy or suspicion?

Talbot's office was cramped, cluttered with textbooks and files, though somehow he'd managed to fit both a large desk, and a small round table in there. We took the table, big enough really only for his laptop, which lay there, lid closed. He placed a file on top.

'Please, hang your coat there if you like?' he said, indicating the hooks on the back of the closed door.

I did so, though when I turned back to him I noted the flick of his eyes, up and down me. Too bad for him I'd come in not particularly shapely jeans and a big hoodie – a deliberate move, because I'd noted his wandering eyes previously.

He sat back in his chair, me on the other seat which, given the tiny table pushed into the corner of the room, was pretty much next to him.

A knock on the door and Talbot called out before the receptionist poked her head in to offer a drink. I declined. Talbot too.

'How are you getting on?' he asked me when the door was once again closed.

'About the same really.'

I'd spoken to him on the phone the day before, explaining about the money I'd been given by my aunt and uncle, and hoped that extra cash, together with any news he had on the other areas, would see us in a decent position we could move forward from.

'I guess you'd like an update on where I've got to?' he asked.

Would there be another reason for me being there? 'Please?'

'Your brothers are okay?'

'Under the circumstances.'

'Good, good.' His relaxed nature grated on me. He opened the file and looked through, as though he didn't already know what he'd find in there. 'I have the final figures now for all pensions, and also a settlement figure for the mortgage. We need to work out logistics for the extra money you've come into, which is in your name, rather than part of the estate, but if we factor that in, the current excess mortgage figure, which I know is the area of biggest concern, is around £80,000.'

'Eighty?' A lot higher than I'd hoped for, and that I'd calculated myself based on the figures we discussed last time.

He turned the schedule around for me to see. I scanned over the numbers.

'The problem is, Jess, the mortgage, like many these days, is quite restrictive. There are surcharges for repaying such big amounts early, perhaps another fee to transfer the balance to you, though I haven't shown that yet. But all these things need to be factored in. Plus, you'll see I've added my fees into the calculation now too, which is everything before today.'

His fees, which were already close to £20,000. What exactly had he done?

'Will the bank transfer that mortgage balance to me?' I asked.

He sighed. 'You'll have to go through some of the process yourself, there's only so much I can do from my side. The key will be to prove your income stream. Do you have a job lined up yet?'

I'd looked online, but I hadn't had a chance to do any serious searching. Until the boys went back to school in a few days I was too busy trying to sort out everything else.

I shook my head.

'You'll need that sooner rather than later to avoid any problems,' he said to me as though speaking to a petulant child who'd already been told the same thing multiple times.

'Problems?'

'Clearly the worst case is that the mortgage provider asks for their money back. Have you spoken to them at all yet?'

I had, but only to understand my options, and I hadn't really taken much of it in properly at the time.

'Not recently,' I said.

'There'll be various elements to consider if they do transfer to you, in order for you to reduce monthly payments. Perhaps extend the term from the current sixteen years, or change to a different product, but... like I said, they could call it back and make you pay if that's their prerogative.'

'But I can't pay.'

'Then you'd need to sell the house.'

I swallowed hard.

'Unfortunately a lot of these big banks have their rules set. Emotion doesn't really come into their decisions. But there will be a way. I can see why you'd want to avoid moving. It's not an easy, or cheap solution. Selling fees, buying fees, stamp duty. It could cost you twenty to thirty thousand pounds to buy somewhere else.'

Was it just me or was he really enjoying putting me down?

'I'm not moving.'

He slowly nodded, as though he completely understood and agreed. He sighed, in such a way as people do when they're about to reluctantly offer help.

'I can make some calls if you like?' he said. 'I told you before it's not my sphere of expertise, but there is the possibility to switch mortgage provider; it might be more simple than moving, and I do have contacts with some specialist outfits. Not your high street brands, you understand, but these are people that you might find more receptive, given your position.'

That sounded good to me, but when I looked back down at the schedule, at the line with his ever-increasing fee, did I really want to sink more money into his services? Surely he wouldn't do anything for me for free.

'Nearly twenty thousand for your fees,' I said.

As I looked up he was staring at me, not blinking. As though he didn't like this kind of challenge, like I was questioning his integrity.

Was I?

'I can give you a full breakdown if you're concerned about costs.' His eyes moved over me again. Actually, what I wanted was for him to stop staring at me like that.

'These are the fees based on the rates I agreed with your parents. But... Jess, I know the position you're in. I know how hard this is for you, and I really do want to help, any way I can.'

He reached out and put his hand on my knee.

I froze.

'It is possible that I could restructure this for you. I'm sure we could find a way, if you really want to?' His hand remained on my knee as he smiled at me, thirst in his eyes. His fingers moved back and forth, rubbing my skin underneath. I couldn't move. My breathing and my heart ramped up.

'What do you think, Jess? For you, I'm happy to make special arrangements to reduce my costs.'

Was this really happening? Or had I misread his intentions, even if to me his actions felt so obviously wrong?

He took his hand from my knee, but only because he leaned forward, hand out, coming toward me, as if to cup my face.

I jumped up out of the seat. He reeled back, shocked by my sudden move.

'Yes, Mr Talbot. I appreciate the offer.'

'Okay, but–'

'I expect next time we speak that you'll have reduced the fees as you suggested.'

I turned for my coat.

'Jess, I'm not sure–'

I spun and glared at him.

'You're going to reduce those fees, aren't you?'

A stare-off ensued. My show of force had rattled him. I could tell by the look in his eyes. But had I done enough? Did I need to threaten him too? I really didn't want to, because there remained some doubt in my mind as to whether I'd misread the situation.

'I'll see what I can do,' he said, sounding a bit pissed off. 'But I *think* I made my position clear. The more you help me, the more I can help you.'

I squirmed at the thoughts building in my mind, then opened the door and walked out.

Really, it was either that, or run up and kick him in the balls.

Perhaps I should have chosen the latter.

My brain remained on fire as I headed home. That little bit of doubt lurked in my mind still, but it was definitely little. The hand on the knee. That look in his eyes. The offer of a reduced fee. A sexual proposition?

I felt sick. I felt foolish. Had other clients fallen for that trick? Did I have a duty to do something about it? But who would I tell? I could imagine a police officer laughing in my face if I said I wanted to report a middle-aged solicitor for putting his hand on my knee. Holster? She probably already thought I was nuts. A conspiracist.

Yet that was part of the issue. A hand on a knee. A hand on the side or the shoulder. An egregious look here, there. A stare on a bus or a train. Small things, some would say, but symptoms of a much larger problem.

I remembered Mum talking to me about men several times in my early teens. All of the warnings she gave me, all of the little tricks too for getting out of awkward, potentially dangerous situations. All of the everyday advice that was second nature to me, and many others. Don't walk alone at night. Don't have your earphones in when walking or running alone – day *or* night. Always have your phone at hand. Cover up on public transport. Be careful taking solo taxis, etc., etc., etc. Unwritten rules to live by, that I'm sure every mother passed down to their daughters.

But what about sons? Did fathers – mothers too – not have the conversation with their sons to tell them what *not* to do? To tell them that certain behaviours were simply not acceptable? Why was it down to potential victims to monitor their behaviours to not get caught out?

On a more personal note, had Mum or Dad ever had such a conversation with Frankie, I wondered? Or had they left it to him to figure out acceptability in his interactions with the opposite sex. I would have said Frankie was a nice, level-headed teenager – most of the time at least – but I had no clue really what went on in his mind. Every girl I knew my age had a story to tell of harassment, and more than a few had stories of much more serious assault. By the same token, would every boy my age know someone who'd committed one of those acts?

More pertinently, with Mum and Dad gone, was it down to me to have that conversation with Frankie to prevent him from becoming an aggressor either now or in the future?

Seriously distracted as I walked along our street, I spotted the man up ahead. He glanced at me, then back to the car he was standing by, before doing a double-take.

I went to cross over the road to the other side, toward our home, those thoughts of the awkwardness with Talbot still playing on my mind, But when the man held my eye, and stepped toward me, for some reason I stayed. 'Can I help you?' I asked him, sounding up for the challenge, to my surprise.

'Jess?' he said, when I was a couple of yards away. He was mid-height, jeans, winter coat. Beanie hat. His face... plain.

I didn't know him. Did I?

'Yeah?'

'I'm... my name's David, I live nearby.'

'Hi,' I said, unease already growing.

'How are you?'

'Fine, really.' Who was he? A neighbour?

'And your brothers?'

'We're coping. As best we can. Sorry, did you know my mum and dad?'

'Yes. I did. Not so much recently though.'

I nodded, even though his answer, his whole manner, seemed a little odd really.

'I'm really sorry for what happened,' he added.

'Thanks.'

'Say hi to Tom and Frankie.' With that he walked off.

CHAPTER THIRTY-FOUR

S till creeped out as I arrived home, matters weren't helped by Frankie's continued weirdness with me. He shut himself in his room for most of the afternoon, and Tom was in and out of his too, giving me plenty of time on my own. A bit too much really, I'd rather have had some company.

As I sat in the lounge, struggling to hold my attention on the TV, I found myself continually looking over to the doorway, outside to that cupboard under the stairs, as though it was calling me in.

Eventually I sucked up some courage, and before I could talk myself out of it I strode across the room, out into the hall, grasped the handle, and pulled open the cupboard door.

Adrenaline surged as I stared inside, but I soon calmed when I confirmed the obvious. No intruder in there. No demon, or bogeyman or anything like that. A few of Mum and Dad's old coats. Walking shoes, wellies. Boxes at the back. What were those?

I got down onto my knees and reached inside. Pulled a box toward me. Old photo albums, from before we had a digital camera. I smiled as I flicked through the top album, holiday snaps from a trip to Malta when me and Frankie were little. Six and three, perhaps. A lifetime ago.

Mum and Dad looked so young, and happy. I could scarcely remember them being like that.

I pulled the box further out, onto the hall tiles. I'd take a good look through all the pictures. Perhaps reminiscing about those days would soothe my troubled mind.

First, though, I grabbed another box. Bills. Water, electricity, gas. Not very interesting. Why had they bothered to keep all those?

I got hold of the last box and dragged it out. Bank statements. Piles, and piles of bank statements. Talbot had shown me some recent ones, though honestly, other than looking for evidence of a purchase from a hardware store of some kind for that damn rope, I'd not paid attention to them much. The only other important thing really was the current balance, which went into the estate pot, the money we needed to help keep our house, and to keep us fed.

I flicked through the papers in my fingers, then I took the box and carried it out into the lounge. With the boys occupied, I spent more than an hour leafing through each page of nearly five years' worth of bank statements. To start with I felt horribly invasive, as though I was delving into private affairs I had no business knowing about. In a way, even with my parents no longer alive, that point remained. But I wasn't looking out of pure curiosity, or to be nosy, I was looking for a reason. *The* reason. Clues as to my parents' problems, clues as to what had caused my dad to make the horrific step to kill himself, if he really had.

By the time I'd finished going through each statement, I had two piles. One much larger than the other. The smaller one contained those where I'd noted something of interest, and all of those were from within the last twelve months. I picked that pile up and looked through again.

Deep in thought, I jumped when I spotted the figure in the doorway. 'Bloody hell, Frankie!'

He was standing there, again. Just like in the night.

'Are you deliberately trying to scare me out of my skin?'

He frowned, as though he had no clue what I was on about. 'What you doing?' he asked, moving into the room.

'Come and take a look.'

He moved over, confusion etched on his face, and took the seat next to me on the sofa.

'Mum and Dad's bank statements?' he said, his face screwing up. 'Isn't that a bit...'

'A bit what?'

'Well you weren't impressed when I had Dad's phone, were you?'

I said nothing about that. 'Take a look at this.' I pulled out a couple of the statements and pointed to the withdrawals. 'I've found three of these from the last few weeks. Cash withdrawals. One for £3,000. Two for £5,000. Those last two were only three days apart.'

'Right before...'

Right before Dad's birthday, I think he'd tried to say.

'That's £13,000. Cash.'

'It wasn't me,' Frankie said, a little defensively.

'I wasn't going to suggest it was.'

He wouldn't hold my eye. Odd.

'Were they doing any work on the house, or anything?' I asked. 'So needed the money for a builder or something?'

Frankie frowned as he thought. 'Not that I noticed. What about Dad's presents? Or a holiday?'

'Not for that amount. And no reason they'd take out cash to pay for things like that.'

'Then who did they give that money to?'

'Who, and why.'

We both went silent for a few moments.

'Anything else?' Frankie asked.

'Maybe,' I said.

I pointed to a transaction on one of the same statements.

'Do you know what that is?' I asked him.

'No idea.'

'I've noticed loads of payments with the same reference. Pretty regular. Particularly over the last year where there's at least two a month.'

'For what?'

'It's a therapist. Yasmine Lowton.'

Frankie glanced at me. 'Like a... psychiatrist?'

'Kind of.' Though I didn't really fully understand the differences between the terms therapist, psychologist, psychiatrist, and the name of this therapist wasn't the same one Mum and Dad had sent me to a few years back. 'I've googled her. She's based in town.'

'Mum and Dad were getting therapy?'

'Mum or Dad, or both, apparently. Presuming that it wasn't you or Tom, that is.'

'No way,' Frankie said, with certainty, a little defensively too, as though he had no problems at all.

'You didn't know Mum and Dad were?' I asked.

Frankie shook his head. 'I feel like... I feel like I don't even know them,' he said, and he looked genuinely upset about that.

'Just because we didn't know everything about them, doesn't mean they didn't love us,' I said. 'Or each other. Everyone has things they don't tell others.'

He hung his head. I put my arm around him. 'What's up?'

'Do you know the last thing I said to Dad?'

Even though his words came a bit out of the blue, his

241

question struck a chord with me. The last time I'd seen my parents had been far from perfect. Dad's party, and the morning after. Mum hadn't even been there to wave me off. I never did find out why, as I never spoke to her again after that except for those few seconds on the phone as she rushed back home after hearing of Dad's suicide. And Dad? He'd hardly been in a great mood the morning I returned to uni either, though thinking now, as I had done so many times, I couldn't remember exactly the words we'd shared, which only made me all the more sad.

'What did you say to him?' I asked.

Frankie scoffed. '"Nah, next time maybe."'

We went silent. Awkwardness and sadness filled the gap in the conversation.

The way he'd delivered the words... regret and self-hatred.

He looked up at me. 'I was in my room. On my phone. He came in and asked if I wanted to go on a bike ride. I don't even think I looked at him. I was too busy texting Meg. He didn't even know about her.'

Silence again.

'He went out on his bike on his own. I left and went over to Meg's because her old man was playing golf and then going to the pub afterwards. Next time I saw Dad...'

He closed his eyes, I think as he relived that moment of walking into the garage.

'And Mum?' he said, eyes still closed. 'I don't think I even spoke to her that day. The last time was the day before when I said good night to her. I didn't even hug her.'

I pulled him close and we sat there a while, not speaking. Frankie's moods continued to be up and down, I didn't get him fully, I didn't know what was happening in his fragile mind, and some of his behaviours worried me, but above anything else I couldn't lose sight of the fact that he was a grieving seventeen-year-old. And he was my brother. I had to be a rock for him.

We released and I looked down at the bank statements again.

'I just want to know why,' he said.

'Me too.'

He looked at me, as though he still didn't trust me. As though he believed I knew something he didn't.

'Frankie, what if... what if he didn't do it.'

'Dad?'

I nodded.

He looked really confused. 'But the police–'

'Police can make mistakes. But... doesn't it–'

'Seem like he wouldn't ever do that.'

I didn't say anything.

'Are you serious?' he asked, looking more worried.

'I... think so.'

'Why didn't you tell me before?'

'Because... I don't know if I'm just crazy, and I didn't want to worry you any more.'

'Why would someone do that to him?'

'I don't know.'

'Is there anything... any–'

'Evidence?'

'I guess that's what I meant.'

'Not really,' I said with a sigh. 'But I asked the police to check some of his things for fingerprints. I just thought... perhaps after that intruder... what if it's all...' I really struggled to get the words out, without sounding crazy, without scaring him.

'So the police are looking into it?'

'Kind of. Not really. Maybe it's nothing. But we have to know.'

'I don't even know if that prospect makes everything better or worse,' he said.

243

I agreed one hundred per cent with that. 'I'll see what I can find out about the therapy,' I said, changing the subject, slightly at least. 'And I'll have a think about that cash. Suicide or not, something caused this to happen.'

'You think it's all related? To what happened?'

'I hope so,' I said, because we really did need some explanations.

Frankie's phone buzzed. He lifted it from his pocket. His eyes flicked across the screen and he looked a little perturbed about something. 'Is it okay if I go out?' he asked.

'With Meg?'

A slight delay. 'Yeah.'

'It's fine,' I said to him.

'I won't be late.' He got up from the sofa and headed on out.

I sat alone, in the kitchen, while Tom played. My mind was a mess, I just couldn't think straight at all. I'd made the leap and tried to explain my thinking to Frankie but I wasn't sure I'd done the right thing, nor that I'd coherently put my thoughts across.

My phone buzzed on the countertop, shaking me back to reality. A mobile number I didn't recognise.

'Jess, it's DS Holster.'

'Oh,' was my lame response. I looked at my watch. Seven thirty. 'Is there a problem?'

'No, sorry to call you late. Can you talk?'

'Yes.' My heart thudded in my chest. An update? But what did I even want the result to be?

'We've done everything we can to process the fingerprints from the items in your home, from the night you had the break-in, but also from... from the garage.'

I think my heart stopped at that point, just for a few beats.

'Did you find anything.'

'Nothing useful. Just the prints from your family members.

A few very small fragments too which we can't really do much with. We also did the house to house, and I've had a colleague go over nearby CCTV towers.'

'That's a lot of work in a day or so,' I said, though I wasn't really sure what my point was.

'I wanted to get the results for you ASAP, because I can see the effect the doubt is having on you. But, Jess, there really is nothing at all that I can see to suggest anyone at all was involved in your dad's death.'

We both went silent for a few moments. I didn't know what to say. Should I be happy?

'Are you still there?' Holster asked.

'Yes. And the intruder?' I finally said.

'Again. Nothing.'

I didn't say another word before the call ended. I couldn't. I really didn't know what to think.

I'd never been so confused, or felt so lost.

Wine. I needed wine. I just needed something to take the edge off my anxiety which had been peaked for... I don't know how long, but which had certainly spiked even further somehow following the day I'd had. I picked a bottle of posh-looking red from the rack in the kitchen. Not a super-posh bottle – the ones Mum and Dad kept for special occasions were in the garage. I wasn't going in there while Frankie was out, even if I'd been minded to have one of those.

I'd got through most of the bottle, still sitting by the kitchen island on my own while Tom occupied himself, when the email came through on my phone. Talbot. I wondered if he'd actually taken the time to write it out – his chubby fingers tapping ungainly on his laptop keyboard – or if one of the paralegals had done the legwork for him.

I read through the email, my sadness being pushed out with

each word as anger swarmed inside me. I heard his condescending voice in my mind.

All figures are now finalised. The balance remaining owing on the mortgage after offsetting all of the various pensions and insurance policies and cash balances, as of the date of this letter, is £87,903. Please let me know, once you have reached agreement with the Bank, how you wish to proceed with this so that we can work toward concluding the matters of the Estate. I would remind you that in the interim, interest will continue to accrue on the mortgage balance and I'd encourage you to seek closure as soon as possible.

I tensed as I reread the formal words. No offer of help with the mortgage now that I'd spurned him. I was on my own. I imagined he'd took pleasure in writing out those words, knowing how impossible it was for me to pay that remaining balance.

The invoice for my fees is attached here, including the goodwill adjustment we discussed.

I turned over the page, my eyes flicking to the bottom. I nearly tore the paper in two. He'd taken off five hundred pounds.

'Bastard,' I said as I slapped my phone down onto the side.

I spotted the envelope on the worktop by the fridge. I frowned and stood up, swayed a little as I walked over. Unopened post. Why was it there? Most likely one of my brothers had grabbed it from the doormat and dumped it there, then forgot all about it.

The brown envelope was addressed to me. I opened it. From the council. Social services. An official appointment for next Tuesday to discuss my custody case, together with a bound, colour printed document outlining the custody process and everything that the council needed to be convinced about the suitability of a guardian. Even scanning through it made me feel sick with worry, particularly given the email I'd had from Talbot.

Was I really suitable? Other than being the boys' blood family, I hardly met any of the attributes. I was too young, I was single, I had no job, I wasn't even sure Frankie wanted me. The only benefit they both got here, with me, was the family home, but was it worth every other sacrifice to stay here? A place that would be forever haunted by memories of our lost family members? Wouldn't a foster family, a loving couple who'd spent years working with kids from all different backgrounds, be able to provide a more caring and suitable environment for my siblings?

'Jess, you okay?' I turned to see Tom in the doorway, worry lining his young features.

'Not really,' I said, downing my half glass of wine in two big gulps.

'Can I help?' he asked, in the sweetly naive way he often did.

'I don't know,' I said.

He looked confused and moved over to me. He wrapped his arms around my waist and I wrapped mine around his shoulders.

'I love you, Jess.'

'I love you too, Tom.'

But I wasn't sure that alone would be enough.

CHAPTER THIRTY-FIVE

FRANKIE

H e left home when it was still light outside, but dusk had arrived by the time he got to Ali's.

Ali's, not Meg's. He'd *wanted* to see Meg. She was too busy. Again. With what?

Why the lie to Jess? She certainly wouldn't have disapproved of him going to Ali's, but he really couldn't grasp why he hadn't simply told her the truth.

Was it because of what she'd said about Dad? That had thrown him. Confused him. Made him a little bit angry, honestly, largely because she'd clearly held that all back from him for some time.

Did he believe her?

He really didn't know. He'd been the one to walk in on Dad. He'd always just assumed the most obvious explanation was the correct one. Had *he* made a mistake?

He tried not to think about it, and Ali provided good distraction. With his parents out at work, they ended up shooting pool in the games room, kitted out for him in the basement of their home. A real teenage haven. His parents weren't exactly mega-millionaires, but their house was at least twice as big as Frankie's family home. Ali's dad drove a Porsche, his mum a Range Rover Sport, both pretty much brand new. Frankie didn't really understand what Ali's parents did for a living. Something to do with finance, and apparently it was his mum who made the most money.

Yet Ali, despite having everything he could ask for, was just like any other kid, and he and Frankie had been best friends for years, well before familial net worth had meant anything to either of them.

Frankie lined up for the pot. Ali still had four of his balls on the table. Frankie sank the black with aplomb, the ball smacking off the rim of the pocket with a satisfying *thwack*.

Ali shook his head in disgust.

'Five nil?' Frankie said, broad smile on his face. 'You need more practice, mate.'

'You sure you haven't got a table at home somewhere?'

'Natural ability,' Frankie replied with a wink. 'Not everything can be bought.'

Ali looked a little offended by that, though Frankie hadn't meant it snidely.

'Another game, or a beer?' Ali suggested.

'Beer.'

'Good choice.'

Ali fetched two bottles from the Budweiser branded beer fridge in the corner of the room and they settled down on the leather sofa, the massive flat screen on the wall in front of them.

'School in a few days,' Ali said.

Frankie took a swig but didn't say anything.

'You seen Dylan recently?' Ali asked.

Frankie had explained about the run-in the other night, though he'd told the same truncated story as he'd given Meg, rather than the whole truth.

'Nah.'

'Once we're back at school—'

'I just need to avoid him. Six more months then we're done.' Sounded easy when he said it like that.

'You know it's all because of Meg.'

'You're saying I should dump her?'

'Is it even worth the effort if you're not getting any action?'

Frankie looked away, a little embarrassed, not just at the situation between him and Meg, but because Ali knew all the details. He trusted him with those details, but he still wasn't sure he'd made the right decision in being so open.

He could trust Ali, couldn't he? Or would Ali tell Katie everything he'd said, who would in turn almost certainly feedback to Meg?

'Ah, shit,' Ali said looking at his phone. 'Sorry, mate. Katie's coming over. She said she couldn't before, but...'

'It's fine,' Frankie said.

'You not seeing Meg tonight then?'

'Said she was busy.'

'Yeah? Obviously not with Katie though.'

'Obviously not.'

He didn't go home. Too early, and his mind was too wired. He headed across town, a near two-mile walk from Ali's place to Goose Avenue. He'd texted Meg on the way to check – or was it recheck? – what she was up to but she'd brushed him off once again. Hadn't given him an explicit lie of saying she was with Katie or anything as obvious as that, but he sensed something was up.

Perhaps it was nothing. They'd seen a lot of each other recently; he didn't want to smother her, even if he couldn't get enough of her right now. Yet he also believed she was being deliberately cagey with him.

At a relatively early hour in the night, the streets were far from deserted, but Frankie was still happy to blend into the darkness in the snicket, looking out toward Meg's house.

No lights on in the front room downstairs – the lounge. No lights on in either of the upstairs windows either – hers and her dad's rooms.

So where was she? She'd claimed to be busy with coursework, and that her dad was hassling her.

He pulled out his phone, shielded the glowing screen with one hand as he typed with his thumb on the other.

If you get your work done, you could come to mine again, if you're worried about your dad?

He stood, staring at the screen as he awaited a response. Noted the blue ticks to show she'd read the message. A moment later the response pinged through.

He's being an arse. Better just leave it tonight, babe xxx

Why was she lying? He put the phone back in his pocket, looked over to the house again, his head filling with unpleasant thoughts.

But then, unexpectedly, her bedroom light came on. The curtains were still open and she rushed across the room to shut them. Once closed he could still see her figure – pottering around the room – beyond the not very thick fabric.

Getting ready? Thinking about the inside of her house, the lack of lights he could see, either she'd come into her room from the bathroom, or from the kitchen downstairs. There weren't any other rooms in the house, other than those darkened ones at the front.

He thought about texting her again, to try and get her caught deeper in the lie he believed she'd started. He didn't. Instead he watched, and watched.

Movement behind him. He whipped his head behind.

A woman, with a dog, had turned into the snicket. Frankie pulled further back into the darkness.

The woman approached. The dog pulled on its lead. It'd smelled him and was trying to get to him. Frankie held his breath. Didn't move a muscle.

The woman yanked on the dog's lead. 'Come on, Sam,' she said, exasperated.

Soon they were gone. She hadn't seen him. A sense of power returned, knowing how he blended so well into nothing.

But that power turned to anger and suspicion when he looked back to Meg's house to see her bedroom light flick off. Moments later he heard the car engine. Saw the lights push across the road from left to right. The vehicle came into view, then pulled up right outside Meg's house. A crappy old Vauxhall Corsa. Too dark to see who was driving, who else was in the car.

The door to Meg's house opened and she dashed out. She opened the back door and climbed in. The next moment the car pulled away. As it moved under a street light, the passenger in the seat next to her turned their head slightly. Just enough illumination, just enough of an angle, to reveal their face.

Dylan.

Enraged. Truly enraged. If Dylan had been standing in front of him, despite the bully's superior physicality, probably superior combat experience too, Frankie believed he'd easily be able to rip the guy's ugly head from his shoulders. He really wanted to as well.

He thumped the brick wall next to him as he hustled along the street, ignored the pain that shot through his bones.

What the hell was Meg doing? Not just the lies, but how could she bear to be anywhere near that guy?

She claimed sleeping with Dylan was a drunken mistake. That's what she'd fobbed Frankie off with. She said she hated him. She knew he did too.

What the fuck, Meg?

He carried on, walking at pace, hate and anger filling his thoughts. He turned onto the street, carried on down. No lights on at the front of 132. So they hadn't come back here. And apparently no one was home.

Good.

He slowed his pace, tried to calm his erratic thoughts as he moved around to the alley at the back of the properties. All clear there, no signs of those little shits this time. Another positive, because Frankie wasn't sure they'd get away with a simple backhanded slap again.

He counted the gates properly this time. Arrived at the back of Dylan's home. Tried the handle. Locked. The wall was seven feet high, broken glass on top of it. He had enough adrenaline in him to climb over and take the cuts and scrapes, but he really didn't want to.

Then he spotted it. The open gate next door. He crept that way, staying close to the wall. Peered through the gap. Lights on in the kitchen at the back, but no one in sight.

He moved across to the other side of the open doorway.

Perfect. As he'd hoped, the wall separating the two backyards was lower than the outer ones, and also not covered in broken glass.

He looked to the house in front of him once more. Still no sign of anyone in the lit kitchen. He took his chance and darted into the yard, straight to the wall, grabbed the top, scrambled up and over.

He landed in Dylan's backyard. Shook his head in disgust. Weeds everywhere, broken paving, broken outdoor toys, bin bags filled with who knew what. Loser. Him and his whole family, all the same.

He moved up to the back wall of the house, to the back doors – an ageing pair of uPVC patio doors, heavily weathered. No lights on beyond.

He tried the handle. Why not? Locked. And he had no clue how to pick a lock. He'd never done anything like this before. But he did want to get inside.

Why?

Because he hated Dylan. He hated him more than he'd ever hated anyone or anything. And he wanted, *needed*, to find a way to punish him.

That was his heart talking. His head? A little more rational. But only a little. He'd wanted to do this for a few days now. Ever since the night they'd had the intruder in their home. Ever since he'd realised his dad's phone was missing. Whatever Jess's theory, it all fitted. Dylan had broken into their home that night, intent on further punishing Frankie following the run-in on the street. Frankie's Dad's phone had gone missing that very same night too. It had to be him.

Yet why would Dylan take the phone?

Why wouldn't he? He was a horrible, thieving bastard. The phone was probably the first thing he'd got his grubby hands on, rummaging through Frankie's room before he'd made a run for it.

Frankie would get it back. And he'd get revenge.

He looked over the rest of the back of the house. The

window to the kitchen was shut. Another ageing fixture. Could he prise it open somehow? He could try. He might not need to. Above him one of the upstairs windows was ajar. Why, on a cold winter's night, he had no clue. Ventilation, perhaps? Or maybe just because Dylan and his family were morons. Or maybe because no one in the area was dumb enough to break in. He parked that thought. Not helpful.

A drainpipe to his right. He could do this.

He grasped the drainpipe, hands high above his head, then jumped up, lifting his feet, knees to his chest, to place his toes onto the handle of the back door. He held the position a moment to steady himself, then, hands sliding up the drainpipe, he stretched his body up.

His hands were only a few inches from the windowsill above. But how to get there?

He took a deep breath, then, before he could talk himself out of it, he shimmied across to the drainpipe, putting the toes of one foot onto the bracket holding the pipe to the wall. He reached up higher with his hands, one on the drainpipe, one on the windowsill. His foot slipped and he was left swinging, scrabbling with his feet. He couldn't hold on, he had to let go...

No. His foot found traction and he heaved with everything he could. Grabbed the window, pulled it further open, and somehow managed to pull his body up and through the open space. He went in head first, his body tumbling up over him as he landed in a panting heap on the cold lino floor of a bathroom.

He took a moment to compose himself, listened. All quiet inside.

He stood up, moved out to the landing. The house was tiny. Pretty much a mirror of Meg's with only two other doors in front of him. Both open. He peeked in the first. Mum's room. Cluttered and messy. He moved to the other. The boys' room. Dylan had two brothers, both younger, but both as brutish as the older, both of them often tormenting kids at school several years older than they were, all the while backed up by the knowledge that anyone who fought back might have to answer to the big man himself.

Frankie hated them all. He stood in the doorway, looking at their cramped space, a bunk bed in one corner, which he presumed the younger two slept in, and a camp bed style single adjacent to it, presumably for Dylan. There was barely enough room for three people to stand in the remaining space and he felt a little sorry for them all. Sorry for their circumstances at least.

No, he couldn't think that. He detested everything about them.

He moved into the room. Other than the beds, the only other furniture in the room was a wardrobe and a set of drawers. Frankie looked through. Soon finished. No luck. He moved to the camp bed. Looked under the pillow, under the mattress. Interesting. A tablet computer hidden there. A bag of weed too. Some money.

Frankie left it all in place.

He looked under the bed.

Still no phone.

He rose up and thought. First and foremost he'd come here for the phone. No success there, but he'd also come to punish Dylan somehow. But how? Break things? Steal something?

Now he was on the inside, those ideas all seemed so... crude. Wrong. And he didn't even know if this stuff was Dylan's or his brothers'. Not that he owed any of them any goodwill.

He took the tablet with him, then moved out to the landing, slowly and quietly down the stairs. Into the front room – a cramped lounge that somehow had a mammoth corner sofa, and a widescreen TV as big as the one in Ali's games room. An Xbox and a PlayStation console too, games cases spread across the floor. Frankie walked across.

A phone on the sofa arm. He picked it up.

Not his dad's.

He sighed. Should he take that too?

What the hell was he doing here?

The initial adrenaline, that red mist feeling, had well and truly dissipated and he didn't want to be inside anymore.

He turned to head back out, then froze when he heard footsteps. Outside. A pause. A key in the lock of the front door.

Shit.

Knife in his pocket? Yes, it was there. But... Frankie dropped the tablet and bolted. Out of the lounge. A quick glance to the front as the door opened. At least it wasn't Dylan. His mum. Youngest brother.

Frankie turned to scarper. The hall light came on and a scream filled the space. He ignored it. Darted into a pokey dining room, toward the back doors. Key in lock, thankfully.

He twisted the key, pushed down on the handle.

'Get out!' came the shout behind him. He didn't look back, but the next moment flinched at the crash above him when the projectile smashed into the door frame. Shards of crockery fell down over his head and shoulders. 'Get out, you piece of shit!'

Pure venom in the woman's voice, rather than surprise or fear.

Frankie pushed the door open and darted into the yard, over the wall to next door, into the alley. Didn't look back at all. He sprinted. And sprinted. And sprinted, until his legs turned to jelly and his lungs ached and he couldn't move anymore.

Then he pulled up against a wall, trying to catch his out-of-control breath, his brain swimming... and a feeling of abject failure sweeping over him.

CHAPTER THIRTY-SIX

Too much wine. I knew even as I opened the second bottle that it wasn't a good idea, but that didn't stop me. With Tom in bed, and Frankie still out, another night of solitude ahead of me, I decided the wine would at least make the hours pass by with a certain distant numbness.

I had no doubt that being at home with the boys day in, day out, was creating strain for all of us. Not long to go before they were back at school and we'd at least get a break from each other. On the other hand, with Frankie out, and Tom in bed, me alone on the sofa in the lounge drinking into a blur, I had no distraction from my continued chaotic thoughts, which somehow intensified rather than dulled from the alcohol.

So much for numbness. Perhaps I just needed to keep on drinking.

As I sat there, my increasingly weary gaze flitted between the TV, the piles of bank statements on the side table by the stereo, and to the door for the understairs cupboard out in the hall. Really the TV may as well have been off as I had no idea what was happening in the romcom that was nearly a third of the way through.

I hit the standby button and the screen turned black. Yet after a few minutes, with the room swaying around me, I realised that at least the background noise had helped keep me calm and grounded.

Alone in the quiet, my thoughts turned more and more to the cupboard, that nightmare I'd had.

Why couldn't I shake the feeling of terror? I'd looked in the cupboard earlier. Nothing in there but junk, but my brain remained unconvinced.

I decided I was better off with the TV on after all. I picked up the remote, had my finger on the power button when a sound out in the hallway made me freeze.

A soft, tapping sound. Like hard nails against wood. I imagined a hunched figure, leathery skin, long pointed nails. I tensed, staring at the cupboard door. Expected it to burst open any second and for a devilish figure to leap out at me.

A devilish figure... How ridiculous, because the face of the figure in my dream was Ed's. About the least threatening face I could think of... except for in the dream, where his features had somehow been hideous and terrifying.

The noise came again. A little louder this time. A little more obvious what it was. Someone knocking – more like tapping – on the front door.

On edge, I got up from the sofa, putting my hand onto the arm to steady me. I shuffled pathetically to the doorway, using the wall to guide me, before rushing past the cupboard door. Only as I approached the front did I realise the absurdity of me being more scared of that damn cupboard than about the unannounced figure outside, tapping on the door like that.

I pulled the security chain over – just in case – before opening up.

'Hi,' he said.

For a few seconds I couldn't speak. Something to do both

with my alcohol-addled brain and with the way the small gap framed his face...

'Ed?'

'Sorry, it's not a bad time, is it?' he asked, looking uncomfortable. Perhaps he could tell I was blind drunk. 'I thought Tom might be in bed already, so was trying not to be too loud.'

'He is.'

Silence again.

'Do you think... I could come in?'

'Yes, sure, why not. Come and join the p-a-r-t-y.'

He looked at me like I was an idiot. Well... I closed the door, released the security chain, reopened. We both hesitated before I stepped aside and Ed came in. I closed the door but then we hovered in the hallway.

'Are you okay?' he asked.

'What do you think?'

'You're drunk.'

'Bingo, bango, got it in one.' I playfully punched him on the arm. Though the way he squirmed suggested maybe it wasn't playful enough.

He shook his head, disappointment.

Join the club, I thought.

Still, he took his coat off.

'Come on through,' I said. I swayed back to the lounge, brushing into the wall not once but twice. We ended up side by side on the sofa, Ed sitting forward, stiff, like someone had rammed an iron bar through him.

I grabbed my wine glass from the coaster on the floor. 'Want one?'

'I... er... I'm fine.'

'Suit yourself.' I took a glug.

'How much have you had?'

'Not enough.'

'Are you sure... are you sure this is the way?'

'Yes, Ed, this is the way to get drunk. I thought you liked me better this way.' I held his eye. I couldn't read the look on his face. Probably because his face was morphing as I tried to focus. Despite my drunken bravado, images of my nightmare – Ed springing out at me – flashed in my mind. Was I right to have let him inside?

'Right, well, I'm here now, so... I wanted to say sorry. For the other night.'

'At the bar?' I asked.

He nodded.

'For being a grumpy git?' I chuckled. He didn't.

'I was out of order. I wasn't myself.'

Out of order? I shrugged.

'Your choice. Whatever. I mean, I've barely seen you for a couple of years, my life is falling apart, but yeah, have a big sulk on a night out. Why not?'

He shook his head. Opened his mouth to respond. I thought. Or maybe that was a hallucination. Or maybe he'd opened his mouth to kiss me.

If he tried that tonight... actually, I really didn't know.

'I know you've got so much going on in your life,' he said, still sounding so calm and... Ed like, 'and the last thing I want to do is make things more difficult for you–'

'Why didn't you tell me about her?'

He paused and held my eye.

'Claire,' I said, my tone not hiding an unexpected bitterness.

His face remained deadpan. 'I guessed someone would have told you. Jamie, by any chance?'

'Maybe it was... maybe it wasn't.'

Ed's body moved sideways, like he was about to fall off the sofa with a...

Smack.

No. Not him moving. Me. My head butted against the back of the sofa. Ed reached out to help me.

'I'm fine!' I blasted. Then, after a moment. 'Why didn't *you* tell me though?'

He scratched his head, looking nervous, worried too. About himself, or me? 'I honestly don't know. I'm really not good at this kind of thing. She's the first... the first girlfriend I've ever had.'

'I'm pleased for you,' I slurred, though he didn't look convinced by my words. 'It's serious?'

He didn't answer straight away. 'I think so... or... it was.'

'Was?'

He closed his eyes and shook his head. 'I'm such an idiot.'

I laughed. 'Yeah. The most intelligent idiot I've ever met. But definitely an idiot.'

'Wow, thanks.'

I tried not to laugh again. I'm not sure he appreciated it.

'The thing is, Jess, I... I didn't think you'd ever be coming home. Not properly.'

What was he trying to tell me? He'd settled for Claire, but now I was back, he was having second thoughts?

'I love her, I do... but...'

'Ed, I didn't come home for *you*. I came home because my dad killed himself, and, I guess, Mum did too, even if she didn't mean it.'

He shrunk, but then reached out his hand onto mine. I didn't move it away. Couldn't be bothered.

'What's happened to you is horrible,' he said. 'I am here for you, and I know you don't think of me like that. As anything more than a friend. That's fine. I think... I think seeing you again simply made me realise maybe my heart wasn't really in it, with Claire.'

He looked up and sighed and looked around the room.

'I've never been so lonely,' I said. Blurted really. I wasn't quite sure where the words came from. 'Or so scared.'

We held each other's gaze for what seemed like an age. Neither of us blinked even.

I knew I was drunk, but... I could certainly do a lot worse in life than Ed...

I edged closer to him. He didn't move at all. I wanted to kiss him. Not because it was him. I would have kissed any man sitting there. I wanted to feel. Feel normal. Feel happiness. Feel passion.

Feel anything.

I leaned in further still, but as I did so my stomach gurgled uncomfortably and my brain took me away from there. To the night of the intruder. That night, Ed had left the bar in a huff. Not long after I'd had the call from Frankie, all in a panic. Then that strange and terrifying dream – a subconscious warning? – of Ed?

Our faces were so close...

I jumped back to reality, and a little clarity, when I heard the front door opening. I shuffled back from Ed, the dejection – and confusion – clear on his face.

'Frankie?' I called out, without thinking, as though it could be someone else walking in, as though I wasn't forever on high alert.

No answer. Ed stared at me. Frankie appeared in the doorway. Even nearly two bottles of wine down, I sensed rage dripping from him.

'What's he doing here?' Frankie slammed, glaring from me to Ed.

'Excuse me?' I responded, hackles raised. Okay, so no kissing tonight. A fight? Why not.

'You know she's never going to say yes, don't you?' Frankie said to Ed. 'She's not interested, mate. Get over it.'

'Frankie!' I shouted, jumping up from the sofa. 'How dare you?'

'It's okay,' Ed said, reaching out for my arm, to pull me back down, but I shrugged him off with an angry twist.

'It's not okay,' I said to him. 'Frankie, you need to...'

But he'd already walked off to the kitchen.

I wanted to chase after him, but instead I stood there, swaying, embarrassed as much as I was angry.

Ed rose up. 'I think... I should probably go. Looks like you've got enough on your plate.'

'You don't have to,' I said, though perhaps the less than convincing look I gave him in return cemented his decision.

'Jess, I'll go. But I really hope... I just want to be there for you. Take care of yourself, yeah?'

I showed him out, then stormed back through to the kitchen where Frankie was necking a beer, the bottle nearly drained already. 'What the hell is your problem?'

He didn't look at me, simply carried on until he'd finished his beer. He clanked the bottle down then glared at me.

'How dare you barge in like that, putting a guest of mine on the spot.'

He scoffed. 'Guest? I did you a favour. Five minutes later and he would have had his hand sliding up your leg.'

'You can be really vile.'

'Whatever.' He grabbed another beer from the fridge.

'I don't think so,' I said, stepping toward him but he turned, beer in hand and the force of the look he gave told me to back off.

'That's what I thought,' he said, flipping the top off with a bottle opener from his key chain. He took a swig then set his glare on me once more. 'How much wine have you had, anyway? Was Ed getting you ready?'

I was mad at him, but pretty much speechless too. Despite my anger, I was disappointed. Not just in him, but in myself. We were both as bad as each other. Both grieving, both tormented, both guzzling alcohol as a means to cope.

If Eleanor Thornby from the council could see us...

Could she see us? My eyes flitted to the camera in the corner of the room as though the local council would do something so sinister.

'It was you, wasn't it?' Frankie said.

'What was me?'

'The phone. Dad's phone. You took it.'

'Took it? What are you talking about?'

He didn't say anything more as he stormed past.

CHAPTER THIRTY-SEVEN

I lay in my bed, in the dark, eyes wide open, the room swirling around me as I tried to battle through my alcohol delirium to keep my focus on the nearly shut door and the sliver of light coming in from the landing. Midnight had come and gone. Three pints of water had settled me, a little. Not enough. I'd fallen asleep more than once before awaking with a jolt. Some sort of subconscious protection mechanism with one part of my brain – the alert, survivalist part – fighting against the other part that craved sleep.

I *wanted* to sleep, but I couldn't let go of the thoughts of the intruder in our home. Of Frankie, mad at me. Of the letter from the council and Talbot and my realisation that seeking guardianship of my brothers was perhaps nothing more than a pipe dream. Me, suitable? In what way?

But in the dark, alone, the most dominant thoughts were those of the ghostly sightings and other unexplained events in our home. Of Ed, leaping out of that damn cupboard. Of my brother's increasingly erratic behaviours, coupled with the warnings to him from the palm reader, Heidi.

How was I supposed to sleep with all that rattling through my mind?

But then, when it happened, I couldn't be sure at first whether I was asleep or awake, such was the confusion in my tired and muddled mind.

A sound. Faint. Too faint to have woken me up. But was I already asleep and only imagining it?

A whimper. A moan. A soft, solemn cry.

Eyes open, staring at that line of light in front of me, I lay as still as could be, barely breathing so as to not make a sound, to give me maximum concentration on what I could hear.

A TV? No. Too... real. Tom? It didn't sound like him... but... who else?

I got out of the bed. The cold air caused my skin to prickle. I stood still. The sound stopped for a few moments and I questioned my senses, considered climbing back under the warm covers when the sound came once more. More harrowing this time.

I moved forward. Reached the door. Pulled it further open. The light caused me to squint. I headed on, the sound drawing me in. Glanced over the banister to the darkness below. No, not down there.

I passed the bathroom, Mum and Dad's room, Frankie's. The sound was coming... from Lily's room?

I froze a few steps away as my heart drummed. Tom's door was near closed. Lily's was wide open, the light from the landing swallowed by the blackness beyond. I wondered again whether I was truly awake, or suffering yet another nightmare, although even if I really was awake it wouldn't be the first time I'd thought I'd heard a voice in Lily's room.

How would I know if I was awake or not? Pinch myself? I did so. It hurt, nothing happened. But so what? Was hurting myself really a reliable test, just because I'd seen it on daft horror movies?

Daft horror movies – fiction, make-believe. Except thinking about them only made me all the more scared, only conjured even more frightening images of what lay beyond the threshold in Lily's room.

For some reason I moved further forward. I reached Tom's door. The sound shifted position. Silently, I sighed in relief. Not Lily's room after all. Tom. Definitely Tom.

Yet as I stared into the darkness of Lily's room, a shape caught my eye. Not a moving shape. A still one. On the carpet, near to the door. I stepped toward it.

Lion. Why was Lion out of the bed?

I edged inside, wary of the dark, picked him up. Sniffed the cuddly toy as if for comfort. Then I placed him back on the pillow, his body just beneath the duvet, tucking him in.

The noise came again. A mournful sob. I followed it. Pushed open Tom's door.

'Tom?' I whispered.

The sound stopped. My eyes adjusted to the dark, his form slowly taking shape under the covers on the bed in the far corner of the room.

'Tom? Are you okay?'

He started crying again. I moved inside, then flinched when I heard a rattle behind me. Realised it was my phone, in my room, vibrating. A ping because I'd just set off the camera. I carried on to my brother. Sat down on the bed. He didn't move as I reached out and gently stroked his hair. 'What's the matter?'

'I can't sleep,' he said in between sobs.

'Shh,' I said. 'Of course you can. You're really tired. It's so late.'

'But I *can't* sleep. I'm waiting for them. Why haven't they come back?'

Because ghosts aren't real, I wanted to say but didn't. 'I don't know,' I said. 'But it's not to punish you. They wouldn't do that.'

'Then why?'

'Maybe they've gone. They only came before to say goodbye, but they couldn't stay forever.'

He didn't say anything to that. Had the idea worked? I continued to massage his scalp. 'They know how strong you are,' I said. 'So brave. But it's time to sleep now.'

I shooshed him a few more times, carried on massaging. Five minutes perhaps?

When he started snoring I ever so slowly crept back to bed.

'Jess!'

The full-blooded shout woke me with a start. Had I even been asleep?

Yes. Tom's room. That was real, wasn't it? I'd fallen asleep after.

'Jess!' Tom screamed again.

I jumped up and raced out of the room, any thoughts of the danger that lurked out there pushed well back in my mind. Frankie emerged as I passed his door. The shock on his face said it all.

I pushed open Tom's door. Flipped on his light. All clear. No one inside. He was up in his bed, panting.

'I saw him,' Tom said, all in a panic. 'The man. He was here!'

Frankie was by my side, his phone in his hand. 'Nothing on here,' he said.

I'd not had a ping either.

'It was just bad dream,' I said to Tom.

'No! I saw him! I really did.'

I had no doubt Tom's reaction was genuine enough, at least to him... 'Go and get in my bed,' I said to him.

He didn't hesitate.

'Did you get a ping just now?' I said to Frankie.

He shook his head.

'We're standing right in front of it,' I added, looking at the camera.

Frankie frowned and glanced at his phone again. 'The system's not armed,' he said.

'What? How?'

'I don't know... did you...'

Had I turned it off earlier? 'Put it on,' I said to him.

He tapped away, looked at me. 'Done,' he said.

'Could you... could you check? Downstairs?'

He looked reluctant, but nodded. Then the next moment, as we both moved, his phone vibrated.

'Working now,' he said.

I went back to my room. Tom was spread out under the covers, eyes closed, seemingly on the verge of sleep already.

I climbed in with him, turned away and pulled my phone close to my face. It buzzed a few seconds later as Frankie entered the kitchen and I watched on the screen in real time as he moved back and forth. Soon he was finished in there, but I continued to watch the empty room on the screen. Continued to listen, as he roamed downstairs.

All still in the kitchen as I stared. All still inside at least, but as my eyes searched, my attention rested on the patio doors. Nothing visible in the blackness of the garden beyond. Nothing... except... the more I looked, the more I was sure I could make out... eyes, nose, mouth... a face near to the glass, looking in.

A ghostly face? Or something real? How was I supposed to tell the difference on a five-inch screen?

I stared, unable to breathe. I think I tried to shout for Frankie but couldn't find the strength.

The next moment I ran out onto the landing. 'Frankie, kitchen!' I hissed, trying to be loud but without rousing Tom.

'What?' he whispered up.

'The back door!'

I ran down the stairs, he got to the kitchen before me. I stopped at the edge of the room staring over. Nothing out there now except the glass and darkness beyond. I glanced at the feed on my phone. No, definitely nothing there now.

Frankie put the outside light on. He looked at me, questioningly.

'What did you see?' he asked.

I shook my head. 'I... I...' I couldn't finish. What *had* I seen?

We took close to another ten minutes to clear the downstairs, the garage and that bloody cupboard under the stairs.

By the end I was cold, shivery, horribly tired, and also had the first rumblings of a hangover. I needed sleep.

But the end result? We were alone, no signs of an intruder. All doors and windows remained locked tight.

Had Tom simply been mistaken this time?

Still on edge, but with nothing else to offer, we headed back upstairs, Frankie moving off first as I hung back. I stopped outside Tom's and Lily's rooms, both doors now wide open. All quiet and dark in Tom's room. Same too in Lily's... except...

My eyes rested on that spot on the carpet once more. The spot where Lion lay.

What the hell?

With an unnerving shudder, I left Lion there and dashed off for my bed.

CHAPTER THIRTY-EIGHT

FRANKIE

The day he'd dreaded finally arrived. First day back at school. First day back since his dad had killed himself. First day back since his mum and sister were killed in a car crash. First day back since Meg had gone cold on him. First day back since the run-ins with Dylan.

Strangely, the latter of all those played on his mind the most as he walked along the frosty ground toward the school gates, where groups of teenagers milled. Frankie, alone, kept his head low. With several minutes to go before the bell went, he really didn't want to interact with anyone, not even Ali. Actually no, there was one person he really wanted to see, even if he felt apprehensive about doing so: Meg.

What the hell had happened to her the last few days? Things had been so good between the two of them in the run-up to Christmas, even despite the tragedies in Frankie's family life. In fact, at first it seemed as though those tragedies had brought them closer.

So why the change? Frankie thought the start had been after the fair, but why would that have triggered anything? Yet since that day he'd received excuse after excuse for why she couldn't meet with him, the last of which was on New Year's Eve, three days ago. Other than a well-wish message for the new year, he hadn't bothered to call or text her at all since then, and she hadn't been in touch with him either.

Yet as he looked up – quickly, so as to not catch anyone's eye – he saw her approaching the gates from the opposite direction. Meg, and three of her 'friends'. Not real friends. Not according to her anyway. More of a school-ground clique that she'd found herself drawn into and struggled to get out of for fear of some sort of wrath. He hated the other girls in that clique. The pretty girls, according to many of the lads, whose idea of pretty was nothing but a doll-like caricature. He knew the real Meg. She didn't belong with them.

He slowed down, trying to time his walk so they'd reach the gates at the same time. The foursome strode on toward him, heads high, faces full of catty confidence.

Meg spotted him. Looked away quickly. One of the girls nudged her, as if to warn her.

'Meg?' Frankie said, stepping in her way to give her no option but to engage. 'Can we talk?'

The four of them stopped. All eyes on him. His cheeks burned red. He avoided looking at the other three because if he did, and saw their likely mocking looks, he'd crumble and skulk off.

'Please?' he said.

'I'll catch you all later, yeah?' Meg said, before splitting from the group as she headed on in.

Frankie rushed to keep up with her. She detoured from the path and onto the soggy grass, likely to try and get away from the constant throngs moving past.

'What's going on?' Frankie asked when she stopped and turned to him.

She could barely meet his eye. 'I think... I don't think this is working,' she said.

'Are you kidding me? Since when?'

She sighed, looked over his shoulder. Embarrassed to be seen with him?

Frankie ignored the cat calls from behind him. So many immature idiots. 'What did I do wrong?' he asked.

She rolled her eyes.

'*You* lied to *me*,' he said to her, trying to contain his rising anger. He hadn't wanted to go this way, but if she gave him no choice... 'Why?'

'I didn't lie to you!' she blasted. That tone wouldn't help him at all.

'No? Last Thursday? I saw you going off with Dylan after you'd sidelined me.'

She squirmed. Didn't deny it. How could she?

'And you've got the cheek to be dumping me?' he said, raw emotion building. 'You're pathetic.' He went to walk away, he needed to regain his composure, but she grabbed his arm.

'You were spying on me?' she asked, clearly angry.

'How could you do that to me? With *him*?'

She closed her eyes and huffed. 'I couldn't tell you because of *this*. Look at how you are!'

'What's that supposed to mean?'

'You're obsessed with the guy! *I* lied? What about *you*? That run-in you had with Dylan. Spying on me. Spying on him too. You know their house was broken into? Was that you?'

How did she even know about that? He didn't answer. Couldn't. She'd see right through him.

'Seems like you know a lot about good old Dylan, don't you?' he said, her screwed face showing she didn't appreciate his heckle at all.

'Yes. Because I told you, our dads are close. Like the other night when I was pretty much forced by my drunkard arsehole of a dad to go to Dylan's old man's birthday party at some shitty rugby club full of losers.'

Was that true?

'Why wouldn't you just tell me that at the time?'

'Why?' she scoffed. 'Because look at you. You're...' she trailed off and calmed. She held his eye. Sympathy now, rather than anger. 'I really liked you, Frankie. I wanted to help you, after... you know. But I don't think I can. I think... I think you need *real* help. And I mean that in the nicest possible way.'

Her anger had all but dissipated, and she reached out and touched his arm, but then whipped it back a moment later when her attention diverted behind him.

'There he is, our very own Romeo,' Dylan called out. 'Mate, it's too late, she's never going to fuck you now.'

A cascade of laughs followed.

'Loser,' Dylan added, more under his breath that time.

Frankie didn't turn. But he did ball his fists, trying to find a way to channel his rage, trying to find a way to keep himself from turning and launching himself at that prick, regardless of how many idiots he had backing him up.

'I'm sorry,' Meg said the next moment, before she turned and strode off to her friends, who remained waiting for her ten yards away.

Frankie followed her movement before his gaze settled on Dylan and his gang a few steps ahead. Dylan turned and gave him the finger, a broad grin on his face.

How Frankie wanted to wipe that look away for good.

He would. If only he could get a chance.

Frankie hated most aspects of school; he had done for years. His philosophy through earlier years of secondary school had been to do enough work to keep Mum and Dad off his back, to keep his head low in class and the corridors to not draw attention of the bullies.

He'd succeeded in both regards for years. Until Meg. She'd been his weakness. At first he'd thought she'd be the making of him. His first girlfriend, and a stunner too. A popular girl. Punching above his weight? Yeah. But now it appeared his brief time with her had backfired spectacularly. Keeping his head down wouldn't see him through now.

He particularly hated PE day. In his younger years he'd held no strong views either way about sport, but as puberty had hit, and the likes of Dylan and the other 'hard' lads had grown muscles and blossomed at physical sports, other kids had been left behind, both physically and socially. Like Frankie. One of the last in his school group to hit puberty, and even now at the age of seventeen he remained scrawny, his features boy-like, not even a hint of stubble on his face compared to some of the other boys who'd been shaving for years.

Frankie knew all of that meant little in the real world. But in the boy's changing room it meant everything. It meant that the obnoxious ones like Dylan would strip off in full view of everyone else and take pleasure in showing their bodies, swinging their dicks around like cavemen, like the appendage gave them everything they needed in life, terrorising and ridiculing others in the process. The likes of Frankie and others cowered in the corners, facing away, hoping not to be picked on. Would leave their boxers or swimming trunks on in the showers. Would just hope that attention wasn't diverted their way at any point. If there was a victim... yeah, Frankie would feel sorry for them. But he wouldn't intervene, and knew no one would come to his aid either.

He took up a spot next to Ali. Neither of them spoke a word as they quickly pulled their PE kits on. Frankie was more than surprised when he managed to make it out onto the school field with nothing more than a couple of sniggers and knowing glares from Dylan and the others. Even the PE lesson itself went fine. Rugby: and Frankie, given his lack of skill, was placed in the lower of the two groups so naturally avoided all the big brutes.

But an hour of rugby on the field in early January meant one thing. Mud. And lots of it. Which meant one more thing. Shower. Frankie would have avoided it if he could, but how when he was caked in thick, brown sludge?

Still, he made the usual decision to leave his boxers on. He had a spare pair in his bag that he'd put on after, exactly for this scenario. Four other boys in the shower did the same. Frankie wiped the mud off him as quickly as he could, making zero eye contact with anyone else, already aware of the growing boisterousness of the big-dick club with their crude bravado, almost homoerotic behaviours.

Frankie hurried out and to the changing room. Had managed to get into his clean boxers before he sensed the change in mood in the room.

Silence. Frankie faced the wall, but he knew Dylan had walked in. Knew Dylan had his eyes on him.

Adrenaline surged through Frankie's blood, but it was definitely a flight rather than fight response that built inside him. He wanted to get out of there. Willed for Dylan – and his minions – to not say or do anything to him.

'Hey, Evans,' Dylan called out. 'You feeling a bit gutted about Meg, mate?'

A few laughs. Frankie closed his eyes and shrank a little. Next to him Ali tried to get his attention but Frankie ignored him.

'I wouldn't worry about it. She was a shit shag anyway.'

Frankie grit his teeth. Picked up his trousers.

'But if you're feeling a bit low... maybe this'll help.'

A couple of gasps, a couple of laughs. Frankie still didn't turn to see what was happening. He flinched when the object hit the peg next to him and landed on top of his bag. He glanced down to the see the poorly constructed noose.

'In your father's footsteps, loser.'

'Frankie, let's get out of here,' Ali said, putting his hand to Frankie's shoulder.

No. Not this time. His muscles twitching, Frankie picked up the noose, turned to face his nemesis. Dylan, towel wrapped around his muscular physique, was flanked either side by his wingmen. Everyone in the changing room stared on. How many of them willed for Frankie to bolt to safety? How many yearned for a fight, regardless of who came out on top? Probably more the latter than the former.

'It goes around your neck, mate,' Dylan said, indicating to the noose, talking to him like he was a moron. 'I thought you'd know all about that.'

Dylan turned to his chums who cackled at the joke.

Frankie tossed the noose across the room. It landed by Dylan's feet.

'Too soon?' Dylan said with a shrug. 'Whatever.'

Frankie took a couple of steps forward. Dylan – a lot of other people too, actually – looked surprised by the turn.

'What?' Dylan said, egging him on, holding his chin up.

Frankie stepped forward again, right up into Dylan's face.

'Frankie–'

He didn't hear whatever warning, or instruction, Ali tried to give him. Instead he swung his balled fist for Dylan's chin – a sweet uppercut that caught the bully off guard and sent him stumbling back. A roar erupted from the watchers – encouraging Frankie on? Somehow the noise helped him. He sent an arcing hook to Dylan's right eye. A straight left to his gut. He managed another glancing strike to his chin.

He could do this. He could really do this…

He went for another huge blow to Dylan's face…

Deflected. And in that moment Frankie's world crumbled.

Even one on one, the odds were against Frankie… three on one…

The goons joined the melee. Frankie took blows to the face, to his sides, to his chest, stomach, back. Dylan shoved him and Frankie stumbled, falling to the tiles with a painful thud.

Dylan, lip bleeding, glared daggers at him, his chest rising and falling with heavy, angry breaths. 'You're dead,' he said. He bent down and picked up the noose. 'Hold him.'

Arms grabbed at Frankie. He tried to fend them off but his brain sloshed, his body weak.

'This is how you use it,' Dylan said, pulling the noose over Frankie's head. The thick rope scratched across the skin on his face. 'So you know for next time.'

Frankie had just enough time to slide his fingers under the rope… then with a vicious yank, Dylan pulled and the noose tightened and dug painfully into Frankie's skin. He coughed and spluttered and clawed at the rope with his free hand, tried to relieve the pressure with the fingers trapped beneath.

'You're a hard man now?' Dylan yelled. 'This is what you get, you piece of shit.'

He pulled harder on the rope, muscles straining and bulging as he dragged Frankie's body across the wet tiles. His feet scrabbled on the floor, his fingers scrambled at the noose. He could nothing. As Dylan, face filled with devilish rage, pulled Frankie out and toward the showers, he caught sight of some of the faces. Shock, horror, sympathy on most. A small number egged Dylan on.

Exactly as he expected, no one came to Frankie's aid.

They reached the showers. Dylan turned the tap on. He knelt down and yanked Frankie's hair back.

'You ever try to hit me again–'

'Shit, Jenkins is here!' came a shout.

Dylan smirked. 'Lucky bastard.'

He got up and, confident as ever, casually strode away, as chilly water cascaded down onto Frankie's quivering body.

CHAPTER THIRTY-NINE

JESS

I'd only just sat down in the coffee shop, hoping to enjoy a drink and a relaxed natter with Hannah, when the call came through. I ignored it at first, as I didn't recognise the number. When the voicemail arrived I tried my best to ignore that too, but with my phone on the table, willing me to pick it up, I lasted less than a minute before I became too inquisitive, and just a little bit nervous.

Thirty seconds later I rushed out of there and toward the car.

Angry, embarrassed, frustrated. I wasn't sure which of those I felt the most. Today – my brothers' first day back at school – was the day I'd planned on starting to get some semblance of my own life back. Top of the list of priorities was finding a job, though – and maybe this was unnecessary really, given the bigger picture – I also wanted to reignite my stagnating social life. I had only seen Hannah once since coming home, and that had been on the less than successful trip to Plaza. So we'd arranged a simple coffee. A chance to meet up in a more leisurely setting, and without the added tension that having Ed and Jamie and Kristen would bring. And without alcohol, which I hadn't touched a drop of since that night before new year.

I missed my best friend. I missed having someone I could talk to unrestricted, unload on.

I never got the chance to. Perhaps my friendship with Hannah was doomed. The last time we'd met I'd had the call from Frankie about the intruder, and had to rush off home. This time, the call from school had me similarly rushing out of the door.

I had not gathered my thoughts by the time I arrived at the school. With lessons still in mid-swing, the school grounds were strangely quiet. Memories of my own time there – good and bad – burned as I walked toward the front entrance. Soon after I headed into the waiting area in front of the headmaster's office where Frankie sat solemnly, alone.

'Frankie?' I said, rushing up to him. I expected to see him upset. Expected him to jump up and to hug me. Instead he barely registered, kept on looking at the floor straight ahead of him. 'What happened?'

After a pause he looked up at me. His right eye had swollen badly. Dried blood caked one nostril, and also a line across his bottom lip. His neck was red raw. His face remained eerily passive.

And then he talked.

'This is absolutely ridiculous!' I blasted to Mr Falstaff, the headmaster, seated behind his big oak desk which I paced in front of, incredulous. 'I've a good mind to call the police.'

'Miss Evans, please if you'd calm down, so we can talk about this properly?' He sounded more worried than anything else, as if he saw me as a loose cannon, about to explode. Perhaps not the best light to set myself in, under the circumstances.

'You're suspending Frankie for two weeks? That makes no sense. How can you not see that?'

'I've suspended both boys for the same amount of time. Honestly, Miss Evans, I think Frankie is lucky. We have a zero-tolerance policy for violence and bullying here.'

'Bullying? That's what those boys were doing to Frankie!'

He shook his head as he spoke. 'There is nothing to suggest this incident was anything other than unfortunate and a one-off. We could have expelled them both for their behaviour, but I am of course mindful of Frankie's personal circumstances.'

'Mindful? Everything you've said to me so far has been entirely mind*less*!'

He sighed, gave me the headteacher stare as though I were one of the unruly kids.

'That... boy, brought a noose to school, put that noose over my brother's head. Dragged him about the changing rooms like that. It'd be a disgusting thing to do to anyone, at any time, but knowing what happened to our dad...' I trailed off as a surge of raw emotion threatened to unsteady my feet. I reached out and held on to the back of the chair in front of me.

'I admit the whole situation is very distasteful, but I'm afraid I don't have enough strong evidence to determine where this noose even came from. Some of the boys claim Frankie brought it himself–'

'That is bullshit and you know it.' I grit my teeth, chided myself for my choice of words. This uppity idiot wouldn't be won over if I chose that path. 'Why on earth would Frankie bring a noose to school?' I asked, a little more calmly, though I found it a struggle.

'Why would any of the boys?'

'Because they're despicable bullies!'

'The problem, Miss Evans, is the lack of evidence for that. Some boys say one thing, some boys say another.'

'Frankie's never been in trouble before. What about this other kid, Dylan Farrelly—'

'I'm not going to discuss the private affairs of another of our pupils with you, as I'm sure you'd not like me to discuss the private affairs of your family with others.'

For a few moments I was speechless. How could this man be in charge of over a thousand kids when he appeared so out of touch with the reality staring him in the face?

'Taking the emotion out of the situation, which I realise isn't easy, one thing we have a very clear understanding of, Miss Evans, is that your brother instigated this fight. Regardless of whatever argument preceded it, Frankie threw the first punches. How can I not punish him?'

'This isn't over,' I said to him, before storming out.

We didn't speak as we headed to the car. Didn't speak on the short journey home. I parked up and turned the engine off and we both sat there, neither making a move to step out into the cold.

'I'm sorry,' Frankie said.

I could tell that, which was why I hadn't exploded at him.

'Two weeks suspension, Frankie,' I said to him. 'I needed this time. I need to get a job, to make some money for all of us to live. You've not even been back at school a day and now this?'

'Because it's always about you, isn't it?'

'What's that supposed to mean.'

He rolled his eyes. 'You can still do what you need to do.'

'Not if I'm babysitting you I can't.'

'I don't need babysitting,' he said, his screwed face showing his offence.

'Are you sure about that?'

He glowered then turned away.

'This probably goes without saying, but you're grounded. No going out of the house without me. At. All. Got it?'

He didn't answer.

'Do you understand me?' I said to him, a little more forcibly.

'Whatever you say.'

We both fell silent. I stared at him, at the back of his head at least, wondering what he was thinking, wondering what I could do to help. Was he falling apart because of my failings as his guardian? What did that say about my intentions of looking after him and Tom permanently?

'I only have one question for you,' I said.

He turned back to me. 'What?'

'Have you told me the truth? About what happened?'

He scoffed. 'Yeah.'

We both paused.

'I'm sorry,' I said to him. He looked a little surprised at that. 'I'm sorry you had to go through that.'

His eyes welled.

'And if you want my opinion, I understand why you reacted like you did. Why you'd want to punch that kid's lights out. I'm not saying it was sensible, but I can understand it.'

His faced turned sour and he looked away again.

'But please, let this be the end of it. Whatever is happening between you and those other boys, you need to walk away from it. It can't end well for you.'

Easy words for me to say, yet I knew how in a school it could be impossible for victims to steer clear of bullies, at least without the buy-in of the teachers – which didn't look likely, did it?

I was about to add to my attempt at support, but Frankie opened the door and stepped out.

I didn't get long inside the house. About enough time for me to lay out the ground rules for Frankie. He could watch TV, play on his console, but only if he'd completed the work that school would email each day. He could speak to his friends on his phone or laptop or whatever, but he couldn't have them over. He'd help me with chores around the house – cooking, cleaning.

By the time we got through all that, with plenty of grumbles and ultimately failed push back from him, it was time for me to go and pick up Tom. A fifteen-minute walk there, likely quite a bit longer going back, with Tom dawdling and complaining that I hadn't brought the car.

'It's not even a mile,' I said to him.

'But Mum used to pick me up.'

'When you were five, maybe.'

'No. This school year too.'

'Not every day she didn't. I bet it was only when the weather was bad.'

'No. Like, every day.'

'That's not true.'

'This is so unfair.'

'That's life.'

'Why can't Frankie pick me up then?'

'What's wrong with me doing it?'

I wasn't sure how to take his lack of an answer. And how could I explain what had happened with his older brother? Tom already struggled with his sleep, without the added thought of a group of bullies tying a noose around his neck.

'Frankie won't be going to school for a couple of weeks.'

Tom stopped and glared at me. 'That is soooo unfair!'

'It's really not, Tom. It's not a treat, it's a punishment.' I walked off. Glanced over my shoulder to see him following me two steps behind, scuffing his shoes.

'How is *not* going to school a punishment?'

'Because Frankie was naughty. He was in a fight and the teachers sent him home. It's not a good thing, Tom. He's in big trouble with me.'

Tom caught up with me. 'A fight?'

I shook my head. How did I explain this? 'Some boys weren't being nice to Frankie. He hit one of them. He shouldn't have. He should have told a teacher instead.'

Tom mulled that one. No question of whether his brother was okay or anything like that.

'Be nice to him when we get back,' I said. 'He's had a tough day.'

'Haven't we all,' he said, the short comment delivered as though spoken by a world-weary adult several decades his senior.

I tried not to show him my smile.

We finally reached home some twenty minutes or so after leaving the school gates.

'Frankie?' I called as we walked in.

No answer. A horrible feeling shot through me. He hadn't disobeyed me already, had he?

'Frankie?' Tom shouted out from behind me.

'Up here,' came the distant reply.

In his room? No, somehow his voice carried differently.

I closed the front door; we took off our coats and shoes. I told Tom to go and get himself a drink and a snack. I headed upstairs. Spotted Mum and Dad's bedroom door open before I reached the landing.

I hadn't even been gone an hour, and what was Frankie up to?

I reached the bedroom door, ready to let loose on him, then paused when I saw the confused look on his face. Sitting on the edge of their bed, he had an old shoebox on his lap. The left-hand doors of the fitted wardrobe were open. Mum's side.

'Before you shout,' he said, looking up at me. 'This is really weird.'

'What is?' I said, intrigue taking over from irritation and anything else.

'Mum had... okay, don't ask me how I figured this out, but there's this panel at the bottom of the wardrobe on Mum's side. Access for something. I don't know. But under the panel there's a hole, going under the floorboards. I was feeling around. It was disgusting and everything, but there were these old sheets, then underneath I found this box.'

Don't ask, he'd said. Because quite clearly his find hadn't been made only in the last hour. So when had he found this panel in the past? Only after Mum and Dad had passed away, or some other time when he'd been snooping through their things?

Though, apparently, he'd never gone so far as to retrieve this box before.

'There's all sorts in here,' he said. 'Most of it from when Mum was younger. Letters from friends, from Nanna and Granddad. Boyfriends too.'

He leafed through the box as he talked. I shivered. Mum's things. Her private things. Clearly put in that unseen place for a reason. How could it be right for her children to now be rooting through, Frankie eager as anything for... what?

But then, if not us, then who would do this? We couldn't keep their room like this, a shrine, forever.

'Ever heard of Harry?' he said, looking up at me with a grin on his face, a yellowed piece of paper in his hand.

'No,' I said, unable to stop myself moving forward and taking the letter from him.

The note was dated well before I was born. Mum would only have been... seventeen. The same age as Frankie. As I read, I didn't know whether to feel nostalgia or squeamishness. Clearly Harry thought a hell of a lot about my mum. Her 'luscious' body. Her 'sweet lips'. Her lacy–

'Bloody hell,' I said, dropping the letter back into the box and trying to remove the thoughts from my head.

'There's stuff in here from Dad too. It's like every love letter she ever received.'

I found reading Harry's dirty thoughts about my mum bad enough, whoever he was, but I really wasn't sure I wanted to know what my dad had thought of her. Not unless it only involved sunset cuddles and bunches of roses.

'These are more recent though,' Frankie said, taking one, two, then three letters from the pile. 'Look at the dates.'

From between ten and twelve years ago. A different handwriting than before, and not Dad's either.

'David?' I said, skipping to the sign-off.

Then I read over the letters.

'You ever heard of him?' Frankie asked me.

I didn't answer. Just read each letter in turn, then over again.

'Jess?'

'This was...'

'She was having an affair,' Frankie said, looking at me. More fascination than hurt or anything else like that on his features. 'Has to be, don't you think? These aren't just... I dunno. He's professing his love for her. Telling her he can't be without her. That he'd do *anything* for her.'

Frankie didn't need to repeat those things, I'd read the words myself.

A sickly feeling took hold deep in my stomach.

'There was a guy outside the house the other day,' I said, my voice sounding way more nervous than I'd intended. 'He said he knew Mum and Dad. Was asking after us. After you and Tom too.'

'A guy? What guy?'

I shrugged. 'I bumped into him. I thought he was a neighbour or something, but I didn't recognise him. He said his name was David.'

'You serious?'

I nodded. Of course, David wasn't exactly a unique name, but still...

'What did he look like?'

Good question. What *had* he looked like? I remembered his beanie hat, his big coat. Everything else about him was pretty... plain.

I tried to explain that all to Frankie.

'I've seen him too,' he said. 'I bumped into him one night. On the way back from Meg's.'

'You're sure?' I asked.

He nodded. 'Who the hell is he, Jess?'

I didn't know. But I determined that I would find out.

CHAPTER FORTY

We all slept surprisingly well that night. Given the day we'd had – me and Frankie at least – I really couldn't understand the reasons for that. I woke feeling physically refreshed, even if I remained mentally exhausted. Tom, up before me, appeared relaxed and content too, no complaints about ghostly sightings, no complaints about the *lack* of ghostly sightings either. Not even any complaints about the fact he had to go to school while Frankie stayed at home.

But then there was Frankie. He woke up in a foul mood. Whatever I said to try and engage him in conversation I received nothing but a grunt, a two-word answer in response at best. He snapped at Tom more than once as they sat watching TV.

With a few minutes to go before I took Tom to school, I sent him upstairs to brush his teeth, then turned my attention to Frankie, still in his dressing gown, laid out on the sofa.

'What's your problem then?' I asked.

No response at all.

'Is this because of school? What happened yesterday?'

'Not really.'

'Friends? Meg?'

I noticed his jaw pulse at the mention of her.

'You're pissed because I won't let you have her over here while you're grounded?'

'I couldn't give a crap what she does.'

Clearly he didn't mean that; his words still surprised me. So something had happened between them?

'Is she... what happened yesterday with that Dylan Farrelly, is that anything to do with Meg–'

'I don't want to talk about it. Okay?'

The anger in his voice told me to back down. I sighed, deciding it wasn't worth pursuing. Not yet, anyway. Earlier, before he got up, I'd considered whether to take him out with me this morning, despite him being grounded. I was going to see Nanna later and she'd have loved to see him. What was the point if he'd be like this?

'You're going to get your schoolwork done when I'm out then?'

He shrugged.

'Right then. I'll catch you later.' I turned to leave...

'Do you think she loved him?' Frankie asked.

'Who?'

'You know who. David. Did Mum love him?'

So was that what had him in a huff? Understandable really, but why wouldn't he say?

'I don't know. But, you saw yourself, those letters were from years ago.'

'Doesn't mean she didn't love him. And... what if they just stopped sending letters. Decided to take their dirty affair into the digital age.' He spoke with real bitterness.

'I don't think so,' I said.

He glanced over to me. 'But you don't know. They could have been together right up until... you know.'

I didn't say anything.

'And even if it ended years ago, it was still when we were around, wasn't it? We had no clue. I didn't any way. I always thought her and Dad were... so real.'

'They were.'

'Apparently not.' He turned back to the TV and sank his head onto a cushion.

Frankie's words rolled in my mind as I drove into town. Of course everything he'd said, I'd already thought too. And the fact I thought I'd seen this guy, and Frankie possibly too?

I called DS Holster.

'Jess, are you okay?' she said, sounding weary. Was she just fed up with me now?

'I think... I might know who broke into our house.'

'You do?'

'His name's David.'

Silence.

'Hello?' I said.

'David? Just David?'

She sounded exasperated already.

'We found some letters. Love letters from years ago to my mum from a David. But I met a man in the street the other day who said he was David too.'

'Jess, are you–'

'Please. I don't know... it might be him.'

A sigh. 'Do you know where he lives?'

'No. But I saw him right outside our house.'

'When?'

'Days ago. Before... before the break-in.'

'You haven't seen him since?'

'No.'

'Can you tell me what he looks like?'

'He was... I don't know. A man. Forties. White. Normal, really.' I felt so lame, but how else to describe him?

'You're not giving me much to work with here.'

'I know, but... isn't there anything you can do?'

'It'd help if you at least get a surname for me?' A pause, then, 'Other than that, all I can do is put word out to our beat officers to be on the lookout around your area for anyone with that description who's... lurking.'

Better than nothing I guessed.

'Sorry, Jess, I've got to go.'

Maybe Holster thought I was crazy. Maybe I was, but I felt like I was finally making progress... but progress to what goal?

I'd made an appointment at the clinic of the therapist, Yasmine Lowton. Clinic? I think that's what therapists have, or perhaps an office? Either way, I'd decided on making an appointment, rather than just calling, unannounced, or showing up unannounced, as I wanted to make the most of the opportunity, to see her face as she gave me her answers. I'd also booked the appointment under my mum's maiden name.

Why?

Hard to answer really. Element of surprise, I think, as though I were now an undercover sleuth or something.

The office – clinic – was small, sparse. Lots of creams and pastel colours to create a calming atmosphere. Yasmine Lowton was in her forties, quite a serious look about her, from her tight face, to her formal office attire. She smiled to greet me, said all the right pleasantries, but it all seemed a little forced really.

We moved into her office. Exactly as I'd expect a

therapist's to look. No chaise longue, but there was a comfy armchair for the client, a more plain office chair the other side of a low coffee table for the doctor to sit and ask her probing questions.

Not today. Any probing would be by me.

'Please, take a seat,' Yasmine said, pointing to the armchair. 'Would you like some water?' She moved over to the cooler before I'd responded.

'No, I'm fine thanks.'

She poured herself a small glass then took up her position opposite me. 'Thanks for coming to me,' she said. 'You've booked for a half hour consultation, so I suggest we use this time to help me find out a little bit more about you, and perhaps we can then discuss how I can help going forward.'

'Actually, I think...' I sat on the end of the chair and sighed. 'I should probably come clean. My name's Jess Evans. You were seeing my parents. I think. Maybe only one of them, I don't know. Andy and Jane Evans?'

Yasmine's face remained neutral as she slowly nodded. Her clasped hands rested on her lap, her legs folded. Calmness personified. 'You look a lot like your mum,' she said.

Not the comment I'd expected. A deliberate attempt to derail me?

'So, you were seeing both of them?' I asked.

Yasmine sighed. 'I heard about what happened,' she said. 'I'm so sorry.'

'You heard? How?'

'I read about the crash online. Your dad... someone told me. They'd heard from someone else and, you know how it is?'

'Not really. My dad only killed himself the one time so that's the only experience I have of such things.'

She didn't say anything to that. I got a strange feeling. Was she holding back? To protect herself? If my dad had killed himself, under her watch... did she have a duty of care? I really didn't know.

'I'm really sorry,' Yasmine said again, her voice a little choked that time. 'But... I'm not sure why you've come to me, and under, I guess, false pretences too?'

'Were you seeing them both? I mean, at the same time, separately?'

She sighed again. 'I know they're not around now, but client confidentiality rules still apply, strictly speaking.'

I'd expected this stumbling block, but to hit it so early on in the conversation didn't bode well.

'But, I guess in a way it's a factual position we're talking about,' Yasmine said. 'I've known your parents for a couple of years, and in that time I've seen them separately, and also together on occasions.'

'But why? Why were they seeing you?'

'This is where I'm going to have to disappoint you, Jess. Think about it like this. They came to me in confidence, to help them. If they didn't tell you the reasons for doing so before, then why would it be okay for me to tell you now?'

'Help them? You didn't do a very good bloody job, did you? Dad killed himself.' The combativeness, and the lack of feeling in my words shocked me. Yasmine too, I could tell, by the nervous twitch in her hands and on her face.

'Perhaps I could ask a question of you?' she said, trying the classic trick of turning everything onto the subject. 'Why do you want to know? Why do you think it will help you?'

'Don't do that to me,' I said, agitated. 'Just don't. I want to know why my dad killed himself. I want to know what problems there were between him and my mum, that led him to doing that. *You* know something. *Please* help me.'

Yasmine shook her head. 'I'm simply not able to divulge any information like that.' She paused, held my eye. 'I will say one thing, though. I was surprised when I heard about your dad. That was... out of the blue. If I'd known he was so close to the edge, I could... would have talked to him about seeking additional help.' She sounded a little rattled at that thought. That she hadn't seen the warning signs, that she'd been in a position of influence, but had failed to act in time.

But then, wasn't that the same for all of us? Mum, me, Frankie included?

I shook my head, ashamed. We'd all let him down, every last one of us. But if anyone who was still alive knew of what had him so troubled, this woman had to be near the top of the list.

'There must be something you can tell me,' I said, almost pleading.

'I'm sorry.'

'What about David?'

A slight frown. A definite reaction, wasn't there?

'Do you know that name? Did either of them ever mention him to you?'

She didn't answer straight away, then, 'I think you should go.'

As reluctant as I was, moments later I stood by the door.

'Jess?' Yasmine said. I paused and turned to her. 'Be careful. The answers you're looking for won't necessarily bring you comfort.'

She knew the name. I had no doubt. Whether from Mum or Dad or both of them, I couldn't be sure. The context? I didn't know that either, nor the seriousness, or even the relevance of it all.

Regardless of all that, I left the therapist's office consumed by anger. At her; at her parting comment. At Mum, at Dad, at Frankie, at so many people. At David.

Who the hell was he?

I went to the nursing home still on edge. I'd planned on visiting Nanna anyway, but my visit had taken on a whole new perspective given recent events.

A kindly male nurse showed me to her room. As always it smelled of musty oldness. I found Nanna sitting in a floral-print armchair, in front of the window overlooking the gardens. Thick jumper and cardigan, a blanket over her lap. She had a dinner tray in front of her, barely a quarter of the food eaten.

'Nanna, it's me,' I called, my voice raised as I entered. She jumped a little in surprise, groaned as she struggled to turn to see me. I reached her and she lifted a hand to my cheek as I bent down to kiss her. Gravy covered her chin. The soft bristles of her cheek tickled my lips.

'Jess, how lovely.'

'Are you okay, Nanna?'

She looked beyond me, as though to see who else I'd come with. Until recently I'd nearly always be here with Mum or Dad or both.

'Just me today,' I said.

'Oh. Yes.'

'Aren't you hungry?' I asked, sitting down on the chair arm.

She leaned in to me. 'It's not very nice. The meat is like cardboard and the mashed potato is like sawdust. Nothing compared to your dad's roasts. He does a good one.'

She chuckled at that and I had a flashing thought – would I need to explain yet again about what had happened?

'You look well, dear,' she said, clasping both of her ice-cold hands over mine.

'Thanks.'

'The boys are okay?'

'They're fine.'

She looked more gloomy. 'You're missing your Mum and Dad and Lily.'

'More than you can imagine.'

She pursed her lips and held my eye and I don't really know how to describe the moment we shared. Painful, poignant, but very, very real. Sincere. More than anything, lucid.

'You know they're still with you. Always.'

'Yes, Nanna, I know.'

She nodded. I really didn't want to go down that path today. So I changed the subject. We chatted for a while about anything and nothing. The weather, the prime minister, cakes. All the while I built myself up to what I really wanted to say.

I felt sneaky.

Finally I made the jump.

'Me and Frankie were looking through Mum and Dad's things yesterday,' I said.

'You were what?'

I repeated myself, louder. She quivered slightly. Either because the volume was too high, or because of the connotations of what I said.

'Not a nice business,' she said, shaking her head. 'I remember doing that after your granddad passed.'

'We found a load of old letters of Mum's. Love letters mostly.'

Nanna smiled now.

'Do you remember a boy called Harry?' I asked.

She raised an eyebrow. 'Yes. A real tinker.' She batted the idea of him away with a swoosh of her hand.

'Really?' I said, genuinely interested.

'Always up to no good. Never got her home on time. Distracted her from school.'

'I thought Mum was always a real goody.'

'Not when she got a boy on her mind. Harry? He was a real charmer, and he knew it.'

'What happened to him?'

She chuckled. 'He went off with someone else. Your mum cried for days. Me and your granddad shared a sherry to celebrate.' She laughed again as she looked off into the distance. I let her reminisce for a few moments.

'There was someone else too, that I didn't know,' I said. 'David.'

'Who?' she said, cupping her ear to me.

'David?'

She shook her head.

'He was more recent,' I said. She caught my eye. 'From when I was younger. Mum never mentioned him to you?'

I noticed a flicker behind her eyes. Kind of a eureka moment as though the name had just clicked.

'Nanna?'

'Yes, dear?'

'Do you know who David is? Someone Mum was seeing?'

She looked beyond me. 'Your brothers aren't here today?'

'They're at school.' Well, not Frankie, but I didn't want to have to explain about that.

'I haven't seen them in so long. No one ever comes to visit me.'

'Nanna?'

She held my eye. Looked... terrified.

'Who's David?'

'Yes, it's a nice day for it. It is.' She turned to look out of the window again. 'It'll soon be spring now.'

Not really. She pushed the meal tray a little further away from her.

'You sure you're finished?' I asked.

She pulled her face. 'I can't eat it. The meat is like cardboard. The potatoes–'

'Like sawdust. Yes, I know.'

I wiped her chin with the napkin then picked up the tray and moved it over to the dresser.

When I turned back around she had her head pushed back, her eyes closed.

'Nanna?'

I sat back down on the chair arm. Held her limp hand.

'Nanna?'

No response.

I sighed. Even riddled with dementia she was a hell of an actress. I leaned over and kissed her on the forehead. 'Love you,' I said, before getting up to leave.

CHAPTER FORTY-ONE

Had I learned anything at all from my round-robin trip to Nanna's and the therapist's? Not really. Other than the mysterious David had clearly played a big part in my mum's life somehow – my dad's too? And that for whatever reason, I hadn't been told about him, and those who did know something, felt they couldn't tell me the truth, even now that Mum was dead.

Which only made me all the more curious. And angry. Betrayed. Hurt.

Determined.

I held those thoughts all the way home, my eyes busy as I drove down our street, looking across the pavement either side of me for any sign of David skulking.

Nothing at all. Perhaps I'd made a mistake in linking those letters to the man I'd met.

A little disappointed, but no less curious or angry, I headed up to the front door, my thoughts turning to Frankie. I really hoped he'd had a productive morning. I imagined walking in to find all his schoolwork done, the washing-up done, house tidy. Frankie taking some responsibility, showing some maturity and contrition.

Yeah, right.

Most likely he'd be watching TV still, not even dressed, or playing video games, or doing I didn't want to think what on the internet.

I opened the door. I took off my coat and shoes and listened. The house was silent. Was he even home?

If he'd snuck out...

I moved toward the lounge. No TV on in there. No sounds from upstairs either.

'Frankie?'

No answer. Except for a creak from somewhere above me.

Nerves taking hold, I moved for the stairs. Climbed up them slowly.

'Frankie?' I called again, loud enough to ensure he'd heard me if he was in his bedroom – or anywhere else – doing something that I really didn't want to walk in on.

Still no answer, and my nerves ramped further as all manner of grim thoughts whirred. The garage. Why did most of the thoughts feature the garage?

But he'd been so edgy recently. Then that horrible incident at school... how close to breaking was he?

Please, not that, I willed.

I reached the top of the stairs. His bedroom door was open. I moved past. Definitely not in there.

Another creak, from in front of me. Mum and Dad's room, where the door was ajar.

'Frankie?'

No response. I reached the door and pushed it further open then put a hand to my mouth as I gasped in shock.

'What have you done?' I said to him. Not anger, more... anguish. He'd trashed the room. Every drawer and cupboard door lay open, pretty much every item inside strewn somewhere on the floor as though a burglar had ransacked the place.

Frankie sat on the bed, a deep glower directed at me. 'You lied to me,' he said.

'What are you talking about?' I replied, even though I thought I knew, yet I really hoped I was wrong.

Please don't let it be that.

He reached over and picked up the paper from the bed next to him. 'I was only looking for more of their things. More information on David and whoever else Mum was screwing. Or Dad for that matter. I expected more lies and dirty secrets. But not... this.'

He tossed the paper toward me. It wafted and flipped in the air, landing midway between us, the paper's sorry flight only adding to Frankie's anger.

I stepped forward and picked up the paper, already fearing the worst. Angry at Mum and Dad for not hiding it better, angry at myself for... everything, really.

I unfolded the paper. A birth certificate. Lily's birth certificate.

'She wasn't your sister,' Frankie said through gritted teeth. 'She wasn't *my* sister. She was *your* daughter.'

CHAPTER FORTY-TWO

Fifteen years old. Young. Impressionable. Madly in love with a boy.

A boy, who, one day, at a friend's house, showed me kindness and affection. After some vodka, I might add. Not a lot really, but then we were young, inexperienced, me in particular.

Did all of my life's problems involve alcohol, one way or another?

I think all girls, perhaps boys too, picture their first time as something special. A comfy bed with sumptuous sheets. Pretty underwear, soft music, candlelight, passion, love and hugs and a warm glow of satisfaction.

I ended up on my back on a cold bathroom floor, the door locked so our friends partying outside wouldn't disturb us, my knickers around my ankles, my bra around my neck, jumper hiked up, my 'lover' on top of me for all of a minute.

Hardly an event to write home about, yet an important event nonetheless, and one I really wanted to happen at the time.

I was desperate for him.

Even if we never slept together again.

Only a few of my friends found out what happened that night, though none found out the consequences.

A few weeks later I missed my period.

A couple of weeks after that I built up the courage to buy a pregnancy test.

A couple of weeks after that, with my daily moods deteriorating rapidly as the weight of the world bore down on me, and with the boy I loved so much no longer interested in me, I told my mum.

Five long, painful years ago.

———

Frankie shot up from the bed, I think aiming to storm out. I stood in his way, my demeanour changing in a flash as raw emotion took hold. 'Sit down,' I shouted.

He came toward me.

I reached out, both hands, and shoved him back. 'Sit down!' I screamed.

He fell back onto the bed, eyes wide with surprise.

'You need to sit and listen.'

'How could you do that?' he said. 'To *her*?'

I wanted to answer but couldn't. I needed to think and to find the right words to explain.

'I remember now,' he said, before shaking his head. 'That summer. You'd been antsy for months already. I thought because of the baby. Mum had told us she was pregnant. I talked to *you* about it. We both agreed it was weird. Wrong, that they were having another kid.'

A tear rolled down my cheek. My legs felt weak.

'You even told me you couldn't believe it either. Couldn't believe they were being so selfish. Fuck, I'm such a gullible fool.'

'You're not, Frankie. You're really not.'

'No? Did you laugh at me behind my back? The three of you, together?'

I shook my head. 'No.'

He scoffed. 'Then at the start of the summer holidays, Mum and Dad did that little presentation to me about the summer camp. How it was a real big treat for me because of my school report. Truthfully? I was so excited. I really thought they meant it. I really thought they were so proud of me.'

'They were.'

'Bullshit,' he said, slamming his fist on the mattress. The feat of anger caused the whole thing to wobble and Frankie's body bobbed up and down, a strangely contradictory reaction to his irate outburst.

'I remember the day she was born,' he said. 'The phone call with Dad, telling me Mum and Lily were okay. That they couldn't wait to meet me. Then when I came home... there she was. My little sister. Except she wasn't.'

He buried his head in his hands. I moved over to him. I wanted to hold him. But he sensed my movement and straightened up and shot me a look of pure hatred.

'I was fifteen, Frankie.'

'And what? You couldn't have your perfect little future compromised?'

I shook my head. 'It wasn't like that.'

'Yes, I think it was. You would have had an abortion, wouldn't you? *Another* one, I should say.'

Well, at the time it would have been the first, but... I sobbed. He was right. I would have done that. I wanted to. 'I was too young, Frankie. I couldn't... I couldn't be a mum for her.'

'And Mum wouldn't let you abort, right?'

I shook my head.

'So the three of you concocted a horrible lie.'

'It wasn't a lie. It was a chance for Lily.'

307

'No, Jess. It was all about you.'

'That's not true.'

'Who was her father?'

I glanced at the birth certificate where the father's name remained blank.

'Jess, who was it? Please don't tell me it was–'

'Jamie. She was Jamie's.'

I wasn't sure who he'd been about to suggest, but his face screwed nonetheless. 'Jamie? That surfer-dude wannabe?'

I didn't say anything.

Frankie laughed. 'I suppose the blonde hair fits at least.' His face drained of emotion. 'Does he even know?'

I shook my head once more.

'So many lies,' he said, then I noticed a flicker in his eyes as though a moment of realisation. 'I see it now. When I look back. I see the way you were with her. So standoffish. You could hardly even hold her when she was little. I thought you were just jealous... but... what was it?'

'Guilt,' I said, without thinking. 'Guilt. The most painful kind. I hated myself. I hated that I'd let her down. I've never forgiven myself for giving her away.'

'She loved you so much.'

'I loved her more than anything.'

'You didn't show it.'

'I couldn't!'

'Why? For her benefit? No. To save your own face. That's all it was ever about.' He got up from the bed.

I wanted to stop him from leaving. I wanted to see this through. Wanted him to see my view. Wanted to reconcile. But I didn't have the strength – physical or mental – to stop him getting past me.

He paused. Then laughed, in such a way as to show his

annoyance. 'How did Mum do it?' he asked. 'And you too? There was no bump on you, but Mum?'

I shrugged. 'Lily was so little. Me too. And you went away toward the end. I... I guess you never knew, so why would you notice...'

'Why indeed? Stupid Frankie, right?'

'No,' I said, hanging my head.

'And Mum? A fucking pillow probably.' He shook his head, disgusted.

I didn't say anything.

He brushed past me. I couldn't move from the spot. I expected to hear his bedroom door slam. Instead I heard his footsteps thundering down the stairs. A few moments later, a bang. The front door?

I rushed out to the landing.

'Frankie!' I shouted.

I got no response. He'd already gone.

CHAPTER FORTY-THREE

I knew it was wrong but I did it anyway. I needed the release. I needed to forget, I needed to escape. I'd finished a full bottle of red before I left to pick up Tom from school. He didn't question my giddiness. We barely talked on the way back. I just wanted to get home and to have another drink.

'Where's Frankie?' Tom asked as he paced from the kitchen toward the lounge.

'He went to a friend's house.'

I really hoped that was the case anyway, though I hadn't heard from him for a couple of hours.

Damn, I really needed another drink.

I finished putting the shoes into the rack, then looked up to see Tom staring at me, distrust in his eyes. 'I thought he was grounded.'

'He is. But he has some course work for school that's really important, that he needs a partner for.' How easily lies came to my lips... 'Why don't you go on your PlayStation for a bit?'

'Okay,' he said, hesitating a moment before he rushed upstairs.

I watched him go, sighed, then checked my phone. Still

nothing from Frankie. I sent him another message, begging him to let me know he was okay. I noticed that the last two I'd sent remained unread.

I went to the kitchen. Looked at the wine rack. My stomach turned over. I didn't want any more of that, but I did need a drink. Gin. But we had no tonic so I mixed it with nothing but a glass full of ice. I took a long sip of the cold spirit. My lips tingled, the back of my throat throbbed pleasantly as the liquor slipped down. My insides burned with satisfaction. My brain throbbed with disappointment. I took another, smaller sip, then I moved upstairs.

I crept along the landing to Mum and Dad's room, being quiet as though not to alert Tom. I went inside. Before I'd picked Tom up I'd already managed to do some tidying while I polished off the bottle of wine, though I hadn't had time to finish. The tidying, that was. Looking at the room now, I wondered what was even the point? Why was I folding and putting away clothes that would never be worn again? At least by no one in this house. Wouldn't it be better to get some black bags and throw everything into those for a charity shop run?

I didn't. Instead I painfully and meticulously put away every item where I thought they belonged, until all that remained were the boxes of memorabilia – photos and greetings cards mostly, but also those more private items of Mum's, and also little Lily's birth certificate which had come out from a box filled with items – and gifts – from her early life.

With tears in my eyes I looked through. Hated myself even more as I read all of the good wishes and messages from friends and family to my parents. Everyone duped by the same lie. Everyone, including Lily herself. I'd lived with the guilt of giving her up for five years. Since her death... I'd abandoned her all over again, the loss too painful for me to even think about. Denial, of the worst possible kind.

'What are you doing?' came Tom's little voice from the doorway.

I jolted in shock and looked up at him and wiped at my eyes. 'Nothing, just tidying. Looking through some old things.'

I tried to close the box but Tom wandered over and sat next to me and pulled the flaps open. We sat in silence for a few moments as he looked inside, though he didn't pick anything out. I wiped at my eyes once more, trying to compose myself.

Tom glanced up at me. 'It's okay, Jess. I really miss her too.'

I said nothing as he wrapped his arms around me.

***

I encouraged Tom to go back and play. He barely hesitated. What a terrible parent I'd make, I thought as I sat in the lounge, another gin in my hand. One of my brothers was being bullied at school, had run off, and I had no idea where he'd gone. The other I couldn't spend any time with because I was too drunk and didn't want him to notice so I made him spend his time in front of a screen.

And I was the one who wanted to be their legal guardian.

Shit!

The letter from social services. The meeting. I'd completely forgotten. How could I be so stupid? I rushed out of the lounge to the kitchen. Rifled through the pile of letters, found the one from the council. I tried to be sober, to think clearly, but I could barely type the numbers out to make the call.

I listened to the rings. Looked at the clock. Five thirty-eight. Would there even be anyone there?

Yes.

'Sorry, could I speak to Eleanor Thornby, please?'

'Let me check if she's still here.'

A click then silence. I wanted to shout and scream. At

myself. I wanted to grab every bottle of gin and wine and beer in the house and chuck it all away. Not that alcohol was the cause of every problem in my life, but it certainly wasn't the solution either.

'Hello?' came the questioning female voice. I recognised.

'Mrs Thornby?'

'Speaking.'

'It's Jess Evans, I'm so sorry.'

A sigh.

'I didn't. I don't know... please, can we reschedule?'

'I have to say, Jess, this isn't the best of starts for you.'

'I know. Please.'

'Are you okay?'

'I... I...'

'Have you been drinking?'

Was I slurring that much? I didn't know what to say. *I need help. Please help.* Perhaps that's what I should have said. 'No,' I went with instead. 'It's just been a really tough day. I–'

'I understand there was an incident at your brother's school.'

'How do you know that?' I said, my temper flaring in an instant.

'It's my job to check on the welfare of you and your brothers. I made a routine call to school. What I heard wasn't exactly–'

'What happened has nothing to do with my application. Nothing at all.'

'Perhaps not, Jess. But I'm worried about Frankie, nonetheless. I'm worried about all of you, quite frankly. Do you think I could speak to Frankie?'

'Now?'

'Yes.'

'It's not... he's not in.'

Silence. Then another sigh.

'I'll come see you tomorrow,' I said. '*I promise.* I will make this work.'

Silence. Another sigh. 'Let me check my diary... 2pm?'

'I'll be there.'

'I hope so.'

The call ended. I didn't move. I couldn't. I thought back to Frankie. The disappointment on his face before he'd left. I thought about Mum, Dad, Lily. I thought about every single person in my life who I'd let down.

I'd fucked everything up. Lily's life. My life. And now that of my brothers too.

Hadn't I?

Or perhaps this was best for Tom and Frankie after all.

By the time I'd got Tom into bed, I'd sobered up, a little, but in place of the numbing alcohol I'd become seriously worried about Frankie. No amount of calls or texts had had any effect. I'd tried my best to persuade Tom that everything was fine, but I think he knew otherwise, even if he chose not to strongly question the bullshit answers I fed him as to where his brother had gone.

With Tom in his room, although not asleep, as I could hear him shuffling around, I tried to sit and relax. Tried to watch TV. It didn't really work. I sent Frankie another message.

Just let me know you're okay. PLEASE xx

As I stared at the screen, blue ticks appeared on all of the messages I'd sent over the last few hours. My heart jumped. Hope? But then no response came. At least he'd read the messages though. That was a good thing, right? At least he wasn't lying in a ditch somewhere.

Unless...

No, I didn't let my brain go there.

But I was getting absolutely nowhere watching TV, so I turned it off, checked the house was properly locked up – except the front door, as I hoped Frankie would be back – then headed to my room.

I sat on the bed, disparate thoughts worming around my troubled mind. Was there anyone I could call? I had no numbers for Frankie's friends, but I could probably try to contact them through social media. The police? I was seriously worried about Frankie, his fragile state of mind, but he was seventeen and he hadn't even been gone for half a day, and Holster already thought I was a loon... plus, would it get back to social services?

Instead, to try and ease my mind from the mess I'd made, I moved over to my wardrobe, felt around the bottom for the little plastic bag. I pulled it out. Stared at the phone inside. Pink, hard plastic case, screen blistered into thousands of pieces of glass, a smudge of red caked across the top.

My insides curdled at the images that conjured.

I wondered about Frankie again. About the lengths he'd gone to in Mum and Dad's room, searching high and low. Had he been in here too? Had he found this phone? He'd never asked about it.

I took a deep breath then took out the phone. Tried to power it on. No juice. I moved back to my bed and plugged in the charger, in two minds as to whether the device was too far gone.

No. It wasn't. The cracked screen came to life after a few minutes. But it needed a PIN code, or a thumbprint ID to unlock it. Clearly the latter was impossible, and it turned out so too was the former, the screen too damaged to accept my attempts.

I thought of another solution. I tiptoed along the landing. Glanced in Tom's room. Asleep. At least he was quiet and his eyes were shut anyway.

I glanced too into Lily's room as I passed, but then quickly away again. I didn't want to think about that right now. I retrieved the laptop from downstairs, took it back to my room. Plugged the phone in.

Still no luck. Even though the unlock code I input into the pop-up on the laptop screen was accepted, I needed to confirm the unlock on the device too, and with the screen so badly damaged, I had no chance.

Frustration gripping me, I lay back on the bed and closed my eyes to think.

CHAPTER FORTY-FOUR

FRANKIE

He'd roamed for hours, unsure where he should go, who he should speak to. Well, one thing he knew: he wasn't going home. He couldn't face Jess. Not tonight. Not after what he'd found.

Five years of lies. How could she? How could Mum and Dad?

His brain rumbled with thoughts as to what it all meant. Five years ago his sister had given birth to a little baby girl. His parents had raised that girl as their own. Jess had swanned it at school, breezed through her exams, before tootling off to university to pursue *her* dreams, all the while pretty much abandoning her daughter in the process, leaving the burden on her parents, holding a lie all that time.

A burden. Is that all Lily had even been to Jess? Poor thing. No doubt her arrival must have caused strain in his parents' relationship. Five years ago for sure. All the way through Lily's short life? Probably. Every time his Mum and Dad had looked into her little eyes they were looking at someone else's kid. Family, yes, but not their child. That had to have caused strain. Problems in their relationship.

The catalyst for Dad killing himself?

Frankie wasn't so sure. Because… why now?

Jess's secret had changed everything he knew about his family. But it hadn't answered the big question. Why had Dad killed himself? Why had Mum run away? She had, hadn't she?

He'd walked past Meg's house numerous times. Hadn't stopped to spy, hadn't the guts to go up to the front door. He'd walked past Dylan's house too. He hadn't stopped there. He'd walked past the gates to Ali's home. Perhaps his best chance of refuge, yet he'd carried on.

He headed through the dark park, and eventually found himself in the town centre. Midweek, in early January, the place was dead. A few of the bars and restaurants hadn't even bothered opening. Those that had surely couldn't have covered the costs of doing so given how few punters were out.

Frankie liked it that way.

He ended up around the back of a run of two-storey terraces. The bottom storey units were all taken up by small shops, from hairdressers to takeaways. The top storey was a mishmash of small businesses and flats, but included the office of Yasmine Lowton, the therapist his parents had used. Apparently.

A rickety fire escape led up to the back door of the poxy-looking unit. He spotted a CCTV camera above the door, but he couldn't care less about that tonight. He climbed the metal steps to the top. Tried the handle of the metal door. Locked. But he hadn't come unprepared for this, and looking at the handle, he decided to see if his recent research worked in real life.

He left the flick knife in his pocket and took out the screwdriver and the hammer he'd brought from home. Used a bit of guile to stick the screwdriver up into the underside of the handle, wedging the thin metal end between the lock and the door. Holding the screwdriver in place, he whacked upward with the hammer, onto the end of the screwdriver, to force it into the lock. A clattering sound, but no luck. He nervously looked around.

No. He was all clear. Who else would be around here at this time of night?

He whacked again, then a third time with a bit more venom. *Crack.*

The screwdriver pushed upward a couple of inches, splitting the inner mechanism of the pin tumbler lock into two. The outer part of the lock-face came loose. He yanked the screwdriver out and used it to poke the broken lock right out of its position in the handle. The metal clanked to the floor the other side. Frankie pulled the door open and braced himself for an alarm.

Nothing.

It's not as though many people would care to rob a therapist, he guessed. What would she have worth stealing?

He moved inside, tried to control his increasingly heavy breathing, tried to control the surge of adrenaline coursing through him.

Could he really do this?

Yes. The hardest part was already over with.

He pulled the outer door closed, left the lights off and used his phone torch to scope out the place. Not much to it really. A reception area. Exit, one other closed door. He went that way. Office.

He moved to the desk, opened drawers and searched through. No computer or anything, but he did find a pile of three notepads. A dictaphone. He looked over the room to a filing cabinet. Went there. Pulled open the drawers. Mostly admin type things. Invoices and the like.

Third drawer down. Client files.

He found 'Evans' within a few seconds. Not very hard because there were three separate entries: *A. Evans., J. Evans., A&J Evans.*

He took all three out. Put the files onto the desk. Opened up A&J first. Typed up notes, but also scans of handwritten notes. A bit of a mishmash of records all in all.

What was he even looking for? Should he just grab all of this and scarper? It could take him ages to read through everything.

Did he even want to? Did he really want to know the most intimate, inner thoughts of his dead parents?

Yes. He did. He wanted to understand. To understand their lives, and their lies.

An entry caught his eye. On a scan of a handwritten page. A name. David Campbell. Circled in the middle of the page.

He glanced over the brief, almost coded notes.

All started with DC.

Tried to live with it.

Made harder with Lily.

Too much guilt.

Tension.

Worse than ever now DC back.

Pressure becoming immense.

J worried about A?

DC back? Frankie thought to the love letters he'd seen at home. To the man he'd bumped into on the street not long ago. The same man Jess had spoken to, apparently.

He thought about all the other odd occurrences...

DC back. David Campbell. Mum's lover. He'd been out of her life since... when? But for some reason he'd come back.

And that was when everything had turned to shit.

But why was he back at all? And why had that caused so much trauma?

He'd take the files and read them in detail for the answers. But first, he turned his phone around, tapped on the screen, and called Jess.

CHAPTER FORTY-FIVE

I woke with a start when my phone vibrated in my hand. I hadn't intended to sleep. What had happened? Well, a bottle of wine and several measures of gin certainly hadn't helped.

I didn't answer the call. I couldn't move quickly enough, my brain still processing the world around me, the unpleasant images from my sleep of my dead daughter not yet eradicated, and my head throbbing too much. My mouth was as dry as sandpaper.

Once I'd recovered – enough at least – I looked at the phone screen. Frankie. In one moment I was both relieved and horrified. Relieved that he'd called me back, finally. Horrified that the time was after 11pm, and, other than Tom, I was home alone.

I called him back.

'Hey,' he said as he answered, and just hearing his voice made all the difference.

'Where are you? Are you okay?'

A short pause. 'Yeah.'

'Frankie, I was so worried.' I did my best to hold back the tears.

'Listen, Jess, I found something.' He talked hurriedly.

'What do you mean?'

'That guy David. I found his full name. It's David Campbell. I don't know what's going on, but I think he's the reason... you know, with Mum and Dad.'

'David Campbell? Where are you?'

No answer. I checked the call was still connected. Yes.

'Frankie? Where are you?'

'At... I'm reading through the notes at Yasmine Lowton's office.'

'Shit, what are you—'

'Just listen to me. It's all to do with him. David Campbell.'

What on earth was he doing? My eldest brother being locked up for burglary was the absolute last thing we needed. How would I square that away with Eleanor Thornby? Yet something about the determination in his voice told me to push that thought aside.

'Jess, you there?'

'Just a sec.' I reached over and picked up the laptop and pushed the power button. I unlocked the screen. Googled the name. Nothing much came up, so I added our town's name and stared at the results in shock and confusion.

'What the—' I said.

'Jess?'

'There're news articles. Quite a few of them.'

'About him? The same guy.'

'Yeah. There's a picture,' I said, opening up the first result. 'It's definitely him.' I looked at the timestamp. 'It's not new though. Eight years ago. Nearly nine.'

'Who is he?'

I scanned over the words, trying to take the information in. I had to read some of the sentences several times over to fully process what I saw, and the horrible and disturbing place where my brain was taking me.

'David Campbell was convicted of rape. He was sentenced to... shit, Frankie.'

'He's out?'

'What happened?' I said to myself as much as to my brother.

'A rapist?' Frankie said. I could hear both the anger and the fear in his words. 'Mum?'

I quickly reread the article again.

'It doesn't mention her. The victim was unnamed, in the news at least.'

'Jess. That guy raped our mum. I know it. And now he's back.'

'Back?'

'Out of jail. And probably looking for revenge.'

This couldn't be happening.

'Frankie, you need to come home. Now.'

'I'm on my way.'

He ended the call. I wished he hadn't because my room, the whole house was plunged into a deathly, choking silence.

Unable to move from my bed because of the fear taking over, I went into the camera app.

Not turned on. Because I'd fallen asleep unexpectedly, I hadn't set it. I did so now, and received a ping a moment later to confirm the system was armed.

But then not even three breaths later and a notification popped up.

Cameras disarmed.

What the hell?

I went back into the app. All I needed to do was tap the orange 'away' circle, but now the app wouldn't let me. I rose up from the bed. Crept over to my door. Even though the landing light was on, downstairs was pitch black. I looked at my phone again. The app still wouldn't respond properly. Of all the times...

I restarted the app as I slowly edged onto the landing. Went into the settings.

'Oh my God.'

For a moment I couldn't move as I stared at the screen. To the settings for our cameras. The list of linked devices that could control the system. Not just two devices. Not just mine and Frankie's. A third device too.

A thud downstairs. My heart jumped. I looked over the banister to the darkness below. Nothing I could see.

When I glanced back to my phone, the app had closed without me touching a thing. I tried to restart it. Error message. I tried to restart again. It did open, kind of. But only to a set-up screen. I'd been kicked out of our own system.

A creak downstairs.

Or was it just the wind at the back doors?

I'd never been so scared...

Hands shaking, I called DS Holster. No answer.

Voice message. No time.

Instead I called Frankie back as I retreated into Mum and Dad's room. Why there? I didn't know. I pressed up against the wall, in the dark. Listened to the rings.

Please pick up. *Please.* 'Frankie?' I whispered when he answered. 'Frankie, I think he's here.'

'In the house.'

'Yes.'

'Get Tom. Get out of there. I'm coming.'

The call ended. Another creak from outside the room. Upstairs now?

I didn't want to move. I wanted to shut and barricade the door, crawl into a corner and hide.

I could do that, but not without Tom.

I had to get my brother.

I took a deep but silent breath then moved to the landing, across the carpet, my eyes never leaving the space below me, where I could see nothing in the darkness downstairs.

I reached Tom's room. Took one step inside...

And spotted him. Standing tall. Right in front of me. I froze in panic, didn't move at all as he lurched forward. At the last moment I lifted my arms to protect me...

Too little, too late.

The blow to my head sent me down... and out.

CHAPTER FORTY-SIX

How long was I out for? Not long. Perhaps not at all, really. I'd never been knocked unconscious before, but I didn't see a wall of black or anything like that. Just the room around me, spinning and blurring, as I struggled to keep my eyes from shutting. Then when they did shut, another struggle to reopen them.

Was there some lost time in between? Possibly.

I fought through my confusion, through the stabbing at the front of my head, and dragged myself to my feet. I put a hand to my temple. Blood.

I looked over to the bed. Empty.

'Tom!' I screamed.

No response. I already knew what had happened. I did my best to rush out of there. To the stairs. Looked to the front door.

Wide open.

'Tom!' I screamed again, even louder, even more panicked than before.

I bounded down the stairs, holding the banister to stop me from toppling.

My eyes searched for something, anything, to take as a

weapon as I gave chase. Nothing in sight. I couldn't delay. Barefooted, empty-handed, I sprinted outside, ignoring the pain in my feet as I stood on loose stones.

I looked left, then right along the street. Movement.

'Tom!'

A muffled cry in response. I raced that way. Off the pavement and into the middle of the road. Five cars down I spotted them. The man, hulking figure compared to little Tom, who writhed in the guy's arms.

'Let him go!' I screamed.

I raced forward. The man tried to bundle Tom into the back of his car but my brave brother fought back and when I was a few steps away his captor thought better of it and swung around, holding Tom tightly to his chest. A shield from me.

I stopped running. Looked into the man's angry eyes. 'David,' I said to him. 'David Campbell.' Strange really, that that was the best I could come up with.

Then my eyes found Tom's and my heart jolted, to see his distress. 'Please, let him go. You don't need to punish us.'

'Punish you?' Campbell responded, confusion above his anger. 'I'm–'

'He's nine. Let him go, please. He's my brother, he's all I've got.' I almost broke down as those words passed my lips.

'Your brother?' Campbell said with a snide laugh. 'He's my son!'

Nausea rushed through me. I felt sick for Tom, for Mum, for Dad. I shook my head in disgust. 'Your son?'

He half smiled. 'She never told you?'

'Even if that's true it's because you raped her. You *raped* my mum!'

He shook his head. 'You stupid girl. You bought their lies too.'

He moved and I flinched, petrified as to where this horrible moment would go next. But it seemed he was only renewing his grip on Tom – a relief, of sorts.

'I didn't rape her. I *loved* her.'

I thought back to those letters. He *had* loved her. That much was evident from his heartfelt and persistent words.

So what changed...

'When your dad found out, about me–'

'No,' I said, shaking my head.

'It's true. He threatened me. I tried to persuade her to leave him. She couldn't. Because of you. Frankie. She had to stay with him, for *you*.'

'This isn't our fault.' Why did I sound so defensive?

'But I would never have left her.' The determination in his voice... 'Instead he concocted the story. Somehow forced her to go along with it.'

'You're lying!'

'I've lost nine years of my life because of them. I won't lose my son too.'

'Please! Just let him go.' My demand sounded so weak and pathetic. I held Tom's eye. Then came his burst of strength. He wriggled and writhed. Stamped. He managed to spin his body around. Lifted his knee and caught Campbell's groin.

Campbell roared in pain and Tom wrestled for freedom. I darted forward to grab him. Tom wormed away, but Campbell came for me.

'Tom, go!' I shouted.

If I could at least block his path... Campbell barrelled into me. I reached out to grab him. We both tumbled to the tarmac. I landed painfully on my back. His hefty weight crushed me. That was when I first saw the knife. Swooshing toward me...

'Stupid bitch!'

I lifted my arm, cowered. The blade slashed across my skin and I screamed in pain.

I thrashed. Tried to get him off me, tried to pull myself out from underneath. My arms flailed in desperation.

I saw the knife above me. Focused on the tip of the blade, plunging down toward my chest...

'Get off her!'

Frankie. Relief washed over me. Fear too. Campbell could hurt me. I'd take that, for the safety of my brothers. But not Tom. Not Frankie. Please...

The next moment Frankie flew across me, diving forward, took Campbell with him and they both rolled across the tarmac, between two parked cars.

I jumped up onto my feet. Looked behind.

'Tom!' I shouted. No sign of him. No response. The sound of sirens pierced the cold air. Up ahead a car approached, its headlights nearly reaching us. Us? No. Just me. In the middle of the road. A head bobbed up on the pavement. A thud and a groan of pain.

'Frankie!'

I rushed between parked cars to the pavement. In the dark all I could make out was a twisting tangle of arms and legs. And a glint of metal in the thin illumination from the street lights.

I raced forward. Spotted the opportunity. Grabbed at the back of Campbell's coat and yanked, trying to pull him away from my brother. I thought I'd managed it but then a flying elbow caught me in the eye. I stumbled back. Lost my footing.

Groggy, I tried to get back up.

Frankie and Campbell were on their feet too. Campbell had his arm wrapped around Frankie's neck. The blade in his hand...

'No!'

Then... how did he even do it? Frankie spun out of the hold, grabbed Campbell's wrist, pushed forward and the blade sank through his coat, into his chest with a horrific squelch.

Campbell spluttered. Frankie lifted his foot and propelled him back, away from him, toward the road...

Smash

I cringed and cowered at the moment of impact. Screeching tyres filled the air. I rushed forward. Frankie too. We stopped side by side on the road. Looked into the arc of light from the car's headlights, to the crumpled figure on the ground. The car door opened and two panicked eyes glanced to me. The woman stepped out.

'I didn't see him. Oh my God, I didn't see him.'

Frankie and I said nothing as she rushed over to Campbell. We slowly moved forward, my eyes never leaving that heap on the ground. The woman, all in a panic, rolled him over. His body flopped, the knife remained protruding from Campbell's chest. The woman screamed.

I looked to Frankie. Recognition in his eyes.

Campbell was dead. We both knew it.

'Tom!' I shouted. I searched in the darkness. Then, from out between two cars, about halfway between us and home, the little shape emerged.

My heart... I don't even know how to describe the relief.

As the flashing blue lights and the sirens closed in, I raced over and threw my arms around Tom's petrified, shaking body.

CHAPTER FORTY-SEVEN

TWO MONTHS LATER

Normal. Normal for us, anyway, but I felt our lives were finally getting back to something approaching the ordinary. The press furore had died down, Frankie and Tom were both back at school. Or they had been at least, though as I stepped off the bus a couple of streets from our home a little after 6pm I expected they'd both be home, waiting for me. Schoolwork done, house tidied, tea made? Probably not.

I found them both in the lounge, movie on the TV, Tom on the floor, Frankie on the sofa staring at his phone.

'Did you have a good day?' Tom asked. Frankie didn't look up from his screen.

'Same as always,' I said, a bit grumbly, but I wasn't going to sugar-coat it. The temp job I had as an office admin for a local estate agents was far from glamorous, far from exciting, but it did pay.

'What's for tea?' Frankie asked, still not looking from his phone.

'You mean you haven't prepared a three-course meal for me?'

He did now look at me, eyebrow raised.

'I'll see what's in the freezer,' I said.

'Oh, it needs to be quick.'

'Because?'

'Because... is it okay if I go out tonight?'

'On a Wednesday? Where to?'

'To Meg's.'

I sighed. At least he'd taken to being honest with me about that. I thought he was being honest, anyway. And I was glad, that after everything we'd been through, he had someone he could turn to, even if they had hit a rocky patch previously. The cause of that rocky patch? I never did find out, though I didn't really want to pry too deeply into my brother's love life.

'Fine. But be back by ten.'

'Seriously?'

'Seriously.'

Readymade pizza was the best, and quickest, I could muster. The boys didn't complain, and soon Frankie left.

With Tom occupied with screen time, I looked over the unopened post. Of course it was unopened, it wasn't as if Tom or Frankie would bother.

A letter from Talbot. I hadn't seen him in person for months, all our communication now through email, phone or letter. Better that way. Perhaps I'd let him off the hook, but at least he'd given me a substantial discount on his fees – not asked for – when details of our experience hit the news. I think perhaps he didn't want to be drawn into the melee by association.

I read over the letter. Confirmation that his work was at an end, the assets of the estate all distributed. With the fee reduction and nearly twenty thousand for selling Dad's BMW, we'd come so close to paying off the mortgage in full. Not close enough for the bank. No one would give a twenty-year-old with no fixed income a mortgage, not even a small one. Luckily Sarah and Duncan had thrown us a bone once more. As reluctant as I was to accept more handouts, I really couldn't see another way, not if we were intent on keeping the family home.

I'd at least insisted that the money wasn't ours, but a loan. I'd pay them back, monthly, interest and everything. Sarah had insisted that was ridiculous. Duncan in the end had agreed to it. Of course.

On a monthly basis, if we were careful, we had between two and three hundred pounds left over for savings. Not bad really, though it did depend on my temp job keeping going.

The doorbell rang. I frowned, not expecting anyone. It'd better not be a reporter, I thought. I'd had more than enough of them. I did also wonder whether it might be one of my friends, or even Blake, who'd made a couple of unplanned appearances recently. I didn't mind, really. I missed him in many ways, I enjoyed his company, though I had no expectations of us ever rekindling what we might have had. We were both so young, and I think our lives were naturally diverging. No point in fighting it, even if he insisted he wanted to be part of my life, offering to sacrifice his own career prospects in the process by ditching his London job offers for something lower paid, and more local to me. I really didn't want that. I didn't want the burden.

Anyway, it wasn't Blake, or any of my friends at the door.

A surprise really. A man. Tall, grey hair, beard over a wide jaw. He held out a warrant card.

'Miss Evans?'

'Yes.'

'DCI Bennett.'

'Oh.'

We'd spoken on the phone. His look was far more... police officer than he'd sounded, as his voice was warm and friendly. I knew why though. He was the police's arse-coverer, as Frankie had aptly put it. Friendly on the surface, as though he really wanted to help us, but I was sceptical about his real intentions, whether that was fair or not.

'I was passing, I thought...'

I looked behind him. He was alone. Passing? I didn't think so. 'Do you want to come in?' I said, regardless.

'Sure,' he said with a smile.

We sat at the stools by the kitchen island.

'We've officially closed out the investigation into David Campbell's death,' he said.

'I heard.'

'There won't be any charges brought against you or your brother, or the driver, in relation to the death.'

A relief. The right result of course, though for a while in the aftermath, I'd genuinely worried whether there'd be some ramifications for us – Frankie in particular, who'd dealt the fatal blow with the knife.

'And what about my dad?' I asked.

Bennett sighed. 'We've done what we can. We'll have to wait and see what happens next.'

'Done what you can?'

'We... we've re-worked what we could, with the benefit of hindsight, and there's still nothing clear, forensically speaking, to indicate that David Campbell killed your father.'

'My dad wouldn't have killed himself,' I said, a very firm belief of mine now. 'That man–'

'I know how you feel, Miss Evans. And... I can tell you that there is circumstantial evidence of Campbell's intent to revenge. We think he took money off your parents, as blackmail, but perhaps that wasn't enough for him. We've searched his phone records and can see calls and messages between him and your mum and dad. Most strikingly, we've found searches on his phone and laptop related to... related to tying nooses. And also a lot of searches related to crime scene forensics.'

I shook my head in disbelief as anger boiled in my belly, though who was it directed at mostly?

'Our findings will be passed to our internal affairs team to consider next steps. I understand there'll likely be a coroner's inquest into your dad's death as a result.'

I nodded. I'd heard the same already. I'd also been told by the lawyer, who Uncle Duncan had insisted I speak to, that we had a good case against the police for their mishandling of Dad's death, and the lack of care toward us taken by the police and probation service following Campbell's release from prison. A civil case, I'd been told, could land us significant compensation. I really didn't know if I even had the energy to think about it, let alone go through with it, and I didn't really begrudge the likes of DS Holster or the other police officers personally for their actions. I did want to know the truth still though. I wanted the proof that Campbell had killed my dad, even though I knew I was unlikely to ever get such clear-cut closure.

'How are your brothers?' Bennett asked.

'Frankie takes everything in his stride,' I said.

Bennett nodded.

'Tom's... he has good days and bad days.'

'A lot to experience for someone so young.'

'That's an understatement.'

He still had nightmares. Still thought he could see Mum and Dad's and Lily's ghosts in the house. Honestly? I didn't believe in ghosts, though I had to keep reminding myself of that every time I heard a creak in the night, or saw a shadow moving unexpectedly.

'It's a lovely house you have here.'

'Thank you.'

'I bet you've a lot of conflicting emotions.'

The pain we'd suffered in the house would never leave us. Perhaps a fresh start would have been better...

'It's our home. We all grew up here.'

Bennett looked up. To the camera in the corner of the room. 'Everything working properly now?'

'As far as I know.' I spoke quite casually, even though I had developed some obsessive behaviours recently, forever checking locks, double and triple checking the camera feeds and the security settings every night before bed, and sometimes through the night if I heard any kind of noise.

Was the paranoia justified? Yes and no. We still didn't know when David Campbell had first broken into our home. Before Mum and Dad's deaths? Though it was obvious he'd had a key, to be able to enter and leave so easily. We still didn't know exactly how he'd figured out how to infiltrate our camera system, either. With the police in damage limitation mode now, and Campbell dead, we likely never would have those answers conclusively.

Bennett sighed. I could tell he had something he wanted to say, but was torn about it.

'The prosecutor has looked back over the rape case too,' he said.

'And?' And I didn't even really want to think about that. Ever.

'With your parents both dead, Campbell too, it's unlikely the verdict could be overturned.'

'Are you saying you think he was telling the truth? That my parents set him up?' I'd kind of expected that angle, as though smearing my parents would take some of the pressure off from the police's failings.

'We know for a fact he was Tom's biological father. We know, based on what you showed us, that he was in a relationship with your mother.'

'Years ago, yes. And that doesn't mean he didn't rape her.'

Bennett shook his head. 'No. And we'll never know for sure. Like I said, the criminal case likely won't be reopened, but keep yourselves prepared. It's possible a civil case–'

'Even if his family, whoever they are, think there's a case to be made in relation to his death, why would they come after us? We were victims in all this. We've lost everything. My parents are dead because... because...'

Because what? Because of the fallout of having set up a man for a rape conviction? A rape conviction following a lie they concocted in order to punish my mum's lover for nearly breaking the family apart? A rape conviction that left such a powerful need for revenge in David Campbell that he came out of prison not only intent on blackmailing my parents for money, but ultimately in tearing us apart by killing my dad so... so what? He could have my mum and Tom to himself?

Except she'd died too. Surely not part of Campbell's plan. I still didn't know where she'd been going that night, but I imagined the pressure got too much. The lies, the secrets, the guilt and regret. Perhaps a blow-out argument with Dad sent her over the edge, caused her to pick up her youngest kids and flee... or had she known of the imminent threat?

I didn't know any of that for sure, but it was the only explanation that truly fitted everything else. My parents *had* set up a man for rape. A man who'd loved my mum. Had she ever loved him?

None of that made me hate David Campbell any less, or feel sorry for him in any way. He'd still chosen to terrorise us, to try to snatch Tom from us, and I truly believed he'd killed Dad, even if it couldn't ultimately be proved.

David Campbell got exactly what he deserved, and whatever the full truth, it was us kids who'd suffered so grievously.

Bennett got to his feet. 'Just one more thing. When we were dusting for fingerprints in here, we took the prints for you and your brothers for elimination purposes.'

'Okay?'

'Your brother's prints matched to a couple of break-ins. One at a house across town. The Farrelly's. The other at a therapist's office in the town centre.'

'You took our prints for elimination,' I said, agitation in my voice. 'Surely you can't use those records for any other purpose?'

Bennett shrugged. I didn't appreciate his nonchalance. As though this was evidence he'd happily use against us if we came at the police too strongly for any apparent failings.

'Why are you telling me this now?' I asked.

He sighed. 'Your brother's been through a lot. More than most teenagers will ever have to go through. Make sure you keep him on the right path. Please.'

Okay, so perhaps I'd misread his intentions...

Still, his words took me back to the Christmas Fair. The palm reader, Heidi. Her words to Frankie about his future, his paths of lightness or darkness. No doubt he'd started down the wrong path at one point, including, apparently, breaking and entering at least twice, plus whatever other indiscretions and criminal acts I didn't know about. I didn't *want* to know about that either.

Those moments out in the street with Campbell... Frankie had saved Tom. Me too. He'd killed a man, would have to live with that forever, but perhaps in that moment he reached his true turning point.

I really hoped so.

We headed to the front. I opened the door.

'What about you?' Bennett asked as he turned back to me.

'Me?'

'I heard you were granted guardianship.'

Somehow. I really didn't know how I'd got that over the line with the council.

'You've been keeping a close eye on us, haven't you?'

Bennett shrugged.

'For now, I'm staying here, in Graystone,' I said. 'My university agreed to let me defer for a year, and I'll finish my degree mostly remotely. After that...'

'You'll be fine,' Bennett said. 'You're an amazing young woman.'

'Thank you,' I said, quite dumbfounded.

Bennett turned and walked away.

'Who was that?' Tom asked, appearing in the lounge doorway, his new-found edginess showing through.

'Just a... friend,' I said.

'Oh.' He disappeared off.

I went upstairs. Turned on lights as I went. Tom's room was a mess, as always. It'd seemed a good idea to remove the partition wall and give him the space from Lily's room too, but somehow he'd more than filled that space in just a few short weeks.

As for Mum and Dad's room? All cleared out, wardrobes and everything. Dust sheets covered the floor. I'd finish the painting with the help of the boys at the weekend, then, once we'd saved enough, we'd get it kitted out with everything they wanted: dart board, foosball, pool table.

I moved to my room. Spent a few minutes putting away my washing, before I changed out of my office gear into jeans and a hoody. I went over to the wardrobe, opened up and took out the box. One of the few survivors from Mum and Dad's room. All of the love letters were gone now, everything from that hidden box, in fact. No more secrets.

No more lies.

But the box of Lily's things... I couldn't part with that.

So many times over the last couple of months I'd tried to put myself in my parents' shoes, tried to convince myself that their actions had been sound, and with their kids' best interests at heart.

They had been, hadn't they?

They'd both sacrificed so much, with Lily, taking her as their own so I could carry on my teenage years like everyone else. But even before that, there had been Tom, and the turmoil Mum's pregnancy with him represented. If my parents really had set Campbell up, could I ever agree with my parents' actions?

Not wholeheartedly, but I could agree that they loved all four of their kids unconditionally, would have done anything for us, anything to keep the family unit together, even if that meant, for my dad, loving two kids who weren't even his. Even if it meant ruining the life of another man. Even if it meant pushing themselves to breaking point when they were left with nowhere to turn to keep the dark past buried.

Kneeling on the floor, I spent a few minutes looking over some of the cards and pictures. Finally I picked up Lion, one of the few toys I'd kept from Lily's old room. I smelled the soft fur. Getting fainter all the time, but there remained a scent of her.

My daughter.

Pushing back the tears, I placed Lion on top, then folded the lid flaps back into place.

I headed downstairs and into the lounge.

'What are you watching?' I asked Tom.

'*Ghostbusters.*'

Perhaps not the best choice for him, under the circumstances, although ghosts didn't really seem to be his problem. Mostly his nightmares now were about Campbell, in his room, in the dark. A very hard image to erase from such a young and troubled mind, even if Campbell was buried six feet under.

I sat down next to him and he cuddled up to me. We watched in silence for a few moments, though I sensed he had something on his mind as the ghostly apparitions flitted across the screen.

'Do you think... do you think Mum and Dad and Lily are still with us? Can they still see us?'

I sighed as I thought about the answer to that.

'Nanna says they're still here,' he added.

'Nanna's very old, Tom. She says all sorts of strange things.'

Though, just like Tom, I hated being alone in the dark now too. My rational side often deserted me at night.

'But what you do think?' Tom asked again.

What was I supposed to say? Yes, Mum and Dad could see us, would always be with us. Perhaps that would provide some comfort to Tom, but then by the same token, wouldn't it also mean that David Campbell – his biological father, but also his tormentor and kidnapper – would also always be with us?

I shuddered at that thought.

'No, Tommo,' I said to him, holding him a bit more tightly. 'Wherever they've gone, they're not here anymore.'

He looked up at me, sadness in his eyes.

'It's just me, you and Frankie now,' I added.

He nodded. 'You won't leave us, will you?'

'Nothing will come between us,' I said to him, holding his eye. 'Not ever. Nothing at all.'

And despite the bumps in the road that I was sure lay ahead for us, I meant every word of that with all of my heart.

THE END

A NOTE FROM THE AUTHOR

Firstly, thank you for reading my first novel, *Lies That Bind,* and I hope you enjoyed it. I know authors are regularly asked where their inspiration comes from and for me, for this book, there were two aspects that I can grasp - which is saying something because book ideas, generally speaking, come to me in magical eureka moments more anything else! But I did know for this novel the type of book I wanted to write. A page turning, darkly atmospheric psychological thriller. Why? Because it's exactly the book that I'd devour myself, sitting on a sun lounger on holiday, or laid out on the sofa at home.

As for the story? Rather than an idea, as such, the story came from a *feeling.* That feeling of being isolated, alone. Lying in bed in the middle of the night and hearing an unexpected noise - *things that go bump in the night.* You know *that* feeling, right? But what if it wasn't just a branch flapping outside, or a window snapping shut from a gust of wind, or a creaking water pipe, but something more *real*, and more sinister...

And thus, *Lies That Bind* was born, from that one simple concept. Although I'm not sure where the rest of it came from, and you wouldn't have read the book, or be reading this page now, were it not for a lot of help along the way. The support of my close family on my author 'venture' means so much to me, and I'd also like to thank the ever eager and supportive teams at both Bloodhound Books and Open Road Media for their input and hard work in taking my creation to completion and publication. Lastly, but perhaps most importantly, I'd like to thank *you,* the reader.

Would I write books if only friends and family read them? Possibly yes, but that's because writing is a very strange bug that effects every writer in different but compelling ways, and I get genuine pleasure from the process. That said it's incredibly humbling to realise that readers such as yourself have spent your hard-earned money on my work, and used your valuable downtime to read my words, and I'm forever grateful for that, especially if you've read this far!

As for what's next... plenty more from me, that's for sure, because that bug just won't let up...

ABOUT THE AUTHOR

CJ Stone is an avid thriller reader turned writer, a former accountant who decided to ditch a 'normal' career for a passion instead. Settled in the West Midlands, and when not walking four-legged friend Rolo, or looking after two boisterous boys, CJ can be found at the kitchen table typing away in creative mode, pulling stories from the ether for others to enjoy. For more information on CJ's work, head to cjstoneauthor.com

A NOTE FROM THE PUBLISHER

Thank you for reading this book. If you enjoyed it please do consider leaving a review on Amazon to help others find it too.

We hate typos. All of our books have been rigorously edited and proofread, but sometimes mistakes do slip through. If you have spotted a typo, please do let us know and we can get it amended within hours.

info@bloodhoundbooks.com